T_)

ATLANTIS PAPYRUS

Whispers of Atlantis: BOOK I

by Jay Penner

In this anthology:

The Atlantis Papyrus

The Wrath of God

The Curse of Ammon*

Sinister Sands

The Death Pit*

(*) may be read as a standalone

https://jaypenner.com

To my father, for his humor and talent, and my mother, for her love.

Jay Penner https://www.jaypenner.com

Printed in the United States of America

First Printing: Mar 2019 / Updated Mar 2020

5.0 2021.11.08.10.03.44
Produced using publishquickly
https://publishquickly.com

JAY PENNER
HISTORY AND FANTASY

Choose your interest! A gritty and treacherous journey with Cleopatra in the Last Pharaoh trilogy, or thrilling stories full of intrigue and conflict in the Whispers of Atlantis anthology set in the ancient world.

THE LAST PHARAOH

WHISPERS OF ATLANTIS

https://jaypenner.com

AUTHOR'S NOTES

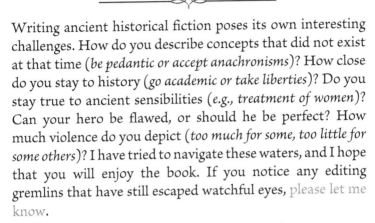

Writing ancient historical fiction poses its own interesting challenges. How do you describe concepts that did not exist at that time (*be pedantic or accept anachronisms*)? How close do you stay to history (*go academic or take liberties*)? Do you stay true to ancient sensibilities (*e.g., treatment of women*)? Can your hero be flawed, or should he be perfect? How much violence do you depict (*too much for some, too little for some others*)? I have tried to navigate these waters, and I hope that you will enjoy the book. If you notice any editing gremlins that have still escaped watchful eyes, please let me know.

ONCE YOU FINISH

I ask for your kindness and support through a few words (or even just ratings) after reading. I've provided review links in the end, and it will only take a few seconds (or minutes). Thank you in advance!

ANACHRONISMS

**an act of attributing customs, events, or objects
to a period to which they do not belong**

Writing in the ancient past sometimes makes it difficult to explain everyday terms. Therefore, I have taken certain liberties so that the reading is not burdened by linguistic gymnastics or forcing a reader to do mental math (how far is 60 stadia again?). My usage is meant to convey the meaning behind the term, rather than striving for historical accuracy. I hope that you, reader, will come along for the ride, even as you notice that certain concepts may not have existed during the period of the book. For example:

Directions—North, South, East, West.

Time—Years, Minutes, Hours...

Distance—Miles.

Other concepts—Imperial, Stoic.

INTRODUCTIONS

PEOPLE

Alexander (the Great)—King of Macedon

Eumenes of Cardia—Alexander's Greek Royal Secretary

Deon—Captain in Alexander's army

Ptolemy—General, Satrap of Egypt

Perdiccas—General, Regent

Seleucus, Craterus—Generals

Antigonus—Governor

TERMS

Kopis—Short sword with a forward-curving blade; plural kopides

Sarissa—12–13-foot long spear

Stade—5.4 stadia = mile (1 stade = ~550ft.)

Cuirass—a piece of armor consisting of breastplate and backplate fastened together

Chiton—a single sheet of woolen or linen fabric worn plain or with overfolds

ΛLEXΛNDER'S EMPIRE ΛT THE TIME OF HIS DEΛTH

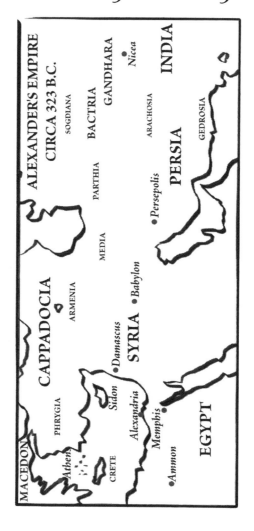

LOCATIONS

---◇---

Locations—Then: Now (approximate boundaries)

Macedon, Greece: *Macedonia, Greece*

Egypt: *Egypt*

Phrygia, Cappadocia: *Turkey*

Armenia: *Armenia*

Media, Persia, Gedrosia: *Iran*

Babylonia / Mesopotamia: *Iraq*

Syria: *Syria, Lebanon, Israel, Jordan, Palestine*

Nabataea: *Portions of Jordan, Saudi Arabia*

Parthia: *Turkmenistan*

Sogdiana: *Uzbekistan/Tajikistan*

Bactria, Gandhara: *Afghanistan / North Pakistan*

India: *India/Pakistan*

Hydaspes River: *Jhelum (Pakistan)*

Hyphasis River: *Beas (India)*

History buff? Don't forget! Go on a virtual tour of all the major locations in the book using a Google Earth flyby. Link in the end.

THE BEGINNING

MACEDON

Twelve armed men surrounded us in the wet courtyard. Apollonia stood weeping with our frightened baby; their sobs drowned by the steady sound of rain on the cracked brick roof.

"Tell her, Deon, tell her about your glorious business," Krokinos said, pointing at my wife. I said nothing. My face burned with shame, and blood dripped from my nose to the rainwater that swirled around my bruised knuckles.

"A bright young man, a scholar even, but all that means nothing because I need to know how you will repay me," he said.

"What is he talking about?" my wife screamed, and I had no courage to answer her. Instead, I addressed Krokinos. "I will find a way, Krokinos," I said, struggling back to my feet.

"How many times have I heard that before, Deon? You think tutoring little rich brats will make the money you owe me? You should have stayed in your world of Plato and Aristotle, and left the world of whores to us," he said, and I dared not look at my wife.

She had no idea what I had done. Krokinos nodded at his men, and two rushed to seize my wife and daughter. "Leave them out of this!" I screamed and lunged forward. Three others blocked my path, and another man kicked the legs under me. I fell, and the men placed their feet on my back, preventing me from standing. I gasped and spat out the mud and water that enveloped my face.

My wife's screams and my daughter's wails mingled with rhythmic music of the raindrops.

Krokinos' goons lifted me to my feet again. He ordered his men to bring us all into our living room. I begged Krokinos, "Let them go, Krokinos! I will repay you!"

"Your house smells of piss," he said, drawing laughter. "I will have to teach your wife to do a better job at cleaning." Krokinos wiped his face with his wet tunic and loomed over me. I watched him with intense hatred.

I could break his bony body like a twig.

Break his bird nose and crush his skull like a crow's egg.

Push a dagger up his—

One of the burly men grabbed my daughter and began to carry her away. My wife fought him, and I struggled fruitlessly. Krokinos forced his palm on her mouth and shouted, "He is not going to kill your little girl, so shut up! I need to talk to you both."

We quietened, and as if by cue, the thrashing on the roof reduced in intensity. "I am an honorable man, Deon. And this is what will happen," Krokinos said, as I strained to look at his face.

"Your wife and daughter will remain my hostages and as servants—"

"No," I struggled against the restraints. Blood rushed into my head like a roaring river through a gorge. He looked on nonchalantly.

"—And you have time until my son turns of marriageable age. If you do not repay me by then, I will sell them to the mines."

I walked quietly, one among the many soldiers in a column that stretched as far as the eye could see. Somewhere at the head of the vast body of soldiers was King Alexander, who planned to take on the Persian empire by marching directly into the lion's den. I hoped that the military conquests would help me earn a handsome salary and make large bonuses. The generals promised plunder, and I would regain my wealth and reunite with my wife and daughter—now in servitude.

A few years, I had promised her, I would be back. I would free them, and we would all live a comfortable retired life. Apollonia had nodded with those lifeless, sunken eyes. I held her hand and enveloped little Alexa's, knowing that if I did not return, those hands would be digging unforgiving earth in terrible gold mines in Ethiopia until they died. And they would never know what it was that I did to condemn them to such a life.

As dust obscured my vision and long, ominous sarissas rattled, I walked into an uncertain future.

PART I

FRIENDS & FINDERS

Circa 327 BC

"…the madness of love is the greatest of heaven's blessings…" –
Plato*

CHAPTER 1.

A FEW YEARS LATER, BACTRIA

Royal Secretary Eumenes shivered in the cold morning wind of the desolate, brown-yellow Bactrian landscape. His leather cuirass and military helmet were useless against the miserable chill. He cursed under his breath—at thirty-six his body was beginning to feel the effects of the harsh climate and the relentless pace of the campaign. Unlike many of his peers, Eumenes had none of the layers of fat and muscle that protected the larger men. His small stature and wiry frame were the joke of many a Macedonian General, and his Greek heritage did him no favors in the royal court.

Eumenes watched as the guards brought the frail creature out of his wheeled cage. He wondered how they ignored the foul stench that emanated from the man, whose skin was covered with abrasions and pus oozed from many wounds. What a fall from glory, Eumenes thought, for the condemned man was Callisthenes of Olynthus—Alexander the Great's court historian, and grandnephew of the famous philosopher Aristotle.

Even though he struggled to walk, Callisthenes seemed to smile and bask in the soft morning sun, ignoring the cold. A dirty mop of hair covered his face, and his visible ribs shook violently as he coughed. He looked up at the sky, muttered something, and then stretched his back. He then slowly reached down to touch the ground and collected the gray dry grass and dust, looked at it for a while, and slapped his palms together dispersing the dust and grass in the air. The guards led him up a grassy, rocky mound before a wooden platform.

They removed his shackles, and he shuffled around. The *Pezhetairoi* encircled the wooden platform and waited for their commander. General Ptolemy would arrive and proclaim royal orders.

But Eumenes did not want to be here.

A week ago, Callisthenes had begged Eumenes for his life, clutching the rusted iron bars of his cage.

Tell me, Eumenes, what fool would die with a magnificent secret if he could barter it for his life?

Take it to the King!

Tell him to spare my life in return for what will make him invincible now and forever!

I may look mad, but my mind has not lost its fidelity, Eumenes, see beyond my wretched state and consider what I have to say!

I promise that you will gain too, Eumenes, believe me!

What Callisthenes had said was astonishing. Whether it came off a fertile or delirious mind was unclear. If what he said was true, there was a strategic advantage in holding it close to the chest. It caused him distress to see Callisthenes this way, for they shared a similar station. Eumenes too had come far from his scholarly origins. At an early age, Eumenes had been the private secretary of Philip II of Macedon, Alexander's father. He had seen the intrigues of the royal court and the growth of Alexander. After Philip's death, he continued to work by Alexander's side. It was as if Callisthenes was like a brother.

Poor Callisthenes. His role was to chronicle the King's conquests and create a royal diary that would live on through the ages. But some time ago, he fell out of favor with the King because Alexander began to adopt Persian customs. The mutual dislike had grown, and eventually, Callisthenes was implicated in a conspiracy to kill

Alexander. Ever since then the historian's life was in a cage, wheeled behind the army like an animal.

Ptolemy arrived, resplendent in his polished metal and leather cuirass and yellow-plumed helmet. He looked at Eumenes and nodded, acknowledging his presence. With dramatic flair he shook his red cape, and then walked up to Callisthenes.

As everyone watched, Ptolemy pulled out the order roll from its cover. Callisthenes looked at the men around him. Eumenes felt their eyes connect—it was as if Callisthenes searched for hope.

"Callisthenes," said Ptolemy sternly, "For your role in the conspiracy against the King, the council sentences you to death. In recognition of your service, we grant you a merciful end."

Callisthenes shook. His lips curled as he tried to speak, but the words died in his throat. The guards had denied water to him the last two days, so no doubt his tongue was swollen. Two men seized him from behind, and one placed a noose around his neck. Callisthenes' eyes bulged from his sockets. The men dragged him on rocky ground, and flesh ripped off his feet. For a fleeting moment, Callisthenes' terrified eyes connected with Eumenes. It was as if they screamed 'coward!' The historian tried once more to open his mouth and say something, but the noose choked his words. Eumenes lowered his head.

Callisthenes was hauled up a platform to higher ground. Soldiers stared at the noble who struggled to preserve dignity in his last moments. Giving Callisthenes no time to speak or say his prayers, the executioner stepped behind, swung a thick rope around Callisthenes' neck, and began strangling him. The historian's face turned purple as the noose tightened around his neck and his frantic hands grasped and fought hopelessly with the tightening snare. Callisthenes' eyes bulged bloodshot and frantic, his tongue protruded between the bloody lips, his tunic soiled from a discharge of urine, and finally his frail body shuddered one last time.

Forgive me.

Eumenes begged Callisthenes in his mind. But some secrets were too valuable to share.

CHAPTER 2.

BY THE HYDASPES RIVER, INDIA

"Deon, are you ready?" asked the rider next to me. But it mattered not to the King or the Gods if I was not. Hundreds of lumbering war elephants loomed out of the mist. Porus, the Indian Satrap of this region, had placed them strategically in the center, supported by his infantry. His cavalry waited on his left.

O Poseidon, I pray thee, may my head not greet an elephant's leg.

It was as if the gods were angry at our incursion into this land. A storm had raged through the earlier night as we crossed the Hydaspes in the dark to surprise Porus. Swelling waters had threatened to sweep me away, and my fear of drowning had added to my terror of crossing. But our deception had worked, and Porus learned of our move too late. Porus dispatched his son, with half his army's cavalry, but we routed them in a pitched battle early at dawn.

Porus' son was dead. And so was Alexander's beloved horse, Bucephalus.

To our right, the Hydaspes swelled. Deep brown water, abundant with twigs, weeds, plants, rats, and snakes, spread far from the bank. The mud, dredged from churning waters, was knee deep in places. The smell of sweat, death, rot, fresh leaves, and wet mud permeated the air. We had moved away from the bank and found drier, flatter ground as we readied to engage.

The densely packed armies, stretching one mile on either side, eyed each other from a distance. The fluttering banners, riders on bedecked horses, blocks of sarissas, colorful plumes on thousands of helmets all gave the scene a feel of great festivity—except that this would soon be an offering of blood to thirsty gods and kings. The first major battle to conquer India was about to begin.

"Look at Ptolemy's wives waiting for him, they are huge!" bellowed someone, and nervous laughter followed. The rider next to me nudged me with the rear of his javelin, "Not quite like the greeting to your wife's arms, Deon?"

Would I ever get back to my wife?

Would I hold my daughter again?

It was as if a snake gently squeezed my chest. Would I be a forgotten unknown lying dead in the foreign mud so far away from home? Would I leave them condemned?

My mind snapped back to the present. The great King Alexander himself would lead the right-wing and engage Porus' cavalry.

General Seleucus would lead the central infantry and target Porus' elephants and infantry. The fearsome phalanx would be crucial in dealing with the beasts.

General Coenus would lead the left-wing cavalry, swing wide, and come behind Porus' Infantry. This would force Porus to split his cavalry, which, as we noticed, remained on his left.

The famed general Craterus, for some reason I could not fathom, was not in the main attacking force but waited on the opposite bank of the Hydaspes. He would cross once the battle ensued and come upon the rear of Porus' army.

We would soon find out if the strategy worked.

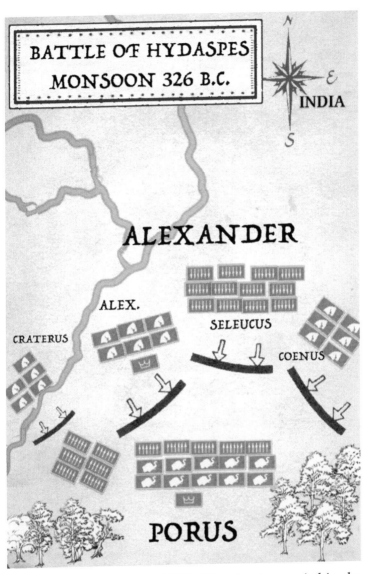

BATTLE OF HYDASPES
MONSOON 326 B.C.

INDIA

ALEXANDER

ALEX.

CRATERUS

SELEUCUS

COENUS

PORUS

"Hold. Wait for command," Perdiccas' voice carried in the quiet. I saw the King's distinct purple plume far ahead and to my left.

What a distinction to fight by his side!

I took a deep breath, straightened my back, and puffed up my chest. My horse stirred impatiently under me—I patted and soothed its neck. The gentle tinkles of the bells attached to the horses, the slight rustling of leaves, the constant sound of swirling waters of the Hydaspes, all gave a false sense of idyllic bliss.

The clouds which had parted to allow the sun to peek closed again and the raindrops began to fall. Then there was the first distinct whistle that prompted the thousand-strong archery to let loose a frightening mass of arrows upon the enemy. We watched mesmerized as the bolts flew across the dark sky and began their murderous descent. I knew our charge orders would now arrive at any moment.

And then there it was—the shrill whistle of attack and the great shout from thousands ready to battle. The horse's' manes glistened as we galloped to engage Porus' forces. Mud kicked up from their thundering hoofs dirtied the ground and men.

The verdant greenery was about to turn bloody and brown.

We angled towards Porus' cavalry, avoiding the elephants and attacking his horses as planned. Coenus split away from us, and I knew the infantry would soon begin its purposeful march forward.

Their cavalry rushed at us with admirable bravery. But their riders were not as well trained. The quiet morning had devolved into a hellish nightmare with the music of death. We swung our kopides and thrust our javelins, and hacked heads and limbs began to pile on the ground. Our Scythian horsemen rained arrows as they rode, and we cut through the enemy's formations. I marveled at the Scythians' grace—they were like lethal dancers on horses.

Thousands fought for the honor of their lands and for their lives. My face was wet with rain and specks of blood, and the faces and bodies became a blur as we swung and slashed. As it is in these battles, the carefully designed formation devolved in chaos at contact. Horses ran amok and trampled men who fell off the saddles. Some dismounted and preferred to fight their battle on the ground.

Soon, the infantries and the cavalries intermingled. The Indian archers struggled with their powerful bows tall as their height. The muddy earth made it difficult for them to anchor the bows and draw the bowstring. We cut them down as they stood.

The Indian mahouts pushed the elephants forward into our phalanx. The beasts, frightened by the bristling spikes, filled the air with their trumpet. Men screamed as the elephants trampled or threw them with their powerful trunks. Soldiers on mounted platforms hurled javelins with remarkable accuracy. I watched in horror as one such terrifying missile swooshed from the air hitting the rider next to me, lifting him off his saddle. He had no time to scream as the spear ripped through his chest and impaled him to the ground. He hung like a grotesque doll.

I came to two more of my men twitching on the ground, and I stabbed them to a merciful death. I maneuvered my horse to avoid the beasts and the missiles. And when it began to struggle and stumble on the wet ground, realizing the danger, I dismounted.

Groups of men engaged in hand-to-hand combat as the horse riders circled.

One of the Indians, still a boy, rushed towards me. Intense hatred burned in his eyes. He swung his sword without control—a child's mistake—and I thrust my kopis into his belly. He screamed, and I twisted before pulling the blade out. He collapsed and began to roll in the ground. I let him bleed.

That was when I saw one of our generals on the ground, trying to fend off blows from a hirsute giant and his companion. As I ran to protect the general, the larger attacker turned towards me. Orange and white paint decorated his forehead and chest, and waist-length wet hair clung to his body. He held a flat, broad sword that dripped crimson in its edges. He turned towards me and swung. The tremendous impact of his sword on my shield sent jolts of pain up my shoulder. The giant lost his footing on slippery ground and fell on his back.

Meanwhile, the general managed to get to his feet but seemed dazed. As he wobbled, the second attacker lunged. I stepped sideways, swung my kopis, and hacked his arm off at the elbow. The Indian screamed. His arm, with the bone jutting beneath the severed muscle, dangled in front of the shocked general's face.

Sharp pain exploded up my right thigh. The giant had recovered and slashed me on my hamstring as he got back to his feet.

I screamed and stumbled.

He gripped and raised his sword to deliver a life-ending blow on my skull. My helmet would be no match for the violence of the impact. But this was not my first battle, and I would not allow it to be my last.

I dropped to my knees, raised the shield, and plunged my kopis into his inner thigh. He recoiled in pain and jumped back. I could not see his face with my shield cover, but I could see the legs. Before he recovered, I swung down with all my might and severed several of his toes.

He fell.

I rose to my feet, ignoring the sharp, terrible pain in my thigh. I swung the kopis at an angle, striking at the giant's neck with force, but the blade hacked half his neck and stuck. I had to use considerable strength to pull it out, and then I hacked him again. And again. And again. Until my fear-induced rage reduced, and his head rolled off.

I then staggered towards the enemy whose arm I had severed. He was rolling on the wet, muddy ground, howling, clutching his almost separated hand. I gripped the general's shoulder to steady myself. Then I put my foot on the Indian's face and pushed it into the ground. After futile thrashing about, his convulsing body went quiet.

We both stared at each other. The general looked dazed. The attack had split his helmet on the side. He looked at me and grinned, as rivulets of red came down by the side of his ear.

"I owe you my life."

"You can thank me later, general Eumenes!" I said as we stood back to back waiting for support.

"What is your name?" he asked.

"Deon, sir. Son of Evagoras."

Soon, others joined us, and we fought the hordes.

What Porus' troops lacked in training, they made up in fanatical bravery. There was no doubt in my mind that most of these wretched souls came from the farm to the battleground. When would they retreat and avoid this needless slaughter? I hoped the battle would be over before the sun reached mid sky.

Meanwhile, our army began to gain the upper hand. The elephants, now running amok among friend and foe, had become a liability. Porus struggled to lead his forces against an experienced and disciplined army.

I was losing blood. My head throbbed, and the world around me dissolved into a medley of greens, reds, saffron, grays, and browns. I collapsed and felt the soft wet mud around my fingers and knees. The pain seemed to disappear into a fog of fear.

Is this it?

Those were my thoughts as I fainted.

My house looks small, yet beautiful, with the mountains in the backdrop. The walls are white, the tiles on the roof have a reddish tinge, and a poorly drawn image of Poseidon adorns the space above the door. There is my wife. Apollonia. It has been years, but she appears unchanged—her long, light brown hair curls and rests on her bare shoulders. She wears an elegant necklace made of gold flowers—it is the one I gave her before we fell on hard times. Next to her is my daughter, Alexa. How much she has grown! All I remember her is as a baby, chubby, fretful, and trying to put her little fingers in my mouth. She runs to me; I ruffle her short hair and pinch her freckled cheeks.

I pick Alexa up and walk up to my wife who holds my hand and leads me into the house. Apollonia is petite. I lean to my right and kiss the top of her head. She says something to me, but it is not clear what she says, but we are suddenly sitting on the floor for dinner. We eat noisily, and my daughter's eyes open wide time to time and my wife scolds me not to tell scary stories. But I tell her something silly, and she laughs with food in her mouth, and it splatters on me. This life is so perfect. Suddenly the floor shakes, and the clay jars and cups crack and turn to dust, the walls of the house vanish, and we are in a dirty, rocky area. There are many almost naked men and women around us, they are dirty, sweaty, and their bodies are scarred. Up ahead is an entrance to a mine—I remember reading about them, gold mines, terrible places with no gods where people go to die. Two burly guards seize my wife and daughter and begin to drag them to the entrance. They scream and shout for help, and my chest begins to beat erratically. I am frantic and try to scream, but no words come out. I try to run towards them, but my limbs do not move, it is as if my body refuses to obey my mind's commands. I watch as their figures become smaller and smaller until they vanish into the darkness. I strain with every strength in my sinews and begin to scream soundlessly, and just then—

I woke up in a makeshift medical tent, gasping for breath. Two of my men hovered from above, staring down with concern. One had his hand on my shoulders, trying to keep me from moving. It took me several minutes to calm down. I drank some water and closed my eyes in relief. A physician had tended to the angry deep gash on my thigh. I asked a fellow soldier on my side what happened. Had we won?

He smiled through a bandaged face. "News is this was a close one. Porus has surrendered. We destroyed their cavalry. Coenus attacked them from behind, and with the help of Craterus, inflicted significant casualty on their infantry."

I sat up slowly, wincing as pain shot up my leg.

"I do not want to spend any more time in India," he whispered surreptitiously, looking around.

I said nothing. While we won, the strain of fighting a fanatical enemy in inhospitable conditions had demoralized the troops. If this ill-prepared army was so hard to fight, how would we face the enormous armies of the King of India?

Besides, in the past two months, many soldiers had fallen sick in the terrible weather. They vomited copiously, their bodies were racked by fever, and some lay where they fell—and the physicians let them be.

Raja Paurava—that was what they called Porus—had surrendered, and the official story was that he responded with 'in a kingly way' when Alexander asked how he wished to be treated. But other accounts told us that the two men got into a shouting match, and the Indian had threatened Alexander that if he were killed or imprisoned, then every tribe would resist us in our march east. And the King, recognizing the difficulty in continuing without cooperation, had decided to give Porus the kingdom back and expanded his territory.

Why fight when we could have achieved that through dialog? I wondered. But I was no king, so my thoughts meant little.

Two days later, the officers' physician visited me, inspected the wounds, and said gravely, "You are unlikely to command any fighting unit soon."

Every few hours physicians cleaned my wound and poured a foul dark liquid on it that caused me to cry in pain. On the third day, the wound began to crust, but pus oozed from it. I developed a fever that lasted several days, but the physicians, who had seen such injuries many times over, knew how to manage it.

I longed for home like never before. Few in the army knew my story and the dire situation of my family. The deadline would expire in less than four years, and if I did not discharge my debt, my family would be sold to slavery. The campaigns were only moderately rewarding, and generous bonuses were uncommon to men of my rank. There were few pillages as most new regions surrendered to the King having known his reputation. I stole when I could, to add to my baggage, but I was still a long away from shoring enough coin to repay my debt. A luxurious life was only a dream.

Ten years of war, and not much to show for it. That realization was stronger today than it ever was. The fervor for battles and conquests was gone. The dreams of making large piles of money had seeped away in the deserts of Persia and washed away in the rains of India. And now this injury would end my career in the army and seriously impair my ability to continue to earn until my return. Imagining my wife and daughter in a caravan of beaten and bruised slaves, shackled and dragged like animals, exceeded all the pain I knew.

I prayed to Dionysus, Poseidon, Zeus—every god that graced the world—to have a plan for me. By the end of a full moon, I was finally able to walk with my crutches. I looked sick, but a soothing bath in the now calm river elevated my mood. I joked with my former troops that if there were anyone that could take on the Indians beyond the Hydaspes, it would be me. This vicious, limping warrior with his fearsome crutches would demoralize the Indian King's army!

On the thirty-first day, an officer paid me a visit.

"Deon, son of Evagoras?"

"Yes?"

He eyed my bandaged thigh. "You are the cavalryman who was wounded a few weeks ago protecting General Eumenes?"

I nodded.

"The General requests your presence at dinner."

At the appointed hour, I hobbled to Eumenes' tent and stepped past his guards. He sat alone at the far end of a small table laid out for dinner. He wore a comfortable, crisp white loose-fitting garment, and there was no customary helmet, cuirass, or kopis.

Watching him in close quarters and in a relaxed environment I was struck by how slight Eumenes was. He was shorter than me, of slight build, and his face was delicate and intelligent. And unlike me, he had a full head of hair, even if an unruly mop of curls. What I noticed most was his eyes—inquisitive and shrewd.

In one corner was a small, expertly carved idol of Zeus—brows furrowed, a thunderbolt in his raised hand, torso covered by a bright red fabric. Eumenes did not forget his Greek heritage. He gestured me to come in.

"I am honored to be here, General," I said as I moved nervously near the table.

"Sit down, soldier. Share a meal with me. We have a few peaceful days before Alexander moves again. So, I thought, 'why not know a man that saved my life?'"

"I have learned too late that saving generals would get me to dine with them." I regretted the instant those words came out of my mouth, which paid little heed to what my head said—be deferential to a general!

He laughed, open-mouthed and free. He had several crooked, yellowed teeth. Only a few years separated him and Alexander. "Considering the results of such an endeavor, that might not be advisable."

I nodded.

Eumenes studied me. He had a bowl of deep-purple, fragrant fruit, and put one in his mouth. He said nothing, and whether by design or unintentionally, he made me uncomfortable, and I fidgeted in my seat.

"You look nervous, Deon," he said, with a sly smile.

"It's not often that a simple soldier is summoned to dine with a general, sir."

"You are not a simple soldier, are you?"

I swallowed. I did not know where this conversation was headed, but my stomach began to growl in the presence of delicious food. I eyed the table hungrily.

"Go ahead and eat, it is rare even we get something like this—do not think the officers feast every day while the soldiers starve. You can answer me later."

I placed one delicious morsel in my mouth and enjoyed the spice of pepper and some other ingredients I did not recognize. "I am but a cavalryman, and have been for a long time, sir."

"I have heard that while you are a great fighter, you are also an outstanding trainer. That is quite a rise from a simple farmer."

"I am humbled by the praise, General."

"And people tell me you are extraordinarily observant of the surroundings around you."

I raised my eyebrows. Eumenes had been inquiring about me. But where his men were wrong was in that I was no farmer, and they had not found out that I was a well-regarded teacher of mathematics and philosophy, and I had memory that never faded with time. I remembered everything I heard, read, or saw. No one knew that, and I had used it to my advantage when I wanted to. Except that all my intelligence had failed me when I ventured into the business of brothels in the desire to make money and lost considerable sums. The foolishness and recklessness haunted me ever since.

But Eumenes' words took me back to a late evening during the Persian campaigns, years ago. I was sitting near a few other very senior men, one of them the great Ptolemy himself. While most of what they spoke was banter, I remembered Ptolemy uttering to someone to his right—

You think Eumenes is a mere bookkeeper, but that man is an astute judge of character. Before you know, he might be the one you bow to.

"Some think it is a gift, but when you are at war for years, the powers of observation leave a great many undesirable memories in the mind," I said, without exposing the nature of my memory.

He stood up and picked a parchment absentmindedly. "Where are you from, Deon? Do you have a family?"

"A wife, sir. Back in Macedon. A daughter who will enter womanhood in just a few years."

"Do you miss them?" he asked, as he read what was in his hand and frowned.

I smiled nostalgically and nodded. Was Eumenes testing me for something?

"She must be awaiting your return," he continued.

"Whether she squeals in joy at the sight of a balding, broken-toothed lout is a question, sir," I said deprecatingly. If only the General knew that my wife was now a servant in my lender's house. My head or teeth would be least of her concerns.

"You are not the most attractive soldier we have, and you could use some hair on your head. Why not wear the hair of some Indian's head that you cut off, eh, Deon?"

"My wife may not appreciate the look of a Macedindian, sir."

Eumenes laughed. "I am sure she is proud of what you do—serving in the army of the greatest king on earth."

What good was pride if my wife never got to see me? If I never saw my daughter grow? If I never experienced some of the luxurious life I had seen the rich live. "I am sure she is, general. So she says in her letters."

My wife's last letter was a year ago, delivered from the empire's messengers, and its contents still burned in my mind.

My dear husband, I hope you are well. May Poseidon protect you and deliver you back to us. Alexa grows by the day, and I worry for her safety as she enters her womanhood. They say the mines are a terrible place, and he threatens that he will sell us there. I pray that King Alexander returns home. We long to see you.

Eumenes grinned as he gingerly ate a mouthful of meat and drank some wine.

"What about your family, sir?"

He seemed taken aback by my frank question. "I have a wife and a son. Both back in Cardia. And just like you, Deon, I have not seen them in years."

He changed the subject again. "So, what do the physicians say about your ability to lead the troops?"

"I cannot lead a charge anytime soon—"

"Then you are no longer useful for the army," He said sternly, as he leaned forward, clasped his hands, and stared at me.

That stung. The realization that I would no longer lead my troops in honor of the King was painful, and now to hear it directly from a general, no less, was a blow—my chest hurt. To lose my position would also dent my earning and jeopardize my mission to free my family!

"I'm only joking, soldier! I lack the natural humor you have, but the army could use a man of your talent. Many talents."

I was immensely relieved. "I am always at your and the King's service. I do not want to go home in disgrace as a wounded, discarded soldier," I said, bowing deferentially.

Eumenes nodded and smiled. "I have the perfect position for you in mind."

CHAPTER 3.

BY THE HYPHASIS RIVER, INDIA

My active military duty ended with my injury. Eumenes hired me as an adjutant, and my job was to support him on a diverse range of topics—from minor administration to military tactics to replaying conversations with other senior leaders, including other generals. My pay was marginally better than as a soldier and with less risk.

While I pretended that I missed combat, I was secretly pleased with gentler duty and the chance to watch senior men at work.

A few weeks after my new role, we had moved further east into India closer to the Hyphasis River. The terrain was quite benign; shrubbery and trees dotted the vast plains, and we passed farmers' fields and abandoned villages on the way.

One morning Eumenes asked me to join him on his early morning walks. We had respite from the rains and chirps filled the air. We dressed comfortably in loose-fitting *chitons* and walked by the river that showed its gentle side, like a beautiful woman quiet before raging at her husband.

"There is a council with seven Indian tribes today," he said, "Alexander wants to know what it means to go deeper into India."

I was surprised. "I thought Porus told him all he needed to know."

"He is not satisfied with Porus' and others' answers about the Indian heartland. He thinks they know little about the vast country. Their fantastical stories are difficult to believe. It has become hard to separate truth from nonsense."

Alexander was aware of the growing resentment among his soldiers who longed to return home with the spoils of war and wanted to know what he was getting into.

Eumenes continued, "He hopes that these tribes have intimate knowledge of the Indian empire beyond the river Ganges."

He then paused as he knelt to pick some wildflowers, and then wiped his hands on his garment. Then, he said, "I want you to join me."

It was an exceptional opportunity to be in the same room with a man who was no less than a god. Eumenes instructed me to pay attention to the words of the translators but watch the behavior of the Indians.

I sat with the stars of Alexander's court—Ptolemy, Perdiccas, Craterus, and of course Eumenes, among others. I was transfixed by Alexander; never had I been so close to the King. We waited for him to summon the Indians. Eumenes noticed me tapping my fingers on my knee and shaking my leg. "Calm down," he said, grinning, "no one here knows you or cares."

Soon, twenty Indians walked in. Proud in their ways, they did not bow to the King. They clasped their palms together in greeting and made their way around the seating. Most of them wore jewelry, and many wrapped their heads in bright white cloth. They had anointed their foreheads, shoulders, and chests, which they left bare, with ash and covered their lower body with decorative tunics wrapped around their waist down to their ankles.

One of them had his head completely shaved but for a small patch of hair on the top of his skull. He was a *brahmana*—a priest or a teacher. He painted his forehead with three horizontal stripes of ash. He came with a boy who looked regal in his bearing.

After the pleasantries, of which they made many, the two sides got to business. And until the sun reached the high point in the sky they conferred. It was fascinating to watch them describe the land beyond the Hyphasis.

The conversations were animated. Men raised voices, others made pacifying gestures, some nodded away in the heat, some ate while conversing among themselves, and as the time progressed most simply stopped listening.

Once the council came to an end and the King bade them goodbye, he ordered that the council regroup later that night to discuss what we heard. Eumenes once again asked me to join them, and when we restarted, the conversation centered on what mattered most to Alexander—what difficulty lay ahead if they marched forward and how might they prepare? The discussion got heated, and I watched in worry as the leaders made assumptions and said things that were simply not true—either on purpose or having heard only parts of conversations. The consensus was that the Indians had told Alexander that he should march east deeper into India.

Eventually, the King turned to Eumenes. "Eumenes?"

All eyes turned to Eumenes. A hint of irritation showed on some of the senior men who seemed to resent the importance Alexander gave Eumenes.

Just a bookkeeper.

"King Alexander, I think there is merit in hearing what my restless adjutant has to say, for he has a rather remarkable sense of observation and memory and may have noticed something we have not. I ask you to grant him permission to speak."

Alexander nodded. His eyes turned towards me, and so did all the others. I could see them thinking,

What did this man have to say that they did not already know?

As I tried to speak, my voice, nervous, squeaked. Seleucus yelled, "Why did you bring a crow, Eumenes!"

That caused much laughter. I was grateful for the distraction. "I am honored to—"

"What happened to your teeth? You could scare the Indians by just opening your mouth!" Ptolemy bellowed.

Seleucus and Ptolemy were not unlike each other—both had noble backgrounds, they were of similar age to Alexander, except Seleucus was bigger and muscular compared to Ptolemy, and had a rounder face. They both competed for Alexander's attention—whether in private or in the battlefield.

Alexander smiled, and my cheeks burned in embarrassment. I admit I am not a handsome man, but women in the past have admired my physique and my rough face, even if that made me appear more a lout than a man of intelligence or refinement. But I would much rather have a laughing King's council than an angry one.

"Be quiet!" Alexander admonished them.

And all eyes were on me.

I cleared my throat and began. "Your majesty, esteemed generals, I observed three things.

"First, there were not seven tribes here today, but four.

"Second, the *brahmana*, who called himself Vishnocottus and the young boy with him Sandrocottus do not belong to any of the tribes, they most certainly found their way into this council through unknown means and came from Taxiles*—"

"I remember them, the priest spoke towards the end, but he was such a bore," said Craterus.

"He was lecturing, the translator looked like he wanted to strangle the man," Ptolemy agreed.

"As did the other Indians—they interrupted him several times," said Perdiccas, and he gestured at me, "Continue."

"Third, I do believe the chiefs may be lying about the ease of our passage from here on, and the *brahmana's* assessment was correct and at odds with his countrymen."

That drew some howls of feigned anger. Craterus stood up and threw up his hands and reached for a cup of wine. He retracted when the King gave him a sharp look and flicked a finger at him. Alexander's eyes darkened, and in his characteristic style, he angled his face from his neck, looking upward at me. "Talk to me about each one and speak your mind."

This was a gamble—and my chance, in my little way, to convince the King that we should return.

I bowed.

"Each tribe in the region has distinct ornamentation—and yet I noticed only four, not counting the priest and the boy. I do not know why they came here with a lie."

"Fascinating," said Ptolemy and the others nodded. An encouraging sign that I had their attention.

"Second, what I found most compelling are the remarks from Vishnocottus the *brahmana*. May I repeat what they said and correlate my observations from elsewhere?"

"Yes, go ahead, and do not ask for permission for every sentence," Alexander said, with a hint of irritation. He seemed not happy with the direction of my speech, but the council was certainly interested.

"The *brahmana* spoke near the end, having stayed silent the entire period, and his voice was lost in the din of cross discussions and other Indians shouting or ridiculing him. This is what he said:

"I would gently disagree with many of my countrymen, King Alexander. The army of Agrammes is larger than they say and more powerful. Allow me to relay the facts:

"You will have to cover great distances, bear challenging weather, fight fierce people who, while they bear no love for their King, seek to preserve their way of life. Finally, the King's army, the extent of which my fellow men do not fully understand—"

Alexander lifted his hand, and I stopped. "You speak these words with confidence, do you remember them exactly as he said?"

"Yes, your majesty. I do. Though of course, I repeat the words of the interpreter."

He looked around, and Ptolemy spoke up, "I remember something similar now that he says it, Alexander."

Ptolemy then looked at me intently as he scratched his testicles from underneath the loose garment. The humid, wet weather caused itches that afflicted men no matter their station.

Alexander muttered something at Ptolemy who looked down at his feet. Craterus began to look at something behind us, avoiding meeting the King's eyes. I decided to persevere. Then I described the army of India, as recounted by the *brahmana*, causing further consternation.

Craterus sighed loudly enough for everyone to look at him. "Those are very large numbers, two thousand elephants!"

"And a thousand chariots?" said Perdiccas, sounding worried.

"And this is just a fourth of the army..." said Ptolemy. I now had their attention, but Alexander's irritation was unmistakable.

"Go on," encouraged Ptolemy.

"Behave like generals instead of teenage maidens fearing their gruff husbands!" Alexander's voice rose at them. But he looked at me and flicked a finger telling me to continue.

I shifted to come closer to the council seating then described the distance to the capital *Pataliputra*.

"That is like crossing Persia all over again, and in far worse conditions!" exclaimed Perdiccas, as he waved a cup in the air.

"Are you sure you are not making this up?" asked Ptolemy—tensed that I was about to push Alexander into a tantrum.

"I pledge on the gods, sir," I said and looked around for support. Finally, Perdiccas spoke up. "He is not lying, I remember fragments of this, but clearly we were not paying attention by then."

"That is because you are a poor drunk," said Seleucus.

"Says the man who soils his tunic after just a few cups!" retorted Perdiccas, but the banter broke the tension, and I felt confident to continue to relay the *brahmana's* words.

"India's climate is unlike Gandhara, or Persia. Your army, as it walks these vast distances, will find the rains, snow, and sun as your first enemy, before you even face the King of India.

"Then come the people. While it is true that the they are unhappy with the king—for they see him as a cruel despot and of lower blood, they are fiercely loyal to their land and will look unkindly upon a foreigner that interrupts their way of life."

"Those chiefs made it sound like we would be welcomed as liberators," said Seleucus. He was imposingly large, and the mass of his golden hair bobbed as he theatrically shook it.

Eumenes finally spoke. "How many of the saints and tribes we have met so far treated us as liberators?" he asked, and no one answered.

"Yes, Eumenes, you have spoken to every saint and tribe, now keep your mouth shut," Alexander yelled at him. Eumenes bent his head, but I could see him suppressing a grin. Ptolemy guffawed. It was a revelation to me seeing these men behave like collegial louts, and yet they were world conquerors. Strange are the ways of life.

"To the south of Agrammes' kingdom are the proud *Gangaridays*. Their capital lies further four hundred miles to the east of *Pataliputra*. While the kingdoms detest each other, there are royal marriages between the two, causing an uneasy truce. You may be god where you come from, King Alexander, but you are an unknown in the heart of India."

Alexander raised his eyebrows and I sensed his mood darken.

The room went deathly quiet. For several moments no man stirred, and my palms turned cold.

"I am only conveying his words, Your Majesty, not mine—" I stuttered.

"Alexander was god even before—" started Craterus, and Perdiccas placed his palm on Craterus' forearm to silence him. There were rumors that Craterus was slowly falling out of favor with the King due to his snide remarks.

Alexander said nothing. I continued.

"Your incursion will embolden them to join hands and face a foreign invader. You have seen the determination of those that have fought you, now imagine people in far greater numbers with the same spirit. These I bring to you for consideration."

I paused and looked around. The council had listened attentively, and many recognized that they had not paid attention to what the *brahmana* had said. But hearing me recount it in exact detail, there came a realization that this priest had spoken in the clearest terms with distances, names, and places, compared to vague generalities and fantastical descriptions of the rest.

"Your recollection is impressive, but why must we believe what this priest said? How do we know he has no personal stake? Is he a spy of their King? We should bring him and the boy back and put them to torture to get the truth," said Craterus.

"The *brahmana*'s descriptions match the most with several reports we have heard in the past year, sir."

Craterus raised his eyebrows. "Go on."

I then recounted in detail my various conversations with Indians from different parts during the campaign, and how those details, from people unrelated, matched to what the *brahmana* said, thereby validating those details.

Alexander was furious. "It cannot be that a single man's account holds sway over all the other men! How do we know you are not making this up?"

Blood drained from my face.

I knew the implications of the angry King—Alexander had murdered one of his closest friends, Cleitus the Black, in a fit of rage not too long ago. And that was not the only time. He had his court historian Callisthenes, nephew of his revered teacher, imprisoned and put to death based on charges which to all of us seemed patently false.

Craterus, much to my surprise, intervened.

"He has nothing to gain from this, Alexander. Let us discuss this further ourselves."

Alexander dismissed me. I thought I had impressed the ruling council—to detriment or profit, only time would tell.

I had, of course, not mentioned one interesting aspect of the council discussions. More than once, I had noticed that the *brahmana* and his pupil made distinct eye contact with Eumenes, Ptolemy, and Seleucus, and had exchanged nods when they thought no one was looking.

They had certainly made prior contact, but I decided to ignore it for I had a hunch what mischief was afoot.

Counter to the wishes and counsel of his *Somatophylakes*, Alexander announced that they would march east deeper into India.

However, without the King's knowledge, the wily generals—I would never find out who, but whispers suggested Ptolemy, Seleucus, and Eumenes—seeded misinformation among the troops that the Indians had strongly recommended the King against proceeding. It seemed they had exaggerated the numbers I mentioned.

The four armies of the Indian King became five.

The five thousand archers became twenty-five thousand.

The enmity between the Kingdoms became a great friendship and unbreakable bond.

The elephants became bigger, faster, more fearless, and far greater in number than ever mentioned. The only thing it seemed they were incapable of was flying.

The fertile but mildly challenging terrain across the Ganges became "impassable mountains and fierce warriors skilled at fighting in the snow."

The *brahmana* became "an expert and a former minister in the King of India's court."

There was even insinuation that some of the Indians in the council were spies for Agrammes sent to assess Alexander and his armies.

It became impossible to tell truth from lie.

The army, exhausted, homesick, and strongly wishing to return to stable governed areas in Macedon and Asia, mutinied. It was unlike anything I had ever seen. They were riotous, insubordinate, and much to the astonishment of the King, unwilling to listen to anything he said. After sulking in his tent for days, Alexander finally relented.

While I worried for my life, nothing untoward happened. I was ecstatic that we were on the way back—though the worry that I had not made enough money to free my family remained. We began our return journey on the Indus river towards the southern seas, followed by a dangerous and long march along the Gedrosian desert with Alexander, while the Navy, led by admiral Nearchus, tracked along the coast.

I was relieved upon seeing the magnificent gates of the most famous city in Mesopotamia.

Babylon.

CHAPTER 4.

MACEDON

Apollonia stood with her head hung low as Diona harangued her about incomplete work. Her husband, Krokinos, stood by his wife not saying much for when his wife flew into a rage Krokinos knew the best course of action was to be quiet.

Diona leaned and poked Apollonia's frail shoulder, causing her to flinch. Apollonia's eyes opened wide—neither Krokinos nor his wife had ever touched her before. Lately, things had taken a turn for the worse. The initial days after Deon left, Krokinos was surprisingly gentle. He let Apollonia recover from the shock and sorrow and allowed the mother and daughter to settle in the servant's quarters. The work was light, and Krokinos had assured her multiple times that as soon as Deon settled the debt, they were free to leave. But he never told her what the debt was.

But Apollonia learned recently that business was getting harder for Krokinos. The world was in a shock that King Alexander had died, and the quarreling among regional leaders had intensified, putting pressure on businessmen such as Krokinos who were now harassed on a regular basis for tax and protection. All this unpleasantness from work bled into the house and mood of the master, and the mistress, had soured. Now it seemed like even minor transgressions were being treated far more harshly than before.

Krokinos tried to mollify his wife, but she swatted away his hand, and he retreated to his study.

Apollonia's back hurt. She had lost weight, and her eyes had sunken. Her once lustrous hair no longer had the shine or the bounce. Each day was a painful reminder of how their life had transformed from idyllic bliss to a glimpse of Hades. Her sadness had transferred to her daughter. The joy and innocence of childhood had vanished under the oppression—her friends had stopped coming to play. The honey chews were no longer available. Alexa was a very quiet little girl now, and her sorrowful looks felt like daggers in Apollonia's gut.

As she returned to the kitchen, Apollonia checked that no one was watching, and then she placed her back to the cold stone wall and began to weep. All she knew was that her husband was far away, and that he was alive, and that after a campaign in a strange, mysterious land called India the army was headed back. She did not know where.

The tears flowed, but there was no one to wipe them away.

CHAPTER 5.

BABYLON, MESOPOTAMIA

The omens were foreboding. It had been several days since Alexander appeared in front of the troops. There were rumors abound in the capital, and generals worried what would happen if he died without anointing a successor. It was now day eight of his fever, and we were convinced these were Alexander's final days. I had seen soldiers die of similar symptoms in the humid swamps of India and the backwaters of Babylon.

The generals moved from a state of disorganized panic to a state of controlled worry on how to rule the empire after his death. Added to this complication was the fact that Craterus, the most respected and distinguished of all his generals, was on the way to Macedon, per Alexander's orders, before the King fell ill. This meant the steady hand of a popular leader was unavailable if there was a full-scale riot.

Eumenes asked that I join him and the others in the King's bedchamber.

Late afternoon the King opened his eyes.

He looked at his senior men—the *Diadochi*—his potential successors. Ptolemy and Seleucus, looking haggard with worry, stood by Perdiccas. The others were on the other side of the bed.

Eumenes stood dressed as a scribe, with a writing parchment in his hands. His demeanor conveyed that he posed no threat and had no interest in the political power play ahead. One could only guess if the others bought this charade, for Eumenes was as ambitious and skilled as any man in that circle.

The King's unfocused gaze wandered among the people clustered around him, and his mouth produced little more than a stream of guttural sounds: the first of any noise we had heard from him in two days.

Ptolemy took the bold step and asked loudly, "Alexander, who do you appoint as your successor?"

Alexander did not answer, instead he looked at his pregnant wife Roxane who stood a foot behind Perdiccas. Even in the fog of his fever, I wondered if the King saw the danger to his barbarian wife and unborn child.

Alexander feebly lifted his hand, the one with his imperial signet ring, and I could see the *Diadochi* tense—was he about to offer his ring to the presumed successor? His hand came half-way from the bed, and at that moment, the light shone briefly on the purple gemstone perched on the ring, blinding some. Perdiccas moved quickly, too fast for the others to react, and knelt before the King's hand. He gripped Alexander's forearm in a sign of deep reverence and kissed his palm. And as if to accept the gesture he gently pulled the ring off Alexander's finger and raised it above his head.

The message Perdiccas sent was unmistakable; Alexander had anointed him, successor.

I could see Ptolemy's enraged expression, but he held back, for Ptolemy was nothing if not a calculative man biding his time. Seleucus seemed dazed, and a fleeting smile passed Eumenes' face.

At that moment, Alexander's hand fell.

It never rose again.

Alexander's death created a vacuum that appeared unfillable. His vast empire extended from Macedon all the way to the border of India. Even the most illustrious of his generals paled compared to the "man-god" who was now dead and had not anointed a successor, even though Perdiccas claimed that role. Alexander had no male heir to the throne to appoint. His pregnant wife was Bactrian and not from the Macedonian royal houses, much to the chagrin of the generals. Her strange mannerisms, accent, and barbarian heritage frustrated them. With the birth of Alexander's child impending but not yet assured, the natural next of kin was his idiot half-brother Philip Arrhidaeus, who exhibited the mental capacity of a 6-year-old.

Ptolemy, who wanted Egypt, received the satrapy of this rich and fertile land by the Great River.

Perdiccas would be regent for the empire and act as the regent protector of the half-wit King Arrhidaeus, who lacked the ability to speak a few coherent sentences, much less to rule.

Seleucus would govern the eastern provinces of Asia.

Eumenes, whom I still served, finagled a surprising victory from the spoils of Alexander's death—he received Cappadocia, with its fine horses and powerful cavalry. He was delighted. He had gone from a scribe to a satrap.

Perdiccas. Ptolemy. Seleucus. I sensed that these men would play a great role in the future of the vast empire.

Craterus and Antigonus were the other two notable characters, but I was unsure what role they would play in the theater that would unfold.

I stayed put with control of a small unit, with the primary purpose of guarding Eumenes through these dangerous times, as he navigated his new responsibility and prepared to leave for Cappadocia when the time was right. I was certain that he would take me with him. But while greater men quarreled for what was theirs, I had my own worry. My earnings were far from enough for pay Krokinos' debt, and the uncertainty of these times made me very anxious. Eumenes receiving Cappadocia was good news—it would get me much closer to home. I planned to ask leave of him, request a bonus for myself for my service, and go to free my family.

I was also planning to ask for a substantial loan which I hoped he would entertain.

It was at this time that I received the next letter from my wife.

My dear husband. When will the gods bring you to us? We hear the King is returning. Our days are full of sorrow and nights wet with tears. Krokinos starves us when he is angry. His lecherous son eyes Alexa. He says you have two years, or we will die in the depths of earth. Please beg your generals to free you. Come back to us.

That letter pierced my heart. They had not known yet that Alexander was dead. I imagined my Apollonia at Krokinos' house, worn, weathered, doing back-breaking work as my little girl probably played nearby. I imagined them shouted at, and I began to feel greater anxiety about returning. But asking to return now would not bode well for me and going back with only a fraction of what I needed to secure their freedom would be risky for me—physically and financially. They had to wait for me some more. We had two years, that was more time than I needed to work out an arrangement to repay my debts.

Meanwhile, embalmers had begun to mummify Alexander's body. They would then place his body in a sarcophagus, housed in a magnificent horse-drawn funerary temple. Perdiccas would arrange for a parade from Babylon to Macedon for burial in the royal tombs.

The tense months began in the fetid, sweltering weather. I had to be patient until we moved to Cappadocia to seek my release and request my bonus and loan. I sent a letter to Krokinos asking him for patience and that I would be returning soon, and an additional message to my wife asking them to wait a little longer.

CHAPTER 6.

BABYLON, MESOPOTAMIA

Eumenes had much to do. Alexander's procession would leave soon and Arrhidaeus—an able commander who was well known to Perdiccas—would lead it to Macedon through Syria. The body was a potent symbol. Whoever had it would gain legitimacy as a ruler.

Perdiccas often muttered that Alexander's mother would crucify him and feed his body to the dogs if the *Diadochi* did not cremate her son in the Argead royal tombs as was the custom in the Macedonian royalty. Alexander's wish to be buried in the temple of Ammon in Egypt could not be honored.

Eumenes was sure of one thing: The Empire would soon erupt into a bloody war, with each general vying for parts of each other's satrapies, or even perhaps the entire empire. Personal relations and ambitions were sure to create fissures quickly.

Even his life would soon be in danger.

Craterus was on the way to Macedon. War with Perdiccas was just a matter of time.

Ptolemy, who received the richest satrapy after Persia, would undoubtedly come under attack from Perdiccas or Craterus eventually—it was simply too valuable a province to stay on its own.

Perdiccas. Ptolemy. Seleucus. Craterus.

He would have to keep an eye on these four—though his allegiance now was to the Regent Perdiccas. Antigonus waited in Phrygia, and no one knew what he would do.

For now, Eumenes decided, he would continue as planned to take Cappadocia under his control, a fantastic region that would be a great starting point for him to build his power and presence. And it was time for him to finally unlock Callisthenes' secret. But there was one problem. It had become impossible to gain access to Callisthenes' papers.

The papers went under Craterus' control just after Callisthenes' imprisonment. When Craterus left for Macedon, he had transferred them to Perdiccas. Neither men knew its importance, but Eumenes could not gain access without arousing suspicion.

He was a Royal Secretary, yet circumstances had prevented him. It was incredibly frustrating.

In his misguided sense of devotion to Alexander, Perdiccas had decided that most of the royal papers that were neither a will nor Alexander's plan, would be buried in Alexander's tomb.

Eumenes thought he could persuade Perdiccas—but he soon thought the better of it. In times such as these friendships meant little, and if the temperamental Perdiccas even suspected something afoot, Eumenes might forever lose the papyri, and his life as well. The gods knew he had attempted several times—bribes, stealth, and even excuses of study for posterity—all were frustrated by Perdiccas' loyal guards. Perdiccas even scolded him once when the guards revealed one such attempt. Further inquisitiveness would only raise suspicion.

So, Eumenes hatched a plan.

Eumenes walked alone through rings of security. He felt miserable with his sweaty wet armpits and itchy scalp. Even the cold marble floors and wavy curtains of the palace did not bring relief. The new Regent had made himself busy administering the empire on behalf of the new King Arrhidaeus and coaxing and cajoling the other generals to take stations and pledge allegiance.

Perdiccas was also waiting nervously to hear from Craterus if he would continue his journey towards Macedon, for he did not want this famous general to turn back for whatever reason.

Eumenes walked along a wide, ornate corridor and entered a large, well-appointed room. Perdiccas' official chamber, once Alexander's. Eumenes felt a tinge of envy—only if he could wield this power and authority!

Perdiccas sat on a flat bench decked with gold-embroidered finery and customary purple cushions, symbolizing royal stature. He dressed in his Macedonian military costume—a deep brown cuirass, purple plumed helmet, and an ornate sheathed kopis on his waist. He pretended to be reading when Eumenes entered.

"Good to see you after many days, Eumenes!"

"Greetings Perdiccas, no doubt you have been busy managing the empire—I hold no grudge for you not meeting an old friend for many days."

Perdiccas raised an eyebrow. Whether it was for Eumenes referring to him as an old friend for he saw himself as the King and deserving of such respect or because Eumenes termed it as a grudge.

"We must talk about the plans for the procession of Alexander's body back to Macedon. Alexander's mother wonders why the wait," Eumenes said.

"That old hag should keep her mouth shut and let me decide what to do!" Perdiccas grumbled.

The stress was beginning to affect him.

He looked haggard with bags under his bloodshot eyes, and his fingers trembled nervously as he paced about. But Eumenes knew that Perdiccas would not take on the Royals so early, as it would be a fatal mistake.

"The body of Alexander is of immense value, and you know that more than anyone else," Eumenes said. This was a touchy subject. Perdiccas looked up, and without expression nodded Eumenes to continue. "It is important that we take the King to his rightful resting place, and that journey goes without a hiccup."

"You are bold to insinuate that the *Diadochi* would attempt something so foolish."

"Do you really believe that no *Diadochi* will attempt to benefit from the King's body?"

Perdiccas stayed quiet. For all his faults, the one redeeming quality was his fanatical loyalty to Alexander, even after the King's death. Eumenes continued to exhort. "Do not be naïve. Times have changed, and it is in both our interests to see the procession reach its destination safely."

Perdiccas sighed. "Go on, Eumenes," he said.

"Plan the procession not just with Arrhidaeus, who I know you believe to be loyal to you, but also with someone else who can keep an eye on that man."

"That may be prudent," Perdiccas remarked.

"Move the procession North along the river before dropping towards Damascus and then Sidon. This will keep the route away from potential incursions.

"Once in Sidon move it North along the sea—always guard the right and watch the sea to the left.

"Reveal the route to no one. It is both our desire that the King rests at his rightful place, under his mother's watch."

Perdiccas and Eumenes then refined the approach, security, and organization associated with the procession. And then came the time which Eumenes waited for Perdiccas to ask.

"Eumenes, this is a good plan. Who might act as a trustworthy eye on Arrhidaeus?"

Eumenes leaned back and crossed his arms. His eyes squinted, and he placed a finger on his lips and grunted dramatically. "I have one name—a man that has worked closely with me and I trust."

"Do I know him?" asked Perdiccas, as he looked intently at Eumenes over the wine cup.

"Deon, the son of Evagoras, who has served as my adjutant. You have seen him several times. He is loyal and a great observer who can report anything that seems out of place," said Eumenes.

"What is his history? I do not remember the details—since when has he served us?"

Eumenes briefly described Deon's background, role, and service record. "Sounds like a good man. He is loyal to you Eumenes, but me?" Perdiccas smiled with a wicked curl of his lips.

"I have no doubt. His loyalty to me extends without question to you too."

Perdiccas nodded.

"I think a talent will ensure that he stays on the task," Eumenes said, explaining that Deon had need for money.

"A talent, you say? That is ten years of his earning!"

"Depends on the price you assign to the task, Regent."

Perdiccas leaned on his cushion and nibbled on a date. He looked outside the window that opened to show the vista of the river. At a distance, the remarkable gardens built on a terrace looked like a forest that hung from the skies. Perdiccas stood and placed his hand on Eumenes' shoulder. Then he walked with the Greek and directed him towards the door. "You have given me much to think, Eumenes. In these challenging times, I am glad to have you by my side. Wait here."

Perdiccas dismissed Eumenes and went back to his table.

Perdiccas completed his plans after considering Eumenes' advice, and that of several others. The impressive horse-drawn funerary temple, over twenty feet wide and fourteen feet tall, and holding Alexander's sarcophagus, would be a remarkable sight as it passed through towns and cities. Three important boxes would go with the sarcophagus.

The first—personally inspected by Perdiccas, would hold a large cache of the most precious personal artifacts—four kopides and a javelin, replicas of Alexander's Persian diadem and scepter, breastplate, helmet, and a copy of the royal diaries.

The second—the most precious gifts bestowed upon the king from various lands.

The third—papers, some administrative, and some from Callisthenes' collection. Perdiccas decided these would act as historical relics.

Arrhidaeus would lead the procession guarded by a contingent of front and rear guard. Following the procession would be the baggage train with the soldier's' belongings, supply, mechanics and road menders, engineers, cooks, cleaners, accountants, treasury officers, translators, wives and children of the soldiers, priests, augurs, physicians, healers, and messengers.

Perdiccas composed his orders.

"… The King's procession shall be guarded by the finest of the cavalry and infantry.

I appoint Arrhidaeus as the officer in charge. He shall have the power and authority of the Regent to direct the affairs of the procession, retaliate against incursion as he sees fit, and deliver the King to his mother. The council rewards Arrhidaeus with ten talents of gold.

To support Arrhidaeus in this task and to act as captain of the rear guard, I appoint Burrhus. The council awards him two talents of gold on success of this mission.

To access, examine, or steal contents of the funeral temple will result in crucifixion."

Perdiccas knew these were not ordinary times, and he had an uneasy feeling that clever Eumenes was up to something. So, he had chosen a man he knew—Burrhus.

Perdiccas remembered Deon—the man with the extraordinary memory, skilled in military tactics and strategy, and close to Eumenes all these years. Close bonds did not bode well in such missions, and high intelligence was often a source of mischief—something Perdiccas had enough to deal with. Besides, Deon's history was difficult to find. There were rumors that he once ran a brothel, and that he was also a teacher. This made the man complex and unpredictable, not something Perdiccas wanted to risk.

Burrhus, another officer recommended to him, on the other hand, was a brute.

Perdiccas' intelligence officers had recounted an example of Burrhus personally crushing the heads of every male member of a captured party. He had then handed the women to the infantry for their personal pleasure and thrown the children off a cliff.

That was what he needed, a man who would obey rules blindly with loyalty but was just intelligent enough to follow delicate orders.

Eumenes was summoned and told of Perdiccas' order. It hurt Eumenes that Perdiccas had ignored his recommendation, but it was not very surprising for Perdiccas was a suspicious man.

Eumenes returned to his station, his mind a cauldron of emotions.

CHAPTER 7.

BABYLON, MESOPOTAMIA

Guards came to my tent one morning and said that The Regent Perdiccas and General Eumenes awaited me in the Royal Palace. I shuffled to the palace, nervous, wondering what this was about. Perdiccas wore a loose-fitting blue embroidered Persian gown, and Eumenes looked every bit a scribe.

I saluted and waited.

"We have a mission for you, Deon," Perdiccas said.

I looked at Eumenes quizzically, but he said nothing.

"Yes, sir," I said.

"You know that we must transport the King's body and royal possessions to his burial."

"Yes, sir."

"We must safely get it to his mother and ensure he finds home in the royal Argead tombs in Macedon."

"Yes, sir."

"We need trustworthy men to escort the procession and ensure it reaches the destination safely."

"Yes, sir." I was excited at where this conversation was headed. If I were to accompany the King's funeral procession, not only would I forever hold the honor of being one of the men to take the King to his resting place, but I would also be home! I would use the opportunity to make more money where I could.

But the Regent did not look happy—he continued dourly. "I had another man in mind—"

My excitement came crashing down, just like the palace of Persepolis when Alexander's drunken officers set fire to it. But Perdiccas continued, "But that fool got himself killed over a dispute."

My hopes were back up. The gods surely played with my emotions. Perdiccas then assessed me coolly with his glassy brown eyes, and said, "I have accepted Eumenes' recommendation that you be the captain of the rearguard."

Thrill coursed through my veins. I bowed and thanked them for the honor.

"Do not disappoint me, Deon. We will also reward you with a handsome bonus of two talents."

Two talents! Glory to Demeter and Poseidon! The two talents, worth nearly twenty years of my salary, would bring me very close to securing my family's freedom. The chance to guard the King's procession would bring glory and help my reputation. And the procession would take me back home. It was as if every god smiled in unison and granted me a divine future.

Perdiccas then sternly described the details of the sensitive and extraordinary mission, and I was tongue-tied by what they entrusted me with. It was as if the gods had smiled at me—giving me a chance to be part of great glory and also help me free my family. Emotions raged in my mind like the rivers in the Indian monsoon. After I accepted the orders and returned, I was soon summoned to Eumenes' quarters. When I hurried there, Eumenes appeared to be in deep thought. He looked at me gravely and asked me if I were truly loyal to him.

The question caught me by surprise—he had never asked me that question before. It almost seemed like an unspoken expectation between the two of us—that he would take care of my well-being and aspirations, and that I would always obey his orders and protect him from dangers he did not see.

"Of course, you know I am, sir."

"So, what do you make of Perdiccas' request?"

"It is an honor to escort the King's procession. The reward is exceptional and will help me and my family. I cannot thank you enough, General Eumenes, I am forever indebted to you."

"Well, Deon, remember Perdiccas chose Burrhus. Unfortunately, that lecherous imbecile got himself killed unable to control what dangled between his legs. He died flopping about like a fish and bled all over the market pavement. Who knows which Babylonian whore's lover he angered?"

Eumenes smiled and his eyes twinkled slyly. That was when it dawned on me that Burrhus was not dead because he slept with some woman, but because if he went, then I would not.

There was more to this mission than what the Regent had told me.

"However, you are an intelligent man, and you must have guessed by now that this is not just about guarding the procession and its contents…"

Silence rang loud.

Eumenes looked around to check there was no one else in the tent. It was a sparse living quarter—he was never the one to deck his space with luxury. He had a comfortable bed, a single faded green cushion couch that could seat two or three people, a large table on which to lay the parchments and other planning material. In one corner, he had a gift given to him by Alexander—a shield once used by the King himself.

He lowered his voice.

"What I am about to ask of you is incredibly sensitive. Do you promise me on all you hold dear—your life and family—that you will obey?"

This was turning out to be the strangest conversation. "You know I will, and you keep me in great suspense, sir."

"I will reveal it all, but first let us seal this oath of loyalty."

With that, Eumenes went back to a corner of his tent and rummaged through a large sheepskin bag and retrieved some cloth, a few iron bars, and an idol.

Next, he created a mini-tent made of gorgeous purple fabric with the embroidery of royalty.

Within this tent, in the center, he placed an idol—that of Alexander. It was a beautiful, life-like image of the King, cut from black stone, showing him in his full battle gear. Then Eumenes lit four wax candles, and the entire structure looked remarkably like a holy shrine to god Alexander.

"Kneel before the King, Deon."

I did.

He made me swear absolute secrecy and loyalty to him and accept misery to all that I love if I betrayed him or the mission ahead.

What was so sensitive that he was going to these great lengths?

"What I am about to tell you has the power to change the course of the empire. I hid this from all so far for fear of what it might unleash, but the time has come to act. Do you truly swear to secrecy?"

"Would you like me to cut off my hand and bleed to death to prove my loyalty?" I said.

Eumenes made a mock show of anger by pointing a dagger at me. He settled down and began. "The truth behind your mission, Deon, has little to do with guarding and protecting the funerary procession," he said, as he relaxed in his seat.

"I imagined as much, sir. I struggled with the thought that you would send me away on guard duty while you were preparing to take charge of your new territories."

Eumenes clasped his fingers and leaned forward, looking at me intently.

"While you will head the rear guard of the procession, Deon, you will also steal something for me from the sacred chamber of the funerary temple," he said, without taking his eyes off me.

I stiffened, and I stammered at what I heard, "Steal... from the King's sacred chamber?"

"Yes. I know it sounds preposterous, but in there is a secret that will change the course of future."

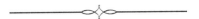

I tried to understand the enormity of the ask. If Arrhidaeus caught me thieving from the funerary temple, he would crucify me. Not only that, this act would ensure that my family either died in the mines or on a crucifixion pole. But to defy Eumenes would certainly pose an immediate threat. It was as if Eumenes read my mind; the master strategist continued. "You worry about the implications of your arrest, and what it means to your loved ones."

I said nothing in response and let the silence hang in the air.

Eumenes waited, and then continued, "No harm will come to you if you were caught and arrested."

"You say that with certainty, sir."

"It is not a matter of if, but when, that the *Diadochi* will turn on themselves like hungry wolves attacking a plump deer that is Alexander's empire. Under such circumstances, a recognized man like yourself, aligned to me, will not be tried and executed, but bartered for favors and returns."

"I see that, General. But the risk is significant."

"Indeed, it is, but let me ask your opinion on something else," he said, as he began to pace around his tent.

"What if what you found helps anoint a single clear successor to the empire, with specific instructions to every *Diadochi* on their role?"

"That would bring peace, rather than mayhem and years of war, of that I am certain," I said, "are you suggesting there is a will that no one knows about, sir?"

Eumenes smiled. His eyes fluttered briefly—a strange expression passed his face. "You are astute. There is a will, written and sealed with Alexander's signet ring and certified by a court historian. And it anoints a single successor and his prime advisor."

I was stunned. Eumenes turned his face away from me as he looked out to the flickering lights of the palace. "The prime advisor is me. That I know. Who the successor is, I do not know."

"And the will is among the contents that go with the procession," I said, pre-empting Eumenes. "How do you know this, sir?"

He looked at me sadly. "Callisthenes was the man who certified the will and sealed it. He told me about it just before he was executed."

I wondered why Callisthenes would say this to Eumenes, and why he kept this a secret so long. But I knew better than to question him. There were details he was not sharing, and it was his prerogative. "So, the will Perdiccas announced after the King's death is—"

"Fake. Made up by greedy charlatans that hunger for the empire, with outlandish and outrageous terms that no one believes."

Eumenes' voice was now low and quiet. "I will have the ears of the new King. Consider the implications to the empire, and to yourself," he said, as he turned towards me. I stayed quiet—breathless. Eumenes continued. "We will bring peace and prosperity, and you and your family will live a life of comfort from the two talents of reward Perdiccas promised. I will continue to employ you if you wish to remain in service. Besides, your wounds have healed, and you seem perfectly fit for the mission."

I sat stunned hearing the story. Surely this was no trickery?

A lie perpetrated on Eumenes by Callisthenes?

Or by Eumenes on me?

I believed Eumenes. In all our years together, he had never given me a chance to doubt him. But the times were different, and we were of vastly different station and ambition.

But a slow anger began to rise in me.

Ten years in service.

All the blood, tears, fear.

I was no ignorant donkey to be swayed by oaths of loyalty and the greater goodness of the empire, while he benefited vastly. Eumenes would attain fame and great luxury while I would start where I was before my debts.

I knew why he was asking me—there was no one else he could trust! The wily Greek knew that the Macedonians had no love for him, and his options were very limited. Besides, if

Perdiccas even got wind of this, he would have Eumenes butchered than to risk his regency.

This was time to be bold, and I took the risk. "What is my reward, sir?"

Eumenes looked at me sharply; my questions appeared to have taken him by surprise. "The two talents from Perdiccas is twenty years of your salary, Deon, and I negotiated that with the Regent on your behalf," he said, and the warmth in his eyes was gone.

Anger began to fill my head, like a snake crawling through a closed space—hissing, flicking. "That was to guard the procession and get it to its final place, sir, not to steal from it and risk being tied to a cross and whipped to death," I said, my voice rising.

Eumenes stood immobile. I noticed him clench his fist and his jaws tightened. I briefly feared for my safety. "You surprise me, Deon," he said, finally, his voice oozing disappointment.

"General. We have both served together and made it through much hardship. Let me share a piece of your glory," I said, mustering my courage, but in a reconciliatory voice.

He took a few steps back and sat down again. The Regent had appointed me to the procession which would leave soon, and if something happened to me as well, Perdiccas would suspect Eumenes that something was afoot. The Regent was no fool and had a terrible temper that no one would risk; not now.

Eumenes leaned back and casually dismantled the shrine with one hand, disgust clear in his gestures.

"What do you want, soldier?" he said, finally.

I had not had the chance to think through what I wanted, but the stakes were high enough for me to gamble. I took a deep breath and stood straight to hide my nervousness. The snake in my head calmed down.

"I have been nothing but loyal to you, sir, and you ask me to risk my life and family for your glory. What I ask for is a generous discharge from your service—and ownership of a small satrapy," I said, knowing that my ambition would surprise him.

Eumenes looked at me for a long time, unflinching.

"I underestimated your ambitions, Deon. I hope this time you will exercise better judgment with the money than to open another brothel," he said, as a wicked smile spread on his face. It was as if someone slapped me. Intense shame and guilt enveloped me, and heat rose up my face. I tried to respond, but my voice quivered.

"I don't care, soldier. We have had a fruitful relationship, and yes, you have my word—ten talents, and a minor governorship if you wish not to continue to serve me," he said.

I caught my breath.

Ten talents! That was a hundred years of my salary. More than enough for a great life—assuming I could live it peacefully.

Then Eumenes stopped, as if he struggled with something. When he finally raised his head for his eyes to meet mine, they were cold in a way I had never seen him before. "This is a contract, Deon. If I find you crossed me, then it is not just you in jeopardy, but so is your family," he said, the threat unmistakable.

We stood facing each other for a long time, saying nothing. I had saved his life. He had saved my career. We had a trusting relationship that had suddenly turned into a contract, and we both had played a role in this. This time, my relationship with Eumenes would be different. I needed to know that he would not cast me away as a lowly soldier—a sand grain in the dunes of history, one among many who the world would never remember. We had a plan. It would be fraught with risk, but I would see it through, and he would act as my protector, watching over me to the extent he could.

No one else would know. No one else would be told. And if we died, Callisthenes' secret would go with us to the heavens, the empire would erupt in flames, and my wife and daughter would die cursing me for abandoning them.

Thirteen days later, the procession made its way out of Babylon on the way to Macedon. A magnificent spectacle befitting the greatest king the world had ever known—and there I was, the captain of the rear guard, with a secret mission to steal an artifact of world-changing consequence.

The procession progressed slowly and steadily first moving north of Babylon after crossing the river, and then westward in a gentle southern slope. At every town, throngs of people came to see the procession. The guards made a protective ring around the grand funerary temple—with its golden panels and figurines of Nike and lions on top of it, and Arrhidaeus often stopped the march to allow people to admire the beauty of the structure or kneel and bid goodbye. In deference to local customs sometimes a priest would take out a replica shield and pass it around the crowd for them to touch it.

The women lamented loudly, the children, excited at this grand procession, laughed and ran alongside, kicking up dust and annoying the guards who swatted them time to time. Rarely did we meet hostility—after the subjugation of

Persia, Alexander imbibed Persian customs, allowed local satraps to continue to govern, and punished the errant, greedy governors who terrorized their population. To them, he was a savior.

Perdiccas had defined a tight security procedure, and my hopes of getting into the sacred chamber vanished—a possibility that Eumenes did not predict. It was sometimes easy to underestimate The Regent because of his bumbling, fiery temperament.

My other hope, much to my own shame, was that someone would attack the procession and I would find opportunity in the melee.

Our journey went past barren lands into a valley somewhere between Babylon and Damascus. The local warlord, Arnobarbus, was new and emboldened with the preposterous idea that the death of Alexander somehow meant freedom and plunder. He planned to attack the procession—except the imbecile was unaware that one of his own men had betrayed this plan.

We stopped in a narrow valley, with gentle sloping mountains on each side. The only way they could approach us was through a gulley from the East, and we set up camp in such a way to suggest a clueless, resting caravan. All the support—the menders, priests, bag carriers, mechanics—received pieces of soldiers clothing and were made to stand guard or be in sleeping position, to give an impression of a resting camp.

Arrhidaeus stationed armed troops just beyond the swell of the low hills and invisible to the raiding party—one contingent of the cavalry on the left flank, and another near the entrance of the valley.

The soldiers of the infantry lay prone as if asleep just behind the motley group of fake soldiers. Arrhidaeus was with the cavalry, and I, with the infantry. At the early dawn at hint of sunlight, we saw the lookout swing his lamp.

We waited in silence.

Soon, the plumes of dust rose at the entrance of the valley, and Arnobarbus and his men appeared.

What mothers bore these suicidal idiots?

They made a tremendous noise, and behind their cavalry, a thousand bandits advanced rapidly. They wore light armor; some held short swords, some poorly made javelins, some tridents, some barbed clubs—it would be comical if it were not a real raid.

Our decoys scurried with dramatic terror and stood in disorganized lines, hiding the real infantry behind. Emboldened by what they saw, and almost rapturous in their excitement, Arnobarbus and his gang of fools, with their flowing dresses and useless weaponry, rushed forward deeper into the gulley with no hint of discipline or military tactics.

When only a stone's throw separated the bandits and our decoys, the lookouts sounded the horns—loud, clear, and rising above the din of the men and horses.

I could see the surprise in the bandits.

They must have realized then that we had tricked them. But committed too deep, like a giant ship on the seas, they could not turn and flee.

The decoys parted, and Arnobarbus saw what was in front. He would now experience what it meant to face a Macedonian phalanx. The bandits ground to an abrupt halt as the frightening mass of concentrated spikes, now pointed towards them, began to move forward rapidly.

And just as the surprised mass slowed down and waited for their chief's direction, they heard another blast of sounding horns and saw a wall of armored cavalry bear down on them from behind and the left. The horrified bandits abandoned all discipline and reacted as immature fighters do—some attempted to flee, others clustered in small groups waiting for the inevitable clash. The horses whinnied and galloped in all directions in terror.

As dust rose and obscured the landscape, I tried one desperate trick—I ran to the funerary temple, now unguarded, and entered the chamber through a maintenance ladder.

I could now hear the clashing of the armies, but in my heart, I had no doubt about the outcome.

The funerary temple's chamber held the gold sarcophagus of Alexander. It was the first time I was so close to the body and the treasured contents. I felt grief, guilt, and excitement at the same time. I removed my helmet as a mark of respect, prayed, and moved behind the sarcophagus. There were three boxes as described. One was magnificently laid out with gold and gems, with intricate engravings on its top and sides. The side facing me showed a royal assembly, with the king at the center, and a host of officers seated around him. The top had the military symbols of Alexander—his cuirass, kopis, helmet and royal plume, signet ring, the royal diadem. I wanted to knock a few gemstones off their fitting using the back handle of my kopis but thought the better of it.

Behind this box was a smaller, less ostentatious box. It was plainer, made of iron, and had metal carvings of a scene—Zeus towering behind a teacher and pupils holding tablets. This was what I was looking for. The box was however under heavy lock, and I could not open it.

I needed a hammer.

I jumped out and attracted no special attention except a few curious 'decoys' for the ones assigned to guard were busy at slaughter.

I paused to watch the massacre. The bandits were pincered between an advancing wall of spikes and an explosive cavalry charge. The foot soldiers, now in a panic, turned and rushed headlong into the phalanx, only to be impaled. As the infantry pushed them back, the cavalry butchered them from all directions. The battlefield resembled a closed slaughterhouse with helpless animals baying within.

Arnobarbus, the chief, was recognizable with his elaborate ornaments and flowing green dress, with its customary lions and patterns of lamps and flowers. His panicked bandits ignored his exhortations.

I found a heavy hammer from the baggage train, ran back, and climbed again into the funerary temple. I swiftly moved towards the box.

I raised the hammer and struck a hard blow on the lock. My shoulders felt a stinging pain due to the impact and the force traveling up my arms, but the lock did not break. And just when I was about to raise the hammer again, the curtains rustled and a tall Macedonian officer, a man I had seen in company of Arrhidaeus, stepped in.

"What are you doing?" he said, the menace was unmistakable.

"Why are you here?" I retorted, in the hope that displaying authority would cow the man.

"I am one of Arrhidaeus' temple protectors, and I'm asking you again, what are you doing?"

His eyes went to the hammer in my hand, and his right hand slowly gripped the handle of his kopis. I knew I had to act quickly before this would escalate and endanger me and my mission.

"I came in to check that no one got in to steal. I asked your name, soldier."

"That is none of your concern, sir. Why do you have a hammer in your hand if you were looking for thieves?" He smirked. I would be foolish to expect a trained officer to fall for weak lies. He moved slowly and cautiously, all the time rapidly surveying the space around me. Once again, a mark of a good soldier.

I waited until he was at an arm's length. There was not much space to maneuver as the chamber wall was behind me, and the two heavy boxes were by my leg. I would not have the time to pull my kopis out and engage him in hand-to-hand combat. "Do not do something stupid and attack your superior officer."

He paused momentarily. "My only superior officers are Perdiccas and General Arrhidaeus, sir," he said, as he inched forward.

"Think of the consequences—" I said, as I tracked his slow movement.

"General Arrhidaeus has complete confidence in me. You knew you were not supposed to be here alone."

"And I told you why—"

"As I said, sir, you have a hammer in your hand, and I think we both know why." He stepped forward. He had enough of the talk, and it appeared he had made up his mind.

I dropped to my knees, taking him by surprise and forcing him to readjust his position in the narrow confines of the chamber. And before he could wield his blade, I brought down my hammer on his right foot with full force.

The heavy iron crushed his bones. His eyes widened, and he bellowed and staggered backward. He thrust his kopis wildly. I avoided the edge of the blade and pulverized his knee with another blow. Screaming, he fell to the floor and tried to push himself back to the edge.

I hopped over the boxes just outside the reach of his arms. He was trying to sit.

I moved behind him, and before he could twist his body to face me, I brought down the hammer on his head. While our helmets did a reasonable job in protecting our skulls from weak arrows, light sword glances, and slowing projectiles—they were incapable of protection against heavy weapons in close quarters.

He tried to ward off the blow with his kopis. Its edge slashed my elbow but did not stop the hammer which crashed into his helmet and cracked his skull open.

He slumped silently. His back arched, his arms and leg stiffened and straightened, and the body twitched for several moments before it went still. The acrid smell of loose bowels and urine enveloped the chamber, and matter from his brain oozed from under the crushed helmet.

I heard noises outside.

I dropped the hammer, drew my kopis and inflicted a deep gash on his forearm. I then sat down holding my injured elbow as blood trickled between my fingers. Four soldiers, and thankfully one of them from the rear guard, stepped into the strange scene in front of them. News spread quickly, and Arrhidaeus' soldiers appeared.

I knelt on the ground, and a physician tended to my elbow. Some soldiers removed the body from the chamber and laid it on the ground.

The battle which raged had begun to slow. Most of the raiders were dead, and our troops were still slashing at the remaining ones who had nowhere to escape.

Someone barked an order to fetch Arrhidaeus, and I asked a soldier to also convey a message to stop the massacre and let some of them go home to tell tales. There was always a fine balance between suppression and keeping the hostile population in check, versus annihilating them and incurring the wrath and continued hostility from their tribes.

It was difficult to perceive the surrounding through the dust and commotion, but before the sun inched further up in the sky, I heard the sounding horns announcing the end of the battle. Arrhidaeus appeared, looking weary and exhausted. They had Arnobarbus in chains, dragged by one of the soldiers.

Arrhidaeus did not come to me at once—instead preferring for one of his men to explain what had happened.

Once they refreshed and Arrhidaeus gave orders for his staff to examine the battleground, inventory the dead and the dying, he walked up to me with a stern look.

"What were you trying to steal?" he asked, his voice a low growl like a beast about to pounce on his prey.

I looked up at him, squinting in the harsh sun obscured by dust, struggling to speak as the fine grains of sand dried my throat and tongue. My hands shook from exertion and weakness, and I balanced myself gingerly.

"It was I who prevented thievery!" I said, mustering as much indignation as I could. I then continued, "It appears your man was attempting to enrich himself when the opportunity presented."

With no one to contradict what I said, Arrhidaeus found himself in a tricky situation. He could, of course, ask for eyewitness accounts on who went in first and who later, and that would weaken whatever I had to say. But doing so would bring out fractures and recriminations against unreliable eyewitnesses. I was confident that there would be no lengthy public trial or investigation.

I was close to Eumenes who would undoubtedly try to protect me if there were a trial, and Perdiccas would support him—and it was unlikely Perdiccas would go against Eumenes and side with Arrhidaeus. I knew his mind was working through the scenarios. He had no idea what I was looking for, but it was reasonable for him to think I was planning to steal some valuables when I had a chance.

"Explain to me what happened then, because we will have to answer to Perdiccas and the Royals."

"That is assuming you want them to know, General, that one of your men tried to steal from the King's sacred chamber."

"Remember you report to me, Deon," he growled.

I was not going to accept assumed authority. "No, General. I report to the Regent. You outrank me, but my commanders are Perdiccas and Eumenes."

Arrhidaeus seemed miffed at my response, but he said nothing on that topic. "Why should I believe you?" he asked, instead.

"We both have been promised ample rewards and a pension. Why would I jeopardize it to steal jewelry from a box?"

He paused to consider my argument. Encouraged, I continued. "When the infantry began to advance, I was at the edge observing the entire battlefield keeping an eye for escapees or spies attempting to infiltrate us.

"From the corner of the eye, I noticed this man quietly and quickly climb up the temple, having separated himself from his group, and disappear into the chamber.

"As you know, we have strict instructions not to allow anyone to enter the chamber alone. Puzzled, I left the side of the infantry, seeing that the battle was in a great commander's control—"

Arrhidaeus' chest expanded slightly at the praise from a fellow soldier. Sometimes even if the mind tells you that what you hear is a lie, the body behaves as if it were the truth. Many of my fellow men who were robbed of their possessions by Babylonian whores would attest to this.

I continued, "When I climbed in, I saw him behind one of the boxes, ready to strike a blow on one of the ornate, jewel-studded boxes with his hammer. There is absolutely no reason for a man to attempt to open a lock except to steal."

Arrhidaeus seemed horrified by the implication. If this were true, it would bring great shame to his battalion. But for now, we were out of earshot from the others who stood quietly and deferentially.

"He seemed very surprised to see me, and when I asked him what he was doing here, he refused to answer. Instead, he raised his hammer and attacked me. There was no question that he was already of the unsound mind to even attempt something so sacrilegious, and then to try to kill me without even an attempt at dialog." I hoped that my indignant voice, coupled with dramatic expressions were effective in seeding doubt in Arrhidaeus' mind.

"I then slashed his arm, and when he lost his balance, I wrestled the hammer from his hand. And then I smashed his foot, knee, and finally his head."

I ended my story. It is always safe to say little to avoid exposing oneself in a lie. He stared at me, and then looked around. He took a step closer and knelt by my side, and whispered, "I know you are lying, Deon. I do not know what you were trying to do but what you say is not the truth. But you are a clever man, are you not? I will keep an eye on you. And the gods will keep an eye on you."

With that, he stood up, beckoned his men, and ordered them. "Take this man's body and leave it on the ground. He does not deserve final rites for what he did."

Arrhidaeus' eyes bored into mine as he said that, and I looked away. He knew I knew he knew I was lying. We were prisoners of our own evil making.

We then turned our attention to Arnobarbus, the idiot chief of a gang of fools. The shackled, scared man no longer brave, tried in vain to reason with Arrhidaeus. The soldiers tied his hands with rope connected to the handle of a luggage cart.

That night, as we rested under the dark skies of Syria, I prayed to the gods to allow the dead soldier's soul into Elysium and asked forgiveness for my actions which I believed to be right in the greater scheme of things.

In the morning, the procession continued onward.

Arnobarbus, dragged along, thirsty, and exhausted, fell to the ground. He had no strength to scream as his skin and flesh shredded over the rough ground, leaving pieces, flecks, and a trail of blood on the dusty earth, and he was soon reduced to a pink stump. We detached his body and left it to rot on the desert ground, letting the scavengers perform the last rites.

Two days later we heard news of our next major destination. We would swing south from where we were and enter Damascus, Syria. And once there we would halt for a few days, replenish our rations, journey to Sidon, and then finally turn North on the way to Cappadocia.

Cappadocia, the region now under Eumenes' command.

I was getting increasingly worried—what if I never managed to succeed in my mission and the procession crossed Cappadocia to the destination at Hellespont? I often wondered if that wily bastard would harm my family if I failed in my duties.

I prayed for the gods to intervene on my behalf.

CHAPTER 8.

MACEDON

The relatively comfortable servant quarter was gone, most of its furnishings stripped away to be placed elsewhere in the house or sold. The token gifts of apparel once every half-year had stopped. They still received enough food to sustain—even if the bread was coarse, and the thin soup smelled of rotten vegetables. They had been joined by two women, both clearly from disreputable backgrounds and from their behavior and utterances, Apollonia guessed that Krokinos, apart from other things, ran a string of brothels. Apollonia kept her distance from them and shielded her daughter. When she tried to persuade Krokinos to let them have their own space, he had only laughed and called her no better than those women and maybe he could put her to work if she were not so miserable and thin. A horrified Apollonia had retreated and never brought up the subject again. But hopes of improvement faded as the tumult in the countryside increased, and the environment for traders and businessmen became hostile.

The berating made way to beating. Apollonia prayed for salvation as her frail body withstood the slaps and the occasional lashes. The curses hurt the mind, and the red welts took time to heal. The eyes lost their luster, and her skin began to show an unhealthy yellow pallor.

It was at this time that she noticed that Krokinos would sometimes linger too long around her and cast his amorous eyes. That she was weak and a shadow of what she once was mattered little to him, for she was just out of his reach for his desires and that made her all the more alluring.

Apollonia prayed every day, but there were no signs of freedom from the gods. There was no new news from her husband, only that he was now somewhere on the way back. The military mail system was no longer functioning reliably, and she had no idea if his messages had been lost.

One day, as ominous clouds gathered on the sky, four unsavory characters arrived at Krokinos' home. There were whispers around the household—these were slave traders from lands far beyond, and here on business.

They stayed for many hours, whispering, eyeing the house servants and slaves, and Apollonia felt the knots tighten in her stomach, and a sense of dread grow in her.

PART II

DANGEROUS JOURNEYS

Circa 322 BC

"At his best, man is the noblest of all animals; separated from law and justice he is the worst."—Aristotle

CHAPTER 9.

MEMPHIS, EGYPT

Ptolemy had settled down in Memphis after his departure from Babylon. While he predicted a devastating battle for the empire, he hoped the greedy generals would spare Egypt and let him rule his satrapy with little interference from either Macedon or Asia.

His fondest memories were in Egypt—the visit to the temple of Ammon, the laying of the foundation of Alexandria, and the sailing on the Great River. He loved this land. He loved the smell of the desert mixed with the pastures by the Great River, the glorious monuments of the past, and the adulation of the people. He also loved how prosperous Egypt was and recognized the advantage of being away from Europe and Asia. They would leave him alone.

The aftermath of Alexander's death was tumultuous. While Alexander wished to be buried in Ammon, Ptolemy preferred that Alexander be buried in Memphis, bringing greater legitimacy to his rule in Egypt; but Perdiccas, deferring to Macedonian customs, wanted the King buried in Macedon. There was also the fear of the wrath of Alexander's powerful mother if the greatest son of Macedon rested in the remote deserts of Egypt.

Soon after his arrival in Egypt, Ptolemy had certain urgent matters to take care of, and dealing with Cleomenes, previously finance minister of Egypt and now assigned by Perdiccas as Ptolemy's adjutant, was one of the first.

Cleomenes was a scoundrel who routinely extorted the Egyptians by manipulating their grain prices, threatening their religious symbols, and threatening to kill the sacred crocodiles of the Great River on the pretext that one of them killed his slave. He often hoisted false charges on local administrators and was also known to cast his immoral eyes on the wives and daughters of the court officials. But for Ptolemy, who had seen such corruption many times before, the one that angered him the most was how blatantly Cleomenes passed on information about him to Perdiccas. It was as if Cleomenes thought Ptolemy's end was near and Perdiccas was the new Alexander.

So, Ptolemy announced the construction of a temple dedicated to Alexander and appointed Cleomenes supervisor for construction. Cleomenes demanded bribes for the award of contract work, imposed outrageous terms, threatened the bidders with imprisonment or worse, and shamelessly used either Ptolemy's or Perdiccas' name to coerce the contractors. Once the undercover inspectors reported to Ptolemy that they had enough evidence of Cleomenes' corruption and would not hesitate to speak against him in an open court, Ptolemy announced that Cleomenes conspired to profit from Alexander's death and had him arrested.

To try to profit from the death of a King still seen as a god was sacrilegious, and no one was willing to protect such a man to their detriment. After a short show trial, a shouting Cleomenes was tied hand and feet, placed onto a raft, just wide enough to lay his body, and left adrift in the center of the Great River. Hanging from three corners of the raft were large pieces of meat.

Egyptian royalties, court ministers, and Macedonian officers alike watched the frightened Cleomenes who now saw the swarms of crocodiles approach the raft, attracted by the wriggling of his ample body and the meat hanging from the sides. Cleomenes wept as the crocodiles began to tug on the meat, and the raft started to tilt. In a final bid to save himself, Cleomenes implored Ptolemy through loud lamentations.

"I swear I will resign from my post and vanish into the wilderness, Ptolemy!"

"I weep for my actions, but gods know that I will forever be true to you, Ptolemy!"

"I will never forget your mercy, and I shall be a slave by your side to my very end, Alexander's worthy successor!" And so forth, while his greedy, terrified eyes scanned the churning waters around him, with hundreds of bodies slithering below the surface and snouts sticking above.

Ptolemy watched impassively while some Egyptian ministers closed their mouth with their palms and giggled.

Eventually, the snouts rose higher in the water and the crocodiles began to push their faces onto the raft. Cleomenes began howling as the jaws began to get closer to him, and finally, a beast lunged out of the water and clamped its otherworldly jaws on Cleomenes' thighs. Cleomenes flailed about and kicked frantically with his other leg to no avail until another dark visage rose and grabbed him by the ankle. Eventually, Cleomenes was dragged into the water, screaming, and the sacred crocodiles he once threatened to have killed now ripped and feasted on his rich flesh.

Ptolemy smiled as he saw the waters turn red. He then turned to matters of greater importance, which was the preservation of his satrapy and legitimacy of his reign. He was aware of the plans to cremate and bury Alexander's body in the royal tombs in Macedon, and that Arrhidaeus handled the construction and transportation of Alexander's funerary temple.

He had been trading messages with Arrhidaeus the past few months.

CHAPTER 10.

SYRIA

We reached the outskirts of Damascus, and the weather was pleasant and a respite from the heat. It gave a chance for the procession to rest and replenish.

My relationship with Arrhidaeus had deteriorated beyond repair. We had quarreled and shouted at each other because his guards would follow me wherever I went, and it gave an impression to the rest of the troops that they could not trust me. There were rumors that I was trying to steal Alexander's personal possessions so I could sell them to the highest bidder.

These rumors could cost me my life if it reached the ears of any of the *Diadochi*.

Four days ago, I had seen some men enter Arrhidaeus' tent. People went to meet the General for many reasons, but what was different was that I remembered seeing them two months ago when we were on the journey through Syria. What made these visitors most interesting was while they were Macedonian, there were subtle, yet distinct signs of Egyptian decorations and mannerisms about them.

The leader wore a symbol seen on members of the Egyptian royal courts. He bowed in the presence of Arrhidaeus, a style reminiscent of officers who tended to Alexander during his trips to Egypt.

So why did this Egypt-based Macedonian officer see Arrhidaeus more than once? The developments alarmed me. I summoned my messenger and asked him to rush to Babylon with a message to Perdiccas.

I addressed Perdiccas thus:

"Honorable Regent,

I have witnessed Macedonian officers from Egyptian courts meet Arrhidaeus more than once. I urge you to send a contingent at the earliest to Sidon and relieve Arrhidaeus of his duty.

Your loyal soldier,

Deon, Son of Evagoras"

Once the messenger returned to me, I planned to send him up to Cappadocia to repeat the message to Eumenes.

I had a hunch.

But I had my mission, my rewards to earn, my family to free, and my master to please—and what this development portended was unsettling.

And today, the men returned at dawn. They spent time in Arrhidaeus' tent until lunch. After lunch one of the leader's henchmen wandered out towards one of the lavatory ditches, and I hurried to him as he went about his business of streaming the plants.

"Greetings soldier, it sure is a beautiful day here!"

He seemed irritated by a stranger's appraisal, interrupting his urgent business by the bushes. "Well, it is—"

"I have not seen you around, did you join us recently?"

He looked surprised. "Well, I have been with Arrhidaeus' guards for quite some time now, you might not have seen me," he said, as he urgently shook his little general.

"Indeed, I am not in the front. I am with the rear guards. Did your lot enjoy the massacre of the bandits as we did?"

A flicker of anxiety passed his face. "Yes, yes, we did," he said, unconvincingly.

He began to walk briskly, eager to get away from me. I kept pace with a friendly, nonchalant attitude.

"Too bad we could not catch the leader. Would have been nice to make an example of him."

"Of course, but sometimes you have to let them go to keep the population happy."

"You are so correct. I know of only two leaders who adopted such magnanimous policies to profound effect. Our beloved King Alexander was one, and I heard Ptolemy was the other."

"Ptolemy is indeed—"

He stopped. "I have to get back to the commander to prepare for evening duties, so if you will excuse me, sir."

"Of course, may the gods be with you."

I knew then I had to do something.

The man emerged from the tent to relieve himself after an entertaining evening with dancers and wine. It was quiet everywhere as the procession contingent rested.

He felt a heavy blow to his head and darkness envelop him.

When he woke, his head hurt, and he was unable to place himself. He realized his attackers had tied him and stuffed a foul rag into his mouth. He struggled to no avail, the ropes were thick, and the knots were well constructed. He tried to use his training to see if he could reach the knots but realized they his captors had expertly positioned them outside his reach.

This was not the work of common thieves.

He took stock of his situation. All he could make out in the darkness was that he was in a narrow path between two boulders, and the ground was rocky. There were no flickering lights of the tents, sounds of chattering people, clanging of the utensils, or the light whinnying and grunts of horses. He realized that they had transported him to a location far away from where he remembered he was.

He heard rustling, shuffling of footsteps, and then the foulness of another man's breath on his neck. He tried to turn and felt a sharp slap on the back of his head, not painful by itself but hurt since the blow to his head had split the skin.

"Keep your mouth shut until we ask you."

That quiet voice sounded familiar, but he was unable to place it.

"And if you shout, we will slowly slice off a piece of your ear. And we may not stop there."

He nodded frantically. There was no point in struggling until he found out what they wanted. Someone removed the gag, and he took a deep breath and shuddered.

"We have a few questions for you, soldier. Answer them, and you can be on your way."

That voice. It sounded… recent. From the sounds and whispers, he figured there were three to four men behind him. Too many for him to try anything adventurous, and impossible if they were all military, which his gut said they were.

"We know you are not part of the procession, so tell us, where did you come from and what is your business with Arrhidaeus?"

He felt a cold fear rise within his bones. "What? I conduct official business on behalf of The Viceroy of Macedon and you—"

A strong hand gripped his index finger and pulled it back violently. The finger bent as far as it could and broke like a twig, the snap clear to everyone around.

One of the men thrust the gag back in his mouth before he could scream in shock and pain.

His eyes bulged from his sockets, and he felt bile rise in this throat. He gasped and took several sharp breaths, rocking back and forth, and finally bent over ready to vomit. Someone removed the gag, and he emptied his stomach. It had been a long time since he was in battle or experienced violence. He had grown soft.

Experience told him that no one withstood prolonged torture.

He had a family.

A comfortable living back home.

And nothing was worth prolonging this.

"You can spare yourself a lot of pain. We have a pretty good idea of where you might be from, but we want that from you before we can trust your answers," said the leader, his quiet voice carrying in the cold.

Through the red haze of pain, it dawned upon him—the voice was that son of a whore who had accosted him in the morning!

He felt strong fingers on his middle finger.

"Egypt! Egypt! I come from Egypt! Stop! What do you want?"

"Good. What are you doing here?"

"We are here on behalf of Governor Ptolemy to see the magnificent hearse, offer our prayers, and offer any support before the procession heads north."

"So, you came here just yesterday to meet Arrhidaeus for the first time?"

"Yes, The Governor was eager to find out if the procession did justice to the King!"

There was silence. It sounded like they were conferring amongst themselves. He relaxed slightly. Much to his horror, he felt someone grasp some of his flesh by his side, and then the cold sensation of a blade against it.

And he felt the blade slice off a piece of his side.

He screamed again, but this time his voice was dead. Tears streamed from his eyes, and his legs and arms began to shake uncontrollably. He felt warm blood soak into his tunic.

"I will ask you again. Did you meet Arrhidaeus here for the first time?"

He rocked back and forth. "No. No, no, no..." He began to cry, his shoulders shaking, and spit running down his lips. "This is our fourth meeting with General Arrhidaeus..."

"Good. Tell us the truth, and it will be over soon, what business does Ptolemy have with Arrhidaeus?"

The man went silent for a few moments, contemplating the situation. His attackers stayed quiet, still behind him, but there was no one grabbing or cutting. With clenched teeth and rising anger, he asked:

"Is it so difficult to guess?"

He felt breathing, but nothing else. Then the leader spoke, "I have no interest in guessing."

The man spat and hung his head low. He knew they would not let him go alive—so he prayed to the gods, begged mercy of those he sinned against, bade farewell to his family, and finally through clenched teeth he described the scandalous plan.

My mind was in turmoil—I had to decide my move. So far, we had seen no sign of Ptolemy's army.

First, I brought to confidence some of my most trusted lieutenants. They were angry, worried, and upset just as I was. Then, I asked them, to find out for me every junior man in the front guard who hailed from upper Macedon or northern Greece. These were hardy men fanatically loyal to their lands and Alexander.

I then dispatched a rider, away from Arrhidaeus' eyes, towards Sidon to check if he could find a battalion at rest. Meanwhile, I knew Ptolemy's agents were frantically inquiring as to the whereabouts of one of their men.

I had one of my men tell the investigators that he had seen the man slip away towards the notorious night market—a place for witchcraft, fraudsters, and whores. A place where fortune-seekers went to consult with questionable shamans, or to sleep with women or boys, but not without considerable risk. The place was known for robbery, murder, and extortion.

Within a day, I got news from my sources that the investigators had dropped the idea of finding the missing man.

Two days later my messenger from Sidon returned, and he reported no garrison stationed anywhere near Sidon, but he did tell me an intriguing tidbit—that local merchants had reported an unusual amount of food grain, fruit, wood, metal, wine, and oil purchases, and that daily merchant caravans headed south of Sidon. It was possible to hide a sizable force in this terrain.

Eventually, we traveled to Sidon and settled at the southern outskirts. One of my fondest memories was my stroll through Sidon's central shopping market. The main path was wide, made of beautiful sandstone, and on both sides, olive trees circulated a gentle fragrance. Behind these trees were buildings and shops built by the Phoenician kings before Alexander's arrival.

The locals treated the trees with religious reverence as there were flowers, beads, purple colored strings, fresh and remnants of spoiled fruit on the ground around them.

I sought out the biggest and best-preserved garment shop in the market and found one with the owner behind the mud stall. The place was grand—cloth cut of the finest fabric, curtains, tunics, all in beautiful colors and brilliant designs hung on the walls and wood poles.

"What would the general like for himself and his ladies?"

The shopkeeper grinned a toothless smile, and I smiled at his shameless tactic. My attire showed no insignia of a general, but he had called me as such—inflating my ego, just as I did Arrhidaeus recently. Flattery made its way, with no regard to rank, wealth, beauty, or gender!

I looked at a gorgeous garment hung on a pole that jutted from the roof of the shop. It was lustrous deep blue and embroidered in gold, depicting two fighting lions—another Phoenician symbol. I decided to buy it, with a deep longing for my wife, far away and waiting for me for so many years.

I told him I would buy it, and he shook his head with great appreciation for my taste. And then I decided to engage the man in small talk. "I heard there have been several merchant caravans going south and they've been buying a lot from the market here?"

The old man nodded vigorously—he seemed eager to talk to me, a ploy to make me buy a few more of his lovely garments for the women back home. "Ah, yes, General. Of course. Lots of purchases of food and materials from here in the past several days. It has been a very good week for us!"

"Tell me, old man, I hear many high-ranking officers were here as well buying your wares."

"I must admit that I profited handsomely. The general who visited me purchased four different dresses for his many Egyptian wives," he cackled, looking comical with his empty mouth and few remaining teeth, like little mountains rising in the Phoenician desert.

"What makes you think he has Egyptian wives?" I asked, trying to sound innocent.

"Oh. It was not hard to guess. Said he was here for a visit. He told me to be quiet when I enquired about his army and why he was here," he said, narrowing his eyes under the bushy eyebrows, holding a palm near his mouth as if spilling a secret, but grinning merrily like a boy up to no good behind the bushes with his neighbor. "Imagine that poor man, troubled every day by four wives speaking in strange tongues. Just imagine the cacophony in his house! Maybe he purchased those dresses to tie them up and stuff their mouths!"

He laughed uproariously at his wit, his belly shook, and his eyes closed imagining that scene—and I could not help but laugh with him.

But this confirmed the presence of a senior officer, even if not a general, in the vicinity in just the last few days. There was no question that there was a garrison somewhere nearby, hidden, ready to strike. But when?

And how would Ptolemy engineer the attack?

I pretended like I was casually curious. "Don't you lie, dirty old man, I bet you wished you had five young wives of your own. Was it just the general or were there many soldiers too?"

"My equipment cannot handle that many!" He bellowed. His breath shaking his great white beard that flowed from his chin to the middle of his chest. "But no... no soldiers. You know that our local king does not like intruding armies."

I nodded. That explained the absence of a garrison within city limits. But it was easy to hide a few thousand men further south in hilly terrain, away from the routes.

"So, what do you think of this one, sir?" He pointed to another shimmering purple dress in the Phoenician style, with no embroidery but had several small metal bells attached at the waist. "You can announce your arrival in style!"

I laughed. I imagined myself like a cow with bells around its neck, as I had seen during the Indian campaigns. "I enjoyed the talk, but I must return. Make sure to visit the procession once it heads this way."

"Of course, sir. And I will bring my wives to it. But they might try to steal the gold!" he laughed again, and I shook my head with mock disapproval.

Your wives would not be the only ones with plans to steal.

I wrapped my purchase, tucked it under my arm, and began to walk away. But he was not done. "Well, it seems tomorrow is an important day—that other general said they would finish their training tomorrow evening and return to Egypt."

That night I summoned my lieutenants and described my modified plan. They then reached out to their allies in the front guard, and some of those men came to me for confirmation.

So far, there had been no betrayal.

I slept poorly that night, my heart was hammering at my ribcage, and it was hard to breathe amidst the anxiety.

That night I dreamt that Alexander's corpse, bedecked in regal purple and full armor, was lying on the dusty ground, and four large hyenas ripped his body apart.

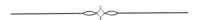

Morning arrived, and Arrhidaeus walked into my tent as I dressed. He seemed anxious. "I'm here to explain the route today, Deon, as there are some changes."

Of course, there was, you pig, I thought, but listened impassively.

Arrhidaeus continued, "We progress west, and then we turn south for a short distance before we turn North again."

"That makes no sense, General. Why are we adding distance? We are already delayed by several days."

He glowered. "The path from here through Sidon is not conducive to the procession, and the road-menders worry that we might damage the wheels."

"The path looked fine to me—"

He cut me off, "Are you a road mender, Deon? What knowledge do you possess to behave like an expert at roads?"

I had no answer to that.

Doubt crept into me—what if I was wrong, what if all this was an elaborate trick played on me? What if Arrhidaeus had spurned Ptolemy's attempt to suborn him?

I pushed aside the thoughts and apologized. "Forgive my tone, General. I am as anxious as you are to reach the destination."

Mollified, he explained the plan. "We will turn south and travel until it is evening. And then tomorrow morning we swing west again, bypass the hills, and turn north onto the main trade route. Do you understand it now?"

I simmered at the condescending tone but nodded. With that, Arrhidaeus barked his order for us to get ready within the hour and prepare to move before sunrise.

He stopped before stepping out of my tent.

"I am also ordering most of the baggage train to take the shorter route and not follow the procession. This will keep us light and help us move quickly. They will reconnect with us once we reach Sidon."

At dawn, the party split to two; most of the baggage train, including children and women, priests, augurs, cooks, physicians, bookkeepers, and some road menders, took the walking path straight northwest to Sidon. The rest of us, the five hundred forward guard and a hundred rear guard, along with the temple draggers, headed west on a different route until we hit the plains near the sea.

We moved slowly until sun appeared at our eye level. Soon, I saw the grey, featureless hills that Arrhidaeus mentioned, stretching a vast distance, as far as the eye can see, and between the sea and us. The General ordered us to halt by the side of one of the hills but stay in formation. The men sat where they were and rested until further notice. I noticed, from the corner of my eye, a flame waving back and forth on the hill. We all knew enough about flame messengers.

My gut told me that whatever would happen would happen very soon. I rode along the periphery of the procession, all the way to the front, signaling the men embedded in the forward guard. My bag was ready with a hammer, a small, sturdy metal rod that would be useful for lock-picking and breaking, some bread, and a vial of physician-recommended concoction that helped heal wounds.

And then, just as the sun began to set bathing us in light orange glow, we heard the unmistakable distant sounds of a march—the rhythmic *clap* of horse hoofs on hard ground, the light thud of footsteps, the change in the atmospheric texture due to dust, just around the corner of the edge of the hills ahead of us.

All members of the procession noticed the sounds and those who were resting scrambled to their feet. At a far distance, we saw a significant military formation turn the corner from the hills, straight onto our path.

Arrhidaeus rallied the troops and appeared at the head, and he asked that everyone come closer to hear him. The soldiers held their breath as the ominous distant sounds of an approaching army neared. They then quickly assembled a tall podium with a ladder in front of Arrhidaeus, and he scrambled to the top, so we could see him and hear more clearly. He began, "Soldiers! Fear not, I have just very recently, only two days ago, received a message from the great Ptolemy who heads the army you see ahead. He wishes to pay his final respects to King Alexander, endow our procession with Egyptian symbols of everlasting life, supply our caravan with rewards for a smooth journey, and send us off to Sidon."

I was shocked.

Ptolemy himself?

I signaled my lieutenants to be ready and rode towards the front closer to Arrhidaeus.

In the waning light of the evening I could not make out his expression, but I knew he was looking at me as I neared his podium. While the front guard looked on, I signaled to the members that pledged allegiance to Perdiccas and me and rode close to Arrhidaeus.

My voice was sound enough to make myself heard.

I addressed Arrhidaeus, "General, may I speak a few words as well on this auspicious occasion?"

I had placed my bet on the fact that he would allow me to speak, knowing that impeding me would create suspicion among the troops. He made a half-hearted gesture of approval.

I faced the men and spoke as loudly as I could, "What a glorious day for us to have the great Ptolemy himself visit this procession! I must add more to the noble reason that Ptolemy is here," I paused to ensure that the entire assemblage hung on to my every word.

Then I expanded my lungs and shouted as hard as I could, "Arrhidaeus is lying. Ptolemy is here to steal Alexander's body and take it to Egypt! You will all be crucified if you let this happen!"

My loud voice boomed across the group. I registered the shock and confusion among the soldiers.

Arrhidaeus shouted, "Insubordinate son of a worthless whore—don't listen to him! He—"

I yelled again, my voice carrying over his. His bodyguards began to edge closer to where I was. No one wanted a battle when everything seemed so hazy. "Why would Ptolemy meet us not in a royal setting in Sidon but hidden plains and hills here?"

There was a murmur of assent. Arrhidaeus was frozen, unable to decide his next action. I pushed on. "Is this how you want to be remembered—impotent men that stood by when an unholy alliance stole their King's body?"

"Enough of your lunacy. Arrest him!" Arrhidaeus screamed. He was trembling and looked frantic as the dying orange sunlight reflected off his glistening cheeks and helmet.

I retrieved my horn and blew it, signaling my troops and lieutenants to act. Immediately, several voices rang out within the groups, sowing fear and confusion, "Arrhidaeus tricked us. Ptolemy is stealing the body. Turn the Funerary temple!"

The situation spiraled out of Arrhidaeus' control. Skirmishes broke out among the front guard, with pushing and shoving, accusations and counter-accusations hurled at each other. The bodyguards whisked away Arrhidaeus, but at a distance, I could see him mount his horse and try to bring the front to discipline. A great plume of dust rose and began to mask the scene, and the entire procession descended to utter chaos.

I galloped to the funerary temple, jumped, and hung on to the balustrade. A guard ran to grab me, but someone from my group clubbed him to the ground. I hauled myself up and entered the chamber.

This time, I knew what I was looking for, and I moved quickly to the corner which had the box with the contents I had waited so long to reveal.

I pulled the metal rod from my bag, inserted it to a gap between the lock and the latch, and then struck it repeatedly with my hammer. After a few powerful knocks, the hinge connecting the latch broke, releasing the lock.

I opened the box, and in it were several papyri, some jewelry (a few chains, rings with precious gems on them, several bracelets), a few larger official parchments I had seen in the courts before, and then a thick, hide-covered, and carefully packaged object.

I retrieved the package as that was what I looked for, and my heart thudded furiously in my chest. I also picked some jewelry with two intentions—warding off anyone who might get too interested in the package and rewarding a few of my closest men.

I stepped out and jumped down, and one of my men scooped and took me behind the lines. The situation had turned into a full-fledged battle by this point, and Ptolemy's forces were upon us. There was no longer any clarity on who was fighting whom—was the front fighting the rear? Was the front fighting amongst themselves and the rear?

Ptolemy's forces were not slaughtering Arrhidaeus' guards—they had formed a protracted line of shield-bearing phalanx encircling us from our left, while the cavalry tried to subdue the guards with clubs instead of swords and javelins.

And then, to my shock, Ptolemy himself appeared in the front of the phalanx and the cavalry, resplendent in his uniform—his purple plume rising high on his helmet, red robe flying in the air; to his sides were symbol bearers with bright lamps, carrying flags emblazoned with ram's head and elephant skin symbols of Alexander. Arrhidaeus appeared on Ptolemy's side and began to exhort his procession to comply and not fight. The sight slowed everyone for a few moments, soldiers absorbing the surreal scene of seeing one of the most revered generals in front of them, now accused of trying to steal the corpse of their beloved king.

It was getting dark, and I realized that there was no longer a possibility for me to prevent the theft of the temple—not without full reinforcements from Perdiccas. Along with two of my lieutenants, I turned my horse, and we galloped away under the enveloping darkness and cover of dust.

CHAPTER 11.

SYRIA

The three of us rode without rest for hours to find a place to sleep and plot the next course. We finally saw the twinkling lights of night lamps—a small Phoenician village less than an hour from where we were. We finally rode into it as quietly as we could, and curious dogs inspected the horses. The homes were far and spread, with some muddy clusters in-between.

We found an isolated house, away from the cluster of dwellings, on the far edge of the town. It was large, styled in the way of Phoenician merchants, with big stone blocks, an archway, and a small courtyard in the front with a dry fountain. Olive trees decorated the garden behind the walls.

We scaled the compound and got to the heavy wooden door, and it seemed unlikely for us to break through it.

So, I decided to try a ruse.

I knocked on the door, and spoke loudly, "Regent Perdiccas' officers seek your help with the King Alexander's procession."

I heard footsteps inside and saw the yellow glow of a night candle under the door. There was a low murmur of a man's voice and another of a woman.

"What do you want? We are armed!" came the gruff male voice from behind the door.

I almost laughed at the absurdity. "We intend no harm; we are only here on orders of the Regent."

"What does a Regent want from a common man in a village?"

"He does not send us to you specifically, old fool! We are collecting household artifacts from each region to include in King Alexander's tomb. It's an honor unless you prefer to forego it!"

It was all nonsense, but I had little to lose. Besides, I did not want to hurt an innocent family.

"What if we are not interested?"

I pretended to get angry. "Well we didn't ride here for hours to be insulted, and if you refuse to let us in, I will have my soldiers forcibly enter the house, and we will set fire to it after we leave!"

I shouted a few military-sounding phrases and had the others yell their response in unison.

After several tense moments, I heard a worried woman's voice. "You promise you will not hurt us?"

"I would not be outside negotiating with you if we wanted to hurt you, but do not test my patience."

I heard the iron bolt release from the latch, and the heavy door gently opened inwards. Inside were a dignified man and a small, frightened woman beside him.

Behind them were two teenage girls—they had to be the daughters. I understood the parents' predicament allowing soldiers into the house. I had to put out the fear quickly before this escalated and anyone else hiding in the house came out to attack us.

"Is there anyone else in the house, hiding, armed?" I asked and deliberately drew the man's attention to my hand on the kopis. My companions fanned out to the large living room and stood quietly near the two doors that went into other rooms.

A flicker of uncertainty crossed the man's face, and one of the girls began to sniffle. "If you are honest with me, your family will come to no harm. But if you are lying, and anyone else comes through these doors surprising us, we will not hesitate to kill all of you and take your daughters away. Is there someone else in the house?"

In a trembling voice, with his hands out in the front to show he would not try anything risky, he said, "My young sons are in the room, and they are armed. I will ask them to come out. They are young. I ask you respectfully not to hurt us."

I nodded. He yelled for his sons to come out and told them to walk into the living room slowly. I moved closer to the wife and held her forearm firmly. The women began to cry. The man stood quietly, tensed, and I watched him to ensure he made no moves.

Two boys, no older than ten, stepped gingerly into the room. They had farm sickles in their hand, useless against soldiers, but I had to admire them for the foolish courage. I signed them to drop the sickles and go to their parents.

Then, I addressed them: "As I have told you before, we intend no harm. We need some food, and quarters to stay for the night. We are not here to take your artifacts or listen to your stories. You behave, and you will all be safe."

There was vigorous nodding from all heads.

"And if you are nice, I might even tell you some delightful stories about Alexander himself, because I used to ride with him!" I said, as I ruffled the hair of one of the boys who stared at us in wonder. The parents relaxed. The man put his arms around his wife and daughters and continued to look at us without expression, but his eyes were no longer full of fear and anger.

"I see your daughter admiring my handsome face, old man, you must have some hideous men in your village," I said, smiling.

That released tension and one of the girls guffawed as she wiped her nose and teary face. The man remained expressionless. He ordered the wife to prepare food.

We ate for the night; a basic staple of salted goat's meat, grain soup, and some strange wine—courtesy of our unwilling hosts. As I watched the woman scurry about, her daughters helping the mother, the sons in quiet attendance beside their gruff, protective father, I could not help but imagine my life had I not enlisted in the army. I wondered if I would ever again experience that simple life. Apollonia was a wonderful cook, and her lamb recipe was the best I had ever known. The image of her face bent over a fire, with her curly hair over her eyes as it reflected the golden light, flashed in my head. I shook it off.

We rested—one of us watching over the others in turn. I made sure to wrap the leather bag around me to ensure no one would steal it from me, and so far, my companions had not asked what was in it and why I was so protective of it.

Finally, late at night when it was my turn to watch, I got my chance to lay my eyes on what I had pursued so hard, for so many months, and with such risk. General Eumenes had ordered me to bring the package intact to him, but I had decided not to obey that order.

I lit a lamp and removed myself from the room, retiring to the front porch. I had locked the family in a room, just as a precaution, and had to admonish the boisterous boys who were insistent that we tell them more Alexander stories. Satisfied that I was alone, I removed the hidebound package from my bag, and gingerly cut the rope around it.

I removed the cover, and inside it was another wooden box, engraved with symbols of the sun and concentric circles with a bull in the center. After a few attempts, I realized that I could open it by gently pressing on the sun's image on top.

Inside the box was beautifully preserved, thick papyrus scrolls, about eight sheets, bound together by an ink-stained deep blue thread, knotted at the top.

I removed the thread carefully, feeling a deep sense of respect for the will of the greatest King the world had ever known.

Then I gingerly spread the eight sheets to see about a quarter of each. The first two were newer and were in distinctly different handwriting. They did not look anything like a will.

Instead, it was a letter from Plato to a man named Axiandros.

Plato? The great Plato?

Greece's greatest philosopher! I had known his work very well as a student of history and a teacher of philosophy before I became a soldier. I recognized Plato's writing and the symbols that represented his work.

The remaining sheets were much older, and the papyrus had aged to a deep brown, but the dark ink on top was still clearly legible. The writing there was exquisitely elegant, with flowing, unrecognizable script in the top half of each page, and bold, beautiful letters in Greek on the bottom half.

It dawned upon me that Eumenes had lied. This was no will—and what he tried to hide was in my hands now.

I separated the older pages and first began to read Plato's letter.

Plato to Axiandros wishes you wonderful harvest.

We have spoken much of my account of Atlantis in Timaeus. Your astute mind, no doubt, has realized that I have grown a tree from the seeds of truth of the wise Solon's account of his meeting with the Egyptian priests at Sais. But I must unburden my mind to you—my trusted sources told me of another fact; that before Atlantis' destruction their king built a new city in the distant desert. There they transferred their treasures and weapons; weapons that seem not of this earth but bequeathed to them by terrible gods. I have ancient papyri that tell, in a most teasing way, where this city lies. These secrets can unleash great violence upon this earth if the benefactors of said secrets were tyrants; besides, as you are aware my old friend, that I am no longer of the sound body to undertake strenuous adventures to unravel this delectable mystery.

After much pondering, many nights of thought, and great consideration, I have concluded that to reveal this would do nothing but to stir malcontents of the Republic and further endanger our peoples. One may

The letter ended abruptly as if Plato had decided not to send it to Axiandros. I sat stunned.

I had read about Atlantis in Plato's works and accepted that Plato had forged the story as a lesson about greed. Some speculated if there was once a real Atlantis. This letter suggested that not only Atlantis was real, in some way, but also that this powerful empire left something behind. That was when the reality pierced me like Zeus' trident— Eumenes wished to seek it for himself and possess the riches and weapons. He wanted to be the next Alexander!

The arrow of the secret had flown from Solon or someone else, to Plato, to Callisthenes, to Eumenes, and then to me— so far unhindered, undiscovered, as if by a miracle or sheer fortune due to the death and failure of others in its quest.

I heard a stirring from the house. Alarmed, I put the papers back into the box and turned back. It was just my tired companions snoring, loud enough for Ptolemy to hear on his way to Egypt with Alexander's body. I turned my attention back to the contents. Next, I delicately extracted the older papyri.

I did not recognize the script on the upper half of each page. The bottom, however, was in an older dialect of Greek—no doubt that this was written long ago.

What came before these pages, one would never know, for it began as if in continuation of a saga that the writer wished for the world to learn. Or more likely, I surmised, Plato only received or preserved the most relevant portions. I began to read.

The Oracles told the Lord that they feared a great cataclysm beneath our feet and fury of the seas around us, for the ground had trembled every so often, weeks on end, a sign of the displeasure of gods for our sins, while the kingdom lay ready to invade every continent, but our plans now at peril.

So, the Lord, alarmed at what he heard, instructed the Council to prepare for the preservation of our riches, our glorious new weapons of war, our knowledge, and our greatest people, secretly from the Egyptians, the chariot wielders of the East, the bull worshippers of the Great Island of the Sea, the barbarians from The North, and wait for the divine signs to rise again.

The Council set sail to find a location, and find they did, far away in the distant continent, inside mountains in the desert. Then, the Lord ordered a city built inside and called it the divine city in the rocks, the new home hidden from the world. While our glorious island may perish someday, our new home shall bloom like a magnificent flower in the desert mountains and spawn a thousand cities.

For five harvests, the architects, masons, builders, and a great many slaves, under the orders of the Council and watchful eyes of the Lord, exploited great domes inside the rocks and seeded them from a hundred ships that set sail.

The Lord put a thousand conspirators, rumor mongers, traitors, and many unknown innocents, to death to preserve the secrets. The task completed, when the multitude of the men and women greeted the Lord and the Council to admire what wondrous place they built for all their future, he called a heavenly banquet in their honor, and but for a few, with agreement from the Council, put them to the sword as they ate.

And then he ordered the city sealed, hidden from the world to see, preserved until he and his Council awaited the omen from the gods, back on the island where the Council and the greatest citizens, unrepentant for what transpired, awaited the signs to go forth, rebuild, and conquer.

But the gods looked down upon this wanton cruelty, this depraved act, this unbridled ambition, this desire to spread death and destruction; and so, they invoked their wrath on the island. When the sun set on the fourth day of the middle of the summer trade, the ocean boiled, and great smoke arose from the rumbling grounds, the birds flew, and the ports shook and crumbled. The Lord, with his Council and first citizens, prayed to the gods, but just as he showed no mercy, the gods showed none.

After seven days of shaking of the ground, liquid rock, red as blood and hot as the sun, spurted from the wounds that opened on the earth, burned all it met, and spared no place of worship or dwelling. And then on the eighth day, as the royals and nobles alike cowered in fear, there was a great upheaval of the earth, and god's terrible power came forth from within the ground in tremendous plumes of fire and ash, and in that instant, the ambitions of an empire vanished as if a speck of dust in a desert storm. As a warning to man's greed, all that was left of a once *glorious empire was an island, now but lifeless rock and ash, like a blind eye as it looked to the heavens in despair.*

Then what they created in distant lands is now only a mighty shell with gold and fire with no soul to nurture, no eyes to behold its beauty, and no king to spread its power.

My heart beat wildly. The next papyrus was not in the flowing prose of the author of the story. This appeared to be a different writer, and his words were simple and urgent.

Down the tongue of my ancestors is a story that talks of the divine city of rocks, and here I have captured truthfully, as Zeus himself attests, the words that I have been told. My search has found truth in many of these words, and yet the find eludes me.

With glorious seas all around, and the great eye beneath his feet, the Lord he towered over the adoring masses, and as the rays of the rising sun shone upon his regal visage, he lay his feet on the spine of the fist that fought the disquiet water below, pointed upon the endless sea, towards the far desert, where a knife's tip awaits, seven days from the sea on burning sands and towering canyons. Three days north from the tip, within golden walls and red rocks, in there they found a magnificent mountain, and a hollow within, where they carved the last city of a great empire and filled it with riches greater than found in all of Libya, weapons not of this earth but designed by the gods themselves, and knowledge superior to all mankind. When the sun sets, the shadows play, the lord he smiles, and smiles away. A smile that welcomes to the doors to a magnificent temple.

The pages ended there, giving no further sign on their provenance, its author, or how he received the information. There were no other papers.

But why would the great Plato guard it so assiduously, if it were a hoax? There must have been some credence to this story. In my childhood, I had heard wondrous stories of lost civilizations, great floods, and hidden treasures—some certainly came from these origins. Briefly, my mind wandered to imagining what magnificent finds lay hidden, but then quickly returned to the present. And that slow anger began to fill my head again—like water reaching its boiling point, bubbling, steaming.

Eumenes had lied.

He had risked not only my life but also my family's, and not had the decency to tell me the truth.

I sat with my back on the wall and brooded. My mind contemplated the alternatives.

I could go back to Ptolemy with this.

Or Antigonus.

Or Perdiccas himself!

Each of those men vied for supremacy, and any one of them would be thrilled with this find if it were true.

I stood up and paced around in the courtyard. The calm skies and the rustle of the trees helped soothe the turbulence in my head. It dawned upon me that my decisions would affect not just my family and me, but the multitude in the three continents. For all his failings, Eumenes was the just among all the others. He was not a career general, was far less bloodthirsty and brutal, and despite his reasons to lie to me, he was the most honorable.

In Eumenes' hands, I felt, this secret may lead to good— peace and tranquility. And those were essential for my retirement! Besides, I had a contract with Eumenes—and there was no guarantee that the other tyrants would believe me or even care. I could not risk their unpredictability. Besides, I could see a reason for Eumenes to hide this from me—what if I had rejected his mission? Who would he go to with such a monumental secret? And if I did nothing, what chance did I have to return unscathed?

The gods surely smiled at the twisted path they laid for me. I made my plans to reconnect with Eumenes, take my rewards, and end this journey, no matter how strange and exciting the story before me was.

But to do that I had to find him.

He had much to answer.

I decided that I would reach Damascus and then plot a course. But for tonight, I was exhausted. So much had happened that I could no longer think any further. I packed the contents of the box carefully, put it back to my bag, and tiptoed to the house.

I lay my head on my bag and let exhaustion take over.

I dreamt a terrible dream that night.

My wife begged and cried, holding our infant daughter, as Krokinos dragged her by the ankles, through dark, wet mud, towards the entrance of a mine. I stood watching them as Ptolemy laughed, holding Eumenes' severed head in one hand and Plato's papyri in the other.

CHAPTER 12.

MACEDON

There was much anguish in the courtyard—loud wails, shouting, and sounds of violence. A guard threw open the door to the basement room, which was now Apollonia's living quarters, along with many other servants of the household. She squinted in the bright light that bathed the dark interior and heard him shout at them to get up and come with him.

Apollonia tapped her sleeping daughter's shoulder, and her heart hammered against the ribs as she joined others heading to the courtyard. There was a large crowd taking up all available space around the central fountain, stone pathways, and shrubs. There was no chirping of the birds even in this early morning, and the fetid air was still with sadness and fear. Krokinos stood in one corner, conferring with several burly men who each wore only a loincloth and had various ornamentations on their ears, wrists, and ankles. A line of armed guards stood in front of a mass of a miserable, forlorn group of men, women, and children who looked filthy and exhausted. They were not part of Krokinos' household and appeared to have come with the men who now stood speaking with Krokinos.

"All of you in a line, and quiet!" screamed one of the guards, and Apollonia and Alexa shuffled along with the rest to stand shoulder to shoulder. The mother and daughter held hands and looked around nervously. No one from the outside group held their eyes, and only a few suppressed sobs emanated until they fell silent under the crack of a whip. For a few minutes nothing happened, and finally, five loincloths came forward and spread evenly in front of the line of twenty-three. Apollonia heard nothing but the roaring blood that rushed into her face and ears, and her chest constricted with fear. The loincloths looked on dispassionately; their black eyes showed no emotion and faces a mute stone wall of indifference.

Krokinos stood hidden behind one of the larger men, his bony visage barely visible. Diona, who had said little so far except to trail her husband and whisper into his ears, finally piped up.

"What are you waiting for? I cannot stand here all day!" and she snapped her fingers in irritation.

The loincloth at the far end of the line reached forward and firmly grasped the biceps of a man and his son—a boy no older than twelve. A wave of gasps rose from the line, and the boy began to shout, "Father! Father!" The man frantically tried to grab the boy, and the loincloth let go of the boy and swung at the man, causing him to lose his footing and fall. A guard dragged the boy to the outside group, and another cracked a whip on the fallen man who screamed and jumped back to his feet. He too was shoved into the mass of miserable humanity.

Many of the women in the line began to cry, and one of them appealed to Diona. "Mistress! What is going on? Please! Master!"

Diona did not respond, and Krokinos walked away to confer with the men.

"Why are you selling us? Why? I have been your faithful—" She began to wail, and it finally dawned upon everyone what was happening. A great commotion arose in the courtyard as some attempted to flee and others began to plead and shout. Krokinos hid among the guards, and the loincloths and their men began to systematically club the frantic crowd to submission as the guards corralled them to a dense corner.

Apollonia began to pray, and her body began to shake uncontrollably. Alexa stood deathly quiet, as if by shock or to shut the horrifying scene unfolding in front of her eyes. The rank smells of fear, urine, sweat, and desperation was overwhelming—and Apollonia hugged her daughter who now began to whimper, "Mother, mother."

In desperation, Apollonia began to shout at Krokinos, "You promised to wait until my husband returns! Master, please!" But in the din, Krokinos did not hear her or pretended not to. Diona, who never had a kind word for Apollonia, smirked and turned away.

One by one, the loincloths grabbed those that they had chosen and shoved them to the guards who pushed them to the caravan. For a while, no one approached Apollonia as she stood huddled with her daughter, trembling with fear, their eyes closed. It felt for a moment that the world was at peace—there was chirping, a gentle brush of wind kissed her neck teasingly, and a horse somewhere neighed. And then as if a monster from the Hades rose to consume all good in the world, Apollonia felt the powerful hands of the slave trader grab her by the waist, and before a sound escaped from her mouth, she felt lifted. In panic, she turned and screamed for Alexa, but her daughter was nowhere to be seen, and her calls were drowned in the cacophony of anguish. She beat the man who held her, but to no avail, and he pushed her hard into the mass of people.

Even as she wailed, another set of guards swiftly forced them to push against each other into a foul dense mass, and then tied the hands of each condemned to the one next. An older man, not from Krokinos' household, fell to the side and the guards raised angry welts on his back, but Apollonia registered none of it, now numbed by shock.

"Leave your belonging, none of it is necessary where you are going!" said one of the loincloths, and the other laughed.

"You will need none of it for the rest of your lives, or whatever is left of it," said another, as he mocked a woman who looked up fearfully.

"Come on, get ready to move!" A guard yelled and hustled the group towards the door. Apollonia looked around frantically for her daughter, but the column was surrounded by dust hindering visibility. "Alexa! Alexa!" She screamed until her voice was hoarse but heard nothing back. Just then, the disheveled woman next to her tapped her shoulder, "How old is your daughter?"

"Nine! She is just nine!" Apollonia said, tears flowing down her cheeks.

"Then she will be in front of the caravan with other children. You will get to see her in a few hours when we stop."

Relief washed over Apollonia. "How do you know?"

"My son is seven. They let us see our children to keep us in check. They threaten to sell the children separately if we misbehave or try to escape."

The dark reality dawned on her.

There was no escape.

As curious onlookers watched, the long column trudged along on a rocky path. Apollonia alternatively cursed her husband and prayed for his return, but feared that it was too late.

CHAPTER 13.

CAPPADOCIA & PISIDIA

Seleucus stood quietly as Perdiccas paced furiously. They had received news from multiple sources that Ptolemy had attacked the procession and made off with Alexander's body. Not only had Ptolemy killed Cleomenes, but he had also now explicitly gone against the Regent's orders, the Royals' wishes, and performed an outrageous act abetted by that treacherous scoundrel Arrhidaeus.

Perdiccas told Seleucus that Eumenes had warned him on this outcome and that a messenger had arrived with a missive a few weeks earlier which he did not heed because it seemed preposterous, but this disaster has struck him just after he had finished an exhausting campaign in Cappadocia.

When the council assigned various territories to the generals, Eumenes had received Cappadocia, but the region, not previously entirely subdued by Alexander, was ruled by an independent warlord named Ariarathes. This mad man, now old and nearing eighty years of his life, refused to cede territory. Since Eumenes was still not a fully battle-tested commander, Perdiccas had asked Antigonus to help Eumenes. But Antigonus, who saw himself senior to Perdiccas, and having never gone with Alexander in the eastern campaign, refused. So, Perdiccas was forced to go subdue the warlord and give the region to Eumenes. He waged a brutal campaign against Ariarathes, and eventually captured him and his family. He also wanted to make an example of Ariarathes to make sure no one dared to go against his orders. The soldiers tied the old man to a wooden crucifixion post, and in front of his wailing family they hacked off his ears, cut his fingers, severed his right foot, and left it a bloody stump. And then they left him nailed to the post, denied him his last rites, and let the animals pick on his flesh.

Perdiccas then put to death most of Ariarathes' family. By now everyone knew what it meant to go against his wishes, and this was a warning not just to his enemies, but also to everyone aligned to him. He spared Ariarathes' young niece and stepson, with the understanding that they would bid his orders.

Then he returned south to Pisidia and was aware of the rumblings in Greece and Hellespont. "Can you believe his audacity, Seleucus? Who does that bastard think he is!" Perdiccas raged.

"Preposterous! You would think Ptolemy had more sense than this."

"He got what he wanted, and then he decides it is insufficient. I intend to put an end to all this nonsense," Perdiccas said, pointing at Seleucus.

"What are you planning to do?" Seleucus asked, his genial face hiding his apprehension.

"I will take both the Kings—Philip and little Alexander, and with the power of their legitimacy behind them I plan to turn the troops of Ptolemy against him and crucify that traitor!" Perdiccas screamed, his face red with exertion, his eyes wild after a bout of heavy drinking. He fidgeted, and his hands shook. He had not shaved his facial hair and looked like an unkempt, drunk soldier.

Seleucus looked at Perdiccas, unsure how to react. Ptolemy was highly respected, and there was no question that the abundant riches of Egypt helped Ptolemy keep his troops happy. His possession of Alexander's corpse made the question of legitimacy a lot more delicate.

But on the other hand, if Perdiccas was stupid enough to march to Egypt, then Seleucus may be able to cement his position as the Lord of Asia. "Do you think that is wise, Perdiccas? To march all the way to Ptolemy and meet him at his strongest?"

"Strength is but an illusion based on his troops' loyalty, Seleucus," Perdiccas snickered. With his trembling lips, he took another sip of wine and then dramatically smashed the cup on the floor.

"But what makes you think they will turn against their leader?" Seleucus asked.

"Is it not obvious? Once they know both Alexander's brother and his son stand behind me, most of their loyal troops will turn. Besides, we have our treasuries to draw from and a large enough force to subdue that scoundrel."

"What about the news that Craterus is preparing to cross Hellespont?" asked Seleucus, as he removed his helmet and caressed the green plumes.

"Yes, I am aware of that, I will find a way to put an end to the adventure of that old fool!"

Seleucus did not voice his doubt of Perdiccas taking on two fronts against powerful, experienced foes. Perdiccas was a good general, but he was no Alexander.

"I do not think it wise to take the Royals—"

"I am not asking for your permission Seleucus."

Once Perdiccas made up his mind, Seleucus realized, it was almost impossible to change the man's decisions. He could also be dangerous when angry.

"As you command, Regent. When do you propose to begin this expedition?"

"Immediately. I want you to work with the senior officers to prepare for departure. Let us bring that dog in chains!"

"I will get on this right away." Seleucus turned to leave, and he heard Perdiccas' voice behind him.

"One more thing, Seleucus. I have a message for Eumenes."

CHAPTER 14.

SYRIA

I left the family and took leave of my companions after promising them significant reward once the situation settled. The journey for a lone rider can be dangerous, for roadside bandits are always on the lookout for easy prey. I took a path that avoided the usual trade routes, and the few that saw me left me alone.

Finally, on the third day, I arrived in Damascus. There was much activity in this ancient city, and it was not very difficult to find a garrison still allied to Perdiccas. The captain was an impressive young man, no older than twenty-five. He was muscular and sported thick facial hair—it was clear he no longer respected the Army's hair rules. Once he found out who I was, he made space for me in his modest living quarters near the northwest of the town, established on the slopes of the hills that rose on this quarter of the city.

After the pleasantries, we got to business. We met in his tent, and Iotros, one of the Captain's men, who I was told had intimate knowledge of the geography of the area, joined us. Iotros had the odd habit of blinking his eyes rapidly as he spoke.

I decided to be as honest as I could be, all the while aware of the intensely valuable nature of what I was carrying. The longer the papers were with me, the greater the danger to me and my mission.

"Before I speak of my mission, I need to know what you have learned so far about Alexander's procession."

They exchanged looks. "Ptolemy took control of the procession—"

"What do you mean took control?"

"He stole King Alexander's body, sir, and offered rewards to those that joined him. The decision had to be made on spot, and most of the men chose to go with him." The captain paused—he had noticed my expression of disgust. As much as I understood the situation, the reality that these men would so readily abandon their cause frustrated me. "You know how it is commander—the men must make a living and pay for their expenses."

Ptolemy—that clever schemer!

"And then he ordered the gold on the funerary temple melted, and other precious ornamentation sold to pay for the mercenaries."

"Where are they now?"

"We do not know, but the last messengers came a few days ago and said the cart is moving rapidly and they should be well past Tyre, safe into Ptolemy's territories."

"Have you heard of anything from Perdiccas?"

"We have received news that the Regent is about to move to Egypt."

That news alarmed me; the situation was escalating rapidly. Eumenes was always loyal to Perdiccas which meant he would be drawn into this one way or the other, I did not know how, yet. I chewed on the chunks of lamb. The captain leaned back on his bench, and I noticed that his right toe was missing. "What happened to your toe?"

"A fine bandit hacked it off in one of the camp raids." He grinned affably. War scars.

"Do you know where Eumenes is?"

Iotros, who was silent all this while, interrupted, "Why did you leave the procession and come here, sir?" he asked, blinking furiously.

The annoyed captain asked Iotros to step back and be quiet. "I have heard you are an advisor to Royal Secretary Eumenes—is that true?" Soldiers not attached to Alexander's campaign were always fascinated by stories, and if someone they met was high up the command, close to the famous men, they met with a hero's reception and could use that to their advantage.

"Yes, I was. And if you must know, yes, I have been in the same room as Alexander, met regent Perdiccas, and dined with Eumenes many times."

His eyes lit up with admiration, and he sat up as if slouching in my presence was somehow improper.

"You must have many interesting stories to tell!"

"I do, but there is a better time. This is like a soldier asking a fellow man whether his concubine has fine breasts, while he is being stabbed in the crotch by the enemy."

He laughed at the bawdy analogy. "I apologize, what else do you want to know, sir?"

"Where is Eumenes? And how do I reach him?"

"His last known position was somewhere near Hellespont," he said, as he sipped wine carefully.

"What is he doing there? He was stationed further west in Cappadocia."

"I do not know, sir."

I felt a sense of dread but did not know why.

That evening I rested in a tent a few hundred steps from the captain's quarter. As the sun set and the cold winds began to blow from the flatlands on the east, I wrapped myself in the barely adequate blankets, secured the package around my waist, placed my kopis in my belt, and went to sleep. Tomorrow would be an important day.

True soldiers never truly sleep, they say, for we are always awake in our minds for the hints of danger. Sometimes late at night, I heard a rustling near my tent, and briefly, I thought this was the sound of leaves in the wind. But I remembered there were no trees anywhere near my location.

When I opened my eyes, I noticed the silhouette of three men approaching and jumped to my feet—though not soon enough. Iotros and his two companions crouched under the tent and walked in. They blocked the entrance, and in the darkness, it was difficult for me to make out how armed they were.

Iotros spoke quietly.

"If you know what is good for you, commander, you will make no noise."

I imagined him blinking rapidly.

"The captain is away on an errand, so do not get your hopes up," said the second man with a gruff voice.

The third man stood quietly.

"Iotros, you should know better than to do this to an officer of Perdiccas."

"I doubt Ptolemy would care."

I was shocked—the man had penetrated the ranks in this region so effectively. "What do you want from me? You already heard everything anyway."

"What did you steal from the procession?"

There it was. "Who told you I stole anything? Was your grandmother on patrol with Ptolemy?"

I could not make out if he smiled, but Iotros was quite the humorless man. I braced for a punch, but none came.

"We've received reports of the leader of the rear guard leaving the scene with a couple of his rascals."

"You're quite the genius, aren't you Iotros? I left because I'm not on the take like you are, drawing a salary from Perdiccas and licking Ptolemy's boots."

He stepped forward, and I took a step back.

"All we want to know is what you stole, people saw you Deon, and Ptolemaios wants to know."

"I doubt that—"

They lunged at me, and before I could parry the attack Iotros punched me hard in the stomach.

They had me tied firmly to a chair.

The situation had turned, and a few days ago I was the man behind the tied prisoner—our gods have a divine sense of justice. There were two low candles burning on the side, their waxy smoke slowly filling the enclosed space of a hut with a low, thatched roof. The gag, which stank, was still in my mouth.

Iotros stood in front of me, his henchmen were outside, guarding. "I'm not the one for long lectures. Let us see what you have here."

He confidently stepped forward, deftly cut the belt, and released the bag. I felt a deep despair; this was not supposed to end this way! Iotros opened the bag, tilted the opening towards the candles, and peered into it.

And then he threw his head back and laughed. "Regent's choice for the rear guard... a swine, and nothing but a common thief!"

I shook my head dramatically as if to convey great shame—whether my theatrics would convince Iotros was another question. I then huffed and grunted—pretending to have difficulty breathing.

Iotros removed the gag and let me breathe easier, he enjoyed the sight of a broken officer turned thief in his control. He pulled out a few of bracelets, beautifully carved with warriors hunting a bull, and some gold rings. "Just one last grab, commander?"

I muttered, "Even a commander needs to feed his family, Iotros."

"You could have stayed back and accepted Ptolemy's patronage."

"My wife is not in Egypt, and I have no interest in learning strange tongues."

He smirked, pulled out the package, and my heart sank. Iotros, for whatever reason, seemed circumspect and was gentle in removing the bindings. There was no slashing and cutting this time. He struggled to open the box and began to get frustrated. I realized that if I did not help him, he might bring his thugs who would not hesitate to break it open.

"Let me show you how to open it."

"You can tell me, sir, I can hear."

I told him so, and he was delighted to see the lid unlock. He removed the inner package and unwrapped the contents.

The last time I packed it in a hurry, I had placed Plato's letter at the bottom, and the ancient pages in the front.

He pulled the first papyrus out and placed it in front of the light, and I gasped. "Do not bring it too close to the flame. You will burn it!"

He pulled it back, and then put his face closer to it, examining the papyrus. I watched him as he read it. His eyebrows bunched, and his eyes darted back and forth. He had the papyrus upside down.

This idiot could not read!

"Every senior officer has to fulfill administrative obligations, Iotros. I carry legal paperwork with me at all times."

He grunted. "Why does this have strange writings on top and what seems to be Greek at the bottom?"

I spoke gently to him. "Iotros, have you been garrisoned anywhere further east?"

"No," he said, and his voice trailed.

I suddenly felt a little sorry for the man. He seemed gentle, recruited when he was young but after Alexander had already passed these areas, and had seen little of the world.

"Some of the areas further east have different tongues, and we sometimes carry orders in multiple languages."

He seemed unsure. It seemed he realized his severely limited world view compared to the man who was in front of him.

"Please leave those papers with me and let me be on my way. You can keep the jewels. I have spent ten years away from family, served our King without question, and I am tired, Iotros. I just want to go home."

"You could be tried for thievery, you know?"

"I know. But I hope you see why I did it. You did it too for Ptolemy, did you not?"

I said that without an accusatory tone. We both looked at each other for a few moments, without hatred, but with the simple understanding that we all sometimes did what we had to. Iotros removed all the valuables. He placed the box, with its papyri, inside my bag. He seemed not to notice my sigh of relief.

He then placed a bracelet inside my bag. "For your wife," he said. "This stays between us until you leave camp tomorrow."

I nodded. He gestured his companions to come in, and they undid my ties. Iotros gave me my bag, and he whispered to them.

And as they were about to leave the tent, Iotros paused, and then he turned back. "Why would you go to Eumenes if you want to see your family? You are signing your death sentence anyway."

"Why do you say that?" I asked, puzzled.

"You have not heard?"

"Heard what?"

"Perdiccas has ordered Eumenes to prepare for war with Craterus."

I was aghast.

Alexander's secretary would go up against Alexander's most respected general.

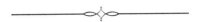

The next morning, I refreshed, fed my horse, packed some bread, and set on my way.

I said nothing of the earlier night's incident and kept a cordial conversation with Iotros. The captain insisted that ten of his crack troops go with me for my safety—and after some thought, I accepted the offer. It was a long way from here to Hellespont and riding lonely on the remote roads was at best foolish, and at worst, suicidal. Animals, starvation, dehydration, ambush, accidents, kidnapping—they were all very likely.

However, this posed a problem I had to solve and solve quickly. Walking around with this package was nothing but trouble, and I might not be this lucky next time. There was no good reason it had to be with me, as I remembered every single word and symbol.

I had to hide it.

So, I concocted a story. I told the captain I had to conduct a ceremony before beginning any major journey. At my request, he gave me two small bronze statues, one of Zeus, and one a local deity, with a lion's face and a human body.

I hiked up the mountain on the western edge of the city, with two of his men. It took us a few hours to reach to a higher point, and when I turned southwest, below us lay this old city. Behind me, the land continued to rise, but to my left, the River Chrysorrhoas carved the mountains and created a valley, before it picked up speed and gushed down.

I followed the river upstream for a few *stadia* and finally waded down to the source. I cleansed myself in the shallow, clear, and running water. I shivered, but it felt wonderful as the sun, now reaching the high sky, bathed me in warmth. I then prayed to Poseidon, asking him to help me on my journey to reach Eumenes and take me back to the arms of my wife. And then, hopefully, allow me to live the rest of my life in peace and luxury.

The gods surely laughed in mirth at my demands.

Refreshed, I scouted for a place to hide the package. An ancient temple on higher ground, carved into a cliffside, was the perfect location—I climbed up to it, found a nook inside and carefully hid the package. Then I covered it with several rocks and packed it in tightly. While a fleeting thought crossed my mind to destroy it, my heart could not bring itself to do it. These papyri were treasures. For now, my memory would hold all the content in my head, secure and safe.

It was time to go to Eumenes. I had to resolve my situation before everything escalated.

CHAPTER 15.

MACEDON

The slave caravan made slow progress through the barren landscape. The daily routine was the same: the guards roused the groups early in the morning, everyone got meager rations of rough bread, watery lentil soup, and two gulps of unclear water. After a few hours of trudging under the watchful eyes of the guards, sporadic instances of beating and berating, the column was allowed to rest for noon when they received another gulp of water and dried goat meat. And then it was hours of walking, again, until nightfall when they were allowed to sleep under the sky, with the guards and loincloths taking turns under tattered camp tents. The warm weather made it difficult to sleep, and the rocky ground further irritated the wounds on the worn skin and jutting bones.

The harmful elements and bad omens had caused fever and dysentery among the slaves, only adding to the misery. The slave traders brought physicians to care for the sick—it would do no good for them to lose their merchandise before it reached the mine owners. Apollonia had grown weak but managed to sustain herself—they gave her a bitter brew made of unknown tree bark to keep her bowels in control.

With each step, she wondered how her daughter was doing.

On the fourth day, the caravan was woken up due to a commotion around the camps. Apollonia looked out and found a military contingent, in full regalia, surrounding them. The captain, a gruff man with all the weariness of the world etched in his deeply tanned face, stood talking to the loincloths who looked angry and frustrated. She could not hear what they were saying, but the conversation was animated, until the point where the soldiers accompanying the captain drew their swords and advanced menacingly at the loincloths. Encountering military units was not uncommon—they often had to stop for patrols and tax posts—but no unit had so far accosted them.

After more frantic conversations now witnessed by every alert member of the caravan, the head loincloth, a giant hirsute man, went inside the camp and came out with sheaves of parchment. On his instructions, the guards yelled at the caravan to stand in line, and Apollonia joined the others. The captain walked along the line and began to shout. "Apollonia! Apollonia! Who is Apollonia?"

Apollonia's heart thudded with surprise and fear, what now? After a few moments of hesitation, she took a few steps forward, and so had two other women—one quite young, and another, several years older than her.

The captain looked at the three women and made an exasperated sign. "Are you all from the house of Krokinos? If you are not, step back."

Two of the women stepped back.

The captain then slowly walked to Apollonia, and the head loincloth loomed menacingly behind. "Are you Apollonia from the Krokinos' household?"

"Yes, sir," she said, weakly.

The captain suddenly reached out and pulled Apollonia's forearm to bring her forward, and she screamed in fear—but he did not inflict further violence. His eyed roamed around her neck. Satisfied, he let go and told her to wait. After further conversations and more shouting, one of the loincloths, a smaller, wiry man, accompanied the captain and mounted behind a rider of one of the horses.

"You will come with me," the Captain said. Bewildered, Apollonia took a few steps behind him before saying, "My daughter!"

The captain did not look surprised—he nodded and said, "I know." The loincloth was back again, this time cursing in his foreign tongue, but cooperating with whatever was going on. He led Apollonia up a narrow path for a short distance to another area, one with a few sorry looking tents. Apollonia's chest constricted in anticipation—would she see her daughter again?

They came in front of a tent, and inside was a huddled mass of children—anywhere from a few years to not yet adulthood. They were dirty, disheveled, and looked on with lifeless eyes.

Loincloth pushed Apollonia forward and said, "Go ahead."

"Alexa! Alexa, my baby!" Apollonia shouted, peering through the darkness. Eventually, she heard a faint voice, "Mother?"

Apollonia almost toppled and fell over a few other children in her urgency to embrace her daughter. Alexa stood in a corner, her hair matted with grime, twigs, food morsels. Her clothes, once a pretty floral gown, had faded and torn in more than one place. There were bruises on her ankle and knee, and Apollonia felt like her heart would explode. She held onto her daughter until she heard the Captain's voice, "We must go."

Under the glare of other loincloths and gruff mutterings of the head, Apollonia and Alexa hesitatingly walked along with the Captain. Once the head loincloth conferred with the Captain for the last time, the Captain directed them to a rider and asked them to mount.

"Where are we going?"

"You will find out. Please get on the horse. Your daughter will sit with you as well," the Captain said.

Seeing the mother and daughter's weakened condition, the Captain ordered a soldier to help them on, and also had someone give them some bread and water. And as the caravan looked on, their dull eyes gauging their fate, Apollonia and Alexa rode away.

It only took a few hours, but Apollonia recognized the landmarks and grew increasingly alarmed—why were they going back to where they came from? Soon, her doubts were answered, for they arrived at Krokinos' villa. They were ordered to dismount, and her daughter clung on to her fearfully.

A guard walked to the gate, and the rest of the group waited. After a while, she heard Krokinos' distinct yet raspy voice. "I can assure you I am doing everything to pay my share, but harassing me every week will do no good!"

The Captain then walked towards the partially open gate and said, "This is about the mother and the daughter."

"I already told you where they were. Why are you back here harassing me again? By Zeus, it is something or the other!" His voice was high pitched and agitated.

The Captain then pulled out a parchment and held it out to the sun. Apollonia then glimpsed Krokinos' beak nose bent over to read, and then after what seemed like an eternity, heard him exclaim and curse.

"It seems the gods want to fuck me for their amusement!"

CHAPTER 16.

HELLESPONT, PHRYGIA

After a long and uneventful journey, I finally arrived at Eumenes' military camp near Hellespont. The sights jolted me at first—it looked like there was recently a major battle. There was still debris at the crest of a valley near the camp, and a large group of men who looked like prisoners of war stood surrounded by armed soldiers. The captain who escorted me to Eumenes told me a most remarkable story.

So, Perdiccas had assigned Neoptolemus, another well-known general, to support Eumenes in his battle against Craterus. I remembered Neoptolemus from one of our earlier days—he smelled of overripe fruit; the man could repel an army with just his odor. He was a slight man, wiry, well-dressed, and he was from a noble family. He wore his hair in a bundle—a very odd sight on a general. I had only seen one other man wear his hair so—Bagoas—Alexander's eunuch and some said his lover. Neoptolemus did not like Eumenes, and he was grudging in his respect.

But it seemed for whatever reason Eumenes suspected Neoptolemus of potential betrayal, and by surprise ordered Neoptolemus to draw his infantry into a formation and be ready for battle. The rest of the troops were horrified when Neoptolemus' infantry turned and marched against Eumenes' main army. Such treachery! In a pitched battle, Eumenes' forces had fought this bastard, and then Eumenes had done something no one ever thought he would. Eumenes sent a part of his cavalry around the battleground and captured Neoptolemus' baggage train—the precious cargo that traveled behind the army, with the soldiers' life's earning, property, loved ones, food, and everything else.

It was a genius move.

Once Neoptolemus' men had realized what had happened, many were greatly demoralized. Their tired bodies and minds realized that not only were they on the wrong side of the battle, fighting against the man they pledged their loyalty to, but now they had lost their life's earnings, and their loved ones too. The captain said that most dropped their weapons and lay on the ground in surrender. The exceptional Cappadocian horse-riding archers quickly cut down those that still fought.

And then the captain said that Neoptolemus and some of his officers made away. That disloyal coward was no doubt going to join Craterus.

By the time the sun moved lower on the skies, the battle was over. Eumenes' infantry surrounded the renegade troops, confiscated their weapons, and led them to a flat area on the lower ground. And now Eumenes was preparing to address the men who once swore loyalty to him but turned against him at the hour of need. Even with all my misgivings, I could not help but admire how far Eumenes had come—he had defeated a full general in battle!

The look of shame and dishonor was plain on the captured faces, but I think more were worried about their baggage losses and what would become of their dear ones now under Eumenes' control.

I finally caught up with Eumenes.

He looked at me from the corner of his eye, and his face broke into a great smile—he signaled me to follow him, along with several of his other senior officers. There were other urgent matters to attend.

We made the captured infantry stand in the sun for much longer, as a punishment to their disloyalty. It was a tactic to let fear rise in them as they waited to hear about their fate. Their families appeared on the higher ground, tied, held hostage, and frightened. I surmised that we might put to death a few members as an example, and exact revenge on the senior officers of the coup. A few officers nailed to the posts even, Perdiccas' way.

But Eumenes had other ideas.

An orderly held a *stentorophonic* horn, so even the men further away could hear his voice. Once everyone settled, Eumenes began. His firm, but gentle voice carried across. "It is not every day that the men that pledged loyalty to their leader abandon him at an hour of need. You are hardy souls that have spent years in the service of Alexander and his greatest officers, and here you are, your reputation tarnished by a coward who abandoned you in battle and placed you in this shameful condition."

He stopped and looked at the assembly before him. Most of Neoptolemus' men looked ashamed, and many hung their heads and refused to look at Eumenes. They fidgeted, scratched their beards, massaged their sore arms, and looked pathetic.

He continued. "But I do not blame you. What can a soldier do if his general asks him to obey an order that conflicts with his conscience? Therefore, I have a proposition to make to you." He took two steps back, puffed his chest forward and swept his arms dramatically across the vista and towards the captured baggage train.

"You can come back to me, take an oath of allegiance to Perdiccas, knowing this time that you shall have no conflict in your minds and that your purpose will remain clear. No harm will come to you, or your family, and I forgive your transgression.

"Alternatively, you may turn your back and join your master Neoptolemus, and we will not pursue you. You may take your loved ones with you, but your material belongings will still be here. We will face you with honor in the next battle. You must make the decision now, for the time of the next great battle is near. Those who decide to be with me may step forward—but you must prepare to fight with a clear mind and heart, with no treachery."

In the next hour, a majority of the deserters returned to us, and there was much rejoice and hugging tears of joy, and relief. A small contingent of men, unable to come to terms with fighting for a Greek master, decided to walk away. They were met with a smattering of jeers, but most of the army watched them in sadness.

Eumenes had gained a new stature in my eyes, but it did not escape the men's minds that this was just a skirmish. The true battle, against Alexander's great general Craterus, was ahead of us. Once things settled down, I finally made my way to Eumenes, filled with mixed feelings.

"You have finally made your way—ugly bastard!" He laughed.

We embraced as old friends as the officers and soldiers alike looked on smiling. I hid my anger, for this was not the place or time to start a dispute.

"You greet me kindly as always, General," I said, as he clasped my back, drew his arm across my shoulder, and walked me to his tent.

"I am now a governor, Deon. Only the gods know what I am supposed to be governing, but Perdiccas has conferred upon me this new title that has little meaning."

On the opposite side of the valley was where we expected the enemy to appear. Craterus was only about fifteen days away. The most striking change in Eumenes was how he dressed. He had mimicked the exact attire of Alexander—the purple plumed helmet, decorative cuirass, sandals—all reminded the men of the King.

As we entered the tent, I asked him flippantly, "Any plans coloring your hair, Governor?"

He raised his eyebrows, grinned at me, and his brilliant eyes sparkled, "Someday, Deon. Do not you know that it is fashion these days for generals to dress like Alexander himself? The way that Seleucus twists his head mimicking Alexander, one would think the dead King is wringing his neck!"

We rested in his comfortable tent. Behind his seat was a large, ornate temple, with an empty throne in it. I looked at him quizzically. His eyes danced mischievously, "My officers feel better when we make decisions in front of Alexander's empty throne as if he were directing the affairs of my campaign."

I nodded. Eumenes had become a formidable force by now, and his uncanny ability to lead his distrustful Macedonian officers was remarkable. There were many veterans in his force; they were a difficult bunch who resented the Greek bookkeeper. But for whatever reasons they stuck by Eumenes.

"You should rest. I am of course intensely curious, but I can wait until morning. There is much at stake, and I want to seek your counsel for what is ahead of us."

"Craterus?"

"Yes. And the happenings around the empire make your expedition extremely critical."

I looked at Eumenes—my anger began to rise to the surface—and it was time to put an end to this fraudulent relation. "If Alexander anointed a successor, Governor, why would you be worried about a battle with Craterus?" I said, looking intently at Eumenes.

Eumenes froze. His expression turned cold for a fleeting moment before he regained his composure. He sighed deeply. "I should have told you the truth right from the beginning."

Eumenes could have admonished me for opening the package—after all, my orders were to bring it undisturbed. But he knew that taking that line would do no good to either of us.

"Rest today—I will hide nothing from you again. Gods and our King shall attest to that truth."

It does not matter; I will collect my rewards and go home. My task is done.

I decided not to press forward. The next morning, well-rested and fed, I joined Eumenes at his tent. He asked his guards not to disturb him. He offered me a bowl of syrup-drenched dates, a delicacy in this part of the world. Intensely sweet, chewy, and sometimes dipped in strong wine, to give the eaters a heady experience.

"Well, Deon, let us get to the urgent matters at hand. What you have found, and how we should tackle Craterus."

I nodded. I knew that my chances of walking before dealing with the Craterus situation were slim. "When do you expect to face general Craterus on the battlefield?"

"Within the next fifteen days. I think Craterus is still reinforcing his infantry and building supply lines."

"Has he not reached out to you, yet?"

Eumenes turned his head and smiled. He was a little man, but his measured gestures had a sense of gravitas to them. "Craterus has reached out to me with promises—I tried to reconcile him with Perdiccas and failed. I am loyal to Perdiccas for now, Deon, and that will not change soon."

"What do you think will happen if we lose?"

"They will most certainly put me to death. Craterus has been sending missives to my veterans, and he has been telling them that my time is over."

"Since when did Craterus decide that his penis was bigger than everyone else's?"

"Ever since old man Antigonus decided every teenage girl in Macedon longs for his."

We laughed, but this was no joke. For me, a threat to Eumenes was a significant risk to my aspirations.

Then Eumenes looked pensively out the tent and sighed. "I am shameful for having lied to you, but it was with reason—no matter how misguided."

"You thought I would think less of you if you revealed that the quest was about laying hands on treasure and weaponry to fortify your chances."

"Or you would think I am an utter fool for pursuing something that sounds ridiculous."

"I have never betrayed you, sir."

"It was a complex time. But it is my fault that I did not trust my most trusted advisor."

After an uncomfortable pause, I spoke again.

"I see no worthier successor to Alexander than you."

His face glowed with pride. "Tell me about what you found. It is exciting, is it not?"

"Sir, you must first tell me about the origins."

Eumenes' eyes glazed. "Deon, you make my mind drift to that chilly night when a filthy, stinking Callisthenes uttered those words from behind his cage…"

CHAPTER 17.

BACTRIA — MANY YEARS AGO

"No force on earth, whether by land or by sea, can defeat a King who finds it…" said Callisthenes, the whites of his manic eyes visible through the cage.

That got Eumenes' attention. He was getting impatient, waiting to hear whatever it was Callisthenes wanted to say, on this chilly early dawn.

"What I am about to tell you is a secret that I have told no one. And you must take my message to King Alexander without delay!" Callisthenes whispered excitedly.

"That is dramatic, but why have you not revealed this before?"

"I waited for the right moment. You, amongst others, should understand that I was wary of what Alexander was becoming. And before the right time arrived, here I was—" he pointed to the filthy floor of the cage.

"I have tried to reach the King to no avail. The guards treat me like a disease, Eumenes," lamented Callisthenes, as he pushed his face forward and peered between the bars. Eumenes recoiled from the odor of rotten teeth. It was as if Callisthenes had a dead rat in his mouth.

"But now this is my life, and only the King holds power over it. And I wanted to talk only to the man I trusted most."

"I am glad. Now hurry up," Eumenes admonished. It would not bode well if any of the King's officers saw him in a conference with Callisthenes.

"There is much for you to gain, as it is for me, Eumenes. Do you promise to take it to Alexander?"

"Yes, yes, now go on." Eumenes tapped the bars with his ringed fingers, impatiently.

"Remember I told you I studied at Ptolemy's academy when I was a youth?"

"This is no time for nostalgia!" Eumenes admonished.

Callisthenes' great mop of tangled hair shook like an aged lion's head. "Please listen. The guards will think I am mumbling incoherently."

He had a point. So Eumenes stepped back slightly, wrapped his cape around him, and faced Callisthenes.

"Did you know I learned to pick locks and climb walls?"

"That is wonderful," said Eumenes drily, as he impatiently shuffled his feet in the cold.

"I used Aristotle's name to get away with defiance to rules, dalliances with women, and trespassing. So, one quiet evening, when most of the academy was away on summer holidays, I decided to find the supposed hidden vault in the sacred area of the academy—Plato's sealed office!"

Eumenes' nervous shuffling stopped.

"I evaded the guards, picked the lock, and got into the chamber. Most of it was empty except for a few bound books of his most famous works, a bust of the man, and an old, delicately carved—"

"Get to the point, in Poseidon's name!" Eumenes hissed. And then he moved closer to the bars and angled his ears to be closer to Callisthenes' face.

Callisthenes stopped to catch his breath and wheezed. "Behind his desk was a brick wall which opened to a hidden chamber with two small rooms full of books, papyri bundles, and a few odd items. I have no doubt the administrators knew of this, but it seems they maintained the tradition of a hidden vault."

Eumenes' interest was piqued. Callisthenes continued in a hurried voice. "I loved that musty room! I spent hours staring at Egyptian and other foreign script and reading fascinating papers in old Greek. On my third visit, I discovered something astonishing. In one corner of the smaller chamber was an innocuous iron box, hidden in a nook, behind a shelf. Difficult for the casual interloper to find. It was locked, but not well enough to keep me from opening it..."

Two guards on patrol walked by, and Callisthenes began to chant while slowly swaying. "By Apollo! By the power of—"

They stared at the mad man, saluted Eumenes, and continued. At a distance, behind the mountains, a gentle glow began to suffuse the sky. Soon there would be activity, and that would not bode well for either of them.

"You need to hurry up, or we will run out of time."

"I opened the box to find some papyrus scrolls. The first two pages were an incomplete letter from Plato, to a man called Axiandros. The rest were from an ancient, unknown author and each page was in two scripts—one I did not recognize, and its old Greek translation." Callisthenes paused and gulped nervously.

"When I read it, I thought my head would explode!"

Now Eumenes was intrigued. "Well, get to it then."

Callisthenes leaned forward; his feral face close to Eumenes. "Atlantis!"

"What?"

"Atlantis," Callisthenes hissed, his expression maniacal.

"What about Atlantis?"

"Atlantis is real, and they left behind an intact city, you fool!"

Eumenes stepped back, and quick anger rose in him. Here he was, risking his life and entertaining the notions of this mad man. He gripped the bar of the cage. "I wish you peace in the afterlife, Callisthenes," he said and turned to leave.

"No!" Callisthenes shouted, and desperately grabbed Eumenes' cape, startling him. "Eumenes, I appear a wretched creature, but have I ever seemed to you as of unsound mind?"

Eumenes paused. Callisthenes was right—there was not an instance he could recollect where this man's behavior bordered madness. But Atlantis? "Atlantis is a story in Plato's book, Callisthenes, we both know that. Scholars have told us it was a warning about the greed of empires, nothing more," he said, with clenched teeth.

"That is because Plato hid the truth!" Callisthenes said excitedly. "There indeed was Atlantis, except Plato did not complete the story and did not reveal all he knew of it."

Eumenes rubbed his stubble, scratched his scalp under the helmet, and tried hard to hide his growing excitement. "So, what is the real Atlantis?"

Callisthenes grinned. He placed his forehead on the bars and stared intently at Eumenes, the whites of his eyes burning through the slowly dissipating darkness. "Procure my freedom, Eumenes, for there is more that I can share."

"While this is interesting, why should Alexander care for a mythical ancient empire?"

"You are no village simpleton, Eumenes, ask yourself why!"

"I have no time to—"

"The ancient scrolls tell the story of Atlantis, and in riddles, they mention the location of a new city the ancients left behind before they vanished. Plato claims that to be true, and from a trusted source. But it is not just a ruined city—"

"New city? Where are these papers?"

Callisthenes made a show of bashing his head against the bars. "In Craterus' possession. That loudmouth has no idea what is under his lock-and-key."

Eumenes groaned. Not Craterus! "What does it look like?"

"It is in a plain iron box decorated with a scene of the great Zeus overseeing a teacher and his pupils. The scrolls are in an innocuous leather package, with the distinct symbol of a bull on it. The box was handed to him during my trial, for safekeeping as royal records and not to be opened."

"He thinks they are pages of the royal diary?"

Callisthenes nodded ruefully.

Eumenes fell silent. There was no question that if he tried anything to get hold of that box, Craterus would not only oppose it but would get suspicious.

"What were you hoping to get from this revelation?"

"My life! If the generals find out then I assure you, Eumenes, we will see mutiny and bloodbath."

"And what do I tell Alexander?"

"Tell him what I told you. And that I had no part in the conspiracy, and that I am giving him the greatest secret of our times, and that I will help him find it."

"You seem to be confident that no one else can decode the riddles."

Callisthenes grinned again. "I have spent years trying to decode them, dear Eumenes. And I assure you that there is only one man on this divine earth who has a clue where the new city of the Atlanteans is."

"You."

Callisthenes slapped the bars of the cage and nodded vigorously. Specs of fine dust flew from his dirty hair, and Eumenes stepped back to avoid the contamination.

"How do you know there are not just a few bars of gold and ten rusted swords?"

"The ancient papers make it clear. If you find the city the Atlanteans left behind, you win the world. Imagine the implications."

Eumenes feigned irritation. "That is vague. I need to know more to be able to report this and provide a sense of impact."

Callisthenes shook his head. "No, Eumenes. There must be a sense of fairness. Alexander may not be swayed by the immense scale of treasures and profound knowledge that this city contains, but he will wish to acquire the fantastical weapons the ancients designed that will make him invincible now, and forever."

Callisthenes stopped again to wheeze and catch his breath, as he stared at Eumenes. "I am sure the King will reward you handsomely for bringing this to him."

Eumenes pressed one last time. "How do I know this is not your delirious mind? That this is a ploy to get yourself out of this cage?"

"If my words are untrue then the King will put me to the cruelest death, so there is nothing in it for me to deceive you."

Eumenes, a great reader of men, sensed the truth behind the frantic voice. Truth, if used wisely and strategically, had the power to change fortunes and empires; but if revealed prematurely to the wrong people, cause great bloodshed in its quest. As the slice of gold appeared on the horizon and the sounds of the early morning became louder, it was time for Eumenes to go.

He bid goodbye to the historian, promised that he would take this to the King post haste and that he looked forward to reuniting with Callisthenes in the royal tents, friends again, and embarking on a grand adventure.

Eumenes' heart thundered in his chest as he walked away, and he did not look back as he was unable to meet the hopeful eyes.

CHAPTER 18.

HELLESPONT, PHRYGIA

Eumenes' recounting of Callisthenes' words matched with what I had read in the papyri and I now had no reason to doubt the Governor. I recounted my saga; the failed attempt during the raid, Ptolemy's subterfuge, my stealing of the papyri, the contents inside, and finally the events in Damascus where I hid the papers in an abandoned old temple by the side of a mountain facing the city. It seemed like he held his breath as I spoke, and when I finished, he let out a gentle sigh.

"Astonishing," he said, finally. And then bitterly complained about Ptolemy. And we both sat quietly for a while, each wondering what to say next.

"So, Callisthenes was not lying, and that is assuming an ancient fraudster did not trick Plato?"

"That is right, sir."

"I have heard and seen the excitement of finding lost tombs with treasure, but nothing on this scale..." he trailed away as if lost in thought.

"There was a reason they were so fanatical about keeping it a secret, and why Plato decided not to reveal it to the world."

Eumenes nodded.

"May I ask something, sir?"

As if he read my mind, Eumenes said precisely what I was thinking. "But how much of what Plato wrote was true?"

I laughed. I too wondered about that.

In his works Plato had gone to great lengths to describe Atlantis—it was beyond the pillars of Hercules; three great concentric water rings from three to one *stade* wide encircled a magnificent temple of Poseidon and a royal palace in the center, an enormous canal three-hundred-foot wide, a hundred-foot deep, and fifty *stades* long cut through the concentric circles of land and water; the stone from the central island was black, white, and red.

"Plato's source was Critias, his grandfather, who supposedly heard it from his grandfather who heard it from the great Solon, who said he heard the story from a high priest of Sais in Egypt. We can expect some loss of fidelity and accuracy with the number of people involved in transmitting the story." Eumenes said.

"Besides, we have no account of Atlantis except in Plato's work. None." I said. For a story so fascinating it was notable there was absolutely no other source for the Atlantis story, and I had read a great many works of famous writers and philosophers. I had even heard that Aristotle, Plato's pupil himself, has scoffed at the story.

Eumenes got up from his cushion and began to pace around. I could see the thinker in him get excited—this topic was far more interesting than what occupied him recently—betrayal, war, murder. "Remember, Plato was a philosopher. He intended to make an impact with his messages. Atlantis gave him a chance to speak of hubris, greed, and divine anger, and infuse his treatise with excitement for the victory of Athenians against a foreign power. Was Atlantis exactly as he described? We cannot know. I do think he exaggerated greatly, but the description of the destroyed city could very well be true, but not at the scale he wrote," he said, as he absent-mindedly picked up his well-worn idol of Zeus and traced his fingers on the thunderbolt.

Exaggerations were very common, as I had seen in my journeys. I had often heard of fantastical beasts, monsters, and all kinds of wonders before my trips to the East, and yet when we arrived there—the men were men, and the beasts were different but nothing of the type the storytellers described. Similarly, I too was confident that Plato magnified the details of Atlantis to appeal to the reader and chose not to tell the story of a second city. And since god destroyed the original empire, there was no way for anyone to call Plato a liar.

"All we know in his brief story is what happened to people of Atlantis, and that they left behind a hidden city. In that hidden city we may find out more about them and the original Atlantis," he said and began to polish the idol in his hand with a beautiful silk cloth that he pulled from a bag.

"The Egyptian priests said they existed nine thousand years ago!" I said, still marveling at it.

Eumenes stopped and looked at me as if I were a gullible fool. "That is nonsense. I have heard a great many stories of our ancestors, and yet except Plato's story there is nothing about a great empire that existed nine thousand years ago."

"Maybe a few thousand?"

"Maybe. I have heard through a famed Phoenician scholar that long ago there existed another glorious city called Tartessos, but it is somewhere near the end of the world."

"What do you—"

A messenger interrupted us. Craterus was on his way and would be here in less than ten days. The two-faced scoundrel Neoptolemus would be with him.

It was time to prepare for Eumenes' greatest test.

Eight days had passed since the battle with Neoptolemus. The time to fight Craterus neared. I debated many times if I should press Eumenes on my release and rewards, but decided not to, given the circumstances.

After the morning war council concluded, Eumenes turned to me. "It is not skills, capability, weather, or terrain that I worry about."

"Then?" I asked.

"I worry about desertion on the battleground."

I had a hunch of what he meant. Eumenes continued, "Craterus is a god to many Macedonian soldiers. I worry that when our cavalry sees the man, they will abandon me and go to him."

"Do you think they revere him so much that they would desert their commander?" I asked.

"Yes. Do you remember Craterus' roles in the siege of Tyre, the great battle of Gaugamela, and so many other battles on the way to and return from India? They love him."

"But still—" I started, and Eumenes cut me short.

"Many Macedonians still see me as a secretary, no matter how much I have proved otherwise!" Eumenes looked sad. I pitied the man—but such was the politics.

"Are you sure that Craterus will be on the battlefield?" I asked.

Eumenes walked behind me and boxed my ear. "You hitch your hopes on the flimsiest of threads."

I hung my head in mock shame.

"You wish that instead of Craterus there will appear a beautiful Greek princess to make love to you on the battlefield," Eumenes continued. The levity helped, but there was no question that the real threat was the stature of Craterus. As we contemplated the situation, I remembered something worth telling him.

"Governor, there is an interesting folklore worth hearing," I said.

He narrowed his eyes and pushed his chin outward. I started, "Long ago, deep in the mountains of Sparta, there was a village. They lived away from war and knew no conflict. Harvest was plentiful, and they reared sheep, goat, and foal to keep themselves full and happy.

"Soon, there arose a problem, for there was an old lion in the nearby mountain that learned of this village.

"He began to come down every so often, menaced the people, and savaged their prized animals. The villagers, untrained in violence, tried to appease the lion with sacrifices."

Eumenes interjected. "What is your point?"

I requested him to listen to me, and he asked me to continue.

"But the lion kept coming, for he knew he could eat with no effort. The frightened villagers now gave him what he wanted. One day a traveler from far away joined them, and what he saw surprised him. He told the chief of the village that he would solve their problem if they rewarded him. The villagers approved.

"The traveler left to a land far away and returned with a pack of wild dogs. The angry beasts snared their teeth and dripped saliva—they feared no one.

"The lion came down again, and he looked at the dogs with arrogance. But the dogs had never seen a lion before."

Eumenes had stopped breathing—he looked at me with his bright eyes, and his face broke into a cunning grin.

The hot sun was on our face, the air still and humid, and sweat flowed down our hair and neck wetting the battle dress. Critters in the grass buzzed and the vast assemblage of troops chattered impatiently. Eumenes fielded an infantry of fifteen thousand men, including three thousand *Argyraspides,* the "Silver Shields," once Alexander's finest troops. The cavalry was a mix of Macedonian and Cappadocian horsemen.

Eumenes had positioned the army along the gentle slopes of a valley. A low hill in-between hid Craterus' and the traitor Neoptolemus' armies. Eumenes had spread misinformation that we would face Neoptolemus and Pigres—a barbarian warlord. The commanders told the soldiers that Craterus had left for Egypt.

Cavalry protected the phalanxes on either side. Eumenes was about to take charge of his biggest, and most important battle yet. Spies told us that the enemy had assumed a classical formation. Craterus' cavalry on the left and Neoptolemus on the right guarded the central phalanx.

On our side, the formation mirrored the enemies. To our extreme right, facing Neoptolemus, was the Eumenes' cavalry. Most of the men were Macedonian.

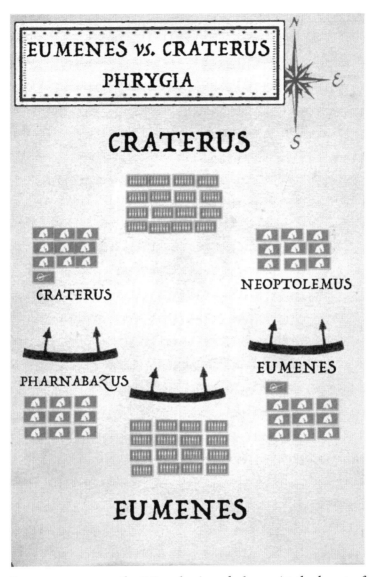

EUMENES vs. CRATERUS
PHRYGIA

CRATERUS

CRATERUS

NEOPTOLEMUS

PHARNABAZUS

EUMENES

EUMENES

In our center was the Macedonian phalanx. At the heart of it were the *Argyraspides*—the silver shields—now nearing their sixties and formidable as ever.

To the left, where I was, was the Cappadocian cavalry led by a man named Pharnabazus. He was taller than most of us and dressed in a deep blue flowing Cappadocian tunic. He was bare above his torso, and his long beard, speckled with gray, conveyed a noble bearing. He wore large brass earrings, his eyebrows were thick and knotted, and he drew dark lines on his eyebrows. Pharnabazus slapped my shoulder in appreciation once he learned of my service by Alexander's side. This Asian cavalry under Pharnabazus would face off Craterus. A Cappadocian told me that Pharnabazus was a royal and had fought Alexander in the earlier years. Apparently, whatever he did had not earned Alexander's wrath, and the man was not only alive but was now fighting on behalf of Alexander's former secretary.

Water bearers went around to quench the thirst of the men. The sun poured fire on our heads and our patience began to thin. There was a commotion in front of me, and I heard one of the riders berate another beside him.

"Don't piss on my horse's leg, you scoundrel!"

"But I had to go! It's your horse, not your wife!"

"But how do you know it's not his wife?" another voice chimed.

"I swear I will come down and give you a beating you short bowlegged dog—"

"Quiet or I will have you whipped!" The booming voice of one of their commanders silenced the men.

We waited.

Eumenes came galloping towards us. He looked every bit Alexander in his attire and demeanor, and the officers bowed in deference. He ordered three of us—Pharnabazus, Phoenix of Tenedos, and me to come before him. He patted his horse, and his weary eyes scanned us as he spoke,

"The time is near. Craterus' forces wait behind those hills, and spotters tell us that they prepare for battle. I intend to surprise them. I will charge Neoptolemus. Pharnabazus and Phoenix, rush Craterus and give no quarter. Let no man escape to tell our infantry or cavalry that it is Craterus that commands them."

He turned to me, "Deon, I know your heart aches to charge and engage the enemy—but I need your counsel. I order you to stay in the middle of the formation and direct the affairs to contain Craterus. But do not engage the enemy unless they break through your protective ring."

"Yes, sir." I felt a pang of jealousy that I would not lead the cavalry attack. While it had been a few years since my injury, deep wounds never heal, and I knew I would never be as effective as I once was. Besides, the years had taken a toll on me, both physical and mental, and the guilt and desperation to free my family had grown stronger and not faded.

"May Zeus protect us from the heavens, and Demeter guide," he said, and turned his horse to return to his wing. We saluted and watched as his cape receded.

We waited for him to charge.

And then we heard the distant sounds of bugles and horns rising above the din of soldiers and critters, and our segment grew deathly quiet.

Our war bugles blared, and there was the same great excitement that reminded me of rushing into battle in India. Pharnabazus signaled the cavalry. The magnificent galloping horses kicked up grass and earth as they charged. Their manes glistened in the sun as they charged. The smell of dug up soil and ripped grass suddenly enveloped my senses. I prayed to Poseidon and asked him to protect me and let me go to my family. It would be a foolish end to my journey if I were to die now.

Eumenes was too far away for me to see, and I prayed that we would meet again, in victory, after this battle.

Our forces climbed the gentle intervening hill and then rushed down the slopes. At a distance, Craterus' troops were not yet in full battle-ready formation. Craterus' cavalry scrambled. Their behavior showed that we had surprised them with our sudden advance. As we approached the flat ground, the enemy finally charged. I could finally make out Craterus. The *kausia* hat he wore was as distinct as the favorite General. As we neared, I noticed that there was a flaw in their formation. Craterus had a significant gap between him and his senior officers and bodyguards.

Why would he—

That was when it dawned on me; our ploy had worked. Craterus thought he would face the Macedonians, whom he would impress and then turn them to his side. I wished I could see his face when he realized that the enemy had no idea who he was. He was vulnerable with a gap by his side that the Cappadocians could exploit.

Pharnabazus ordered his lieutenants to charge the gap. Meanwhile, the rest of the cavalry met in a great clash. I stayed in the center, commanding a small group. Swords glinted and connected, missiles hurtled in the air, and a great noise engulfed the space. Craterus' cavalry was no slouch, and the fight was even. The injured and the dead soon littered the ground. The screams, moans, neighs, clashing of metal, thundering hoofs on the ground, all intermingled to create the now familiar cacophony of battle. It was the music of death in the theater of Dionysus.

I faced a Macedonian who charged me after slipping through my protective ring. When he missed his blow, I hacked his shoulder open like ripe pear and shredded the skin. Flesh and blood embraced the sharp iron like a coat in a cold winter. He fell to the ground, and I turned my horse towards the fallen man. I raised my javelin and thrust it through his chest, and a bold fountain of blood erupted from his mouth. He convulsed, and his eyes lost their light.

I turned my horse and looked back. The Cappadocian cavalry had formed an arc around Craterus' troops to prevent a breakout. The longer he fought, the higher the risk. If they routed our cavalry, this would be the end.

I spotted the hat in the far corner. The Cappadocians had exploited the gap well and isolated Craterus. His officers fought to get closer without success. I marveled at his dexterity when he blocked one attacker with a sword and thrust his javelin into another. He exhorted his men and brilliantly maneuvered around his attackers—and I began to worry that if we did not contain him, the tide would turn. But as I watched, a Thracian managed to poke Craterus, and the General lost his balance. I watched as his hands failed to grab the harness and he tumbled to the ground.

Craterus tried to get up, but his horse, panicking without its rider and harassed by a Cappadocian, kicked the general in the head. Craterus' *kausia* flew, and he was thrown back like a rag doll in a comical drama. My heart felt like it would explode with grief. On the ground lay bloody, alone, and unrecognized—one of my idols. From the corner of my eye, I noticed a horseman charge towards Craterus.

"No!" I screamed; my voice unheard in the din. The horse delivered an aimed kick to Craterus' exposed face and smashed it to a pulp. His body began to twitch. I rushed towards Craterus and by me was a trusted officer of Eumenes whom I ordered to guard Craterus' body. Craterus' men saw what happened and they began to dither—news of his fall spread amongst the cavalry. Many lost the will to fight, and unable to retrieve their fallen leader, they began to withdraw. Eumenes' instructions were clear. If the Cappadocians achieved victory on their wing, they were to aid Eumenes' cavalry. Leaving a small force behind, we rushed across towards Eumenes' cavalry.

The situation there was grave. Many were dead or dying, and groups of soldiers were fighting in pockets. There was no sign of victory, but all that changed when we caused a great noise and attacked the enemy from behind.

When they heard that Craterus was dead, the troop's dedication began to falter. The battle turned and then became a slaughter. There was no mercy as we hacked, thrust, and stabbed away at their one-time companions. Severed limbs, intestines, heads, and torsos began to pile up as soldiers stepped over them. We chased Neoptolemus' cavalry which ran to the protection of their untested phalanx, and we broke the pursuit as it would be foolhardy to attack a fresh phalanx without the aid of our own.

I then made way through the debris of the battleground and found Eumenes, standing with his head bowed. He had removed his helmet, and his wet, matted hair fell slick on his blood-stained cape. I dismounted and walked towards him. He was bleeding from his elbow and thighs.

On the ground lay Neoptolemus, his body covered in many gashes, and his neck cut wide open. His eyes looked like glassy marbles but with no joyful light in them.

One of the officers whispered to me. "Eumenes engaged Neoptolemus hand-to-hand and killed him!"

I looked at Eumenes with profound admiration. He looked at me and broke into a grin, and then spat blood on the ground. But there was one more matter to attend to. I walked to Eumenes and whispered, "Craterus."

He arched his eyebrows, and then, accompanied by some other officers, joined me as we galloped to where Craterus lay. When we reached, Eumenes hurried to Craterus, limping, and stood over the mass of red. He ordered two soldiers to pick Craterus and place him on a gurney.

Craterus reminded us of our mortality, and that no matter how great a man, we all serve at the pleasure of God.

I wondered who was next.

And then Eumenes held the fallen general's hand and bowed. At that moment, Craterus stirred. He let out a guttural moan like a deeply wounded animal, startling us, and tried to open his swollen, fractured right eye. His mouth coughed up dark, thick blood. There was still life in this fighter. Clouds slowly moved over the fiery sun and the glint off Craterus' earring faded.

It was a sign from the heavens. To my great surprise, tears rolled off Eumenes' cheeks. My eyes welled up as well, and I pretended to survey the landscape.

"O Craterus! What fool were you to array with that incompetent traitor Neoptolemus? Why did you force me to bring upon you this fate, my friend?" Eumenes lamented. Craterus stirred and sighed. Eumenes placed his palm over the fallen general's skinned forehead. He then thrust his kopis into Craterus' chest—a final gurgle came from Craterus' blood-filled throat. He kissed Craterus' forehead, and we stood around, heads bowed.

In one day, the little secretary had outmaneuvered Alexander's greatest general and vanquished another.

But it was also time for me to get my dues and leave.

Eumenes performed last rites and sent Craterus' ashes to his wife. Then, before local looters arrived at the battle scene, Eumenes' men scoured the battlefield to strip the fallen of their weapons, jewelry, and any fine clothes. Finally, late in the afternoon, he summoned me to his tent. He rested his wounded leg and clapped as I entered.

"You have come far from managing papers for Alexander, Governor," I said, with genuine respect and affection for the man. I had noticed his conduct on the battlefield—as cunning and clever as he was, he was also a decent man, unlike the cruel tyrants among the Macedonians, Perdiccas coming foremost to mind.

Eumenes smiled. He had had his hair trimmed short.

"Did a pretty girl from the baggage train ask you to cut your hair?" I asked.

He rubbed his fingers through his scalp. "Neoptolemus tried to grab me by the hair. I did likewise and pulled him down to the ground."

The hair was a liability.

"It is a problem you should not have to worry about, Deon." He grinned and then continued, "The Macedonians will never accept my command with absolute loyalty, will they?" he asked, and his voice dropped low.

"You know the answer to that, General."

"Perhaps Zeus wishes me to burn Alexander's empire and build my Greek empire on its ashes and bones?"

His eyes blazed with ambition, and desire burned hot in him. But we both knew that under the present circumstances, there would be no Macedonian empire run by a former Greek bookkeeper.

"How do you see this develop, with the Regent on his way to Egypt?" I asked, curious to see what he thought.

He gazed towards the far hills towards the south, thoughtfully. "If Perdiccas wins, our joint forces will take on the others. But if Perdiccas loses, his army will splinter—some will go to Ptolemy, and others will go to Antigonus. Unless I muster significant new reserves, there is no hope for me to grow my army."

"Which makes your quest to find this new capital of Atlantis even more crucial."

"What do you know about building an empire, or even securing a country, Deon?" He said, surprising me with the change in direction.

"I can offer a commentary or two about building armies of babies, that would not be a bad—"

"Not the time," he scolded me; chastised, I returned to the topic.

"I'm a soldier, not a king, sir."

"You build an empire by conquering lands. You conquer lands using great armies. You build great armies by finding the best men and rewarding them well. But that is not enough. Once you conquer, you must hold cities and ports. To hold them you must fortify them with walls, siege towers, guards. And then you must protect the citizens, supply your troops, secure, and expand the roads, canals, forts. Then you must administer it all. No one hands you an empire ready for use."

"I imagine the immense complexity and the need for money, sir."

Eumenes nodded. He stretched his leg and grimaced. The physicians had padded his thigh with poultice and tied a tight cloth, and yet the blood seeped through it. He took a sip from his wine cup and relaxed on his seat; he was bare above his waist, an uncommon sight for this slight man. Rivulets of sweat flowed down his hairless chest.

Eumenes continued. "You must then encourage trade. You must find sources of revenue, cultivate them, protect them—gold, grain, slaves, spices, women, all tenderable value. You must decide on taxes, impose them, ensure no one is cheating; but to raise adequate tax revenue, you must appoint administrators, revenue collectors, accountants, and inspectors. And all that takes more troops and money."

I suppressed my smile watching Eumenes deliver his speech. It was as if he imagined a large audience in front of him. He continued, gesturing, and swinging his arms. "You have learned this by now, Deon, that your troops are only as loyal as you can reward them."

I nodded. Most soldiers were mercenaries for the highest bidder.

Eumenes continued, as he smoothed the creases on his dress. "A leader must not only forge alliances and define strategy, but also help troops expand their loot. We now face a major war, and we have no king. The men with the most money will not only rule Europe and Asia, but they will execute the rest of us without hesitation. The victors will establish legitimacy as they please."

"I understand."

"You realize that finding this city is critical for our very survival. We have a chance to define our destiny."

I nodded. Eumenes then picked a jug of water from a clay pot by his side and took several gulps. His face was red and glistened with sweat. Small droplets of sweat tickled the nape of my neck and balding head.

He wiped his face with a towel and continued. "You would have no idea where it is, would you?" he asked.

"Sir, if I knew where it was and wanted to betray you, I would be sitting on Ptolemy's lap now."

His eyes dropped for a moment, and his cheeks flushed at that admonishment. But I had not endured everything I did only for him to question my loyalty. We paused, and I helped him stand up. He winced in pain from the injury, but we knew that recovery needed both rest and exercise.

He began to limp within the spacious tent.

"Now let us return to the topic we have been waiting to talk about," he said.

I was ready. It was time to let Eumenes pursue his ambitions and let me go. "Plato is a mischievous creature—he will cause many to search for the original Atlantis," I remarked, smiling.

"Including you," Eumenes said, and while his lips curled in a smile, his eyes conveyed no mirth. "You have to find the location of the first Atlantis to understand where to find the second," he continued, as he lifted an idol of Zeus to his eye level and inspected it.

My heart palpitated. My mission was to bring the secret to Eumenes and go home. Finding the Second Atlantis, as exciting it may be, was not the original contract. I gathered my composure.

"I was to go home at the completion of this mission, sir," I said, as I hunched and put my palms together as if in prayer.

"Circumstances have changed—"

"We had an agreement, sir!" my voice rose. The guard outside peeked in.

"As I said, circumstances have changed, and I am unable to reward you and let you on your way," he said, refusing to match my anger.

The veins in my temple began to pulse. I clenched my fist behind my back. "Can you please discharge me then, sir?"

He shook his head like a master at his disobedient pupil. "You will go nowhere," he said.

I rubbed my face as the reality dawned on me. My temple began to throb. "But we had an agreement, sir! I looked upon you as Alexander, and my family will die if I do not return!" I shouted.

I had to return!

Two guards stepped in.

Eumenes turned to them, "Stay outside unless I ask you to come in."

They both glared at me as they returned to their post. Eumenes leaned and placed his palm on my shoulder.

I recoiled.

"Listen to me, Deon, your best chance is to continue the mission. If you succeed, I promise you that I will reward you far beyond anything you ever imagined."

"Why is it my best chance, sir?"

"If you return now, coinless, do you think you can free your family? You know that I cannot let you defect to Ptolemy or Antigonus. Who knows what stories they might hear about you?" The threat was unmistakable. Even if I somehow managed to deal with my lender, I would always be under threat from one of the *diadochi*.

My face felt hot like coals.

"You become a king, and I return to the graves of my wife and daughter," I said, now facing him. I ground my teeth until it hurt, and my shoulders throbbed from tension. I knew he would not touch me—not with what I hid in my head.

"Don't be dramatic. Your family will be safe, as long as you complete this quest."

"How would you know that?" I hissed like a trapped snake.

"Because I do," he said, "now shut up and listen to me!" His eyes lit by a maniacal glint and gone was the gentle face, and in its place was the strident reproach of a commanding officer.

"But why me, sir? Why not send some of your other trusted officers."

"I need them by my side because these battles are not over yet. Do you think Antigonus is out there scratching his withered balls and whoring around? He will come after me next. Besides, no one else knows of this."

"What?"

"Yes—and it shows the level of trust I have in you. I cannot set anyone else on this task. You have the mind and the skills. We both need each other."

I persisted. "Why not go along with your army? Would that not be the safest thing to do?"

Eumenes exploded. "Do you think I'm a stupid road mender, Deon? Do you think a goat's arse is in my skull?" he screamed, tapping his head vigorously.

"No, sir, but—"

"How prudent do you think it is for me to move my entire army and draw attention? Besides, where would I even go? We should search first without anyone noticing. I will move the army once we know the exact place and know that to be true!"

There was no way out for me.

Eumenes was in a desperate situation and I was his hope.

We listened to the hum of grass bugs. Eumenes gestured me to sit, and I refused. He continued, "It should not take a military genius to understand what any of those men would do if they came to the possession of this city. You think there has been enough blood spilled already—this would be nothing to what someone like Antigonus will unleash."

Finally, my shoulders slumped. The best course of action for me, my family, and while it sounded pompous—even the empire—was for me to find this Second Atlantis. "What if it is too late for my family? Can you keep them safe?" I asked, and his expression softened.

"You give me too little credit, Deon," he said.

"Sir?"

"You think I had no idea who your family was or where they were?"

My fingers tingled with fear and dread.

"I did not—"

"Be quiet," he said and then walked to a shelf. He made a show of searching for something in a large leather bag. He began to mutter, "Could your family be safe? How would one know? What if they are not?" I was puzzled by the behavior, and just then he pulled out a parchment and held it up.

A letter!

I reached out, and he pulled it back. It felt childish, but Eumenes had not finished what he had to say. "I arranged for a messenger to bring a letter from your family," he said, and his eyes smiled, "so control your tongue before you berate me again."

I took the letter, and my hands shook.

"How recent?"

"Not too long ago, only a few weeks," he said, and relief washed over me like a soothing waterfall. I opened it gently as if it might crumble and vanish into the air.

My dear husband. Poseidon keeps us alive, and his mercy wrenched us back from the filthy hands of a slave trader. We thank General Eumenes for his generosity. The messenger says you will be with us soon. Why do the gods punish us so? Alexa asks every day when her father will appear from behind the trees. I pray that you will not abandon us for these years have been terrible and my body can only survive so long. Send us a letter.

The words opened a grievous wound in my heart.

My wife was blameless.

My child was blameless.

It was I who put them there, and only I could set this right. Sorrow welled up my chest, and for the first time in many years, tears fell. The drops turned to a flood as I hung my head and my shoulders shook. The Governor said nothing as he waited for me to regain my composure. I wiped my eyes and face with my sleeve and looked up. Eumenes placed his hand on my shoulder and I did not push back.

"We live for our loved ones, Deon, there is nothing to be ashamed of," he said.

I nodded.

"Your debtor had sold them to a slave caravan, but I paid part of your debts to secure them back. They will be safe, for now. I have no desire to hold your family as ransom, but we find ourselves in a wicked world."

"Are they here with you in this camp?" I asked, hopeful but knowing the answer.

"No. They are back with your lender. I have enough to worry about than to have them with me at this juncture. They are safe, and they await you. As I said, your debt is not fully paid, but they will stay and continue their obligations to the lender until you return."

Burning hate rose in my belly for Krokinos who, after all, had decided to sell them without waiting. But it also dawned upon me that Eumenes had left me with little choice. He had not freed them, but only secured a temporary relief. My wife was still with Krokinos. Eumenes had at the same time helped me and yet held us all hostage. I took several deep breaths and calmed myself. We paused our conversation as I penned a letter to my wife.

Apollonia, the star that shines so brightly in my life. Not a day passes without longing. I am well and with Governor Eumenes. I will return within a year with a handsome bounty that will settle our debts and let us lead a life of dignity. My heart is filled with shame for what I have wrought upon you, and the gods punish me daily. Be strong for us, for our daughter, and pray that Poseidon's mercy remains with us. I ask Krokinos for kindness and patience.

I knew Krokinos would read the letter, and I had to make sure there were no recriminations. Once the letter was turned over to a messenger for the next dispatch, we returned to business. Eumenes ordered for some fresh lemon infused water which brought relief to my parched, angry throat. We sat down and continued. I knew Eumenes would now turn his attention to the affairs far south, where Perdiccas was getting ready to attack Ptolemy in Egypt—another worrying development we had to contend with.

"I want you to meet Perdiccas and relay our victory to him. Ask him to hold off the attack on Ptolemy if he can until we regroup."

I did not look forward to meeting the Regent, but I nodded my assent. "When do I go on the search, sir?"

"After the message to Perdiccas. And when you are away on the search, I will move my army south to meet him in Egypt."

"Why should I not go on this mission instead?" I asked. Going to meet Perdiccas in Egypt would only add to the time.

"I need a trusted messenger to reach Perdiccas and to ensure he does not do something stupid until I have mustered my strength. Without Perdiccas our quest may be fruitless if I cannot hold what we find."

"Do you think you will win against Ptolemy?"

"Perdiccas may be foul-tempered, but he was Alexander's best general. With Seleucus by his side, and me as well, Ptolemy will crumble."

"Assuming Seleucus does not betray Perdiccas," I said, knowing the ephemeral nature of the alliances.

"Of course. Which is why we need to forge our destiny. I will also provide you with a small number of experienced bodyguards for your journey to Egypt."

"Can I trust them?"

"They are as trustworthy as I could gather. I will also be sending orders, in my authority as the governor of Asia-Minor, to grant you safe passage for your journey."

I thanked him. We still had the outstanding questions—

How do we find the Second Atlantis?

How would we guard it?

What do we do with it?

It would be of no use if we found it, only to have it stolen.

"And one more thing, Deon, I have found the perfect person to help you in the search. She brings skills you will find invaluable."

"She?!"

Eumenes then refused to answer any questions. With a sly grin, he said that he had administrative matters to attend to and that he would introduce me to 'her' next morning and help us prepare for the journey south. I was angry that he kept me in suspense, but also intrigued. Eumenes did not make such choices without reason, and more importantly, on matters of such great import.

As any man might attest, I did allow my mind to ponder upon who this woman might be. Would she be a goddess, with a perfect face, her hair lustrous, breasts firm and big, fecund hips, and a curvaceous behind? Or knowing the games the gods have played on me, she would breathe fire, and be big enough to eat me if she were hungry. I hoped not.

I was a man without companionship for a very long time. My encounters with women in Persia and Gandhara had not gone well. My one attempt to have a mistress had failed after a handsome soldier from my regiment seduced her. I then limited my involvement by availing services for payment, and after a terrible curse on my genitals after one such union I had finally given up on any womanly pleasures. The next morning, I had to control my curiosity and irritation as Eumenes introduced me to my bodyguards. Four from the Cappadocian cavalry, and four from the *Argyraspides*.

The split between the Macedonians and the Asians was how Eumenes would keep betrayal at a check. Once we met with Perdiccas near Egypt, my bodyguards would stay back until Eumenes arrived with his forces, and I would continue onward with my mission—with 'her' presumably.

Finally, late in the morning, Eumenes finally summoned me to his tent. He was alone, serious, and gestured me to sit by his side. "Deon, the time for you to travel is near. Do you feel comfortable with the bodyguards?"

"One of the silver shields is a bit boorish, but they appear committed."

"Good. Tell Perdiccas it will take us two months or more to arrive there, but he should wait to join us."

"Why can you not use the mountain top messengers to relay a quick message?"

"Because those relays are broken. Antigonus' forces have infiltrated the countryside, and I cannot trust what is relayed back and forth."

I nodded.

Finally, the time to meet my companion arrived.

"Are you curious to meet her?"

"My erection can only hold so long, Governor."

He laughed, throwing his head back, and then shaking it in admonition. "You will treat her with respect," he said and pointed his kopis at me.

"You do realize that having a woman by my side poses a significant risk. The world is hostile, Governor, and you may have noticed that."

"I am aware, but I want you to meet her. You have the memory and muscles Deon, but that alone is not enough."

"Are you expecting that she seduces everyone to giving up their secrets, throw their weapons down, and do our bidding?"

"I am not assigning a prostitute or a seductress to you."

"I do not need a housemaid to clean behind us."

He smirked. "I am appalled that you think so lowly of women. Do you forget that Alexander's mother is still a formidable force? Or that Adea, still sixteen years of age and wife of our mentally incapacitated king, is a thorn in the commanders' sides?"

"They are not common-born, and not out in the wilderness with no army behind them, sir."

"There is a good reason I have chosen her. She has traveled widely and has seen danger. Stop complaining now," Eumenes said, in mock admonishment. He grinned and clapped for a guard. After what seemed like an eternity, a head peeked through the tent. She tentatively stepped in, head bowed, and greeted Eumenes. "Greetings, Governor Eumenes. Reporting as asked, sir."

She did not look at me.

I had imagined a withered maid with parchment arms, or an emaciated slave looking like a dried orange. She was none of it. She radiated an aura that bellowed, "Not a slave."

Eumenes acknowledged her and said, "Deon, this is Eurydice." Eumenes must have registered a surprise on my face, so he clarified. "No, I have not secretively taken the Macedonian Viceroy's daughter hostage, this is not her."

Eurydice. I was sure it was not her real name.

She was petite, with long dark hair that fell to her narrow waist, mesmerizing green eyes, light olive skin, and a face that was more reminiscent of the beautiful Persian and Sogdian women. She had a delicate nose, not quite Greek or Persian. She had modestly covered herself with a fresh, unadorned cream gown that draped around her upper body, and until her knees. She wore little jewelry—two small hanging earpieces, and a modest necklace with little flower-beads.

"Greetings, Eurydice," I said. Nervous. She raised her eyes to me. Clear and inquisitive. She was judging me just as I did her. I wondered what she saw.

"My greetings to you, commander."

Soft, gentle voice. I imagined her to be a progeny of a Persian, Macedonian union. I began to worry. Not only did I have a difficult quest, I now had to manage this delicate flower. What was Eumenes getting me into? Was she Eumenes' spy?

Eumenes intervened to fill the silence that encompassed the tent. "Eurydice, perhaps you should tell your commander your abilities."

She nodded. "I speak eight tongues, commander, and I can wield a knife," she said, as her eyes sparkled mischievously.

Eight tongues! Sorceress? Do I put this pretty little creature on my lap as I ride hostile territories?

"I can ride a horse just as any man can," she said like she read my mind.

"Deon, I told her that she would act as your translator. She will be invaluable in learning enemy troop movements and decipher any gossip." He winked, and I nodded. So, Eurydice knew nothing, and I had to figure out how to use her skills without exposing the truth. I understood Eumenes' intention—often interesting stories of the past are buried in fables, tales, poems, and songs of the region—and someone with the knowledge of many languages would be a great asset. Eumenes had masterfully assessed a gap in my capabilities.

"Eurydice, do you realize that this is a challenging task? We will first meet the Regent Perdiccas in Egypt, and then head back again and regroup with Eumenes." I asked, putting on my officer's tone.

"Yes, sir. I am aware of the risks."

"And that this will take several months…"

"I am aware of that as well, and I am at your service."

Eumenes interjected. "Deon, she is not a slave, so treat her with respect as you would any honorable woman."

I nodded with some irritation. What did he think I was? Just because I tried to open a brothel did not make me a whore monger!

The absurdity of it all. "Do you know the dangers of this mission? Why did you agree to it?"

"Yes, sir, I do. I owe the Governor," she said, cryptically.

I looked at Eumenes quizzically, but he offered nothing else. "You will have plenty of time on the road to learn about each other. For now, I suggest you prepare for your journey and leave at dawn," he said and dismissed Eurydice.

She turned and walked out of the tent. We would meet at the first light of dawn and begin our long journey back to Egypt.

"Can she handle this, sir?" I asked, still unconvinced.

"I am sure she can convince you that she can. She is no delicate flower, Deon, of that I am certain. Take good care of her, take advantage of her skills, and do not pry into her past as there is pain that must not be surfaced," he said, gravely.

I decided not to press further, but could not resist asking, "Is her name Eurydice?"

Eumenes laughed. "Her name is of no consequence, Deon, but know that she will be of great service to you and that I share a bond with her father. Treat her well and protect her."

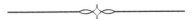

At dawn, the group assembled by Eumenes' tent. We were all heavily armed and supplied—cuirass, kopis, javelins, shields, knives, protection orders, food, water.

Eurydice had changed; she wore a shorter pale blue tunic, and unlike most women's open skirts, she had tied the garment around her knees on both sides making it easy to mount horses or run if needed. Her hair was an unusual bun. A long, serrated dagger, uncommon among the troops, hung from her waist clipped to a thick leather belt. She was a strange sight—a gorgeous warrior.

Eumenes came to greet us, but first, he pulled me aside. "The fate of the empire rests on you now, Deon. I trust you more than anyone else, and I hope the gods protect you. I will await news from you."

"I will do everything in my ability to reach Perdiccas, and then proceed to solve this mystery for you, Governor. You may be our best hope to preserve Alexander's empire."

And my family.

There was pride in Eumenes' eyes; he smiled, stepped forward and firmly embraced me.

"When all this is over, I hope to visit you in your magnificent villa by the seas," he said, and I grinned.

Or in the afterlife.

He addressed the group.

"Your mission is to ensure Deon reaches the Regent with great speed. You are under his command, and I expect that you pledge your unquestioned loyalty to him. Remember that enemy forces are along the coast. May the gods grant you safe and uneventful passage."

I led the group—Eurydice beside me, and the bodyguards in a split formation of four in the front, and four behind. As the horses galloped, I looked back one time, seeing the little Governor stand still and watch us as the dust obscured our path and sweat blurred my vision. Our long journey to Egypt had begun. And on the way, I aimed to collect clues and hints that might point to the start of my quest—only the gods knew if this would bear fruit or if we were pursuing an allure that never really existed except in the fertile mind of an ancient fraudster.

CHAPTER 19.

JOURNEY TO EGYPT

The journey to Egypt from Hellespont took us through varied landscapes. The greenish, grassy mounds and flatlands changed to more rugged, mountainous regions as we came closer to the borders of Syria to turn south towards Egypt through Phoenicia. We stayed away from the coast, for that was often the preferred path of other armies. The route had not yet become dangerous, and the hills offered cover and secrecy. Once in Syria, we moved inland, and the lands here were fascinating. As we rode south, to our right were green mountains, not full of trees or thick with foliage but matted with dull, uninspiring shrubbery. To our left were the unending flatlands of Syria—a land with nomads, fierce tribes, and bandits. Here, between the flatlands and the mountains, we found that the ground was not so benign—it was rough, rocky, and the roads were far less traveled, making it difficult for the horses and men. Water was scarce, and the sun beat down with a vengeance. The dust was fine with the smallest of grains, and with no water to keep it glued to the earth, it rose and pinched the eyes, nose, coated the lips, and parched the tongue. In such terrain we rode with speed. At this rate, it would take us another forty to sixty days to reach Egypt, and with the gods' favor, we would face no major obstacles. But even then, the mornings and evenings showed the beauty of the world, as light reflected on the land, bathing everything around us in a red-orange-yellow glow.

But of course, the travel was not without incidents.

This woman frustrated me. Her feminine appearance was a lie—a rebellious fire burned within her and she had again disobeyed my direct order not to interfere in a skirmish. I would have any other soldier whipped, or even executed by now for insubordination, but I had to deal with her on the Governor's orders and for the skill she brought to the search.

"This is the third time—third! If this happens again, I will have no mercy on you for being a woman, I will have you beaten," I shouted at her. She stood quietly with no expression in her face.

She still held a bleeding ear in her hand—the one she had sliced off an attacker.

A demon in a dainty form.

The others stood around, perplexed but admiring her courage and willingness to put herself in danger.

"Why? You realize your role in this journey is not that of a soldier, like the others," I said, pointing to the other men.

She said nothing, and I was losing patience.

"Do you want me to send you back with word that your value is outweighed by the danger you pose?"

"No, sir," she said, softly.

"Well then stay within the protective covers—"

"I can protect myself, sir—"

"What did I tell you? Your role is not to fight, but to aid me in decoding local speech to ensure our journey is without peril. That is all!" I shouted.

"Yes, sir."

I dismissed her. She dropped the ear to the sandy ground and walked back to her small tent. It was difficult to believe that this woman was any kind of a fighter. But a fighter she was, and my few attempts to understand her history were unfruitful. I remembered my conversation the day after we departed Eumenes' camp.

"Where are you from, Eurydice?"

"A village west of Persepolis, sir."

"Where exactly? I am quite familiar with Persia."

"I don't really know, sir. I moved around."

"Who is your father?"

"He was a local chief, sir."

"You do not look entirely Persian."

"My father spent time with the Greeks, sir."

"Which of your parents is Greek?"

"Mother, sir."

"Are your parents alive?"

She hesitated. "No, sir."

I had become tired of questioning her and let her be. If she did not want to talk, I cared little to force her. Instead, I enjoyed her feminine presence—to watch her lovely eyes, her beautiful smile or irritation, her soft voice, and everything that was contrary to the rough band of boorish soldiers.

The Governor had entrusted me with her, and she had helped me several times in this journey as we navigated safe routes. I would tolerate her for now.

"How did you learn so many languages, Eurydice?"

"We moved around when I was a child. I had the ability to learn the local tongues very quickly, sir."

I watched her green eyes as they looked downwards to her feet as we sat to eat. I had asked her to come sit with me while the others created a perimeter.

I heard some sniggering but let them be.

"Were you a slave?"

She seemed taken aback by the question.

She was. Who is this woman?

She chewed slowly on the lamb chunks before answering. "I was, sir."

"Where?"

This time she did not answer. I shifted my position—she seemed nervous, but I sat next to her. I had to know who this woman was and if she posed a threat. I placed a finger below her chin and raised her face towards me. In those eyes I saw anger and her face reddened, but she said nothing.

"Where?" I said, this time with a harder voice.

She looked at me and finally answered in a measured voice, "Syria. Phoenicia. Nabataea. Egypt. Cappadocia. I was rescued by Governor Eumenes."

My questions after that elicited very little response, and she finally said, "No more, sir."

We had spent several nights with various local tribesmen, listening to their stories and legends, much to the frustration and irritation of my companions. They did not understand why, and I told them that often messengers hid secret codes and that tribesmen warned in songs—only fools would believe that story, but they knew not to question their commander.

So far, I had no luck. Barely any story I heard was of interest or matched to the scrolls—and those that we heard, fables from Babylon and elsewhere—were too fantastical or vague to help in the search for the second Atlantis or the original.

On this day, we sat around a fire, entertained by the local tribe. The men's hawkish eyes, beak nose, and wide mouths made me wonder if they were brothers, or if their whole tribe married among siblings—but I refrained from asking such questions.

The chief was a tall, leathery old man on whom hair grew from every visible surface, like grass on fertile river banks. He regaled us with stories and bawdy poems, some in mangled Greek, and some in a local dialect which Eurydice translated with embarrassed discomfort.

I goaded him to tell me ancient songs of his ancestors, and that those were what I found most enjoyable. A few songs were interesting, but nothing useful, but one, which he said came from his great ancestors from the sea, was next.

His deep voice merged with the crackling of the fire as he sang a folktale. He stood and swung his arms up and down, letting his white robes flow in the gentle night wind. Eurydice translated the song to me.

O beautiful moon of the water,

You were the pride of the Seas,

You were the eye of the gods,

Yet your men were blind to their deeds,

What cruelty, what ambition,

Thy hubris at divine displeasure,

Even when the earth shook, and the birds cried,

Even as the rocks burned, and the trees died,

Yet your men they were blind to their deeds,

And your mighty men carved into the rocks,

A new lord's abode, in the knife's tip,

For their gold, their bronze, and their sacred silver,

But god is the master, god is the giver,

Your land is His, not for the king to keep,

You displease the gods, your innocents weep,

Then fiery anger rose from the sea,

Smote your homes,

Burned your bones,

Once a moon for the birds above,

Now a blind eye, my beautiful love

We were mesmerized by the voice and the deep longing in it, as if in a distant past the man had experienced whatever he sang, in another life. For a few moments there was silence and just the sounds of flames and the smells of warm, smoke-infused wind from the burned wood.

When Eurydice translated the poem to me, it felt as if the finger of the gods had brushed my back—my hair stood up and a chill coursed through my veins. I remembered those words from the papyrus as clear as day.

…towards the far desert, where a knife's tip awaits, seven days from the sea on burning sands and towering canyons. Three days north from the tip, within golden walls and red rocks, in there they found a magnificent mountain, and a hollow within, where they carved the last city of a great empire.

And the last line from the older story.

now but lifeless rock and ash, like a blind eye as it looked to the heavens in despair.

I turned to the chief, "What a beautiful song! Your voice is a gift of the heavens."

He accepted the compliment graciously, and his men nodded approvingly.

"This poem, is it about an island? You will pardon my ignorance of the background."

The old man was enthusiastic to answer the questions. "It is. It is about a beautiful island, shaped like the moon, in the deep blue waters of the Aegean. And then the legends say the gods burned it, and all that was left was like a blind eye, whatever that means."

"Does this island really exist?"

"I do not know. We are land dwellers, captain. But our people say that long ago, there were men from the far seas, and that this song is a story of their ancestors."

"What is the Knife's Tip?" I asked.

The man adjusted the wood, and the embers cracked and reignited the fire, sending small sparks to our faces.

"The Knife's Tip?"

"Yes, your song mentioned a Knife's Tip—or that was what my translator called it," I said, glancing at Eurydice.

"Ah, yes, she translated it correctly! The Knife's Tip is the end of something long and strong, like my penis!"

And he laughed uproariously at this very clever ending, and the men joined. I laughed along. Eurydice shook her head.

"Do you know where this Knife's Tip is, so I can find some treasure for myself?" I said, flippantly.

The old man turned serious again.

"Well, our people around these regions, from Syria to Nabataea to Libya, call the edges of sharp mountain ranges as Knife's Tips. There is one nearby, but there is one much further North, there are more in Egypt, and there—"

"But are they all within days of walk from the sea?"

He looked surprised at the question, as it was oddly specific. "You take the poem too seriously, commander," he said, laughing, "yes, the one to the south of here is within days of walk from the sea, but then so is the one far north, and two in Libya."

I nodded. "I just enjoy these stories, they keep my spirit happy in all this darkness," I said.

"Well, if you must waste your time and look for a mythical king's mythical treasure, then the nearest one is a few days walk from Sharuhen near Gaza," he said.

"You may not find that King's house," yelled another man, and then he dramatically looked at his companions and said loudly, "but you may find his penis there," pointing to the old man. They cackled again.

"Oh, make sure you have no wives following you," another man said, eyeing Eurydice, "she may not appreciate you being penetrated by another man!"

I got up, looked behind and patted my bottom frantically, much to their roaring laughter.

After the mirth died and we exchanged parting pleasantries, I sat down to contemplate what I had heard. I had no time or manpower to scour the continents. I decided at that time that the prudent course of action was to complete the mission at hand and begin the search in the Aegean.

But how? I did not know yet. The seas were vast.

The next morning, we continued southward, but not before I made the tribal leader explain to me again the locations of three different Knife's Tips—including one that was in visual distance, a hazy outline far away from where we were, tantalizingly close but agonizingly far.

I watched as the man blinked his unfocused eyes. Blood seeped from a deep gash in his throat into the dry cracks in the ground.

One of my soldiers.

Appointed by Governor Eumenes himself to guard me on this mission, now about to come to an ignominious end.

Eurydice stood behind his head.

Her face was flushed red.

Her nostrils flared, and her chest heaved.

Her hair was disheveled, and her attire was torn in two places.

A prominent bite was clear on her neck.

She held her blood-soaked serrated dagger in a white-knuckled grip.

"Execute this bitch!" shouted one of the dying man's friends, and he lunged at Eurydice and backhanded her viciously. She staggered and fell but made not a sound—I ordered my men to restrain him.

"You should call a court," he again, and some others nodded—although unsurely.

I put on my helmet and ordered everyone to stand back. I then walked to Eurydice who still lay on the ground. Her sand matted hair hid her face.

"Stand up," I said, and then when she did not move, I bent forward, gripped her under her arm and pulled her to her feet.

I then addressed the soldiers.

"There will be no court—"

"She murdered one of our men! Who does she think she is?" The man's friend shouted again, his face red with anger.

"Keep your mouth shut or I will have you whipped for insubordination," I warned him. That silenced him and the others. The gurgling sounds as air escaped the dying man's severed throat was distracting. His hands were beginning to twitch.

"He was not her master and had no rights over her. Governor Eumenes assigned her to support me in this mission just as you were. You have seen her skills, and her conduct has always been honorable, even if sometimes insubordinate—" I said, as I turned to her.

She stood bowed. I continued, "I see no reason to call court. He did not win her as a spoil of war, nor buy her in trade, or pay for her services. He tried to rape her and that is as plain to see as the afternoon sun on this desert. The gods willed that she defends herself, and she did. Does any man here believe otherwise?" I said, and no one answered.

I then pulled out my kopis and stabbed the dying man to end his life. As a respect to service rendered until now, we stood around him with our heads bowed and prayed to the gods.

Eurydice looked away and spat on the ground. I ignored the disrespect.

"Go back to your tent and rest, Eurydice," I said, and then spent time with the rest of the men explaining my decision and calming inflamed tempers.

Then I headed to Eurydice's tent. When I entered, she scrambled back to her feet. She looked at me with great sadness—her eyes were wet, but there was no anger in them. I moved forward and gripped both her arms gently, and she began to weep. Her body shook, and I stood paralyzed unsure how to react. It had been a very long time since I held a crying woman. For a fleeting moment I wondered if this is how my wife would face me once I returned home.

I let her be until she finally pulled back and wiped her face.

"We will see this through together," I said, quietly.

We rode hard. To our left, the dusty Nabatean desert stretched as far as the eye could see; Egypt, our next stop, was ahead. Eurydice had elevated herself—she had gained the group's respect, her opinions showed intelligence, and her courage gained our admiration. I began to understand why the Governor demanded she go with me—he had seen in her a fine mind and a skilled operative. Besides, her language skills were invaluable.

We stopped only occasionally to rest, and with a little sleep each night, we arrived near the Great River. The signs of a major siege and battle were all around us—deserted roads, checkpoints, and fearful eyes of children and their parents.

At dawn on the fourth day after we entered Egyptian borders, we joined the final stretch to the south to a route to take us to Perdiccas, who, we were told, was near the apex of the tributaries of the Great River. The landscape had changed from orange and yellow hues of the desert to lush greenery, with olive and fig trees, lentil and other grain fields, and flower gardens dotting the banks of the river.

When we reached a fort called the *Kamelonteichos,* the scouts told us that after a failed attempt to capture the fort and cross the Great River, Perdiccas had moved his army south opposite Memphis. This was a worrying sign—while I disliked the Regent for his cruel ways, he was a very capable commander. I had hoped that Ptolemy's troops would turn and defect to Perdiccas. That had not happened.

I had heard that three senior leaders were with Perdiccas—Peithon, Antigenes, the chief of the *Argyraspides*, and Seleucus—and yet why was this force unable to destroy Ptolemy?

The signs became clear as we turned south and went along the route that the army had moved. There were funeral pyres and ditches, with hundreds of bodies, many half-burnt and left unceremoniously—stripped of their battle gear and clothes, and many thrown in the shallow hurriedly dug up ground. In the rising heat of the morning, the acrid stench of burned bodies and rotting corpses permeated the air, and we retched as we passed them by. This disgraceful abandonment and mistreatment of his dead men left to the vagaries of nature rather than proper rituals sickened me and only strengthened my hatred for Perdiccas.

That was not the end of what we saw as we progressed further south.

Rows of crucifixion posts had been dug into the soft earth, and on each hung a severely beaten and murdered soldier. Whether this was for disobeying an order, for just not pressing forward, or something else—I did not know. One of the men, bloodied and hung on a crude post, stirred and moaned as we passed by. Unable to ignore, I thrust my kopis through his chest to give him a merciful end. We then inspected forty bodies for signs of life and ended six more lives. We prayed for them all.

As we neared Memphis, we saw the signs of Perdiccas' army on our side of the river. Across the river was the formidable fortress of the city, behind which were the grand temples built with golden colored sandstone and topped with white limestone that shone brightly in the sun. There, in plain view, was the army of Ptolemy. I had no doubt that the wily General was there, among his troops, taunting Perdiccas and scheming how to defeat the Regent.

We got through two check posts, and from the look on the faces and the defeated body language of the soldiers, we concluded that Perdiccas' hopes of a rapid, decisive attack and submission of Ptolemy had been dashed. But once he found out Eumenes' victory, I was sure there was no question that they would be energized and would wait until they were supported by Eumenes' army.

Finally, after moving slowly through grimy, hastily constructed makeshift tents, lavatory ditches, and horse sheds, we arrived close to the senior officers' quarters. The generals' tents were obvious with their elaborate construction, orange flags that lay limp on the hoisted poles, and the number of guards.

At the final checkpoint were a group of heavily armed men led by a heavyset man who was naked from the waist up, and wore a dirty, blood and mud-stained waistcloth. He was bald, clean-shaven, and wore large gold rings on his ears. He held a big, spiked club in his hand, adorned by unsightly copper bracelets.

I imagined that the Pharaohs wept in shame at this specimen.

It was the strangest sight, an Egyptian captain of a Macedonian guard assembly, on Perdiccas' side?

"Stop there," he said, accompanied by two guards. The others surrounded my bodyguards.

"Greetings, I come with a message from Governor Eumenes to the Regent. These are my companions," I said politely, but authoritatively.

He stood still as if he had not heard me.

I was impatient.

"May we proceed? It is critical that we meet him at once."

"Get down." His words were gruff and firm. My bodyguards sensed the tension and one of them yelled at the man.

"Let us through, you fool! If Perdiccas finds you delayed us he will nail to you the posts and let you rot."

"What message?" he asked. His guards assumed a combative position and drew their swords. I had to be tactful, for I did not know what was causing this hostility. Were they worried that we might be Ptolemy's henchmen?

"Tell message. We will allow. Order, no let anyone."

There was no point in me getting angry with this Pharaonic barbarian, and the worst we could do is escalate the situation. There was commotion at a distance. However, we were unable to get any closer.

"Eumenes has defeated Craterus and Neoptolemus. He will arrive in a month's time. We need to speak to the Regent."

Something registered with the brute.

"Wait. Move, guards kill."

He turned and sauntered towards the generals' quarters. The guards, who looked afraid of this man, stood rigidly making no eye contact and showing no signs of friendliness.

We would have to wait.

CHAPTER 20.
MEMPHIS, EGYPT

The Regent's camp was tense. Inside, Perdiccas raged at his most senior officers—Antigenes, Peithon, and Seleucus. Outside, a hundred officers of the army had assembled— angry, sullen, and waiting for the outcome of the discussions inside. The last few days had been disastrous. First, they had failed to take the fort up North and lost many men. Then, they endured exhausting overnight marches to get near Memphis.

Perdiccas had then tried a signature move of Alexander—he tried to get his army across the Great River to surprise Ptolemy's forces. But the swift currents, rising silt from the bottom when Perdiccas attempted to use elephants, opposition from Ptolemy's army on the opposite banks, the crocodiles in the river, all frustrated that effort. Hundreds had died again in vain, washed away or snapped up by the crocodiles.

"Shame on you!" Perdiccas screamed, his face red with exertion, hair disheveled, and the veins of his neck throbbing. He had removed his cuirass and helmet, and his hand trembled as he pointed an accusatory finger at Antigenes, the aging, respected leader of the *Argyraspides*. "Silver Shields, indeed, you are not fit to fight an army of donkeys! What use are you if you cannot muster your men to fight?"

As Antigenes stood silently simmering under the insult, Seleucus stepped in. "That's enough Perdiccas. They are exhausted, and this strategy of trying to cross the river has been nothing but disastrous. We have lost many good men already."

"That is because your unfit bastards cannot walk across a shallow river fast enough. They will sit and eat all day," Perdiccas shouted and turned his ire against Peithon.

"And there you are Peithon, weak rat bastard—"

Peithon lunged at Perdiccas, and the two grappled each other, punching, and kicking before Seleucus stepped in to separate them.

Perdiccas stood breathing heavily. Saliva dribbled from the corner of his mouth and wet his unkempt beard.

But now Peithon began to scream at Perdiccas, spittle spraying from his mouth. "You would not be fit to be my father's dog, incompetent scoundrel! Look around, so many deaths due to your stupidity. You are no Alexander—and there is Ptolemy, mocking us from across, and we watch as our men are washed away or eaten by crocodiles. What kind of glory is this?"

Seleucus, who was silent so far, joined in the tirade. "Wake up, Perdiccas! This expedition is a lost cause. Unless we know Eumenes' situation in Cappadocia, we should retreat, make a truce with Ptolemy, and bide our time."

Perdiccas picked up a clay pot and smashed it to the ground. "Yes, Alexander's appointed successor and three of his so-called senior men will tuck their penises between their thighs, get on their fours and run, in fear of an illegitimate bastard child whose father would not even own him. That is what cowards propose! We will keep at it until all of us are dead, or Ptolemy is in chains and hoisted up a hanging post."

"Perdiccas," Seleucus began again, trying to calm the Regent down when an Egyptian captain poked his head under the tent and requested an audience.

Seleucus stepped out, and there was silence as the generals calmed down. Perdiccas, refusing to meet anyone's eye, sat on a couch and drank. Wine dribbled from his chin, and his hands trembled.

Then, Seleucus stepped in and gestured for Peithon and Antigenes to join him. Perdiccas, curious but angry and unwilling to inquire as to what they were conferring about, sat sulking on his couch.

In a short while, Seleucus stuck his head inside the Regent's tent and said, "I will be back Perdiccas, there is an urgent matter to attend to."

CHAPTER 21.

MEMPHIS, EGYPT

General Seleucus appeared much to my relief. I may have preferred Perdiccas himself, but the Regent's most senior man was good enough. The General looked tired—he had shaved his head very close to the scalp; his naturally full, curled hair absent on his skull, and there were dark circles under his eyes. The left side of his face was slightly swollen—I knew the signs of rotting teeth and the pain they inflicted on the men. It made them irritable, and in rare cases drove them to madness and suicide. He walked gingerly, sidestepping pools of mud and water, and finally approached me.

Eurydice and I dismounted from our horses.

I removed my helmet and saluted the General. Seleucus, usually amicable, said nothing and looked at Eurydice who bowed to him.

"I am Deon, Governor Eumenes' adjutant, and that is my companion, General. It is good to see you."

Seleucus grunted. I thought the frosty reception was odd—had the Egyptian brute told Seleucus nothing? "I know who you are. Tell your men to dismount and follow one of these guards to the soldier's quarters."

That was an unusual request, but I asked them to follow the orders. Then it was just Eurydice and me.

"The gods do not favor us here. What is the message from Eumenes?" He asked while scratching his stubble.

"Governor Eumenes has defeated Craterus and Neoptolemus in Hellespont, sir," I said, barely able to hold my smile as I thrust my chest outwards.

Seleucus looked up in surprise, and his eyes searched mine for deceit. "Defeated? Alive or dead?"

"Both dead."

"I am in no mood for dark humor, soldier," said Seleucus, still not believing me. His square jaws were tense.

"I swear, sir. It is hard to believe but governor Eumenes prevailed, it was quite extraordinary—"

He cut me off abruptly. "Eumenes defeated and killed them both, are you sure?"

"I was on the battlefield and oversaw the cremations."

"Astonishing…" he said, and it was, to anyone who heard what happened. I nodded.

"What is Eumenes' plan?"

"He will join your forces in a month, and he has asked that the Regent hold and not press to conflict until then."

Seleucus laughed ruefully. He swept his hand in an arc. "Too late for that. I doubt the drowned, eaten, or crucified soldiers care."

The grim surroundings told the story.

"What do you think of Perdiccas?" Seleucus asked, surprising me.

This was treacherous ground. "I—my loyalty is to the Regent, through the orders of Eumenes who I serve, General."

He nodded.

"Wait here," he said. And before I could protest that I wanted to see Perdiccas myself, Seleucus turned and walked away briskly. The Egyptian brute and his guards now surrounded us.

I could not understand what was going on.

"What is your name, captain?" I asked the brute, who was now eyeing Eurydice and me.

"Nekh-Aser," he said, "your wife is pretty."

Eurydice, who was quiet all this time, looked at the man who was a time-and-half her height, and said firmly, "I am not his wife."

"Then maybe I take you," he laughed, displaying his sharp teeth and looking around at his guards as if he had made a great joke.

They laughed nervously.

CHAPTER 22.

MEMPHIS, EGYPT

Perdiccas was in an animated discussion with Alexander's widow Roxane about difficult camp conditions. How he wished he could drown the woman in the waters, this was not the time to be worrying about comfort! After calming her, he sent her away and turned his attention to pressing matters. Antigenes and Peithon were still outside, and he did not know why. But soon, he heard Seleucus talking to them, and he shouted, "What are you all scheming about now? Drawing up terms of surrender?"

Seleucus shouted back, "Give us some time Perdiccas, we're dealing with a military matter."

He summoned the men back to the tent. "What were you talking about that is so important?"

"It is time we draw up terms of negotiation with Ptolemy," Seleucus said, his voice cold with a hard edge.

Perdiccas had calmed down a little. He had smoothed his ruffled hair and adjusted his *chlamys* draped over his shoulder.

"Why? We have enough troops and materials available to wait. Let us hold ground until we hear from Eumenes."

Seleucus hesitated, and Perdiccas noticed that Antigenes made a slight gesture to Seleucus at that moment, as if asking him to be quiet. "What is it?"

"It's nothing. I was distracted."

Perdiccas' anger began to build up again. It was plain as night and day that Seleucus was hiding something. Perdiccas was no fool, and he had a hunch.

"What are you hiding, you wretch? Do we have news from Eumenes?" he asked.

The men said nothing, and Seleucus' eyes darted to Antigenes and Peithon who were now aware of the news from Cappadocia.

"We have news from Eumenes, don't we?" Perdiccas shouted gleefully, "The way you bastards are fidgeting tells me that the little master defeated the fools that went up against him. And you cowards want to sign a surrender before he arrives with reinforcements!"

Surprise at the Regent's astute observation was evident in Seleucus' eyes. "What Eumenes accomplished changes nothing for us, Perdiccas. It is too late," Seleucus said quietly.

"I was right! It changes everything! Our troops will be energized, and we can crush Ptolemy with our combined forces!" Perdiccas yelled, his voice trembling with excitement. He absentmindedly picked an empty wine goblet and took a swig, and then threw it on the ground in irritation.

"I have serious doubts that the news will energize our troops to get into those waters again, besides, how long can we hold on until Eumenes arrives?" Peithon started, and Perdiccas exploded.

"Shut up. Shut up, ungrateful dog fucker! I should have put you to the sword in Persia, and here you are, traitorous scum trying to abandon me!"

Seleucus, now angry at Perdiccas' crass behavior and belittling of his peers, stepped in again. "Perdiccas, the troops will not fight. Waiting for Eumenes is pointless, and we will have a mutiny in our hands. Antigenes has asked his

Argyraspides to stand down, and we demand that you enter into negotiations with Ptolemy."

At that, Perdiccas erupted into uncontrolled fury and began to scream at Antigenes. "Antigenes, old son of a whore, how dare you disobey my orders and stand down the troops without my knowledge? This is it! I will have you crucified, you scoundrel!"

He lunged forward and grabbed Antigenes by his throat while screaming for the guards.

Seleucus nodded at Peithon.

Peithon moved behind Perdiccas, thrust his arms under the Regent's armpits, and yanked Perdiccas backward, lifting him off his feet. As the shocked Perdiccas struggled, Antigenes stepped forward and grabbed a sarissa leaning on a tent pole. The aged chief of the *Argyraspides* then thrust the sarissa deep into Perdiccas' chest in an oblique angle.

Blood erupted from Perdiccas' destroyed heart. But Antigenes, blinded by his anger, removed the spear and thrust it again into Perdiccas' abdomen and sliced it upward, almost missing Peithon who dodged the spear tip that emerged from Perdiccas' back.

"I did not serve Alexander to be insulted by a filthy motherfucker!" he screamed and then repeatedly stabbed the Regent until Perdiccas' ruptured intestines began to spill out of his belly.

Seleucus pulled back a gasping Antigenes—his face like a beast from depths of the underworld—with his silver hair and beard red with Perdiccas' blood. The air smelled of lilac, rose, iron, and sweat, and the curtains waved in patterns of red.

Peithon let go of Perdiccas, who dropped dead on the floor, with the long sarissa sticking out of his stomach. And as he fell, Alexander's signet ring slipped off Perdiccas' finger and rolled into a dark pool of blood.

CHAPTER 23.

MEMPHIS, EGYPT

There was commotion at a distance, but I could not make out what was happening. I then saw a few men, their faces bright and smiling, run to their tents while whooping with joy. I looked at Eurydice and laughed. My news had lifted the spirits of these beaten and exhausted men. Relief surged through my body. We could rest a few days and enjoy the hospitality of the Regent. And then we would turn and head back to the seas to find that elusive city.

I would then go home.

A group of soldiers parted with respect. Seleucus walked towards me, his face still sullen.

There were visible streaks of blood on his fabric.

He kept wiping and rubbing the stains which looked fresh. He refused to meet my eye.

"General, what is going on? I—"

He ignored us and turned to the Egyptian. "Arrest and hold them until further notice."

I felt as if a great power sucked the life out of me. I stood shocked as Seleucus, with not a glance towards us, turned and walked away. "Sir, what is going on?" I shouted. Seleucus did not respond.

Nekh-Aser moved towards us, and the other guards drew their weapons. He yanked Eurydice's hair and grabbed her breast. She screamed, and he smirked at me as he tried to drag her.

I exploded with anger.

I swung my fist upward and smashed it into his face.

The Egyptian let go of her and staggered back in surprise. He looked at me with wild eyes and punched me in the gut with astonishing force. An incredible pain shot up my body, starting at my belly and rising all the way to shoulders and through my face. I collapsed over the muddy ground.

Another powerful blow on my back pushed mud up my mouth and nose, and at a distance, before I lost consciousness, I heard Eurydice cry, "Stop! Don't kill him!"

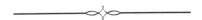

When I regained consciousness, I realized I had been tied and placed near a makeshift wooden stage, and on it stood none other than Ptolemy, bedecked in Macedonian attire. He was within earshot, though that meant little as my mouth had been shut with a foul rag and all I could do was emit guttural sounds. As a hush descended, all eyes turned on Ptolemy, and I watched him.

Ptolemy looked at the sorry multitude standing before him. Their defeated eyes and haggard faces looked up in expectation. The campgrounds were squalid. Heaps of bodies lay exposed, and sickly smell from the funeral pyres permeated the air.

The fine ash of the burned dead clung to the faces and dry lips of the living.

Under his banner, Ptolemy began, "Ptolemy stands here not as a victor, but as a defender of the land that the council granted.

"You have braved great misery, all because of a man who forgot that Alexander is no more. What foolish ambition caused a brother to turn on brother?

"As I speak, my men bring you food, blankets, and medicines to tend to your souls and your bodies. They also bring the urns with ashes and bones of your brave fallen soldiers. Take them to their loved ones!"

He paused.

For this theater, Ptolemy had shunned his Egyptian attire. Instead, he donned the traditional military uniform — gold-plated cuirass, yellow-plumed helmet, a red cape, and an ornate sword. For Perdiccas' men, this was a scene that took them back to the times when their leaders were all united under a magnificent king.

The men cheered with boundless joy at Ptolemy's words. Seleucus, Antigenes, and Peithon stood by Ptolemy to show solidarity.

I watched with disbelief at the turn of events. These men had ended Perdiccas' life—so much for loyalty to the Regent. There was no doubt they were plotting their next move already.

Several soldiers wiped their tears.

Ptolemy continued—

"Your leaders, my beloved peers, have brought before Ptolemy a proposal. That Ptolemy becomes the new Regent and assumes the role of the protector of the two kings. But Ptolemy has refused! For Ptolemy's responsibility is now towards Egypt," he said, as he gestured behind him. "Ptolemy proposes Peithon and Arrhidaeus to that role!"

The crowd cheered Ptolemy's magnanimity again. But I knew that behind this modesty was an astute understanding that anyone proclaiming themselves Regent to the empire would find themselves in great danger. Ptolemy, the cunning schemer, had put away immediate risk to his position.

"That is not all. I have received news from messengers of Eumenes that the Greek is now on his way here. He, no doubt, wanted to join Perdiccas."

There was outrage from the crowd, who, at this point, had no desire to become part of another war against Ptolemy. Any friend of Perdiccas was now their enemy. Men in the crowd, some planted by Ptolemy himself, shouted and decried Eumenes.

"Death to Eumenes!"

"That dirty Greek scoundrel has no limit to his ambition!"

"Drown that whore's mongrel in the river!"

"Send that bookkeeper to tend to the books of the underworld!"

"Put an end to Perdiccas' friends!"

After urging the crowd to be silent, Ptolemy made a show of conferring with the others. Then he ended the suspenseful wait. "The council sentences Eumenes to death and proposes to execute Perdiccas' closest confidantes."

My chest tightened at what I heard. Suddenly, we were in danger, my family was in danger, and Eumenes, who I had served for so long, was in grave danger.

"To those that desire, Ptolemy invites you to join him for a feast and become part of his army. And those who want to return to your lands, Ptolemy wishes you safe passage, and no harm will come to you."

The crowd went wild, and there was energetic jubilation. Under his fluttering banners, the satrap of Egypt looked on with a smile.

Seleucus, who was within my earshot, rolled his eyes at Peithon and mimicked Ptolemy, "Now Ptolemy will sit on the throne and let the mortals kneel before Ptolemy's giant penis!"

Peithon laughed and made an obscene sign with his hands.

Ptolemy ignored them and then turned to one of his adjutants. I could not hear what he said, but the adjutant looked at me as Ptolemy spoke, and he nodded vigorously.

I pissed blood for two days after the beating. But the local physicians took diligent care of me, in what appeared to be a room somewhere in the Memphis Palace. The room was bare but clean, and much to my relief Eurydice was in an adjacent room. Nekh-Aser had beaten her, and her face was healing from the bruises. The guards took care of us and fed us thrice a day. Our conditions were far more comfortable than what we had expected.

There was no doubt that we were prisoners. There were guards always outside the room, and one of them warned us of terrible things if we tried to escape. Nekh-Aser had once peeked into my room, grinning maliciously. But there was no further interaction between us much to my relief.

I worried each night that we were losing time.

For me to complete my task and return to my family.

For Eumenes to take control and put an end to the blood and tears that would envelop the regions soon.

For Eurydice's safety.

What was the plan? Why were we here? I would know the answer soon. Eight days after our "comfortable incarceration" a messenger visited us.

"The great Ptolemy requests your presence."

The great Ptolemy? As if we had any say in the matter whether we wanted to be in his presence.

The grand palace was bigger and airier than the one at Persepolis. The open, gigantic halls were twenty to thirty men high. The walls were of a beautiful orange hue due to the nature of the stone. On either side were statues of Egypt's Pharaohs—kings that lived long ago, even before my ancestors. The large stone slabs of the floor were cold to the feet. The builders had affixed ornate stone lamps on every pillar. I could not marvel at what a great empire this once was, and such glorious men inhabited it once.

The hallway ended in a large hall of pillars rising high up to a decorative ceiling.

On the far end was a wide staircase, and at the bottom on either side were majestic sphinxes. I had heard that there was a giant sphinx somewhere north of Memphis, built by a pharaoh long ago.

On the top of the stairs was Ptolemy sitting on an imposing stone throne. He looked small and insignificant. Egyptian chaperones stood next to him holding lamps.

It was a strange scene.

Afternoon sunlight poured from an opening in the ceiling. As I tried to go up the stairs, two guards, holding long spears, stepped in front.

"Let them up," commanded Ptolemy.

I made an obscene gesture at one of the guards. Eurydice kept her head high and tiptoed by my side. It was unclear what Ptolemy wanted from us.

"What is your lovely companion's name, Deon?"

"Eurydice, sir," I said.

Ptolemy raised an eyebrow. "Do you mock me, soldier?" His eyebrows squeezed disapprovingly.

Eurydice looked confused, as was I.

Ptolemy registered the confusion, threw his head back and laughed. "Ah, you do not know, my wife's name is Eurydice as well. I have a fondness for that name."

"The Viceroy's daughter?" I asked, referring to the Viceroy of Macedon.

He smiled—Eurydice and I laughed in relief.

And then Ptolemy whispered, "Alliance of convenience."

He leaned towards me and covered his mouth conspiratorially. "Tell no one, but I prefer the name Berenice better," he whispered.

I had no idea who Berenice was, but we nodded.

"You may sit," he gestured to Eurydice, but she stood where she was.

"I trust your journey has been uneventful until you arrived here, of course, Deon?" he smirked.

"Yes, sir."

"You look thinner than I remember you."

"I cannot say the same to you, General," I said. Ptolemy had put on some weight; his handsome face was now pudgy—the luxuries of Egypt weighed on him. His usually shaggy light blond hair was now carefully coiffured, and he wore a shiny green silk scarf around his neck. He wore a thick black eyeliner and a large golden ring on one of his ears.

He looked offended, but then recovered and rubbed his cheek absentmindedly.

"Why do you think I wanted to talk to you?"

"I do not know, sir. You think I know something that will help you against Governor Eumenes…"

"Ah, Eumenes. Governor now? What is he governing, goat sheds?" Ptolemy remarked. And then he turned his gaze towards the far nothing. "Why would I care what that little bookkeeper is up to? Craterus was stupid, and Eumenes got lucky."

Luck had little to do with it. Eumenes had outmaneuvered his adversaries.

"I suppose so, General."

"You do realize that the Egyptians think of me as the new Pharaoh."

"I suppose so, Pharaoh."

Ptolemy bristled at my insolence. I realized that I had to control my tongue considering my precarious position.

"I apologize, sir. I do not know why I am here. We were messengers who arrived too late and would like to leave as soon as we can."

Ptolemy nodded. "And where do you plan to go?"

"Somewhere North. Away from everything."

"Away from Eumenes too?"

"Yes, sir. We have had enough coming between the battles of great men."

"You are a bright man, Deon. But let us say your presence here has nothing to do with the message you brought from Eumenes."

The hair on my hand stood up, and a chill gripped my bones. I heard the rustle of the light blue curtain, and from the corner of my eye saw a man step out from the shadows.

Arrhidaeus.

"We meet again, Deon."

"Not under the best circumstances, General." I wanted to hit the treasonous bastard on his face.

"I gather you two are good friends, but we have other things to discuss," Ptolemy interjected. "What I am most curious about, Deon, is what did you steal from Alexander's funerary temple?"

So, there it was. Eurydice cast a sharp look at me.

"I'm not sure what Arrhidaeus has been—"

"We both know what you were up to," said Arrhidaeus, flexing his palms.

"What was I up to?"

"Your first pathetic attempt was during the raid."

"I was only protecting the contents from an intruder." That was a lie, and we both knew it. Ptolemy was no fool, and this charade was clear to him as well.

"The time for grandstanding is over," said Ptolemy. "We know you stole something."

"I took nothing," I protested. But in my heart, I knew that Ptolemy and Arrhidaeus knew a lot more than I gave them credit.

"We know you stole something during the transfer in Sidon!" Arrhidaeus shouted, turning red.

"Transfer, indeed! Do you have no shame for saying so Arrhidaeus? And you accuse me of stealing!" I shouted back. I moved forward, and two guards stepped in-between.

"Remember who you are speaking with," Ptolemy warned.

I muttered under my breath.

"So, what did you steal?" asked Ptolemy again. But this time the smile was gone.

I sighed. "Jewelry."

"You know better than that. All you had to do was join me, and I would have rewarded you," Ptolemy scoffed. One of the attendants stepped forward and began to fan him. Arrhidaeus moved closer to the fans.

"It was an impulse, sir."

"I see. Well, Arrhidaeus, it seems we have a common thief here?" Ptolemy asked Arrhidaeus in a mocking tone.

Arrhidaeus responded. "What can I say, Ptolemaios, we wasted all our time on a rascal with loose morals!"

Ptolemy stood up. And with an exaggerated motion swinging his arms and swaying his hips, he pretended to walk away. He and Arrhidaeus were having fun at my expense. My cheeks burned.

Just before the curtains Ptolemy stopped and turned. "But wait, there was one other thing. We heard there was some document that you might have possession of. Is that true?"

I froze. Eurydice was now staring at me with an upset expression. She must have realized I had not been truthful about the mission.

"I do not know what you mean, sir," I said, looking at Ptolemy.

Ptolemy stood still. His eyes had gone cold and distant. He nodded to someone behind me, and for some time, there was nothing but absolute silence.

Eurydice gasped, and I turned.

Nekh-Aser walked from an antechamber by the side of the throne.

He was pulling something.

He finally dropped the rope, and I looked at the thrashed and bruised figure lying on the floor. A low moan came from his crushed lips.

Iotros.

That man who confronted me in Damascus and took me for a common thief because he could not read my papers. Nekh-Aser's spiked club had ripped chunks of Iotros' flesh off his back and thighs. The rest of his body was purple. The inquisitors had pulled the hair off his scalp, revealing skull underneath. They had gouged an eye.

But tortured breath still emanated from him, and I prayed for his end. I clenched my fists. Ptolemy's amused expression at what he had sanctioned ensured that I would not bargain with the man.

Nekh-Aser walked behind and slapped me on the back of my head. I looked up at Ptolemy and decided to take a different tactic. "Since when did Egyptian dogs get the authority to strike Alexander's soldiers who stuck by you and the King's side?"

Ptolemy flinched. No matter what our differences were now, we were all together for a long time, serving the same King.

"Nekh-Aser, enough! Await my orders," said Ptolemy, and the brute scowled at me as he stepped back. He made a show of intimidation by flexing the muscles of his broad, hairless chest. He then swung the club back and forth and his eyebrows danced.

"You need to tell us what you stole, and why it was important. I know that Eumenes, that cunning snake, is up to something," Ptolemy said.

"I already told you, sir."

"Iotros here was quite clear that you had several papyri that you guarded. He said they had two different writings, though unfortunately for us it seems the fool could not read."

"That is because those were official papers from Regent Perdiccas. It had two languages on it, Greek and Persian."

"Where are they?"

"I threw them away, too much trouble."

"Is there a reason for a Regent to send administrative papers through the captain of a procession?"

I said nothing.

Ptolemy continued. "I know you to be very bright. You should remember every letter in those administrative papers." He accentuated the words 'administrative papers.' He looked at Arrhidaeus, and they grinned at each other.

I stared at a pillar behind him.

"You test my patience and take advantage of my patronage." His puffy face turned a dark shade of red. "You have two days to think and come to me with the truth," he finally said, coldly.

Ptolemy turned to Nekh-Aser. "And if I am not satisfied with Deon's answer, the woman is yours. And once you are done with her, and I am still unsatisfied with Deon's answer, he is yours as well."

With that, Ptolemy stood and walked away. Arrhidaeus locked his eyes on mine, and I thought there was pity in his eyes before he vanished behind the curtains. Guards restrained us and began to march us back to our quarters.

Nekh-Aser strolled to my front, towering over me. He smirked and turned to Eurydice and flicked his tongue between his yellow teeth. He traced his finger—from her forehead, along the bridge of her nose, and all the way to her waist. Eurydice began to tremble. I seethed as he bit her lips, while thrusting his hips on her. He stepped back, laughing. "That man," he pointed to Iotros, "not last too long, but you I make," he said. He then tapped his forefinger on one of the metal tips on his club.

Nekh-Aser walked towards Iotros. He swung his club and smashed Iotros' head—splattering the contents of the man's skull on the pristine floors of the palace.

The guards took us back, but this time we were together. At first, I wondered why. Ptolemy must have surmised that if we were stuck together, Eurydice might wear me down to come up with the truth. Even report what she learned from me.

Pressure on the mind before pressure on the body.

Ptolemy's threat had frightened us. But right now, I had to handle Eurydice and come up with a plan. And for the last quarter of the day, she sat shooting daggers with her eyes at me.

Sullen, silent, and angry.

"When were you going to tell me the truth, sir?" she asked, her chin resting on her folded knees.

"Never. The plan was to let you go on your way once I was closer to what I was seeking."

She seemed surprised by my honest answer, and her demeanor softened. She rested her back on the wall, tucked her feet under her thighs, and cast her eyes to the floor.

"You are willing to let that beast rape me and die for a cause I would never know."

"You're not dead, are you?"

"You lied and deceived me even though I was loyal to you," she said. Her intense green eyes focused on me.

"We are at war, Eurydice. And Eumenes sent you to support me in the mission. It is not your place to question my decisions," I retorted with irritation.

"I am now a soldier and not a trusted partner as you told me before. You were lying then."

This woman sounded like my wife!

I stood up to flex my limbs, and through the little window, I could see the Great River beyond the palace walls. The greenery across the river was a contrast to the yellow sands beyond.

"You are my partner Eurydice. I would not have guarded you with my life if I did not see it that way."

"So why am I not privy to your mission? And does it matter anymore given our circumstance."

"I am not going to let that animal harm you."

"That is not under your control, is it, sir?"

I nodded. And then I walked towards the door, which had a little opening of its own, and peered through it. As I expected, there was Nekh-Aser and a younger Egyptian who I had seen the past few days. The two conversed in short sentences in their language. I went back and sat next to Eurydice. She was still sulking—irritated at my dismissal of her concerns. She pretended not to recognize my presence but instead began to examine her palms.

"Those are lovely palms," I said and saw her trying to suppress her smile.

"They may be smooth but not as smooth as the back of my head," I continued, imitating Eumenes' voice. She guffawed.

"Inside that smooth head is a deceitful mind." She said, feigning anger.

"As that may be, I promise I will reveal the truth in time. For now, we must figure out a way to escape."

She raised her eyebrows.

"Why not tell them what you know, what do you have to lose? Let the generals quarrel."

"It is not that simple because you don't know what this is about. They will shackle and drag us along until we serve their purpose, and then put us to death. We will not be screaming for days if we are lucky."

"What makes you so sure?" She asked. But her tone conveyed her doubt.

I ignored her question. "If the wrong people find out my mission, there will be a far bloodier war that will engulf the continents. Have we not had enough?"

"Yes, but we are immaterial actors on the stage of gods and kings."

"That may be so, but right now this insignificant agent knows a secret to the play that the others do not. And you are safer not knowing it."

Eurydice's eyes bored into mine.

"Why do you risk so much for this, what is in it for you?" she asked.

I paused and considered my options. Eurydice had proved to be a trustworthy companion. She was bright, and my lies would only hurt my chances.

I took a deep breath.

"General Eumenes promised me a generous retirement," I said, hoping she would not ask for more.

Eurydice continued to stare.

"It seems like you accepted a great deal of risk to make some money. Is your family in trouble, sir?" she asked. There were times she spoke like a royal, which made me question her background. But here she was, with me, facing the same terrors.

I sighed. "Yes. A terrible lender controls my wife and daughter's fate, and I am in significant debt."

She blinked.

"You do not seem like a gambler, what did you do to incur such debts?" she asked, encouraged by my momentary truthfulness.

I opened my big mouth and spluttered what I did not want to reveal. "I opened a—a brothel, I thought I would—" I blurted. And then I looked away.

For a few torturous moments I heard nothing. And then for the first time, I heard Eurydice laugh—a full-throated, uncontrolled laughter.

I turned to her. It struck me how beautiful she looked as she laughed, unabashed, open-mouthed and loud. Her laugh had settled to a chuckle as she looked at me. "I could never imagine you to be a pimp!"

"I am not a pimp!" I protested.

But yes, I did try to be one. What was I thinking, O Poseidon?

"Are you going to try to sell me too, sir?" she pouted, putting her hands together as if I had tied them. "I will fetch a good price as a whore."

I swatted her hands away. "Enough! That is a life I left long ago. I was younger, naïve, and stupid. Yes, I thought it was a lucrative business on a trade route. I learned the hard way that you need a lack of moral compass to make money from it," I said. I hope that my serious voice conveyed business-like ambition.

"Hard way, indeed," she said and began to giggle.

This woman.

"It was a long and hard road, Eurydice!" I admonished her, but soon we fell to fits of laughter.

Absurd.

She nodded and leaned back on the wall.

Silence.

"Eurydice?"

"Yes?"

"I know so little about you. I think me revealing my filthy past earns me the right to know something more."

She nodded, and I could see her struggling with what to say next. Eventually, without meeting my eyes, she asked, "What do you want to know?"

"Tell me about your childhood."

There was a pause, and sadness showed in her face as she placed her chin between her drawn-up knees.

"I grew up in Persia. My father is Phrygian but was part of the Persian forces. He married my mother who came from a Greek trader's family."

"Do I know your father?"

"No," she said curtly, and continued, "I grew up happy, among brothers and sisters, and a difficult but protective father."

"Did he teach you the dagger skills?"

She smiled. "Yes, but it was another man that taught me how to wield it as I do."

"A man?" I hoped no jealousy seeped through my voice. She raised her eyebrows at me, and I thought her lips curled in a barely perceptible smile.

"Yes. He was a father when mine was no longer around."

I felt ashamed.

"Where are your parents now?"

Pause.

"Dead, I think. I do not know. I was snatched away from them when your—" Her eyes welled up, and I hesitated. I placed my palm on her shoulder as she gathered herself. She continued, "When your King Alexander crossed into Asia, my father was among resistors who lost to an attacking force. I was captured along with others and sold to a wealthy merchant."

It was like someone had punched me in my stomach.

"I—I did not—" I stammered.

"I did not see you in the raiding party, so you are safe from my dagger," she said, smiling, as she wiped her tears with the back of her hand.

I did not smile. "I am sorry for your pain."

She patted my shoulder as if to say it was not my fault. I had one more question. "Is your name Eurydice?"

She laughed. "I have a different birth name, but I was called Eurydice since I was a child."

"Why?"

"We lived in Macedon for a while. My mother loved the name. What else do you want to know?"

Eumenes had warned me from prying into her life, and I could see that the wounds were still raw. I also did not know how much of what she said was true, but I believed most of it.

"Let us talk about our lives some other time, and I can share more of my stupid stories."

She nodded, and we sat quietly for a while. I decided to change the subject.

"I have noticed no extra guard except those two and the two at the night shift, have you?" I asked her.

"No. But I have heard them mention a larger contingent outside the palace chambers."

The light detail outside our room was surprising, but they may have thought that we had no chance of getting out. Showing some leniency might gain better cooperation. Allow the two prisoners to talk until they scare each other.

"Have you ever spoken to them?"

"No. There are things they need not know, but I did learn much about them," she said, her eyes glinting.

The golden sun was midway between the zenith and the tree lines. We looked at each other and pondered what tomorrow might bring.

I knew something was churning in her mind, and eventually, she tapped me on my shoulder. "Sir?"

"Yes?"

"I have an idea," she said, with a mischievous smile.

It was late in the evening; the sun had almost set, and all that remained was the orange glow reflecting off the sandstone walls. One of the servants came to our room and placed a candle in a decorative brass jar set at the corner.

Nekh-Aser and his companion were getting ready for the end of their shift. Eurydice and I prayed to our gods—for safety, success, and well-being. The strain on what might become of us weighed heavily on our minds, and we had only a day left before Ptolemy summoned us.

The moon rose, bright and yellow, though some saw the rise of a colored moon as an ill omen. I moved next to Eurydice, and we began to breathe in and out to calm ourselves down.

Eurydice's eyes began to flutter and close, and she knelt on the cold floor; her head bowed, and her torso began to sway.

I walked to the door to check the guards on duty. Nekh-Aser and his companion sat quietly, looking bored and ready to go home. Now Eurydice began to shake more often like a spirit possessed her.

She began a mystic chant.

These actions were reminiscent of oracles and mystic priests of Egypt. I ran to the door and shouted in anguish to the guards.

"Spirits!"

Alarmed, they scrambled to their feet. Nekh-Aser was tentative, but the younger guard, who had taken some fancy to Eurydice, rushed to the room.

Eurydice was in a deep trance. Her body quivered, and her mouth opened and closed in a silent chant.

The younger guard stood mesmerized by the vision: a beautiful and sensual woman on her knees, swaying rhythmically, her bare midriff glistening with sweat, and her face enchanting in the gentle glow of the candle, the fading sunlight, and the rising moon.

Eurydice suddenly threw her head back, her lustrous black hair flew in the air, and she raised a slim hand and pointed at Nekh-Aser accusingly. I was awestruck—the arched back, the firm and proud breasts beneath her chiton, the sensuously curved hips—I could not take my eyes off her.

"*Thak-el sah-ahk-khaut!*" She growled, in Egyptian royal tongue, the way I heard it spoken by the nobles and the priests, startling both the men.

"Kneel, you mortals."

Nekh-Aser, confounded yet vigilant, looked around unsure how to react. His companion had kneeled even though she had not commanded him. Nekh-Aser then firmly gripped the knife in his belt, stared at me menacingly, and asked me to stand in the corner opposite his side.

I moved slowly behind Eurydice, and he locked his eyes on mine until I stopped. And then he kneeled.

"The goddess commands me to give you a message."

Eurydice jerked her head forward, some of her hair falling on her face, her back arched, and both hands now raised with her palms making a boat and pointing towards the frozen Nekh-Aser. The other man sat still, hypnotized. The Egyptian brute, his mouth agape as he knelt and stared, tried to interrupt, "Goddess—"

"Be quiet, insolent child!"

Eurydice moved forward and struck Nekh-Aser on his face, stunning him.

I too sat down to show my respect to the gods and bowed my head and clasped my hands. She then turned towards me, her eyes wide, and her teeth open in a snarl. I faced her boldly, and this time she delivered a stinging open-palm slap to my face as well. I fell backward, mumbled my profuse apologies, and kneeled. She turned towards Nekh-Aser again.

"Your woman loves you as the Great River loves the denizens of this glorious land."

I noticed Nekh-Aser jerk briefly at her mention of his woman.

"A life stirs in her."

His eyes widened with surprise, and I noticed that his caution had slowly turned to fearful obedience. It always fascinated me to watch how the gods instilled awe even in the most fearsome beasts.

"Six moons before your mighty son sees your affectionate face."

Nekh-Aser's face lit at the mention of a son, a great honor for the household and often a necessity for the preservation of family in grim times. From his mannerisms, I knew he came from a primitive part of Egypt where parents took pride in their sons, and tribes cast away those with only daughters.

She then crawled on her knees towards Nekh-Aser, sat straight with her legs folded, and stretched her right arm to gently place her palm on his head.

"I foresee danger. I see walls all around you, enclosing you in a blanket of black."

Nekh-Aser jerked. I noticed his muscles tense, and he began to sweat.

"A child lost in a deep mine, earth collapsing, entombing you."

The Egyptian began to tremble, and copious rivulets of sweat drenched his body. He was choking and gasping for breath. I was surprised to see his reactions.

"These images foretell a dark omen. The goddess sees Osiris' evil brother rise from the bowels of the earth, make his way into the womb of your wife, and strike your warrior son before he sees the light of Ra."

Nekh-Aser jerked in terror, unsure how to react to the frightening news. "No! That cannot be true, mother goddess," he gasped.

"There is a way to send Seth back to the underworld where he belongs."

I had seen similar spirits in bodies elsewhere during my brief time in Egypt. Often the goddess demanded money, grain, gold, or in rare situations even slaves, as restitution to the divine in return for comfort and protection.

Eurydice turned her gaze towards the other guard, his face adoring, and his body transfixed.

"Bring me the candle jar."

He stumbled towards the heavy brass jar on which the lone candle shone and brought it to her.

She carefully dipped her middle finger into the pool of hot wax, and then as we watched, wiped it on Nekh-Aser's forehead, and began to hum a hymn in a quiet voice.

"Prostrate before me, and may your ears hear my words."

Nekh-Aser prostrated. He was still breathing heavily and sweating profusely. Eurydice moved to his side and began to press two fingers on his body, starting with his shoulders, in intervals. And each time, she would exclaim a word. She then ordered the other guard to place the brass jar in my hands and asked me to hold it on my head.

She then moved closer to Nekh-Aser's waist, while chanting a hymn. She placed both her palms on his back and while looking at me, growled in a low, soft voice.

"Ahk-an-Ra."

In that instant, Eurydice moved at lightning speed.

She pulled the knife from the prostrating Nekh-Aser's waist and stabbed him. Simultaneously, I jumped and smashed the brass jar on the other guard's head.

He collapsed like a rock.

I turned my attention to Nekh-Aser.

Eurydice had stabbed him deep in his shoulder and hung on to his back, but she was unable to extricate the knife out of him. The powerful man would become dangerous very quickly.

Nekh-Aser bellowed as he rose.

I swung my brass jar and connected to his chest causing him to stumble back, pinning Eurydice to the wall behind. His eyes were now wide open, enraged at the duplicity in the name of his gods, and he managed to land a powerful punch on my shoulders. I almost lost my balance but recovered.

He was not yet in control due to the pain, surprise, and with Eurydice now trying to gouge his eyes.

I swung the heavy jar with all my might and connected with tremendous impact, and I heard his jaw break—the sound of a fracturing bone I knew so well from the battlefield. His yellow eyes went wide, and his scream died in his mangled jaws. I raised the jar and hit his head—and Nekh-Aser collapsed.

I wanted to kill him but thought I heard some sounds outside. We had to leave.

I shouted to Eurydice, "Let us go!"

She sprang to her feet, and we both ran out the door. There was no one in the corridor, and the vast halls were empty. It was dark except the dim candles. We soon turned into another quadrangle that led to the outer walls of the palace and found a side gate guarded by sentries. Getting past them was no great challenge, as no one recognized us, and Eurydice was able to expertly speak in their tongue.

Our excitement began to subside as we walked out to the cooler air, with stars shining above, and the moon bright and beautiful. We did not know how long this freedom would last, as there was no doubt that within the next hour the new shift would find the men and raise the alarm. We had to find a way to get out of Memphis and go somewhere out of Ptolemy's reach. But for now, we enjoyed the freedom and were very proud of how we had engineered a miraculous escape.

After a few hours of quiet walk, we found a place to rest.

It sunk in that we had just escaped tortuous death, but now Ptolemy would hunt us.

I looked at Eurydice admiringly. "That was a brilliant plan," I said, "and awe-inspiring performance. You speak their tongue so well."

She giggled. The first one in a long time. "And I was amazed at how accurately you recollected all the guards' dialogs in a tongue you do not know."

We had pieced information about Nekh-Aser listening to his conversations and Eurydice had found a way to use it against the brute.

"Well, our plan worked spectacularly, at least until now," I said quietly, "the question is how long we can stay ahead of Ptolemy's hounds."

"Where do you think we should go?" she asked.

Ptolemy looked at Nekh-Aser, who now sat recuperating on a clay bed.

The Egyptian had been under a physician's care for over thirty days, had lost weight, but not the glowing hate in his eyes. The royal physicians had taken care of his stabbed shoulder, allowing the Egyptian some movement of his hands.

But his mouth—that was another matter.

The physicians had created a contraption out of iron wires that held his broken jaw. They then secured it in place by creating a harness that went around his head. It made Nekh-Aser's face appear like a grim, deformed creature from an offensive play.

The Egyptian had suffered. At night he often wondered what felt worse—the terrible pain in his face, or the shame of falling to a ruse. He had often lain awake, fantasizing the many ways he would torture and kill them. Even the gods of the underworld could not imagine what he would do to them. But it was a mystery to Nekh-Aser why the Satrap allowed him to live, and who now stood looking down at him.

It was as if Ptolemy read his mind. "You wonder why I let you live."

Nekh-Aser nodded, barely moving his jaw, and all that emanated was a grunt. He shifted on his uncomfortable bed, now cracking and wet in places with his sweat.

"The search parties have returned empty-handed."

Bowed head.

"But I am not surprised. Deon was a captain in Alexander's army, and he is well trained in the art of deception."

Nodding.

"And the woman, she is a mystery, but she is no innocent."

Eyes raised. Anger burning through.

"It is a shame she made you look like an imbecile."

Growl and spittle through the iron wires.

"While your stupidity got us into this situation, your anger makes you the right person to find them."

Slow nodding.

"In twenty days, you will be on your feet and seek them."

More nodding and grunting.

"Choose your men. Be discreet."

Nodding.

"No one, absolutely no one must know what they tell or find."

Nodding.

"I have debated many times whether I should send a different search party instead of you. But the times are delicate and I do not want more people involved. You have been a faithful and talented officer so far, and I trust you to keep this quiet."

Nekh-Aser felt relieved. He drew a line across his neck with his flat palm, and Ptolemy shook his head.

"Do not kill them once they confess. I do not want them to trick us again."

Shameful nodding.

"They seek something, and I do not know what."

Raised head and eyebrows.

"Find their destination."

Anger flashed on Nekh-Aser's face. But his chance of revenge?

"And no, I do not want us to meekly follow them to see where they go, for they might deceive us again. Deon knows we seek him, and he will keep a watchful eye."

Nodding.

"You have to keep them alive until they lead us to whatever they are seeking."

Nodding.

"Once I have the truth, do as you please."

Tortured smile.

"If I find out you killed them before we uncover..." Ptolemy left that hanging, and he turned towards the door. Nekh-Aser's eyes tracked Ptolemy's face.

At the entrance, looking fearful, stood his pregnant wife. Two burly Macedonian guards stood by her.

Satisfied, Ptolemy turned and walked out. The Egyptian brute laid his head back in relief.

He would track those scoundrels. And he would not wait once he did.

He would torture, break, watch him beg for mercy, and kill him slowly.

He would take her, inflict such horror that she would hope never to be born again.

Too bad his pregnant wife might die at the hands of Ptolemy, but such was life. It was his concern for them that brought him such humiliation.

And pride mattered more to Nekh-Aser than anything else in the world.

PART III

WATER AND DUST

Circa 322 BC

"Let me not then die ingloriously and without a struggle but let me first do some great thing that shall be told among men hereafter." –Homer, The Iliad

CHAPTER 24.

ALEXANDRIA, EGYPT

Forty nights had passed since our escape. We evaded checkpoints and managed to reach the outskirts of the new city founded by Alexander.

Alexandria.

That Ptolemy's forces had not caught us told me that he had not ordered a large-scale hunt. I guessed he wanted to keep this quiet for now. But tonight, under a beautiful moon and gentle breeze, I decided that I would reveal the truth to Eurydice. She had not asked, but I knew it bothered her that after all this time together, I would not tell her the entire truth.

I had indeed grown fond of her resilience, skills, and loyalty. And in no small parts to her cooking skills and how she tended to me. In our limited interactions with outsiders, we were husband and wife. But we had privately not behaved as such.

As much as my love for my wife stayed undiminished, I was drawn to Eurydice. Intimacy had been rare since I left on King Alexander's campaign.

With Eurydice it was different.

I knew that she knew I was attracted to her.

She had curtly dismissed my awkward overtures of intimacy.

My mind wandered to what Governor Eumenes was up to. Was his army still progressing south? Did he know

Perdiccas was dead? But tonight, we sat with our backs to an abandoned well wall. We had stolen some food from a roadside seller. I felt guilty, but we had no other choice until we figured a way to own more barterable tender.

I had nothing with me. All my earning was in Eumenes' baggage train and accounting books. Iotros had stolen most of the jewelry that I had stolen from the funerary temple. And Nekh-Aser had cleaned the rest of our belongings after our arrest.

After over ten years in Alexander's service, I was, somehow, completely coinless.

My mind returned to the present.

"This night will be different," I said, my voice emphatic. I laughed as Eurydice inched away from me, putting distance between us.

"No, Eurydice, I did not mean that way," I protested. A faint smile passed on her face in the reflection of the moonlight. I held her hand and pulled her towards me, and she slid back without a fight.

"I know you've resisted asking me what I was hiding from you."

No response.

"I am going to tell you. Now."

No response.

"My wife ran away with my neighbor, and he's threatening to return her to me."

Punch on my shoulder.

"My neighbors wrote to me when I was on the way from Babylon. They said my son was growing to be the most handsome boy."

Smile. Knowing what would come next.

"He couldn't be my boy then. So, I'm trying to find the scoundrel who—"

"Enough," she said, with mock anger.

I sighed. It was time.

"Part of our job was to deliver Eumenes' message to Perdiccas. And your job was to keep an eye for deceptions on the way."

She nodded.

"And you did that. But those trips to the village councils, listening to ancient folklore and bawdy songs? Nothing to do with Perdiccas."

"I thought as much, sir."

"Call me Deon. You were never in my command, and this formality brings risk."

No response.

"My real quest is to a find a lost city. It is deep in the mountains somewhere and is full of treasure and the most advanced weaponry."

Silence. I was surprised she said nothing. And then she spoke. "When will you be serious? At some point, you should—"

"That was no joke."

She looked at me incredulously. "You are looking for a mythical lost city?"

"Well, I call it the second Atlantis, built by the Atlanteans."

"Who?"

"By the people of a long lost empire that was called Atlantis—"

She cut me off. "Indeed, and you believe it exists?"

"That is what we are to find out."

"How did you learn of it? How do you know it is true? Why do you need to find it?"

At a distance, dogs began to howl.

"That is a long story. One of King Alexander's court ministers gave a clue to Eumenes. I found ancient papers that supported that account when I was in Damascus."

"And those documents are reliable?" she asked, inching closer.

"They look real. And they portray a story a great Greek philosopher later masked into something else."

"What if it was all made up?"

"It could be. We will never know unless we find out. And if it was a fake, at least we went on an adventure," I said, mimicking a galloping horse with my hands.

"One that almost led to torture and death. And might end up leading to your family sold to slavery," she said, putting an end to the levity.

I rubbed my hand on the soft dusty floor and then clapped my hands gently. Her shoulder touched mine. It sent a warm flood of arousal through my very being, and I had to control the sensation between my legs.

"But it didn't. And I will free my family, whatever it takes. We live in a harsh, unforgiving world. Would it not be a departure to go on a quest for finding something rather than killing someone?"

"But if what you said is true, the discovery would unleash more fighting and killing."

I had no response to that.

"There really is a grand hidden city in the mountains?" She asked, her voice hushed, as if speaking aloud would magically cause Ptolemy to appear in front of us.

I grinned. The curiosity had gotten the better of Eurydice. "The legend says it is literally inside the mountains. They carved a city inside and sealed it!"

"And it is full of treasure?"

"Immense. And it has weapons of great power."

"And that is why Governor Eumenes wants you to find it?" she asked, and her warm breath teased my cheeks.

"Our world is far better with Governor Eumenes in charge. You saw what Perdiccas did. You know what Ptolemy can do. I know that the other generals are as bloodthirsty as the next."

"I am indebted to Eumenes," she said firmly.

"He may be the best King we will ever have."

Assuming he does not kill my family.

"And he needs the money and weapons to build his armies and fight the others," she said.

Very smart.

"And we are his only hope. Now that Perdiccas is dead, the other treacherous bastards circle him like crocodiles."

"What will you do after you deliver the secret to him?" She asked, slyly.

"I will first return to free my family. Then I will kill the lender and his sons for what they put my wife through. And finally, I will retire in luxury," I said, stretching my back and placing my hands behind my head.

Only if it were that simple.

She nodded.

"And you will be amply rewarded as well," I said, looking at her.

"Assuming we are still alive."

"That is a minor detail," I remarked, and we both snorted like pigs.

Her voice dropped to a whisper, "How do I know you will not dispose of me once you find this place?"

I turned to her. It was a fair question. I cupped her face in my palms, and she did not resist. "I swear on the gods that I will protect you as I know you will protect me."

Just when my loins decided to turn this moment into something more, an old voice boomed from somewhere behind us. "Who are you?"

She pulled away from me, and I rose quickly. It was time to keep moving. It was time to navigate the marshes and get to Alexandria.

I grabbed the terrified man by his throat and pushed him against the cracked wall. He understood simple Greek, but he understood my gestures even better. Onlookers stayed away, not wanting to be involved in the dispute.

"Where is your father?"

"Not live here! Not here!" croaked the young man, just out of his teens. Gangly and taller than me, but no match for my strength. His light brown skin glistened with oil, and the eyeliner made him effeminate.

I slapped him on his head hard and twisted an ear, causing him to howl. "He owes Tharbazus money."

"Ow! No! Ow!"

"Father?"

More pressure on the ear. And I pulled my curved knife out and brought it to his groin—and he finally saw the light of the divine sun god, Ra. "Yehudi quarters! Mistress' house!"

"Where in Yehudi quarters?"

"Behind blue-roofed grain shop! All know blue-roofed grain shop!"

"You lie," I said and gestured with my knife making him wince and instinctively push his thighs together in protection.

"No, no, real!"

I sheathed my knife, much to the young man's relief. I let him go and hurried back to my employer, a colorful man named Tharbazus—a local lender of a very unsavory reputation. This was no time to go to the Yehudi quarters—I would need Eurydice's help. I walked along the narrow streets and arrived at Tharbazus' house.

Tharbazus' angry, lazy eye turned towards me. His tugged on his long gray beard and admonished me again, as he did every day since he employed me as a collector. "You did not find him because you forgot the directions," Tharbazus growled at me, his bony finger targeted my forehead.

"No, I did not forget the directions, Tharbazus. He no longer lives there."

"Eh?"

"THAT MAN NO LONGER LIVES THERE."

"That rascal owes me four copper coins."

"I will find him. It seems he is hiding—"

"Eh?"

"HE IS HIDING IN THE YEHUDI QUARTERS."

"Find him. You can keep a coin. Where is your wife today?"

"I told you she is not my—SHE IS FINE. COOKING."

My daily job of collecting monies owed to Tharbazus helped me build savings. Collection was a lucrative business in a rapidly growing city, and my odd contracts for other disreputable characters helped me make coin quickly. But it was a dangerous job, and the odds of Ptolemy's men finding me increased by the day. Living in a mostly foreign area helped me stay hidden from the nearby Egyptian garrison. And no one was conducting door-to-door searches.

Not yet.

We sat for dinner. Eurydice was a good cook, and she made delicious meals with the dry meat, olive oil, salt, and some strange peppers she found at the local market. But she did not enjoy cooking for the entire household which consisted of the ornery man's wife, four daughters who still lived with them, and an invalid son whose eyes never left Eurydice.

We had little time to plan. Eurydice was busy during the day in the house, and I was out threatening and cajoling the indebted. At night, she slept in a large hall with the rest of the women of the household, while I put up with the snoring of the old man.

But today the family was out on a courtesy visit, and apart from a daughter and the invalid son, the house was empty. We sat together as she washed the grain for the next day. It had been a month since we had a meaningful conversation. I stared at the son until he retreated to another part of the house.

"Busy days?"

She wrinkled her nose. "I will poison the food if that cackling sorceress yells at me one more time."

"Just a few more days. Patience."

"You've told that thrice already."

"Well, plans change. I think we have enough tender for the next journey."

"You have not yet told me what was in those papers, and you were supposed to!" She complained in a rushed whisper.

"I will. And then let us talk about the plan."

As the lamp flickered and the milky white orb rose in the sky, I recounted the story starting with how I met Eumenes. It felt wonderful to unburden myself, share it with the woman who deserved to know it more than anyone else.

She listened with rapt attention, utterly captivated, and interrupted me only once a while. I left out the ignominious part of having tortured Ptolemy's henchman. And then, as the cold moonlight bathed the kitchen through the oblique window, I repeated the page that spoke of the location, using a tune I had made up in my head. A soft, lilting lullaby.

With glorious seas all around, and the great eye beneath his feet, the Lord he towered over the adoring masses, and as the rays of the rising sun shone upon his regal visage, he lay his feet on the spines of the fist that fought the disquiet water below...

She held her breath as I finished. Her face took on a dreamy expression. Away from the hardship, fear, running, there was something to look forward to. Now that she had context, Eurydice could share her views and recounted fables influenced by events of a distant past. We sat late into the night theorizing, challenging each other, and formulating a plan for what would come next.

It felt exhilarating.

Finally, at some point later into the night, with the oil wick slowly dimming as the fat ran out, I gently held Eurydice's waist and pulled her towards me. She did not resist, and as my heart hammered in my chest, I put my lips against hers.

She did not react at first. And then her soft lips pressed hard against mine.

It was an exhausting conversation, but Tharbazus had information and connections in the quarters few could match. I had to get him to introduce someone to me. The old man lazed in the afternoon sun when I approached him, and he chewed on a nut with his remaining teeth. He swatted at a seagull that tried to steal from the breadbasket placed next to him.

"I need to speak to an experienced sea captain," I said.

"Eh?"

"I NEED TO SPEAK TO AN EXPERIENCED SEA CAPTAIN."

"Why?"

"I MUST VISIT Athens."

"What? You have friends here?"

"NOT FRIENDS, ATHENS."

"Why sea?"

"TOO FAR AND DANGEROUS BY LAND."

"Ptolemy and others going at it like mad dogs?" He grinned as he made a lewd gesture with his fingers. War was good business.

I nodded. His lazy eye drifted to the lands far away, and the good eye bored into mine.

"It is an expensive voyage over the sea."

"I have the—I HAVE THE COIN."

And then he peered at me suspiciously.

"Have you been stealing from me?" he said, waggling his bony finger.

"I AM NOT A FOOL TO STEAL FROM THE GREAT THARBAZUS. I JUST NEED HIS HELP."

Tharbazus grinned.

"I need you for my business. You are very good."

"I will steal your daughter."

"Eh?"

"I WILL BE BACK."

He made a dismissive cluck on his tongue. We both knew I would not be returning.

"I will introduce you to Thefeni. He has contacts among the naval traders. But keep your coin ready."

I had no doubt Thefeni had an arrangement with Tharbazus.

Eurydice and I paid a visit to the man.

I thought Thefeni would be a fit, tall, seafaring warrior, and he was anything but. He was a huge man, my age, grave and full of self-importance. Beady, suspicious eyes and thick colored lips adorned his swarthy face. He had trimmed his dark mustache and short beard with care.

He greeted me warmly, his eyes searched my face, and his mouth opened wide. His belly shook as he exerted himself to stand up from his comfortable dewan. "Welcome. I am always at Tharbazus' service. He has told me that I must take good care of your needs."

"Thank you. And this is my wife."

He eyed her greedily—his gaze lingering on her midriff for too long and she stared back. "Yes, yes, please sit down. Please. What can I do for you?"

We sat on the colorful cushions in his open tent, overseeing the beautiful green waters of The Great Sea. The port of Alexandria was busy with many vessels going about their business. The air was pungent with the smell of dry fish and seaweed. There were hundreds of people engaged in maritime trade all along the port. There were several triremes whose flags fluttered in the breeze. Ptolemy was reinforcing the regional garrison to prevent invasion from the sea.

"We must go to Athens, but not by land due to the current political situation," I said.

His large head bobbed, and his wide nose moved up and down. "Very true. Very true. No place is safe these days."

"How long does it take for the direct route to Athens?"

Thefeni rubbed his ample cheeks and shifted his large bottom. He turned towards an assistant who stood nearby and spoke something in Egyptian.

Eurydice's face turned red. *"I am not his whore, and if you talk like that about me again, I will cut off your penis."*

Color drained from Thefeni's face. He mumbled and then crumbled under our steady gaze. "Just a compliment. My sincere apologies. Your wife is divine, very divine indeed!"

"Let us talk in a common language."

"Of course. Of course. There will be no more mistakes. Ah, what were you asking about? The direct route from here to Athens?"

"Yes."

"You see. That will be problematic. Very problematic. Athens is in trouble, and there is no longer an active trade route between here and Greece."

"Surely there must be some traffic? I have not heard that Egypt has cut off the grain routes."

He nodded. "That is true. That is true. But the captains are very wary of taking on anyone not known to both Greek and Egyptian authorities."

"But an important man such as yourself can make arrangements."

He grinned. His eyes went to Eurydice but averted under her glare. "Of course. Of course. But such exceptions need the satisfaction of many people." He rubbed his palms gleefully and the gold rings on his chubby fingers jiggled. Here came the haggling. His eyes sparkled.

"You have not yet told me the arrangements," I asked.

"Oh yes, arrangements, yes, of course, arrangements. Your timing is most fortuitous. There is a grain ship due to leave tomorrow night. It will dock briefly in Crete in four days, and reach Athens three or four days later, depending on the wind on its sails."

I did not tell him that our ultimate destination was not Athens. We only wanted to see the islands on the way. He offered us honey-dipped dates, salted fish with pomegranate, cloyingly sweet wine. I nibbled on the dates and sipped on the drink.

Thefeni's assistant returned to whisper in his ears, and the fat man looked at us through the corner of his eyes. His eyes darted away when I caught him looking at us. "I apologize, something came up. Please stay here, and I will be back. Shortly, very shortly." He bowed and vanished.

I stood up and walked outside the tent to watch the people. Workers were busy clearing the path for a wide road. I could imagine how magnificent it would look once ready. Dinocrates of Rhodes, Alexander's architect, had laid out plans for its construction. One of the significant features, I had learned, was a magnificent royal way. The project was slow in its execution but was finally beginning to take shape under Ptolemy. There was also news that Ptolemy would make Alexandria his capital.

But before I ran out of patience, Thefeni returned, looking gleeful. "Many apologies, great apologies, where were we? Ah, the next ship. Tomorrow. Tomorrow night."

"They leave at night?"

"Not night, not at night. But all loading ends at night. They sail at the first light of dawn."

"What of food and shelter?"

"Small space in the cabin. Small but enough. Food from the galley kitchen, all included in the price of course. It is a luxury indeed. Luxury." His head bobbed with enthusiasm as if he were sending us on a royal tour of the Great River.

"Very good. I thank you for making the arrangements. What do we do next?"

"Of course, Of course. Any friend of Tharbazus is a friend of mine. But we must settle the price," he said, looking apologetic.

"What will this cost us?"

Thefeni went back to rubbing his ample jowls. He put on a great show as he tensed his eyebrows and tapped the table. "For you, forty copper coins, royal standard."

The swine.

"Fifteen," I said.

Thefeni's generous body shook with mirth as if I had made a great joke.

"I will be laughed out of the harbor, laughed," he protested, looking very anguished at my counter. "It is a fair price, much lower, much lower than my standard!"

Eurydice shook her head. I kept a stoic composure.

"All we want is a ride and little else. Forty is preposterous."

"Not at all. Not at all. Make a reasonable offer. If I accept fifteen, then Nismet here will murder me for my incompetence and take over my business." Thefeni and his assistant both laughed, no wonder a worn-out well-practiced joke.

"Eighteen. Not a coin more. I have traveled the world, Thefeni, you are not dealing with a village idiot."

"Not at all, not at all. My heart bursts with love for any man of Tharbazus! Bursts!"

Eurydice looked at me and rolled her eyes. Tharbazus had told Thefeni that I was a thug, so I wondered where Thefeni's love came from.

Thefeni sighed loudly. He stretched his arms and made a great show of tumult. And then he whispered in Nismet's ears.

"Eighteen. I accept." He stood and enveloped me in a sweaty, foul-smelling mass. The stench of Perdiccas' half-burned troops was preferable to Thefeni's body odor.

"I will pay five in advance, five after we board, and the remaining eight to the captain when we disembark."

"Five now is too low. Very low." He protested and thumped his chest like a bad actor.

I held position, and he relented. I paid him, and we turned to leave.

Thefeni made sure to remind us.

"Ship leaves harbor as soon as the moon reaches halfway, make sure to be there. I have made great arrangements, very great!"

A cool wind blew from the open sea. The moon was past the zenith. The grain ship was busy with activity.

It was a beautiful vessel—painted on each side with various Egyptian deities and Greek gods. It was a large ship with at least three levels and tall, impressive masts.

Eurydice and I watched, hiding under an inverted boat supported by logs.

Men stood on the sides, slaves lighted lamps, supervisors yelled and screamed at workers to complete departure procedures, and soldiers milled around. Sellers crowded the areas hawking their last-minute wares to the sailors—sweets, clothes, magical potions to perform like a bull, perfumes—Alexandria lived night or day.

A rough man, the captain I guessed, stood at the bottom of the loading plank shouting angrily at a harried Thefeni.

I strained to hear the conversation.

"They are not on board, Thefeni, you are testing my patience!"

"Meurius. Meurius. What if they slipped past your eyes?"

"No one slips past my eyes, are you stupid? You have been here before the moon rose. My sentries have been on watch. No one has seen them."

The furious captain continued his tirade.

"You have delayed my ship. The winds are picking up, and we will not be ready to leave in the morning. I must pay my crew an extra day because of your nonsense. Tell your military goons to get off my ship, or there will be hell to pay!"

I watched Thefeni consider his options. He signaled an assistant who went up the loading platform into the ship.

The captain had his arms crossed and continued to shout at Thefeni, who now looked like he would rather be flogged.

We then watched heavily armed Macedonian soldiers come to view. My heart beat rapidly as each man stepped off the loading plank and stood on the ground.

The last man was a giant. And he had a strange contraption which tied his jaws to his skull, like a monster from children's stories.

Nekh-Aser.

The Egyptian towered over a terrified Thefeni, and I could not hear what he growled through his broken jaws—thanks to my handiwork.

"I swear, I swear they came to me. He and his witch of a wife."

And after a few testy exchanges, the soldiers got ready to leave. I heard Thefeni whine one last time.

"Will I be compensated in some way for trying—"

Nekh-Aser backhanded Thefeni, who screamed in terror and fell to the ground. He grunted as one of the soldiers kicked him in his large behind. His assistant stood paralyzed.

Nekh-Aser stood straight. He then turned and looked around slowly, and at one point I sensed his eyes connect with mine. Eurydice stiffened beside me. I held her hand.

But of course, in flickering night lamps and torches, all Nekh-Aser would see was a play of shadows. He turned, and his men vanished into the darkness.

We waited until all men left and the lamps on the ship went dark. The sellers disappeared into the night. We made our way to the far western quarters that was still developing and inhabited by the poor and the wretched.

A willing homeowner allowed us in, accepting us as vagrant travelers, in exchange for a coin—a steep price for what was nothing but a little mudroom.

We waited until our nerves calmed.

"How did you know?" asked Eurydice.

"Have you ever seen an experienced merchant accept a counter less than half his price and barely haggle?"

She looked at me thoughtfully.

"Thefeni is Persian. I have haggled with more than thirty-five Persian merchants for reasons big and small, and not one of them settled like this. I can tell you the opening and settled price on every transaction in the last ten years."

She smiled. "He must have received word that there was a reward on our heads when we were there."

I nodded. "And he sold us out."

We had come within a finger's width of capture and torture. We had to get back on the ship tomorrow. I was sure no one would come back looking for us.

But first I would visit the fat man.

Thefeni stayed at an opulent house close to his tent. I knew he lived alone, a detail he had shared with me while looking hungrily at Eurydice. He had no guards for the house. Alexandria was not a haven for thieves—the rapidly growing trade and construction businesses employed most people. Thievery was not worth the risk of capture and execution.

Local protectors walked the streets now and then, keeping an eye for unscrupulous elements, but no one was around now.

I climbed the wall and tiptoed towards the door. A quick inspection of the open windows, left so to allow air, showed Thefeni asleep on a large bed, with nothing but a loincloth.

He snored with his mouth open, and his stomach rose and fell rhythmically.

It passed my mind that as he slept fitfully, we might be in the hands of Nekh-Aser, in torture, or already dead.

I used my tricks and opened the lock.

And then I tiptoed to his room.

I rushed across the floor and thrust a thick cloth into his mouth.

Then I punched him hard on his belly.

Thefeni's eyes opened wide, and his neck snapped up. He tried to scream, but nothing came out.

I punched him in his belly again—he doubled in pain and pulled his legs up to his stomach.

I then thrust a finger in the ring that hung from his ear and ripped it off.

He screamed in agony; the shouts muffled under the rag.

Then I straddled him.

"Scream, and I will stab you in the eye."

He nodded vigorously.

I removed the gag, and he heaved. Nothing came out except guttural sounds, and he threw up on the bed. The stench was overpowering.

"Answer my questions, and I will walk away."

Nodding.

"How did Nekh-Aser find out about us?"

"W-Who?"

"The Egyptian."

"Reward. Ten gold coins. Y-You and your wife... Please..."

"Does the whole city know?"

"N-N-No. Discreet. Big merchants, traders…please…"

"Name of the grain ship captain?"

"Meurius, yes, Meurius, great captain!"

"Honorable?"

"Yes, yes, yes."

"Does he know who I am?"

"No. He has no idea. None."

"Will you speak of me to anyone tomorrow?"

"No, no, not at all," he grunted and held his ears to stem the bleeding.

"If there is even a hint that you opened your mouth, I will hunt you down, slice you piece by piece, and feed you to the crocodiles."

He nodded, and then placed a palm over his stomach and began to nurse it.

I stood up to leave but asked him one last question. "Does the Egyptian know Tharbazus employed me?"

Thefeni bowed and began to weep.

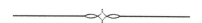

I ran to Tharbazus' house. I ducked behind narrow alleys, avoided startled dogs, and jumped over the occasional sleeping vagrant. It was a quiet night, bright enough for me to run without the help of a torch.

It was quiet in Tharbazus' house. I checked to ensure no one was watching the house.

And then I tapped the door.

Wake up!

I whispered through clenched teeth.

"Tharbazus, wake up, this is urgent!" I tapped on the door several times, using the ring on my finger to make a metallic sound on the iron lock on the door.

I heard the bolt click, and his wife peered through the door.

"Deon?"

"You need to get out now. Where is your husband? Tell everyone to leave!"

I made my way into the house. "Wake everyone up."

She did not panic. I admired her poise—this woman was accustomed to dangers because of her husband's trade.

"What is going on?"

"This is not about your husband's work. The military is looking for me, and the man who heads the soldiers now knows I lived here. And he is a very, very evil man."

She nodded. And without question, she roused the household quickly and efficiently.

Everyone was present except—

"Where are your husband and son?"

"They went on some business south of the city, expected to return in the morning."

I cursed. "We cannot wait. Do you have a place you can go to, a secure second home?"

"We have a small farmhouse no one knows about, further west."

"Go there, now. Avoid the main street, stick to alleys. All of you."

"Are they in danger?"

I looked at her calm face in the flickering candlelight. She was strong.

"Maybe. I will watch the house and warn them if I see them heading this way."

She gathered some bread, meat, a few candles, coins, and herded her family out the door. I watched them dissipate into the night and sighed with relief.

I found a well-concealed viewing point nearby.

And I waited in silence.

I did not have to wait long. A small group, hunched in the darkness, wearing capes, approached the house. I could make out that they were dragging two adults.

Tharbazus and his son.

Nekh-Aser was behind them, kicking and punching. Tharbazus resisted, but one of the officers pulled the boy to the side and made threatening gestures. Tharbazus relented, and soon they were inside the house. I felt helpless. There was little I could do from here. As I mulled my options, the men streamed out of the house. Nekh-Aser paced around, agitated. He made several gestures at Tharbazus, who, it was clear, had no satisfactory answers to the Egyptian.

How could he? We were not at his house, and he had no idea where we were. But he must have taken some comfort in the fact that his family was no longer in the house.

They made the son kneel on the ground. Tharbazus continued to make frantic gestures.

Nekh-Aser lifted his spiked club and brought it down on the son's head. The boy collapsed, and his father sagged and fell to the ground in a heap of despair.

Nekh-Aser did not stop.

He turned towards Tharbazus and swung again, like a crazed executioner smashing a bull's skull as I had seen in some rituals. The swinging continued until all that was left of the lender was chunks of flesh and shattered bone, splattered on the dry Alexandrian ground.

I vowed on all that is holy that I would wreak a terrible revenge on this godless man.

We learned that Nekh-Aser had left Alexandria to go to the eastern town of Heraklion. Did Tharbazus mislead them in his last moments? I would never know, but if he did, I prayed eternal happiness for him and his child in the afterlife.

I asked Eurydice to stay hidden, while I resolved our travel plans. It was not hard to find Meurius near the docks. I followed him at the markets as he went about his daily business.

Meurius looked every bit a veteran Greek captain. Curly hair, dignified stubble. He walked with a slight limp. He dressed more in a manner akin to the Egyptians, no doubt to please the land he was doing business with.

I finally caught up to him.

"Greetings, Captain Meurius."

He jerked at my sudden intrusion. His eyes narrowed. "Greetings. And you are?"

"A fellow soldier. Never had the privilege of working for *Navarch* Nearchus."

He raised his eyebrows at my mention of the famed Alexander's admiral. Nearchus had led the King's navy from the Indus on the journey back to Persia.

"It was you the military was looking for yesterday."

Astute man.

I nodded. And a sly smile spread on his face.

"How did you know I was with Nearchus?"

"Your tattoo."

He glanced over his shoulder. And there was a distinct little figure of a boy holding two twigs and standing on what seemed like a raft — a symbol I had seen on the soldiers aligned to the Navy.

"Where were you?"

"Riding through Gedrosia with Alexander."

"A terrible journey."

"Even gods make mistakes."

We both smiled ruefully. That desert voyage had cost thousands of lives.

Meurius walked into a fruit seller's stand. "I did not think you would notice a little symbol."

"People say I have a good memory."

"Not better than my wife. She remembers what I did fifteen years ago," he said, as he picked an orange and inspected it.

We both laughed.

"How did you come to this business?" I asked.

"I discharged after we reached land. Got tired of war. Made some connections, used the money from the campaign and started this enterprise. Good so far," he said, looking at the harbor, his new livelihood away from the blood and tears.

"I need your help, Captain."

We continued to walk along the busy path. Someone behind was shouting, "Pottery! The finest pottery from Cyprus you will ever see!"

Meurius kept his head down as we walked. "You are a wanted man, why should I take the risk?"

"A minor dispute. They will not come back looking for me." I hoped he would take me at my word.

"The trip is not free."

"I understand. I will pay what I promised Thefeni."

"He will not be happy."

"He does not need to know."

Meurius nodded and pointed at me. "If the soldiers come back I will hand you over to them. I cannot risk my business and employees, even for a fellow soldier."

"I understand. When should we embark?"

"Wait until the sun sets. I will look for you once we turn off most of our lamps."

"I will be with—"

"She is not your wife—"

"No. But she is dear to me."

"I do not know what you are up to, but I do not want to know," he grinned.

"Thank you, captain. Someday I will repay you."

"I hope I will not come to regret this," he said, without expression.

"I promise that you will not. But you should know our destination is not Athens."

"So where do you plan to disembark?"

"Somewhere after Crete."

It was now time to ask that critical question. "Are you aware of any island shaped like an eye, on the way?"

I waited in anticipation.

Captain Meurius raised an eyebrow.

"An eye? Well, I don't know about an eye, but there is an island not far from Crete that looks like one. Long ago I heard they used to call it Stronghyle, the round one, you can see for yourself."

Excitement crept up on me but I did not show it to him. Would this island be the ghost's eye? The land of the original Atlantean empire? We would soon find out. "Wonderful, we may disembark there."

The Captain continued, "That is an unusual request. That island gets very little trade traffic due to the poor harbors and very deep water by the cliffs. What are you looking for, there? It will cost, you understand."

"I understand."

"Where do you plan to go?"

"Phrygia. Through Halicarnassus."

"Ah, there is some traffic that way. But be careful—you will come across the military and pirates."

How wonderful.

But things had gone better than I hoped. Unless Meurius was another dirty double-crosser, we would be able to move forward. I thanked the captain and headed back to Eurydice, who, I knew, would be waiting with a tense stomach.

We bought fresh garments before boarding, and apart from what was in the bag, nothing indicated that I was a soldier or Eurydice anything but a farmer's wife. I wore a light *chiton* but no *chlamys,* a basic leather belt, and tied sandals. She wore a cream tunic that ended at her knees, a *straphion* to hold her breasts, and a leather belt that looked no different than mine. We purchased a simple threaded necklace made of fake gemstones and two earrings because she complained she did not want to look like a boy. She had cut her hair to shoulder length after I warned her of the risks of long hair when in fights.

It was time to say goodbye to Pharaoh Ptolemy.

I had never seen such deep turquoise.

The sea extended all around us, and a pleasant breeze whipped our face. We watched the ripples on water as the grain ship sailed on its way to Athens, now past Crete.

"Glad to share this second meal with you both," I said, as I greeted the captain and his right-hand. They bowed in acknowledgment.

"Always glad to share stories with a fellow soldier. You both appear to be enjoying your time on the deck," said Meurius.

"The isolation in the cabin was a comfort for the first three days, and then we could take it no more."

They laughed. We sat on worn wood stools around a little meal table. Eurydice joined us, and the men kept a respectful distance unsure if she was high born. The meal was broth and salted fish, it stank, but we were grateful for the hospitality.

Even the lousy beer tasted excellent. Conversations in the previous meals centered on our personal lives and military experiences. Nothing that was particularly interesting. But today I wanted to explore the legends in this region to see if I could glean anything useful.

I turned to the Captain. "So how active is this trade route?"

"Very active. This is not new. It has existed for thousands of years," remarked Meurius.

"Egypt sends grain, gold, papyrus, ivory. Greece sends wine, olive oil, pottery," added Theocydes.

"Has Egypt always owned these routes? I have heard of fantastical stories of the great Pharaohs."

Meurius made a dismissive sound. Who could surpass the Greeks? "Exaggerated stories. Some Pharaohs traded with Phoenicians in Tyre and Sidon. Legends say there were, long ago, even greater seafaring nations."

Eurydice's eyes connected with mine for just a fleeting moment. "What seafaring nations? Weren't our forefathers, the Myceneans, and the Ionians the lords of the sea?"

Theocydes expanded his chest and furrowed his brows like a teacher imparting great wisdom to his ignorant pupils. "Yes, they were good seafarers. But there was another group, small but powerful, and controlled the waters. They influenced our forefathers. They traded with most ancient posts."

"Never heard of them."

"They only exist in memories and stories told from father to son."

"What happened to them?"

"No one knows. The underworld opened and swallowed them!" Theocydes laughed and looked around. No one joined him.

Meurius shook his head at his lieutenant's flippant answer.

"The veterans of the sea talk of a story where these ancient men's greed angered the gods, and a great fire came upon them."

My heart began to beat faster, but I kept my poise. Eurydice spoke for the first time.

"I heard a similar fable in my childhood, what is yours?" she asked, shifting her mesmerizing eyes between the men.

Theocydes now felt the urge to share his knowledge. I was not about to stop him.

"You must tell me your legend, Eurydice. I am sure it is most interesting."

Lay off the charms, old man.

"A man must show his wares first," she said, batting her eyelids. It was the most shameless flirtation, and we all knew it. Theocydes laughed, and Meurius shrugged.

"The stories say the sea people became very wealthy through plunder and dishonesty. They mistreated the people they traded with. One day, the enraged gods brought fire upon them and destroyed their empire. Their peoples vanished from history."

That was interesting, but nothing particularly groundbreaking. My spirit fell. But Eurydice would not let go.

"That is not much of a legend. Not even interesting."

Meurius laughed, and Theocydes feigned outrage. He rolled his eyes, threw back his luxurious graying hair, and scratched his beard.

"Well, it seems the lady wants to hear the bombastic stories rather than realistic ones!"

"No one likes to hear boring stories," she retorted.

"Agreed. Let me tell you the fantastic story about what happened to these so-called masters of the sea."

My ears perked up again. I took another swig of the beer and nodded at Meurius, who encouraged his lieutenant. "Well, Theo, they want to hear, and we have nowhere to go," he said, gesturing at the blue expanse all around us. The sun was beginning to set, and it was exquisite.

"Long ago there was a great Pharaoh named Sakho-pet—these Egyptians and their names!" He shook his head, and Meurius agreed.

"The invaders raided the Egyptian coasts. Their boats were five times as tall, ten times as long, and ten times faster than the Pharaoh's. They harassed the Egyptian navy, the farmers, and traders all the time."

He grinned at the incredulity, and we smiled along.

"The people rose in revolt against the Pharaoh, what kind of a God was he if could not stand up to these heathens?"

"No good, no good at all," I said and swallowed a large piece of fish.

"So, he tried fighting them, to no avail. Then he tried negotiating. He sent two of his sons, ten of his finest Generals, his beloved daughter as a hand in marriage. He also tried to bribe them with gold and silver."

"The Pharaoh appears not of sound mind—" I began, Eurydice slapped my wrist and Meurius held a finger to his lip.

"Keep your mouth shut and listen. This is a legend!" admonished Theocydes. But his eyes sparkled with mirth.

"The king of the sea invaders was a tyrant and saw no point in negotiating from a position of strength. He displayed great cruelty on the negotiating party. First, he had the generals flayed in full view of the Egyptian navy and had their bodies thrown into the ocean. Then, disregarding counsel, he placed the sons in a cage, overhanging a cliff of their island city. They starved to death. As a final act of degradation, he had the princess stripped, whipped, and sent back in chains. Humiliated, she leaped to her death from the ship and became one with the sea." Theocydes stared at us, willing us to imagine the horrors.

"What a nasty man," I said. If there was a kernel of truth, it was despicable to mistreat negotiating parties. As ruthless Alexander was, he often treated the surrendering people with kindness.

Theocydes knew he had a captive audience. The attention of a beautiful woman and a compatriot fueled his storytelling desires. The heavenly hues and the strong beer helped.

"This enraged the Pharaoh, but there was little he could do. The sea invaders dwelled on an island protected by an invincible navy. He tried to starve the tyrant's kingdom by preventing grain shipment from the coasts. So, the sea invaders' king wrought terrible havoc. Flying demons launched from the invader's boats and crashed into the Pharaoh's towns."

"What do you mean flying demons?" Eurydice asked, almost reading my mind.

Theocydes chuckled.

"Who knows? Legends say they came streaking from the sky and set great fires when they landed. Nothing like anyone has ever seen."

I looked at Eurydice.

A wicked king.

Came from the sea.

Terrible, almost magical weapons.

"This is much more interesting," said Eurydice, playing with her hair, and pouting her lips.

This woman.

Theocydes continued, "That was not the end of it. The sea invaders often launched vials of foul sickness into the coastal populations. The people developed terrible afflictions, bled from their orifices, and died imploring gods.

In despair, the Pharaoh decided to do the only thing left—appeal to the mercy of his gods."

"Let Anubis swim up to this island and bite the king's buttocks?" I said and drew angry admonitions from the captain and his lieutenant.

"Deon, let us not insult their gods."

Chastened under six pairs of glaring eyes, I focused on the fish and hung my head.

"Anyway, he held a great feast at the palace, summoned his highest priests, and made a pact with their demon god."

"Why not with the good god?"

Eurydice slapped my hand.

"I will crack your skull with that grain ladle," scolded Theocydes, but he continued. "Who knows, Deon? I am telling you a story, so listen. If the god destroyed the invaders, the Pharaoh would sacrifice ten thousand of his people."

"He thought the sacrifice was better than the destruction of his entire Kingdom?" asked Eurydice.

"That would be my conclusion," said Theocydes. The sun was about to set, a small sliver of red peeked from the edges of the boundless sea.

The Captain rose from his seat and went downstairs on a task, asking leave of us for the night.

Theocydes continued.

"Soon after the pact, the sea invaders' island began to tremble. And Seth compelled an enormous fire to explode from beneath the seas and engulf them. Their king and citizens perished in three days, and their brutal reign ended. Egypt was free, and the seas were open for trade."

"What happened to that island?" I asked.

"The legends say that the gods left behind a king's blind eye. Whatever that means."

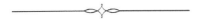

"We will first encounter a small island on our way," said Meurius.

"How small?"

"Too small. We have never seen any inhabitants there."

I thought about that. There was no way a little island would be the sea invaders kingdom.

"But after that, we will encounter the one you want to disembark on."

"Have you ever been there?"

"No. But I have heard there are some minor settlements."

"Yes, that would be the one."

If nothing else, we would use that as a point of transit to go on our way without entering Athens.

Meurius was kind enough to steer the ship to get closer to islands. We first saw two islands, one larger and one smaller, but of no exciting feature. Then Meurius steered the ship slightly eastward.

"We will reach before sunset, so get ready to disembark. Pack food and water. Take blankets as it gets chilly in the nights."

We thanked him and prepared to leave the ship. Theocydes bid us goodbye, and we stood on the deck in anticipation. Tailwind was favorable. As the sun shone in cloudless skies, we saw the first distant visages of the much larger island ahead.

As we got closer, I noticed that this was an unusual formation. We were passing by a tiny island, but on either side, not too far away, were imposing cliffs in a giant arc.

My fingertips tingled, and I gestured Eurydice to join me. As the ship neared, the features became much clearer. The imposing cliffs were part of a large circular island. In the middle of this ark, under the seas, was the hazy feature of a sunken island.

My stomach tensed as I watched.

A big arc.

Sunken, hazy land in the middle under the sea.

How would it look like to a bird?

Like an eye.

Blind eye.

I remembered the words in the letter and muttered them.

My spine tingled, and I looked at Eurydice. She was staring at the landmass around and ahead of us. But I did not know if she had made the connection or even if she remembered the letter or poem.

I brushed her elbow, and she looked at me. I moved closer, bent my head low, and whispered.

As a warning to man's greed, all that was left of a once glorious empire was an island, now but lifeless rock and ash, like a blind eye as it looked to the heavens in despair.

She jerked as if touched by a thorn and her eyes lit up.

We bid goodbye to Meurius and his crew.

"Whatever it is that you two are up to, I hope the gods bless you and keep you safe," he said, and saluted me in a gesture of kinship.

"I am grateful for your support and wishes, Captain. May you have a prosperous life, and may Poseidon bless you and your family," I said, as I saluted back.

We clutched our belongings as we made our way down the ship. We waved as they sailed, and then turned our heads to the massive towering cliffs.

There was an ancient, yet visible, worn path cut into the walls.

We reached the flat ground by sunset. The climb was exhausting, but the view was spectacular. We forgot our mission and other horrors and sat by the ledge to watch the sunset. It was getting cold, but holding Eurydice was an incredible feeling.

I hoped she felt the same.

What would become of us at the end of this journey was in the hands of powers beyond our comprehension. I would take Eurydice, and my beloved wife Apollonia, to someplace where I could wed a second woman. As if she read my mind, Eurydice turned and smiled. We rested for the night after a dinner of dried meat and dates.

There was much to do.

In the morning, when we stood by the cliffs, it was clear that the island was a large arc, and we were at the center of it. Now that we were here, we had no plan on what we would do next. The clues would not be sitting there for us to find as soon as we landed.

If there were any clues at all.

Far ahead were desolate mountains. To either side was undulating land with sparse vegetation.

"Where should we go?" I asked.

"Well, we could go straight, or we could go to our left or the right."

I slapped her bottom, and she squealed. "Let us go North. I see nothing ahead," I said, we had to begin somewhere.

We turned left and walked North. The earth was a tapestry of colors—black, red, and white. The surface in many areas was white and pockmarked, like hardened ash. But the walk was not strenuous, and we kept pace. The sun inched up in the sky, and we saw no signs of habitation, though the path looked man-made.

I began to worry.

Are we going to die here?

Is this island cursed?

My head filled with these thoughts when Eurydice tugged on my hand. "Look."

At a distance, the island curved sharply to our left, but up ahead on a low hill we saw several little dwellings.

"Thank you, Apollo!" I said and fell to my knees.

She rolled her eyes. "Were you that worried?"

"Yes, Eurydice, if you have not noticed we are somewhere in the middle of the Aegean Sea. And this island was once destroyed by divine fury."

"You are not a bright traveler," admonished Kadmos, the elder in this little hamlet of thirty people. We sat by the shade of his small hut. Three men had met us on our arrival, and after satisfying themselves that we meant no harm, they welcomed us.

They were Spartans and spoke my tongue with an amusing accent. Kadmos wore nothing but a loincloth and paid no heed to his jewels hanging down.

"Indeed, I am not," I said, "but surely some ships would get us on our way to Phrygia?"

"No. There is little trade from here that makes it worthy of ships. Once every eight to ten days there are small fishing and grain boats that go to Crete, and a few to Athens."

I placed my face in my palms and rubbed my stubble. The second man, much younger, pleasant, and courteous, spoke up. "There may be another way. Did you come here from where you disembarked?"

"Yes."

He looked at us without another word. And then he ruffled the hair of his naked little daughter who came running and placed her on his lap. She hid her face in the nook of his neck and peeked from the corner.

They all smelled pleasant—like they had rubbed an aromatic oil on their bodies.

Eurydice smiled at the little girl, and she smiled back.

"You have not gone up the mountains?" He asked.

"Which mountains?"

"The ones you said you saw when you climbed the cliffs."

"Ah, yes. They looked desolate."

"There is an old, but a larger colony on a hill behind what you saw."

"Who are the settlers, and will they accommodate us?"

"Spartans. We have not been there in years—bad blood—but the town has grown, and there is some trade."

"What is the best way to get there?"

"Skirt along the eastern edge until you reach the hills. Or if you prefer to stay hidden, go the way you came and proceed eastward." He was confident and clear in his instructions. I believed him.

"How long will it take?"

"A full day to reach the base. And then half once you begin the climb, or more, depending on how fit you are."

The little girl was now on Eurydice's lap and was examining her earrings.

"Are there any other villages on the way, aggressive ones?" I asked as I looked around to make sure they were not lulling us into a trap.

"None. The island has only two settlements. Here, and Thera. The rest of it is not conducive."

"Thera?"

"That is the name of the old town on the mountain," he said, as he gestured his daughter to go to her mother.

We rested for the night, courtesy of Kadmos and the villagers. They were very interested in hearing about Alexander's campaign. For these isolated people, the stories of Babylonia, Persia, and India were mesmerizing. I may have exaggerated a few details of my heroism, but there was no one to contradict me.

Eurydice rolled her eyes and wrinkled her nose at times, but I paid no heed.

Late in the night, I walked out of the hut to stare up, and what a spectacular sight it was. Absolute darkness around us, the sounds of the seas below, and innumerable stars twinkled above. I have often wondered what they are, and the truth eludes me. Are they souls of the dead? Are they distant giant fireflies? Or are they more suns, just like our own, but only much further away?

I prayed to Poseidon to help us decode the ancient scribe's tantalizing clues.

CHAPTER 25.

ALEXANDRIA

Nekh-Aser sat in a tent with his men. They had been loyal so far—though a couple of them had objected to his ways. He would deal with them later. The old man had misdirected him, and he had spent days looking for Deon and Eurydice outside Alexandria, but it was as if they had vanished. No one in the surrounding villages had the slightest idea. He had then returned to Alexandria to check again, and the last few days had yielded little.

But today that had changed. The fat man who had pointed him to the grain ship was back again and said he had news. It was a pleasant evening. They had set up a tent near the shores away from the main harbor. Nearby, laborers paved the way for the most magnificent pathway that ran east-to-west. The news was that Ptolemy would soon shift his headquarters from Memphis to Alexandria. The din was maddening yet comforting.

Thefeni sat on a plush cushion along with his assistant. Nekh-Aser tried to project professionalism, though he would have preferred to whip Thefeni.

"News?" Nekh-Aser uttered the word under his contraption.

"Indeed. Indeed. A most interesting one," said Thefeni, rubbing his palms.

"Good."

"What a pleasure, such a pleasure bringing this to you, sir." His head bobbed, and Nekh-Aser wanted to punch him.

Thefeni's assistant fidgeted on the corner of his seat. Nekh-Aser flicked his palms to tell Thefeni to hurry up. He had no patience for the typical Egyptian barter.

"First there is the delicate matter. Very delicate. Of compensation," Thefeni said, "you benefit, and we benefit." He pointed to his assistant who shrunk under the Egyptian's gaze.

Nekh-Aser's muscles tensed, and the man seated next to him placed his arm on the Egyptian's shoulder. "Captain, how about I conduct this on your behalf?" he said.

Nekh-Aser looked at him, and back at Thefeni. He let out a breath.

The man began, "I am Polymedes, a very recent addition to the Captain's team. We are grateful for your help."

Thefeni beamed. To hear a military-man speak with such politeness was a change. Polymedes had the hallmarks of a well-read, well-traveled man—he looked impeccable in his uniform. Coiffured hair and gold rings on manicured hands exuded sophistication. Thefeni felt great relief for dealing with this Greek than the Egyptian brute.

"Very honored to meet you, Lieutenant, you have the most regal bearing, very regal indeed."

Nekh-Aser scrunched up his face. Polymedes bowed and smiled. "Now let us discuss compensation."

"Of course. Of course. The reward was ten gold coins, most generous indeed. But times have changed—"

Nekh-Aser rose. "Pig, let me give a reward!" He growled and his words slurred. He reached for his club, and Thefeni jerked in horror.

Polymedes gripped Nekh-Aser's arm and said firmly, "Captain, let me handle this. His excellency Ptolemy demands we deal with this sensitive matter."

Nekh-Aser quietened again.

"Continue, Thefeni," said Polymedes.

"The value has increased," he whispered. Then he furtively glanced at Nekh-Aser who now looked on with disgust.

"Increased by how much?"

"Not too much, not too much at all. Twenty gold coins is a very fair number."

"That is not very fair, sir. You are taking advantage of us," said Polymedes. He stood and crossed his arms.

"Not at all, not at all! Why would I be here if I did not want to help you wonderful gentlemen? Thefeni gets nothing," he said and bobbed his head in unison with his assistant as if they were pained at Polymedes' insinuation.

"You seek much reward, sir. Not nothing."

Thefeni spread his palms and smiled. "A small reward to take care of us, very small," he said, pointing to his assistant again, who seemed ready to run.

"Fifteen. Not a coin more." Polymedes said firmly.

Thefeni looked offended. "Twenty is the value, twenty, Lieutenant. Fair offer for a reasonable officer."

Polymedes' eyes turned cold, and his demeanor changed. He stepped forward, and Thefeni shrank on the cushion. Polymedes dropped his voice. "Would your nobility like to negotiate this further in our dungeon?"

Thefeni's face lost its color, and it seemed like his assistant was about to faint. "No need for more negotiation, none!" he declared. "Fifteen it is, indeed, for you most gracious officers of this great Kingdom." He bowed and clapped.

Nekh-Aser pretended to spit on the ground close to Thefeni's legs. The fat man retreated to his cushion. His assistant's eyes transfixed on the iron cage that held Nekh-Aser's jaws.

Polymedes intervened. "Tell us what you know. I hope it is worthy of the reward."

Thefeni nodded. He tugged on his meaty ear and the rings jingled. "We know where Deon and his companion went."

Polymedes nodded as Nekh-Aser looked on. "Go on."

"They boarded captain Meurius' ship the next day—that is, four days ago."

Nekh-Aser threw up his hands in surprise. "Joking!"

"Not at all, sir. Not at all. Those conniving bastards returned to board the same ship. They knew you would not check there again. That rat Meurius must have received a big payment. Very big."

"We will deal with the captain later, but how do you know this to be true?" asked Polymedes.

"Of course, of course, one of the Captain's men saw them come on-board and converse with the captain. He also found out more by talking to the captain's hand."

"What else did he find?"

"That their destination is not Athens. Not at all! They are disembarking somewhere on the way. They want to go to Phrygia."

"Phrygia?"

"That is what he heard. Phrygia, indeed."

Nekh-Aser and Polymedes looked at each other. This was getting intriguing—what were those two up to? Where did they plan to disembark?

"If we find that you are lying, then I will have you in chains and deliver you to the Captain. And he is not gentle with liars," said Polymedes, as Nekh-Aser nodded and caressed his club.

"May the gods burn my house if I lied, may they burn my hands! I did not lie the first time, and not this time," protested Thefeni. He bounced on the cushion and the assistant nodded furiously.

"We will find that out," said Polymedes.

"And now, kind sir..." Thefeni patted his considerable stomach.

"Of course," Polymedes whispered to an adjutant who returned with a small bag and handed it to him. Thefeni stood up after much effort and ambled up to Polymedes who gave him the bag. Thefeni counted the coins. He huffed, and his lungs labored as he picked each one and examined them.

"But this is only ten coins, only ten!" Thefeni protested.

"Your information does not tell us where exactly they will disembark. We have the whole sea to consider."

"That was not—"

Nekh-Aser walked behind Thefeni and struck him with a short whip. The fat man yelped. He then dropped the coins in a little bag that hung from a belt on his waist and walked out muttering. His assistant followed in relief.

Nekh-Aser turned to Polymedes. "What up to?"

"I have no idea. But there are few islands between here and Athens on trade routes."

"Crete?"

"That is the best guess. But there are some other islands further ahead, like Thera, which has some people."

Nekh-Aser strained to control the ever-present pain in his jaws. "Reach commander of Ptolemaic fleet."

"I will take care of that, sir," said Polymedes as he adjusted his chlamys and smoothened his hair.

"Leave in Bireme. Take soldiers, investigate Crete."

"Yes, sir."

"Bring them unharmed."

Nekh-Aser imagined Deon and Eurydice led out of a boat and seeing him. Polymedes was about to leave but stopped at the tent entrance.

"Sir?" He addressed Nekh-Aser.

"Yes?"

"We should check Thera too just in case."

Nekh-Aser grunted in agreement. Polymedes could check anywhere he wanted as long as he brought those two back.

CHAPTER 26.

AEGEAN SEA

We woke up to rains. Eurydice and I finally had time to converse in private. We found a rocky area with little natural caves and sheltered in one of them.

The rain created a sheer curtain that reduced visibility. Streams gushed from higher ground towards the cliffs. The smell of earth as water mixed with the mud was pleasing. But they brought unpleasant memories of the Indian monsoon.

It was time to plan our next steps.

"The stories tie up to the papyri," I said. Eurydice sat opposite me. She had tied her hair to a bun, and droplets clung to her cheeks.

Gorgeous.

"Theocydes' legend appears to have originated from similar sources," she said. She fiddled with her toe ring and continued, "The reference to the eye in the papyri and then in his story. The distinct features of this island. All these make me think we are on the right track."

"I agree, but not only that. The colors of the rock on this island match Plato's description of Atlantis. They all link!"

"Yes!" She said, her enthusiasm returning.

"We must figure out the direction that the priest refers to, for that is the next destination."

"Yes, can you recite those words?"

With glorious seas all around, and the great eye beneath his feet, the Lord he towered over the adoring masses, and as the rays of the rising sun shone upon his regal visage

She narrowed her eyes and concentrated. We began to debate the meaning of the words.

"The glorious seas all around and the great eye beneath matches well with where we are. Who is the Lord?" she asked.

"The King? Or a high priest."

"Did he float above the people? Did the poem not say towered over the adoring masses?"

"Well, they could fly if they had magical powers," I said, but in my heart, I had little confidence in that theory. I had traveled many lands and had heard a great many magical stories—but not once had they been real. I remembered from my reading that Herodotus, our famed historian, had said there were ants the size of dogs in the deserts of India, and others had talked of fantastical monkeys. And yet while the foliage of India was different to other places, her people were no more beasts and the ants no larger than anywhere else.

"What it means is he was at a greater height—a platform or podium constructed for prayers," she said. That was smart thinking and made sense to me.

"So somewhere on this island, they made a platform. And on that, the Lord stood and pointed towards a destination."

The rain had stopped. I stood up and looked around, hoping for a sign. "The question is where. But it seems clear to me that this Lord did the ritual at dawn, and he was facing the sun—so he was facing east."

"Maybe where he stood was destroyed?"

We did not know if the arc was a leftover from a larger island whose center god destroyed and sunk into the sea. If that were the case, then the high priest's platform no longer existed. I felt I was missing something but was not sure.

Then we debated the next few lines.

...and as the rays of the rising sun shone upon his regal visage, he lay his feet on the spine of fist that fought the disquiet water below, pointed upon the endless sea, towards the far desert

"Well, it says 'spine of the fist' which means there must be something that feels like a spine and goes down."

"Or does he mean a person's spine? Human sacrifice beneath his feet—" I stopped. It added no clarity to the discussion. We listened to the slowing rain and watched the sun's rays peek through the clouds and form a golden path on the waters below us.

"Without a place to start, we are stuck. If we cannot find the general direction, then the entire world is open to us! We will never find the true destination," I lamented.

She grabbed my hand and pinched the forearm.

"You are a very bright man, and you have so many ideas, you cannot give up. We found this island, did we not? That is the starting point. We should walk along the island, and something will give us clues to the next."

"Yes, goddess of Memphis," I said, and she pinched my shoulder. "You are right. Sitting here will do us no good. Let us walk along the edge of the path we came from, tomorrow, and go around the island."

"Why not go to the east as they said?"

"Because I want to cover everything. We do not know if we missed anything on the way. Besides, I want to be sure we don't meet hostility too early."

We bid good-bye to our hosts, resupplied, and began our long walk. We paid close attention to the features around us. Small hills with the strange white rocks with holes in them. Red cliffs with a thick gray coating on top. Anything to make any connection to the verses. But there was nothing.

After an entire day's walk, exhausted, we halted near the southern edge of the island. The beauty had worn off, and wariness and doubts set in. So far, all we had was that this was the island.

The next morning, we decided to walk across and reach the south-eastern edge, and then walk back North. The cliffs here were not as deep as on the western end, and the earth sloped down to the sea. As we trudged along this jagged path, seas to our right, we marveled at the desolation of the island.

Was this once the heart of a formidable empire?

We broke for lunch, ate our meager rations, and affirmed our plans that we would continue this way. There was some old pottery that I wondered could be from a town that existed long ago before the fiery extinction. We stood atop this higher ground and looked to the south and east.

The island curved eastward. Like the brow of an eye.

Many little hills to our left. Larger hills far to our North-East. The same that we saw when I climbed up the cliff from the ship. As we progressed on uneven ground, Eurydice, who was silent so far to conserve energy, spoke up. "Could the Lord be on top of a mountain?"

I paused. "Go on."

"Imagine that he got up a mountain, and then looked eastward."

Why did this not occur to me before? "Then the congregation could be below him..." It added up.

She caught up to me. "And if that mountain exists, then we can confirm this," she said, standing still, and looking around.

"If it still exists..." I said, sounding doubtful. But again, there was that nagging feeling at the back of my head that I was missing something. I hoped that the revelation would come to me at some point.

"Those mountains?" she pointed to the large formations ahead.

"We won't know until we get near and on top."

"Let us go near them then!" She sounded excited, and it rubbed on me.

We rested for a while. We got up and made our way to the southern edge of the hills as the sun crossed the zenith. We finally arrived at the foot of the mountains at sunset. There were two connected mountains, and the base extended to the sea. We then walked along the edge of the mountain near us until it reached the sea.

When we got near the water, I noticed something interesting. The mountain jutted further out to the sea than the rest of the island.

We then walked back south, away from the hills, until the entire formation was visible. I then asked Eurydice to stay on the land, while I waded into the water. I took careful steps until the water was chest high and looked at the formation.

The mountain pushed further into the sea like an extension dipped into the water.

That tingling sensation in my head intensified.

What is it?

As I stood contemplating, it finally flashed to me.

The thrill that I felt when I read the papyri.

The same thrill when I saw the cliffs of this island.

Now it all made sense.

I ran back to the shore and grasped Eurydice by her shoulders and shouted.

"We have to find the path to the top of the mountains."

She searched my face. "Tell me!"

"Not yet, Eurydice, not now. Not until we are on top of the mountain."

"What did you realize?"

"I do not want to test my fortunes with the gods, please follow me, and I will explain."

She sulked but did not press the matter. I had invoked gods and wanted to ward off bad luck. I let the breeze dry me though it was cold. I was now confident that the papyri were true.

"And that means we should climb and get to the town," Eurydice said, bringing me back to reality.

Were they friendly there? What would we face?

It had been more than ten days since our departure from Alexandria.

That night I dreamed that I was floating high on the azure seas. Beneath me, a raging conflagration engulfed the entire island.

Thousands screamed as they burned to death.

We resumed our journey in the morning.

There was already a well-worn path to the top since a town flourished there, but it was an arduous climb. We met a few people on the way who gave us curious glances, but none were hostile, and there was no armed presence.

We reached a point on the climb that was an intersection of two mountains–one to our right, and an even taller one to our left, which did not end at the sea. So, we continued right. The sun went past the zenith when I noticed the first structures. The ground leveled and began to dip. It was a most spectacular sight! The town, also called Thera, perched on the descending slopes of the mountain with the vast blue seas on either side.

It was a modest town with a central cobblestone path made of whitish stone. On either side were basic, rectangular houses, built of stone blocks. Men wore simple white robes around the waist, and the women wore tunics that left their upper body bare.

There were a few shops further down the slope along with a temple dedicated to Apollo cut into the rock. Worshippers congregated in the courtyard.

We went in.

"You appear to be new here," the priest said, and we both nodded. And then he engaged us in small talk.

We made up a story of nomadic travel, and I made vague references to a past military career. The priest agreed to board us for the night for a modest payment. The priest was chatty, and while he knew little about the town or the islands past, he told us to explore the central path until it ended. The next morning, we woke early and readied ourselves for the sunrise.

We walked down the slope along the central path which ended after a short distance. The unpaved road descended, and the ridge became narrower on either side. The view ahead was breathtaking.

My heart thumped as I descended. I stopped when it became too dangerous, and the mountain ended in a cliff that protruded into the sea below — the same protrusion I had seen the earlier day from the water.

When I turned, there was the unmistakable spine of the mountain. A King could be on higher ground, people lower on the slope, and he could point down the spine to open seas. The extension was like an inverted fist that dipped into the waters.

The gentle light of dawn finally led to the sun peeking in distant horizon and rising over the water. The skies were magnificent.

A light layer of blue on top.

Yellow below that.

And then orange-red.

I understood why the Spartans chose this place to build a town. Apart from the strategic advantage of height, it was too beautiful not to!

From where I stood, the sun was at an angle to my left. This meant that the ridge was towards the South-East. I held Eurydice's hand as I watched the mesmerizing sunrise, and I let my mind try to put it all together.

Every line from the documents.

Every story I heard.

Every geographic knowledge I had.

Every conversation with captain Meurius and his crew on direction and positions.

They all had to meet and give me an idea of where I would reach land if I went in the general direction pointed by the ridge.

And as the wheels in my head turned, it all began to come together.

He lay his feet on the spine of the fist that fought the disquiet water below, pointed upon the emerald sea, towards the far desert, where a knife's tip awaits

That was when I knew our next destination. It was going to be a long journey ahead of us. My heart danced in my chest, and my face broke into an idiot's grin. Eurydice had been watching me without a word, and she finally had enough.

"Can you tell me now?"

I looked to her, still grinning like a fool. "Yes, and I have a lot to tell you."

I took her to the western slope of the mountain overlooking the arc of the island below. We found a sandy spot that was devoid of grass. I picked a dry twig from one of the shrubs nearby and asked Eurydice to follow me.

My mind was clear, as clear as the morning skies.

"First, let me explain why this is where the king or the priest stood. Thank you for talking about the mountains."

She beamed with pride.

I told her how the larger mountain could not have been where the King stood, for it did not extend to the sea. And then how the one we were on jutted out as if there was a fist that met the waters beneath.

And how there was a spine that sloped down.

And how this ridge, and the formation below, pointed towards the east.

And how this was on the island that looked like a blind eye.

And how the island was so sparse, and it looked like a fire had burned the rocks. So, I concluded, this had to be the place. Eurydice's face glowed with anticipation—our harrowing journey was bearing fruit. She had asked me one question, a very astute one, and one that had bothered me a long time, so I had to address that.

"Remember you asked me what if there was a mountain in the center of this arc, but sank beneath the seas? And what if that was the high platform? If so, then were we in the wrong place?"

"Yes, that has bothered me," she said.

"Well, if that mountain was in the center, then no extension of it would have a spine that dips to the waters below. The details would not match."

She nodded thoughtfully.

"I do not think there was a mountain in the center at all; there may have been an island, nothing more. This," I pointed to our location, "is where we need to be."

She agreed, and I continued.

"Now let me tell you where I think this city is…" I said, and I shook my hips and moved my eyebrows like a Persian dancer and pumped my fists. She laughed.

"You managed to decode that? How?" Rays reflected off the limpid pools of her green eyes.

I pointed a finger to my lips, and she glanced around before leaning forward. It was time to describe the next part of my thinking. "Pay attention." I drew a circle on the sand, rubbing the twig enough of a visible indentation on the ground. Then I drew sixteen lines dividing the circle as she watched.

I began to explain like she was my student. It was great to bring out the teacher in me. "If I extend each line over the seas, they will end in some distant place, on land, correct?"

"Yes."

"So, you can imagine this circle and its lines to represent all corners of the land and the direction."

"Hmm…yes."

I pointed to the cardinal lines.

"See these big lines? I have drawn them to align with the sun and the North Star. The line point forward is towards the rising sun, and the one to our left, the North Star. The spine descends to the sea below is not quite to the east—it points slightly to the right, so the south."

"South?"

"Well, that is the direction that is opposite to the North Star. West is where the sun sets."

She nodded. She had no formal training in philosophy or mathematics, but she was bright enough to grasp the idea.

"We came from Alexandria, through Crete. I remember the sunrise and sets, the wind directions, and the Captain's words—we sailed North-West to get here. Is that too hard to understand?"

"Not at all, not at all. When a fine, almost bald, officer explains," she said, mimicking Thefeni's accent and mannerism. I laughed.

"Be serious!"

"I am most serious, of course very serious, sir," she said and rubbed her palms while arching her eyebrows.

"Eurydice!"

She snorted like a pig, and I returned to my explanation. "That is the direction the Lord pointed to, and he pointed following a landmark—this spine."

"I understand now."

"I know from Ptolemy's, Anaximander's, and Hecataeus' maps that the south is Egypt and Libya. Somewhere there—" I pointed to the West and North, "are Greece, which long ago was Mycenae, and Macedon."

I continued, "To our east are Phrygia and Cappadocia, but they are away from the direction of the spine, and there are no deserts there."

"These details are beyond me."

"Now let us match this geography with politics. If the Atlanteans wanted to build a second city, and were already at war with the Egyptians, would they try going there?"

"No."

"They worried about the Mycenaeans—would they go there?"

"No."

"Cappadocia and Phrygia are possible but have no deserts. Libya and Egypt, as I said, are to the south. Where else could they go?"

She gripped my shoulder. "Eurydice demands that you tell her, soldier, for Eurydice has no idea," she said, mimicking Ptolemy.

"Phoenicia. Anywhere from the entrance to Egypt to Tyre, Sidon, or even a little further North. That is the only place that remains, and we can most certainly eliminate the vast regions of Libya."

"Are there no islands from here to the land?"

"There is Cyprus. But it does not have deserts, canyons, and nothing seven days from the sea."

Then she realized something. "We came through Phoenicia!"

"Yes, but of course we had no idea. The descriptions tell us the rest. They land near a desert, which is how that region is. And then they walked seven days until they meet big hills."

"There are so many hills there."

"But there is one that I recollect the locals called the Knife's Tip, based on an ancient term."

I grabbed her hands and had her slap me.

"Why did we not check it when we were there?" she asked, pulling her hands back.

I turned and saw some inquisitive morning walkers. A child ran to us and stared at the circle I had drawn until his mother admonished him to come back.

"Because that term is not uncommon. Remember what the tribal chiefs said? There are many called *Knife's Tip*. It refers to jagged hills that sharply narrow at the end. I had little to make much of it."

"And our mission was first to reach the Regent—"

I nodded. The bright orange rising in the sky hurt our eyes, and we moved to sit beneath an olive tree. Lost in thought, we spoke nothing for a long time, only looking to the sea, the people, and time to time at each other.

"Now that we have a start, a path, and an end, it is time to get out of here," I said, as reality sunk in.

There was a presence behind me.

"The mornings here are like god's paintings, are they not, sir?" said the man, impeccably dressed in a crisp white tunic, well-groomed hair, and very Greek in his demeanor.

Theocratis told us that he was a merchant who traded with Egypt, Crete, Cyprus, and Phoenicia. He said he was a protégé of Cleomenes until Ptolemy put the man to death. He said he was here on behalf of Ptolemy's navy to see if they could set up a trading post and a small garrison here. I was alarmed, but it soon became plain that he was here on other business.

I called myself Demodocus, and Eurydice said she was Alexis. We said we were travelers and that I was a cook before I left to tend to fields. I said I had recently left Alexandria after working as a farmhand.

"I heard that there were two travelers on the island and sought company. I find it difficult to understand the way these people speak," he said, jerking his thumb at the town.

"It is an accent, typical of people who settled here long ago from Sparta."

"Very interesting. You look Macedonian, and your—" he looked at Eurydice, who surprised me this time by saying she was my wife.

"Ah, yes. Where is she from?"

"I met her during my campaigns with Alexander."

"You were with the great King Alexander?"

"I was. I fed the army all the way to India and back."

"I am honored to meet you, sir. There are many men in Governor Ptolemy's forces like you. Very impressive, honorable men."

I shook my head, "I was only a cook, but I accept the compliments," I said, and then remarked on Ptolemy. "I thought he was Pharaoh now."

Theocratis sniggered. "Well, he decided not to take the title. He calls himself the Governor. I wish I could meet the great man, but he is busy these days."

"Why did he send a merchant on military work?" I asked.

"I am a merchant, sir, but I did spend time in the military under Cleomenes. I am familiar with the Aegean."

"Why here? There is not much–"

"Ah, you land warriors know so little of the sea!" he exclaimed. His eyes darted to Eurydice as if to say, *look how dumb your man is*. I must admit I felt a pang of jealousy for Theocratis was a handsome, young, wealthy man—everything I was not. Perfect blond hair fell on his bright eyes, and he wore expensive garments and gold rings.

Even the embroidered footwear seemed exquisite.

I worried he might even seduce Eurydice.

"Please educate me," I said, with mock diffidence.

"This is a strategic island in the Aegean at the intersection of several trade routes. Have you not heard? Antigonus is flexing muscles in Greece and Phrygia. Ptolemy wishes to hold Egypt—so the control of the Aegean is critical. Ptolemy hopes to establish control here and deter foolish adventures from Athens."

"I am a cook and a farmer, Theocratis. The ways of our leaders escape me."

"Why don't you two join my men and me for lunch? It would be an honor to have Alexander's man with us," he said, as he gestured towards the town.

A free lunch, who would say no? Though it seemed strange that a wealthy merchant would care about a cook and a farmer. Or Alexander's name carried such reverence to those who never had a chance to ride with his army.

We dined with Theocratis' crew—five well built, Macedonian soldiers and an Egyptian. He said there were two galley masters who led the oarsmen, but they were on the ship. The made-up tent had a long rickety table at the center, and we sat on borrowed stools.

Theocratis said they would soon sail once a supporting vessel arrived to set up a basic army post.

The conversation was boisterous, and each man tried his best to impress the only woman at the table. Eurydice enjoyed herself but spoke little. No matter the reasons, it was still vital that we guard our secrets. The salty smell of the seas mixed with the aroma of local herbs, bread, olives, dates, lentil soup, and cooked fish.

"What is your plan, Demodocus? Are you both going to settle on this beautiful island?" asked Theocratis as he chewed on his food.

"No. We wish to move on. Somewhere East."

"How? Few trade ships these days."

"What do you mean? I thought grain ships still moved around."

"Very few. Athens wants to squeeze Egypt. Ptolemy, likewise, is holding merchants from leaving our ports."

My chest palpitated. My fears that hostilities were escalating among Alexander's successors was coming true.

He continued, "Besides, I am certain that our garrison will prevent any vessels not bound for Egypt."

"Well, that poses a problem," I said, looking at Eurydice. She furrowed her brows.

"Not if you tell me where you want to go unless that is a great secret," he said, and his men sniggered.

A server went around the table filling the cups with an awful local brew. She was naked from the waist up and slapped the hand of one of Theocratis' louts that tried to grab her wrist.

"Could it be that Demodocus is Athens' spy trying to run from Ptolemy?" One of his men chortled, "The secretive spy couple!"

I had to put an end to that. "We would be the dumbest spies then, dining with officers from Ptolemy's navy."

They laughed, and I decided I had to take my chances. "So where are you headed next, Theocratis?" I asked, chewing the hard bread, and sounding as nonchalant as I could.

"It depends," he said.

"Depends on what?"

"We have planned two potential routes before returning home. One, a scouting trip towards Phrygia. Other, towards Phoenicia, as Ptolemy wants to control the region. Sidon is likely."

My ears perked up.

Sidon? The gods were finally smiling upon me. "Sidon. Some of my wife's family are near Gaza."

"Does your wife have any sisters?" shouted one of the men, and the table howled.

Eurydice responded, "I doubt she will want you. You are too old." At that, his companions rubbed his greying head and mocked him.

Theocratis lifted his hands for everyone to settle down. We had not finished our conversation yet. "We came with another vessel which will return to Alexandria soon. It leaves soon as the winds are favorable in case you want to return to Egypt."

"I am grateful for your offer, but we do not want to return to Egypt, at least for now. But we would be grateful to join you for the Sidon trip."

"Excellent! It would be an honor to have you with us. We are yet to decide on our next course and will let you know by tomorrow. Where will you go in the meanwhile?" he smiled, gesturing towards the expanse around us.

We watched the island recede. The distinct "fist that fought the disquiet water below" was evident when seen from the sea. I wondered if that was what an escapee long ago saw before his words made their way into the verses. I could not believe our good fortunes, and we both had prayed to our gods for smiling upon us. It was an irony that an Egyptian navy vessel was helping us—only if Ptolemy knew!

Eurydice and I had more than once smirked and sniggered at the turn of events. But we also hoped that Theocratis would not get into trouble for having helped us.

Theocratis was a good host; the only time he frustrated me was when his men tried to persuade us to disarm. This was for all our safety, he said. I refused, saying that we were no pirates and it would make no sense for me to take on them on open seas. They relented, but I decided to keep my belongings, weapons, and my "wife" close until we arrived at Sidon.

The winds favored the journey. The vessel was an impressive modified bireme with twelve oarsmen on either side. A single sail emblazoned with Ptolemy's insignia of a man with a ram's top powered the boat. The builders had painted a green wolf either side of the hull.

The oarsmen were all Egyptian and Greek slaves. Hiring citizens had become expensive for dangerous sea work. There was plenty of opportunity in booming Alexandria—it was likely that these men were here on accounts of debt or other crimes. The masters treated the oarsmen well given the importance of their work. They kept to themselves, which was odd, as rambunctious camaraderie was quite common.

The seas were calm for the night, and we sat clustered on the deck for dinner.

"Where from Sidon are your wife's relatives?" asked Theocratis, as he broke his bread to small pieces before eating.

"Further west, a few days. We hope they are still there."

"And if not?"

"Then we may come back to Egypt to settle. You could even offer me a job. I am a competent trainer, and not bad with my hands."

"I could use a skilled hand. I have a feeling you may be back in Egypt even before you think," he said, grinning at both of us. I did not like him but did not know why.

"Why so?"

"Oh, where would you rather be in this climate? In the uncertain hot sands of the Levant, or the stable, growing cities of Egypt?"

He had a point.

Eurydice and I found a corner on the back end of the vessel, and we took turns sleeping.

My dreams were becoming increasingly unpleasant. In the last few weeks, the end scene always had me holding Eurydice, as my wife and daughter were dragged away—it was as if the gods were telling me that I was building companionship in abandonment of the ones I swore to protect. I often despaired going to sleep, but those images spurred me further to not only prevail but to take this quest to a happy end.

At some point in the night, Eurydice woke me and whispered that we were moving.

I thought we would stay afloat for the night. The moon was behind me, which was a little odd, as I expected it to shine to our left.

I stayed awake, unsure what was nagging me.

Dawn arrived, as did ominous clouds at a distance.

But I did get a glimpse of the rising sun, and instead of piercing our eyes, it was far too much to our left. The crew was navigating south, no doubt. The wind was picking up, and I made my way to the front of the galley, squinting my eyes as water sprayed on to the deck. Theocratis and two of his men stood looking at the dark, rising waves, and I noticed one of the men flinch as I neared them. "The sea is angry," I yelled over the sounds of the swells and the gust smashing against a rocking boat.

"Poseidon is not a happy god today," said Theocratis, pointing at the waves. "Afraid of the water?"

"I am no fan of seas and storms."

"Neither am I, but these are common occurrences."

"The winds seem to favor going east, so why are we headed south struggling against it?" I asked, pointing to the sun, and then arcing my finger to the south.

The man on the right, he had never mentioned his name, shot a glance at Theocratis.

"I, well, the oars master thinks this is how we should travel to avoid the worst of the storms, and then we turn again in a day."

They had not refuted my observation that the vessel headed south.

"Ah. I know little about all this," I said. "How long will this last?"

"It depends. A day at least."

I made a sign to Poseidon, and they laughed.

I then turned towards Theocratis, "A day, of course. Indeed, a day. Would I know more than the officers of the Navy? Not at all, not all," I said, and I rubbed my belly.

Theocratis' eyes flickered before he broke into a grin. I returned to the back of the vessel, and we stayed there for some more time.

Eurydice followed me as we walked holding the railing. The skies had gotten darker, and lightning streaked at a distance. Theocratis was with three of his men. They huddled under a makeshift tent on the deck, buffeting them against the gust. As we approached, I noticed them stand up and one of them gripped the hilt of his sword.

We did not enter the tent. I held onto a mast pole, as the rain began.

For a moment, it all brought back memories of the battle against Porus in India.

The greenery.

The swollen, brown river.

Elephants in the mist.

The dark clouds and the rain that began before the whistles of the battle.

But we were not in India, and there was no army to face, except an angry sea and sky.

"Why are you here?" Theocratis asked. His demeanor had changed, and his stance, look, and the way he moved gave away his military background. He inched back and picked up a sword behind him.

No more games.

"Why are we headed to Egypt, Theocratis?"

"Who told you that?" he shouted. And one of his men began to move towards me.

"Tell your man to stay where he is," I said.

Theocratis signaled, and they stopped.

The hostility was unmistakable. I looked around quickly; no one else was visible. The oarsmen and their masters were below. Two other officers were in the back.

Four against two. Or four against one-and-a-half considering Eurydice's size. I pulled my kopis out and pushed Eurydice behind me.

I reached back and felt the cold blade of her serrated dagger. A brand new one, very sharp, as we had purchased it before our departure from Egypt. Earrings, necklace, and a dagger. Fine purchases for a woman.

There was little space to maneuver where we stood. The vessel narrowed in front, and Theocratis and his band crowded the deck. One of his men kicked the supports of the makeshift tent, and we were now in the open.

A steady rain began to drench us, and the winds became ferocious. The vessel rocked as the waves slammed against it. Theocratis and his three men spread themselves as best as they could.

Theocratis stepped forward. "Listen to what I have to say."

"You can do that without coming near, go ahead."

"You are acting strangely. We are only turning south to manage the storm."

How stupid did he think I was?

"Time for lies is over Theocratis. I was not the advisor for one of Alexander's smartest generals for nothing."

He smiled. A mirthless, cold smile as rain splattered his hair over his eyes. He spat some water. "It is in your best interests not to fight."

"Why not?"

"Cooperate, and the Governor promises leniency."

I realized that Ptolemy had ordered him to bring us back alive and in good condition. Then I remembered something from our conversation from a few days ago. "Who will you hand us to?" I asked, as I wiped my face and steadied myself.

"Ptolemy. I will secure your safety and take you to him in Memphis."

Liar.

"And you promise not to inform our capture to captain Nekh-Aser."

"Of course."

He knew Nekh-Aser.

"How could you deliver me to Ptolemy in Memphis, if he is already on the way to Triparadisus as you told me a few days ago?"

The vessel swayed as a large wave slammed against the sides. Theocratis' men formed a chain to support each other. His demeanor changed. Gone was the polite negotiator.

Each man drew his sword and held it low.

"You have a choice, Deon, to secure your life, or die a painful death if you do not cooperate."

"You know my name too, how magical. It seems to me that there is no choice."

He ignored me. "Prolong this, and I swear you both will wish you were dead."

"You sound like that dirty pig, Nekh-Aser."

They inched forward.

The Egyptian officer to my far left.

Macedonian next to him.

Then Theocratis.

And then another Macedonian.

What fools we had been as we dined with them.

I nudged Eurydice to my side, and she held her blade in the open.

"Your whore holds that knife like she holds every cock!" yelled the Egyptian, drawing laughs from the others.

"Maybe if you had any dignity you would not be a Greek's bitch," she shouted back, mimicking my comments to Ptolemy in Memphis.

The Egyptian only laughed.

Then Eurydice spat at him and made a gesture. The Egyptian seemed deeply offended and screamed at her; then he charged.

Theocratis still held his ground and shouted, "Stand back! Stand back!"

But it was too late. Eurydice ducked his swing, and the momentum caused the Egyptian to lose his balance. Before he could react, her serrated knife glinted as she plunged it into his abdomen and sliced it upward.

He screamed and staggered back, and Eurydice stabbed him again, right between the legs. The Egyptian howled, and fell, writhing on the floor.

"Get back," I yelled, and she moved back to a narrow side passage on the side, ensuring only one man could engage her at a time.

The Macedonian to my left went after Eurydice.

Theocratis and his lieutenant stayed.

It was time to act.

I lunged on the wet, slippery floor towards them. Theocratis jumped in the front, and I kicked him hard in the stomach.

He flew back and fell.

I stood straight and turned to the lieutenant.

He raised his sword to parry my attack and realized too late that I had a knife in my other hand. As I struck a blow to his sword with my kopis, I thrust my blade into his chest.

He looked down in disbelief.

Not a sound as he dropped like a rock.

Theocratis was back on his feet. I could not turn to see what was happening with Eurydice.

The despair on his face showed. Nowhere to run.

I closed in on him as he stepped back. All his bravado stuck in his throat. My senses were right—this man had lived a comfortable life for too long, and he thought he was a real soldier.

The Egyptian's wailing dissipated in the lashing rain and crashing waves.

I watched Theocratis as I closed the distance.

Then I sensed a presence behind me. One of the oars masters was back on the deck through stairs that was closer to the sail mast. He stopped when he saw the sight in front him. I pointed my kopis towards Theocratis and knife towards the oars master. He seemed in shock and prepared to run.

"Don't run. Step slowly towards me and listen to what I have to say."

He hesitated.

"I said come forward, or you will face the same fate as those two," I said, pointing to the two men on the floor. He squinted at the bodies and the blood mixing with the rainwater that drained to the sides.

I signaled him to walk to my side and make an arc, between Theocratis and me. "Did you know that your commander planned to put you and your crew to death once you arrived at Alexandria?" I asked as thunder cracked above us.

"What?" The oars master sounded alarmed.

"He's lying!" shouted Theocratis, but still too scared to advance on me.

Where was Eurydice?

"You were part of a find and retrieve mission, and due to the nature of the secret, since you saw us, he would put you all to death."

The oars master stood frozen, unsure of what to make of what he was seeing and hearing. But the doubt in his mind was enough to keep him from trying anything stupid.

"Go down, say nothing to anyone. I will explain. No harm will come to you from me," I said.

"The governor wants him and his woman, there is no danger to you."

The oars master seemed in a trance, not listening, as rain beat on his chest and back. Shakily he walked back, all the while staring and saying not a word.

I hoped he would keep his mouth shut.

It was time to deal with Theocratis.

"Listen Theocratis, or whatever your name is, you have one chance to be truthful."

"Do you think you will get away with this?"

"All I have to do is join Antigonus and Ptolemy can do nothing."

Theocratis would know that to be true. He had no leverage over me, not here.

He wavered. "What do you want?"

"What we agreed on. Take us to Sidon—well, not exactly Sidon, but nearby, and we will let you go."

Silence.

"I have no desire to kill you Theocratis—"

"My name is Polymedes."

"Polymedes. You can go your way, and we will go ours. Now stay where you are and ponder over it."

He did not move. Facing him, I walked sideways towards the pathway where Eurydice had vanished.

With my kopis pointed forward, I began to walk backward, holding the ledge. And then Theocratis, no, Polymedes, did the inexplicable.

He lunged at me like a mad man.

I swung my kopis, but he had an advantage over me, and his strike dislodged the blade from my hand. I reached forward, grabbed his neck, and gripped his forearm with my right. He was unable to strike me with his sword. Polymedes may not have been an expert, but he had the strength of youth in him. We fought on the slippery floor that rocked us like an angry mother swinging her baby. We spit, strained to see each through the curtains of water, and grappled each other.

I was beginning to tire.

"Stop it! Save yourself when you can," I shouted, as I swallowed water.

"I was not sent here to save myself. Now surrender and give up." He shouted. It seemed like the gods of the underworld possessed him.

Or Nekh-Aser.

I had had enough.

I dropped on a knee, and he slipped. Then using all my strength, I rammed my head to his belly and pushed him against the guardrails. As he struggled, I wrapped my arms under his knees and lifted him off the ground.

Then I threw him overboard.

Polymedes shouted as he fell. But I had not thrown him far enough, for he managed to grip the barrier. He hung on the side and began to scream, "Lift me!"

I pulled my knife out of my sheath and looked down. I felt no pity staring into his frantic eyes. I placed the edge of my knife on his knuckles and sliced off his fingers like I cut vegetables. The sharp blade ripped through the tendons and cracked the bones.

He screamed in terror as he fell into the dark waters below. He frantically tried to grab the oars, but the powerful waves knocked him and pulled him away. The rain beat down on us, and Polymedes' shouts went unheard. His head bobbed in and out of the swelling seas and his hands raised in desperation.

I watched as he vanished behind another swell.

Then I ran to find Eurydice. Two figures were lying on the passageway.

No, no, no, no, no.

The Macedonian lay on her and his bulk hid her body underneath.

And there was blood. Everywhere. Pooling and not washed away even with the rain.

CHAPTER 27.

MACEDON

Their rescue from the slave caravan seemed like eons ago. The letter from Deon that he was well had lifted their spirits and kept Krokinos at bay. The relief was short-lived, for Krokinos was getting impatient again. The improved treatment had lasted only a few months, as the promise of repayment along with a handsome bonus had lifted Krokinos' spirits, and for a while, he saw Apollonia and her daughter as valuable possessions worthy of a modicum of kindness. But just as the foliage changes with the weather, so did Krokinos' mood and attitude as the winds got colder.

On this day he was losing his mind.

"Where is that bastard husband of yours? He sends an armed contingent to my house to pay a portion and layers that with promises. It has been months and I see no man walking through those doors with my money!" He screamed. He looked like a vulture about to pick on its prey, his head bobbing and beak nose moving back and forth as he gestured angrily.

"He will come, master. Why would he take the effort to send those men and pay a portion if he did not intend to return?"

"But he has not returned! I do not need an expensive servant and her useless daughter!"

Apollonia's face reddened at the slight and the remark on her daughter, who, still not yet of age, toiled like any grown woman.

"She works hard—"

Diona, who stood by Krokinos while he harangued Apollonia, now joined.

"She eats more than she works! The wench casts amorous eyes on my son and no doubt plans to steal him and our fortunes along with him!"

"She is too young for those thoughts, mistress!" Apollonia's voice rose.

"Who do you think you are, you whore, raising your voice!" Diona lunged forward and grabbed Apollonia by her hair and yanked. Then she viciously began to slap her, all the while cursing and drenching them all with her spittle.

Apollonia collapsed at the assault, and Diona let go—her chest heaving, face red, and her eyes ablaze with hate and a sense of power. Then she turned at her husband. "Why are they still in the upper-level quarters? What royalty are they that you decided to indulge them?"

"I was expecting Deon to return anytime, and it seemed like—"

"Seemed like what, husband? What makes you think that that charlatan will return to fulfill his fake promises? How long do you think you will coddle these princesses?"

"I am not—"

Diona would not allow Krokinos to finish whatever thought he had. "Are you trying to sleep with her? Aren't your whores enough?"

"No, by Zeus Diona, I never have—"

"Then move them to the basement! Let them stay with the wretched, and I swear if that son of a street donkey does not return in the next few months we will sell them, and this time it will be final! Final!"

"Yes, I will. I understand. I agree. Now let me take care of this and stop nagging me!"

The couple quarreled for some more time as Apollonia lay in a puddle of tears. Eventually, Diona left, leaving Krokinos alone with her. The sobs intermittently broke the dark mood in the room. Apollonia felt Krokinos' breath near her hair and his cold deathly grip on her shoulder. Apollonia tensed, and sat up facing her tormentor.

"Diona is worried, rightfully so. Our situation is far from what it used to be, what with all the happenings around," he said, and then began to caress Apollonia's back. She felt bile rise in her throat and saw the dirty lust in Krokinos' eyes. Apollonia shirked back. Krokinos did not stop, and this time he reached forward and grabbed Apollonia's breast, whispering, "I can make it better for both of you."

She recoiled, pushing his hands away. "Please do not lay your hands on me," she said, meeting his eye. Krokinos was stunned at the display of resistance, and the rejection stung him. Rejection from a woman who would be a slave! Undeterred, Krokinos pushed himself on her, this time trying to disrobe Apollonia. With all her might she struck him on his chest, causing him to lose his balance and fall. Krokinos scrambled to his feet and began to shout, veins pulsing under his temples and throat.

"You harlot! Your husband borrowed money so he could employ a hundred whores like you, and you think it's beneath your dignity to spread your legs for me!"

Apollonia took a sharp breath. The words sliced her like an executioner's blade—she had long suspected what Dion had done, and she had heard innuendoes but treated them as lies. But to listen to it from Krokinos' mouth confirmed her fears, and once Krokinos cursed her some more and left the room, she began to gently rock and cry. If she were to be put in a slave line again, she would end her life and kill her daughter.

From the next day, they were moved to the basement—a large, windowless, squalid room that held many others who lived in these abject conditions for unknown transgressions. Their life changed once again, and this time they were no better than disfavored slaves in the house. The living conditions were abysmal, and food only fit for beggars.

Filth, beatings, and an endless demand for work were companions as each day passed with no news of her husband.

CHAPTER 28.

CAPPADOCIA

Eumenes was distraught. It had been months since Deon had left, and there was no news of him and Eurydice since their escape from Memphis. Perdiccas was dead, Ptolemy had prevailed, and now through a twisted turn of events, he was alone.

How cruel were the gods? His defeat of two great generals had meant nothing. In the recent conference at Triparadisus, the constellation of warlords, governors, and satraps had singled him as the enemy. The council carved Alexander's empire like an elephant's carcass—Ptolemy received Egypt, Libya, and the lands beyond; Antigonus—Asia Minor; Seleucus—Babylonia all the way to the skirts of India; and a host of others received pieces here and there. But Eumenes' loyalty to Perdiccas and his hand in the deaths of Craterus and Neoptolemus had sealed his fate.

The news was that Antigonus was preparing to march against him.

Remarkably, Eumenes' army still stuck with him. They saw a cunning, kind, and capable leader and believed he would prevail. Eumenes was unsure, for it seemed the world conspired against him, and the odds seemed insurmountable.

Unless Deon found the second Atlantis.

If it held the suggested treasure and weaponry, Eumenes knew he could change the scenario at once. He might even be able to forge alliances with unwilling partners.

He would first finish Antigonus. That would secure him enough power to demand the surrender of Ptolemy, and then Seleucus.

Eumenes would be the lord of all Europe and Asia.

Greater than Alexander.

Now only if Deon returned.

So, Eumenes devised a strategy to reconnect with Deon. His officer was last known to have been in Alexandria. If he died, then there was nothing else to do. But what if he were alive? Where would he go? He also thought that Deon, if he were alive, would avoid areas that were hostile to Eumenes.

Libya?

But Libya was outside Eumenes' sphere of influence.

Greece, Macedon, Sparta, and on his way to Cappadocia?

Those regions were outside his control, but he could have spies in Cappadocia watch out for Deon.

What about Phoenicia? All the way from the borders of Egypt until the Northern borders of Syria.

That was a distinct possibility. Anything further east was Seleucus' territory and out of bounds as well. All those areas were possible by sea from Alexandria. Eumenes' instincts told him that a new city built to replace a seafaring empire had to be closer to the shores than far inland.

The only logical region would be Phoenicia before it fell under the firm control of one of the satraps.

Eumenes summoned fifty of his most trusted men, captains, and lieutenants. These men he had led for many years, helped them profit during the campaigns, and they had stuck by him at all costs. Them he directed thus:

They were to undertake a most secretive task to find Deon and Eurydice. They were to spread along the Phoenician coast and conduct their inquiries and search. If they made contact, they would assume Deon as their new commander until Eumenes arrived.

Ten in Antioch.

Ten to cover Tyre and Sidon.

Ten near Gaza, at Sharuhen.

Ten near the sea at Egypt's border.

And ten to travel the lands in-between and around, with no fixed territory.

It could even take one to two years, Eumenes told them. If they received news of Eumenes' death or imprisonment, they were to disband and go wherever they pleased without shame of abandonment. Each man received a talent, enough to last them many years; a handsome payment.

But if they found Deon and Eurydice, then Eumenes would move his army to join them.

"Once we are together again," he told them, "you will witness the greatest change of fortune in history."

CHAPTER 29.

AEGEAN SEA

No, no, no, no, no.

I ran towards the bodies, wrapped my hand around the man's neck and pulled him off her.

There was blood—on her face, chest, stomach, legs—everywhere. It was as if a monster gutted a horse and held it over her body.

"Eurydice!" I yelled and shook her face. Then I placed my palm on her chest.

She was breathing. Her chest still rose and fell. She was unconscious.

Thank you, Poseidon!

I dragged her to the back where there was more space and placed her head on my lap. And then I protected her face from the falling rain. I do not know how long I sat that way, but after a while, she stirred. And later, she opened her eyes, looking disoriented. Once she realized it was me, she smiled.

Relief washed over me.

I examined the dead man. It was as if he had stood and let her butcher him.

I threw him overboard.

She had a few nicks to her forearm, but none too serious. That man had no idea who he was up against like so many others who had underestimated her. I held her and let her recover.

Then I went down the rickety ladders to the lower deck.

The crew listened to me with rapt attention. Whether they believed me or not was immaterial. They knew that Polymedes and four of his men were dead and that they faced the duo that killed them. The two other soldiers had laid down their arms and were willing to listen.

The senior man, with his weathered face and gray beard, finally spoke, "How do we know you will not murder us as well once we take you where you want?"

"You do not. But I have no such desire, and you have my word."

"Where do you want to go?"

"South of Gaza, where the land curves up from Egypt."

"That is a long way. What will happen to us once the naval commanders realize we never came back?"

"I doubt they know you and your slaves. Stay away from Egypt for a while, and they will think the sea swallowed you."

He looked at his associate and the other men.

"Who pays us?"

"You will receive your payment from Polymedes' purse, and you can also divide his men's belongings."

They nodded.

Then one of the men spoke up. "Who is your master?"

"Antigonus one-eye," I lied.

With Perdiccas dead, it was my hunch that the tide had turned against Eumenes, for now, at least. And then I warned them. "If I suspect trickery, know that I will gut you, and feed you the entrails. Do not test me."

They nodded.

I pulled aside the senior man. There was another order of business to take care of. "I need your services, and I can pay you very well."

I then told him to meet Eumenes and ask the Governor to send support to the Knife's Tip. We agreed on payment terms, and I explained the location of the Knife's Tip. He explained how we could shelter in Sharuhen, a mostly abandoned town near Gaza, for the time being.

"I now need you to help my wife," I said.

I had to take care of my many-tongued little demon.

"You look much better," I said, as Eurydice and I sat with our backs to the cabin wall. The sail was smooth after the storm had passed.

"My aunt would say that every time I took a bath after several days of reminders. But yes, I feel much better," she said, smiling.

"You sound like you were fond of your aunt."

"Yes, she was the one who managed to get me freed," she said, as her eyes drifted to nothingness.

"Eurydice, I worry about how you attack men. You do realize that they are stronger, and if one is able to grab you then they can easily kill you."

"I know. That is why I was taught to evade, run, let them underestimate me, and then gut them," she said, and I laughed as I shook my head. There was not much I could do to dissuade her from risky situations.

"Will you tell me your story someday?"

"Someday. Why do you need my past when I am here with you in the present?"

I held her hand gently and entwined my fingers in hers.

"I know so little about your family," she said, "tell me more about your wife and daughter."

I spoke of them fondly—of my wife's gentle nature, her wavy hair, her strength through the years, her wonderful smile, our beautiful baby. I had to gather myself a few times. The gentle rocking of the boat had lulled both of us into a sense of calm.

Eventually, I nudged closer to her. We sat quietly for a long time. Then she spoke up, "This reminds me of my father."

"What?"

"Whenever my mother disciplined me with her olive branch, I would sit crying by the wall, and my father would sit next to me and say nothing."

"You said he was tough," I said.

"Yes, but he never once laid his hands on me in anger. After I calmed down, he would lean and kiss my forehead. I wish—" She wiped a tear and I let her be.

The sail to the south of Gaza was uneventful. The crew kept their word, and through judicious use of water and food, we made it to land in five days. I kept a watch on Eurydice, but those were five happy days.

We bid goodbye to a relieved crew after we landed. We consulted with local Bedouin tribesmen on how to get to the Knife's Tip. There were no armies nearby for the leaders had returned from Triparadisus.

The oars master went to Gaza to get a horse and go North, while we trekked to Sharuhen.

It took us a day on the barren landscape.

Sharuhen was an old decrepit fortified town occupied by local tribes. These tribes kept their independence from the

Egyptians, Phoenicians, Greeks, and Macedonians. The fort was crumbling, and there were many abandoned buildings inside. Isolated from the main trading routes, it was the perfect place for us to stay until we plotted our next journey.

For the next sixteen days, we stayed at Sharuhen. Once a few days we visited Gaza in the late evenings to replenish our supplies. I worried about Ptolemy's spies detecting us because Gaza was not a large town. Most of the population had fled after Alexander's siege years ago.

On the sixteenth day, I was at a local meat shop, haggling with the seller who had no recollection that I had been there four times already. But such was their custom. As I prepared to pay the man, I sensed someone behind me. Before I reacted, a strong hand gripped my forearm, preventing me from drawing my weapon. I recognized the sharp tips of three blades—one on my back, and two at the waist.

There was nothing I could do.

"Walk with us," hissed the man. Then they shoved me ahead. They had covered their faces.

Nekh-Aser's men?

Bandits?

Local warlords?

We walked to a desolated spot behind low lying hills. The leader ordered me to sit, and one of the men secured my wrists behind my back.

This was it.

Then the leader came to the front but did not remove his cover. His eyes gave away that he was Greek or Macedonian. But then so were many of Ptolemy's men.

Too many damned Greeks.

"Do not attempt anything funny."

"There is not much fun one can have with his hands tied behind his back."

The corner of his eyes wrinkled. "We are looking for the woman you are with."

What?

There was no point lying, and they must have seen Eurydice during our trips when we came together.

"She is my wife, what do you want with her?"

"Our master is in love with her, and wishes to marry her," he said, and the others nodded.

What?

I heard guffaws from the other men. What was going on?

"Who is your master? I said she is my wife."

"He is a dirty old man, but he pays for our livelihood. He thinks she has beautiful breasts and would be wonderful in bed."

My face reddened. This made little sense. "Tell him I am her husband and that it is against the law to force her away from me!"

What an absurd conversation. One of the men turned to his leader, "Which law does he speak of, sir? Is this Greece?"

The leader stood and pranced, "No, does not look like Greece at all!"

"Or Macedon?" The man asked.

"No does not look like Macedon at all!" the leader said, placing his palms over his eyes and peering.

They all laughed.

Then the leader turned to his men. "Looks like he loves her. Tell us you do, sir, do not be shy."

Laughter.

What was going on?

"Yes—what is this all about?"

"Oh, look at his red face like a teenager, except you are a crusty old bastard. Your penis is probably already dead."

More laughter.

I sat fuming; angry, confused, and unsure of the danger. Then the man removed his cover and broke into a giant smile.

"How are you doing, commander Deon? Very much in love it seems."

I heard great laughter, and in my confusion, I smiled but stopped. Who were these men?

"Governor Eumenes sends his regards."

After much merriment and teasing, we settled down to business. I was giddy with happiness and excitement.

Alkimachus explained Eumenes' plan. Eumenes had the foresight to tackle this as best as he could, and he had succeeded.

The first order of business was for us to regroup with the rest of his team. I sent three men to relay the message to the remaining forty, and Eumenes. I hurried to Eurydice, as we had to move and make a new home while we regrouped.

The news stunned and thrilled Eurydice. Two days later the seven-member squad met with us, and we broke camp in a desolate stretch far away from the roads. They had horses and knew where to get water.

The plan was for the rest of the battalion to arrive in small groups, and to meet us near the Knife's Tip. We would have lookouts to help herd everyone.

Alkimachus finally could not contain himself as we sat for dinner. "Well, Eurydice, it seems our commander here is deeply in love with you."

I placed my palms around my ears; there was no stopping these idiots.

She giggled.

"He was outraged when we said we wanted you for our master."

"How angry?"

"His face was redder than a pig's arse."

Howls of laughter.

I could not help but feel embarrassed as she looked at me and blew a kiss. That set them off.

"We cannot have a leader running around with an erection!"

All that brought back memories of a distant past during our campaigns. The campfires, the bawdy ribbing. It was wonderful to be back among my men.

"Well, Alkimachus, I must warn you and your men that she is a little demon. Talk too much, and she will slice you like little bread pieces."

"I am not a little demon," she protested and pouted. But she loved that. It was a name I gave her after she butchered the soldier on the ship.

"A pretty, vicious little demon," I said, and I reached out to her hand, much to great approval of the audience. And then I mock-scolded them, "I am your commander, how about some respect?"

We sat late into the clear winter night, talking, and strategizing. I had not told them what exactly we were set to do, but that they would have to follow me.

I thought to myself.

How would all this end?

CHAPTER 30.

KNIFE'S TIP

The landscape changed as we neared the Knife's Tip. Yellow sand made way to gold and pink cliffs. Immense, reddish rock rose from the earth, and the ground became rougher. It had taken us six days as the papyri suggested.

I understood why they called it the Knife's Tip. When seen from an elevation, the jagged mountain range tapered sharply as it ended to our right. The place was beautiful and foreboding, and somewhere in there was what I wanted.

Between the smaller hills where we stood, and the hills of the Knife's Tip, was a valley. As we took the sights, I could not but marvel at the location and how the ancients chose it. I interpreted the papyri's 'a day ahead' as proper for someone on foot so that it would be less than half the day for a horse rider. I was confident that our destination was in the towering mountains we could see far ahead. At this point, I had no idea where to look and what to look for.

Just over a day from the bottom of the Knife's Tip we finally arrived at the foot of the largest mountains. We rested for the day, and I decided not to go on a search mission until we regrouped with the rest of the squad—all fifty. Instead, I would spend time with Eurydice to decode the final pieces.

We were so near!

That night, after setting up camp under twinkling stars, Eurydice, and I decided to walk and debate. I recounted the next set of verses that alluded to the location.

Three days north from the tip, within golden walls and red rocks, in there they found a magnificent mountain, and a hollow within, where they carved the last city of a great empire and filled it with unimaginable riches, weapons the world had never seen, and knowledge superior to all mankind. When the sun sets, the shadows play, the lord he smiles, and smiles away. Pay heed my prince for in that smile lies the door, the path, the way to new Atlantis

What did that mean? Now that we could see the surroundings ourselves, we had a better chance of guessing it right.

"We're in the right place, we are!" I exclaimed, "It took us a day on horses, a walking party would need three or more. And we came through sandstone canyons. Now, look at the red rocks around us!"

She agreed, and energy surged in me. This would all end soon, and I would be home.

"'There they made a hollow within'—that seems obvious," she said, and I nodded. The story was unambiguous in that the city was inside a mountain.

"The tricky part is the next one—and it seems we have to wait for the sun to set for it to happen."

"So, when the sun sets, the gods appear in the sky and smile?"

That was what I thought. But it was too obvious. "I don't think so. Remember Thera? No one was floating up in the sky. What does it mean he appears and smiles away?"

We were both at a loss. We debated many useless theories.

That the sentences meant nothing. A ruse.

That something magical appeared on sunset.

The Lord meant a star that appeared precisely above the spot on the mountain.

The Lord meant the moon, and that something would happen on the day when the full moon appeared after sunset.

The Lord was an immortal and came out every day after the sunset and laughed.

That the line only meant that the Lord smiled when he was still alive, before the destruction of Thera.

And so on. None made much sense after we pondered over it and led us nowhere. Tired, we decided that we would watch the sunset from an elevated point the next evening.

The first of the four other squads finally arrived that night guided by an outpost messenger at the Knife's Tip. By morning the entire group of fifty had assembled—a testament to Eumenes' foresight.

Suddenly, it felt like the gods were smiling upon us. We could now secure the find until the governor arrived. I was gleeful. While uncovering the second Atlantis would be thrilling, being a satrap was even more enjoyable. I imagined my two wives and daughter shooting adoring glances at me. At night I watched the twinkling stars, and I fervently hoped that my family was still safe. It had been a while since I had heard from them or Eumenes, and my mind alternated between fear and hope. My squad asked no questions—I would soon have to reveal to them the mission. My only nagging worry was someone was following us. Was there any other way for someone to be on our track other than the oarsmen?

A foreboding sense of danger washed over me. Then I remembered something from my conversation with Polymedes in Thera.

There was a link, and it would only be time.

O Poseidon, I pray thee, protect us.

I split the group into ten teams of four and spread them at various points of the valley and the canyon entrance. The remaining ten stayed with Eurydice and me to act as our bodyguards and to help us run errands.

We were restless the next day waiting for the sunset. There were still many unresolved questions. Were we near the right mountains? Were we supposed to be in a specific place for the evening? Were we supposed to do something at sunset? Many questions and no answers.

And we were running out of time, for I was sure someone was following us.

I decided to scale the hill with Eurydice, and two men, well before the sun began its descent. These celestial beings always fascinated me—what was the sun? How far from us was this ball of fire?

The climb was not strenuous but took effort. We made it before sunset and sat on a rock. I only asked the men with me to watch the mountains and tell me if they noticed anything strange. It was a vague instruction, but that was all I was willing to part with now.

We watched the mountains as the sun slid across the skies. It looked as if the hills were on fire. The light and shadows created a changing tapestry of colors as the sun slipped beyond the horizon. Where did the sun go? That was a mystery for the wise.

While the views felt like the gods designed them, we saw nothing that helped our cause. My temples throbbed squinting at the sun and staring at the mountains. The men reported nothing unusual either.

We hurried down the slopes before nightfall as the cold winds intensified. "What could it be?" I asked Eurydice, hoping she would have an answer.

"Nothing... there is nothing but emptiness here," she said, sounding forlorn. I worried that we had made it all this way and our excitement of yesterday had begun to wear. But we had reached here after a long journey, and we would persevere. We waited until the next evening, but this time climbed a different hill. The two men went with me again. I am sure they wondered what we were up to.

Once again, we watched as the sun slid across the sky.

It was beautiful.

The colors were captivating.

The vista was inspiring.

The outcome was disappointing.

I was getting frustrated—we were losing time, and we were stuck. And to add to that was the senseless banter of the two soldiers. I called them the dog and the goat; one sounded like he barked, and the other one whined and bleated. They were lewd, much to my annoyance, and not particularly concerned with the presence of a woman.

"Those mountaintops look like Nubian nipples," one of them opined. The other one bleated, "End your fantasies about Nubian women with a thousand nipples."

I shook my head and kept watching.

"There, that one is a pig," the dog said.

"More like a donkey if you ask me," the goat responded.

"Definitely a pig. A loud, ornery red pig."

They both howled and bleated, and I finally could not hold my irritation.

"What are you both talking about? Keep quiet."

I heard shuffling of the feet.

"We apologize, sir. Keeping ourselves busy. We were talking about the shadows…"

"You were talking about pigs," I said, still annoyed.

"Yes, sir, the shadows on the hills made one like a pig's face." I heard juvenile guffawing.

"Which shadows—what are you," I stopped mid-sentence. I stood up and turned towards them, and both dog and goat stepped back alarmed, afraid that they had enraged me.

"We're sorry sir, did not mean to," goat stammered. I slapped them on their shoulders with great affection, grinning at their confusion.

I turned to Eurydice.

"Eurydice. The Lord smiles upon us too." I said.

Now I knew exactly what to look for.

At night we were unable to sleep with excitement.

"It was right there in front of us," I said, laughing.

"Clever writing. Not so obvious," she said.

We both sat huddled in front of the flickering fire, and I watched the flames reflect in her eyes.

She looked beautiful.

"When this is all over, what do you want to do?"

She looked at me, surprised at the question, but said nothing. She placed her chin on her knees and sighed.

"Will you come with me?" I asked. It was time.

"Where?"

"Wherever the Governor sends me, or back to my village."

Her eyes fixed on mine. "I will not be your mistress as you walk back to your family."

"I am not asking you to be."

"Then what are you suggesting?" she asked, searching my face.

"I ask your hand in marriage," I said, without hesitation.

She blinked in surprise, and her mouth was half agape. The crackling of the fire broke the occasional chirp of a night bug. "You say this with no other hidden purpose?" she finally asked.

"None. I know you have reasons to doubt me, Eurydice, but of this I am sure."

"You already have a wife."

"The law allows me to wed you as my second, so long as you and my first promise not to kill each other."

She scoffed. "The law allows royals. You are not one."

I laughed. "You are right. We will go where they allow it. I swear on the gods."

She made a dismissive gesture. Polygamy was not uncommon in her heritage, but it was not very prevalent where I lived.

"You will not abandon me?"

"Only if you continue to cook that terrible concoction you made a few days ago."

She laughed. But she had not answered. So, I asked again, "Eurydice, will you take my hand in marriage?"

Beyond love, there were practical reasons for her to marry me. If I managed to complete this quest successfully, I could give her material comfort and protection.

"Yes," she finally said, the color of her face changing to match the red embers.

The next evening, we were back again. This time I enlisted four more men and had each one climb to a different vantage point. Then I gave them the instructions.

"Look at the big red mountains as the sun gets closer to the horizon. I want you to look for the appearance of a face formed by shadows on the rock. It should look like a smiling face of a royal—a man. You should not have to imagine, for I expect that when the face appears, it will be clear and distinct as day."

"What is all this about, sir?" asked Alkimachus.

"I will reveal it all soon, Alkimachus. I need you and your men to trust me."

"As we always have, sir," he said, and ordered his men, "use your whistles and draw attention. Be sure, or I will have you flogged."

We began another watch, but this time a lot more hopeful. But as the evening wore, there was but one whistle, which turned out to be a false sighting. I did not admonish the man, as it was easy to see why he mistook what he saw for a face.

Disappointed, but not defeated, we waited for the next evening. Our supplies were running low—we could only camp here for another two nights. Then we would have to scour for food and water. So far there was no news of any intruders to the valley, except a few stragglers who we scared away.

We changed the viewing spots, and I positioned two more men than the evening before. And then we got back to the watch. The beauty was no longer alluring—it became boring and tedious. The sun was orange. The sky was blue. My arse itched sitting on the rock. The birds chirped and so on. None of it was exciting.

The evening progressed, and so far, we had one false whistle. We stared at the mute rocks and the jagged edges mocked us in defiance.

And finally, the sun began to set again—the bottom of the orb now hovering above distant horizon. I threw a few stones in frustration. Eurydice placed a consoling palm on my shoulder. "I want to drive a sarissa down the writer's throat," I said and dug the earth with my kopis.

I shifted my position and looked around. Was this it? A huge chase for nothing based on a writer's fertile imagination? Would I lose my family and Eumenes his empire based on a malicious pig fucker's old papers?

But all other details had made sense!

As I sunk into despair, there was a whistle again.

And then once more.

And then again, the third time—the urgency unmistakable. It was from a new lookout to our North-East. We scrambled down the hill we were on and rushed to the new one. It was imperative that we get up to the spotting point before the view vanished.

But we were too late. By the time we ascended, the sun had almost vanished, and whatever the soldier saw was no longer visible.

The lookout stood biting his nails. "I swear, may Zeus strike me, but it was the distinct view of a face with a crown," he said, worried about our displeasure.

"Where?"

He pointed to a region on a massive mountain right up ahead. It was about a quarter from the bottom and difficult to make out any features in the falling light. But his insistence gave me great hope, and we were back to waiting another day.

But my hope was also changing to worry. Every day we lost was a day gained for an unseen enemy. I was also sure the soldiers were questioning their work, and idle minds led to untold mischief.

The next day went without incident. There was no news of any armed parties in the vicinity. I was unable to hold my excitement as the evening arrived. There was a moment of panic when clouds threatened the skies but cleared soon after.

I asked Eurydice and Alkimachus to join me. The lookout took us to the viewpoint well in advance of sunset, and we settled.

I could sense the soldier's nervousness. He was biting his nails like a hungry dog attacking bones. I told him to relax.

The sun finally began to descend over the horizon.

The shadows cast on the rock face of the hill ahead of us began to transform the view.

We watched in suspense and anxiety.

And then there it was.

As the sun reached a point in the sky, the golden rays played on the corners, and an image appeared. I heard Eurydice squeal, and the soldier's face lit up. He began to jump up and down like a little boy.

"I told you, sir. There!"

I was transfixed. In that slant of light was visible a distinct face of a man wearing a crown.

The eyes were wide open.

The nose straight and imperial.

The smiling mouth unmistakable.

I remembered the words again. Now they sounded beautiful.

When the sun sets, the shadows play, the lord he smiles, and smiles away. A smile so welcome as the open doors to a magnificent temple.

The ancient builders had fashioned the rocks in a way to create the visual. It was breathtaking in clarity and secrecy, and a testament to their prowess. I knew then that the second Atlantis was now within reach.

A ledge from the side of the cliff face ended just below the left eye. The ledge itself extended on the face of the mountain for a distance, and I guessed that there would be some entrance at the end of the ledge. And we would have to find a path to reach it. As we all marveled at the sight, the shadows began to shift and part by part the face vanished. The Lord no longer smiled, and the view turned into dark, jagged rocks. But we laughed. We laughed like we had not for a long time. I turned and hugged the soldier who turned into an uncomfortable statue.

"I will reward you," I said to the beaming man. It was getting dark, and we had to get down the treacherous slopes. We would climb to the area of the Lord's face as soon as sunlight appeared.

We watched our steps and made our way to the valley floor. As we walked towards the horses, I heard a whistle again.

Another sighting? That cannot be—

Instead, it was a signal that a messenger was coming our way. Once he arrived, the messenger dismounted and rushed to me. He was sweating in the cold, tension writ large on his face.

"I have an urgent report to make, sir."

"Go on."

"Battalion with seventy to eighty raiders, cavalry, and infantry. At the far entrance of the canyon."

At nightfall, I assembled the men. I left two lookouts atop hills closer to the entrance of the canyon. While I had not personally announced the find and told the lookouts to keep it a secret, I knew that most probably they had heard of what had happened. No one had asked me anything, but there was no question they were waiting for me to tell them something. They huddled in a tight circle around me. A lone torch burned in a soldier's hand. It was time to make a speech. "A contingent of Ptolemy's force is at the entrance of the valley, preparing to strike. I expect that we will face assault before noon. Whether we journey to our afterlives or the bosoms of our loved ones, we will do it with bravery. Our duty is to the man to whom we have sworn loyalty. I know you wonder why the governor has you here."

I paused and looked around. The men stood without a word, and many soldiers nodded. By late tomorrow some of them would be dead. "Eumenes stands tall as a leader, a Greek he may be, but he has shown exceptional bravery and mercy while surrounded by scoundrels who would think nothing of extinguishing millions in their quest for the empire. They have condemned him to death, but Eumenes has conjured a brilliant plan to fight and defeat them. You wonder why you are here, amidst desolation, away from the main force."

I paused, making sure every man hung on to my words. "In those mountains is a cave with a prophecy written in stone by messengers of the Oracle of Delphi. We have learned that tablets portend something: that in times of great tumult, where the world is at the edge of war among many greats, the one man who holds these tablets will summon fearsome gods to his side, and that the man who holds it must be Greek. No one here doubts that we are in perilous times and that Ptolemy, Seleucus, Antigonus, and others vie for Alexander's empire. And who among them is Greek?"

Many in the crowd murmured. In the flickering torch fire, I watched the awe and sensed fear in the men. I hid my deep shame in taking advantage of their gullibility, but it was necessary.

"You have no higher calling than fulfilling an oath to the man that has protected you, fed you, gave you purpose. Tomorrow we fight Ptolemy's men lest those scoundrels find the place and destroy it. And with that done, we shall reap the benefits of our courage—and you, men, will be wealthy and powerful beyond your wildest dreams!"

The men stirred. Many whooped in excitement and raised their spears and swords. I sincerely hoped that Eumenes would bequeath upon them great riches as I had just promised.

Alkimachus stepped forward and spoke. "The men are with you, commander. We either live to great glory in the service of a benevolent master or die a greater death with pride and loyalty."

Once the tents became quiet, I conferred with Alkimachus, who I knew was hiding his urge to ask me more. "Alkimachus, it is imperative that I head to the hills well before sunset. That means I will need to break away from the battle if it is still in progress."

"If I may ask, sir, what exactly are you looking for?"

"You will know as soon as I do, Alkimachus, have faith."

"Should I join you, sir?"

"That is a noble thought, Alkimachus, but I need you in the battle."

He asked again. "How many do you need to be with you?"

"None. Eurydice and I will break away once the battle is in our hands. I want you to continue to lead the men on my departure and await my return. No one from the enemy must escape, and this information cannot leak until Eumenes' arrival."

He understood the stakes.

That night I held Eurydice for a long time. I told her what to do if I died in battle—that she should escape and seek shelter with Antigonus One-Eye's forces, and do what she can to free my family. While One-Eye arrayed against Eumenes, they still respected each other. I surmised that she was safer there than in the hands of Ptolemy.

I told her how much I had come to treasure her company, and she said she was honored to be by my side. We had come so long, our prize so tantalizingly within reach, and the gods had one final test for us.

Only Dionysus knew if our embrace was to be our last.

PART IV

ROCKS AND BLOOD

Circa 321 BC

"He looked at the walls,

Awed at the heights

His people had achieved

And for a moment – just a moment –

All that lay behind him

Passed from view."

—Epic of Gilgamesh*

CHAPTER 31.

KNIFE'S TIP

We woke early and made rapid progress along the edge of a large mountain and arrived at an entrance to a canyon. Then we corralled into a narrow path flanked by towering golden canyons. We had discovered this place a few days ago, and I hoped my strategy would work. The path was about eight to ten men wide where we were.

I had all our horses moved to the rear, to another exit out of the canyon on the eastern end. The horses would be a disadvantage here.

The sun warmed our backs. I was at the head of the formation, with Alkimachus beside me. I placed Eurydice in the middle, much to her irritation, but she could not persuade me otherwise. I told her that this was not going to be a skirmish.

We looked plain, without our military regalia, emblems, or adornments. To the enemy, I hoped we looked like an untrained cohort of rough men drawn from the farmlands.

They outnumbered us more than two-to-one, but we had the advantage of nine days. I had learned something precious during Alexander's campaigns.

Do what the enemy cannot guess you will.

Nekh-Aser sat straight on his horse. Ptolemy's flags fluttered—Alexander with ram's horns and elephant scalp headdress. The Egyptian squinted, eyeing Deon and his ragtag mercenaries far up ahead in the narrow path. Polymedes had never returned from his mission, but the other ship that docked in Thera and returned had reported that Polymedes had left Thera with two extra passengers— a man and a woman. As luck would have it, he had learned about their new destination through Ptolemy's spies.

And he had caught up to them, finally.

Nekh-Aser did not like tight spaces. There was something about them that distressed him since he was a child. His father had once locked him in a crypt as punishment—the terror of that moment had never left him. And that harlot with Deon had reminded him of all that again. The troops waited for an order, and Nekh-Aser knew in his gut that an ambush lay ahead, but he was unsure how. His lookouts had not spotted anyone on the rims. Besides, the cliffs were steep, and there was no way anyone could attack them from the top.

His spies had found no sign of large armies in the vicinity—it was all very puzzling to Nekh-Aser.

What was Deon doing here? Why this suicidal attempt?

The restless hoofs of the cavalry clicked on the rocks. Nekh-Aser's lieutenant controlled his impatient horse. "May we attack, sir?"

The subordinate's question irritated Nekh-Aser.

"Ambush," he said, straining against his painful jaw cage. He signaled the lieutenant to come closer. "Send thirty, wait for whistles."

The lieutenant picked thirty men and a leader and had them move forward as a line six deep with five horses in each. "Blow the whistles when you want us to join," he said, and the leader bowed.

Nekh-Aser hoped that this affair would be over by noon. He pulled by the forward party leader's side and growled. "Capture leader and woman. They die, you die."

"Yes, sir."

Nekh-Aser nodded to the lieutenant who raised his sword in the air.

"Move!"

The thirty rode towards the entrance of the canyon. Their measured progress on the uneven, rocky ground was to avoid injuring the horses. The leader of the cohort eyed the sides for an ambush.

They soon entered the passageway a few horses-wide, but the enemy had retreated. "Halt!" the leader shouted. "I do not like this," he said, as he adjusted his helmet and stroked his beard.

"Sir, look," a soldier said, pointing to several items at the entrance of the next passage. The retreaters had strewn about bags, crude spears, and camping paraphernalia.

"Looks like they ran in a hurry," said the soldier, grinning.

The leader considered the possibilities. It might be true that the enemy saw their strength and ran, or it was a pathetic attempt of a ruse. Could this clever man Deon have sanctioned this childish attempt? They surveyed the area and looked at the cliff walls but found nothing. Finally, the leader signaled them to move forward. Three horses in each line entered the narrow passage.

The canyon closed in and towered over the riders. The steep walls bore deep cracks. It was cool, and on the sand ahead were many footprints of men running. The leader signaled his men to trot forward faster.

Finally, the entire group was well within the empty canyon. The nervousness eased. A few riders amused themselves by shouting and hearing the echoes.

"It all makes sense," said the leader, addressing the men behind him. "They chose a place from which they could decide to fight or flee. Let us proceed to the end of the passageway, ensure it is clear, and then return to the captain for his orders."

They continued several steps. A low whistle floated in the quiet air. The leader turned to admonish the idiot—

"Ambush!" he screamed.

Ahead of them, and behind, men appeared from the walls. They wore military helmets, held sarissas and swords. Many carried large bales of grass. The messengers blew their whistles.

The leader yelled, "Half with me, other half behind!"

The enemy on both ends set fire to the bales and rolled them forward. The horses panicked and refused to charge ahead. Then the first volley of missiles came hurtling from either end.

Several men fell screaming, and the remaining riders struggled to control the horses. The enemy changed tactics again. They formed two tight lines that trapped Nekh-Aser's party in-between. The leader realized that these were not a ragtag bunch. The battle became one-sided in no time. The advancing enemy impaled, stabbed, and hacked away at the disorganized invading party. Some men caught fire and ran like human torches, screaming and flailing. The air soon filled with the smell of charred flesh, burnt skin, flaming hair, and screams of desperation. The leader dismounted and tried to bring order. Amidst the madness, he thought he saw a woman disembowel one of his men.

Who were these people?

A well-built, almost bald man rushed towards him, appearing like a monster from the smoke.

This must be Deon, the leader thought.

Their swords clanged, but Deon was far more skilled. After a short struggle, Deon grabbed the leader's throat and kicked the legs under him. The leader stumbled and fell, and his helmet flew. He felt someone grip his hair and pull him away.

The leader gagged due to smoke; his eyes burned, and he struggled to see. He saw Deon over him, and he raised his hands to thwart a final blow. Deon stopped short and brought his face close to the fallen man.

"I have a question for you. Tell me the truth or say your prayers."

The leader nodded fervently. He was not going to die for a captain who had sent them unprepared.

Nekh-Aser watched as a waft of smoke rose in the distance. Expanding shrubbery fire, he thought, and paid no heed to it. He and his men waited for the whistles, or for someone to appear at the entrance of the canyon. Finally, Nekh-Aser saw a rider at the entrance. The man waved and then blew the shrill whistle several times.

Nekh-Aser raised his sword in the air and nodded to his men.

"Move forward," yelled the man. Ptolemy's banner rose high, and the column began a slow march towards the canyon entrance. Nekh-Aser felt his loins stir at the prospect of bloody vengeance.

Whether Alkimachus did his job was yet to be seen.

CHAPTER 32.

KNIFE'S TIP

I prayed to the gods that Alkimachus would prevail against Nekh-Aser. I had left the force under his command as Eurydice, and I slipped away from them and made our way along a rocky incline. The path led us to the area where we believed there was a passageway into the hidden city.

The walk up the incline, skirting the face of a rocky mountain, was strenuous. We had little respite after a brutal, intense battle, and there was no time to lose. Our bloodied attire blended with the red rock all around us. After what felt like an eternity, chest burning and calves hurting, we arrived at a narrow ledge. The farther corner ended in a shallow cleave of the mountain. There was no path forward. We had to gain a foothold on indentations on the vertical wall and move higher up to the ledge near the door. Eurydice looked scared, and I was no fan of great heights either. But we had come all this way, and I was not going to return. We made our way taking our time to find the right support. After several heart-stopping moments, we finally made way to the ledge. The huge stone slab was ahead of us, and it was at an angle to the mountain. The corner of the slab was raised outwards with a slit hidden behind, invisible to anyone except those that were on the ledge. A single person could squeeze in. It was ingenious.

My heart thundered as I gripped a stone overhang and swung inside the opening. It was narrow and short, so I balanced myself and helped Eurydice through. We rested and laughed with relief. So far, today, no one had stabbed us, hacked us, set us on fire, and we had not fallen down a cliff.

The narrow passageway went a distance, and we moved cautiously holding our hands over our mouth and nose to protect from the fine dust. The walls were cut from rock, and I scraped myself twice. After about two hundred steps, before it became completely dark, the passage opened into a chamber that was dimly lit through an opening that channeled sunlight inside.

We had stepped into another world.

The small, musty room was empty except decorative patterns on the roof. I felt the presence of ancient gods in the darkness. No one had been here since the founders had sealed it. Eurydice sensed my trepidation—she gripped my forearm and then knelt; I followed. We prayed that no harm comes to us, for we were here on orders of our superiors, in love for family, and desired greater good of the peoples.

There was an ornate stone lever on the wall next to a wide stone door. We gripped the handle of the lever and pulled, but nothing happened. It was rigid—thousands of years had degraded the structure, and I worried if we were stuck after coming so close. But I examined the lever and noticed fine sand in the hinges. I cleaned the hinge by blowing on it. The fine craftsmanship was visible; smooth circular patterns hid bronze hinges underneath.

We tried again—but nothing moved. I sensed the ancients laughing at us.

"There may be another way to unlock the lever," said Eurydice. We began to inspect the stone walls. We started at each end, feeling the surface for anything unusual.

"Here!" Eurydice whispered, and I raced over to her. The engineers had carved a smooth dial with notches, into the wall. Once again, we blew into the ridges of the dial to clear the passage. I placed my fingers and turned it to my right—it did not move.

O Poseidon, may your power move the dial!

I directed all my strength to my wrists and twisted it. The dial clicked and turned. Then I heard something release inside the walls. I sprinted towards the lever like a young athlete from the famed games of Athens. We both gripped the handle again and pulled it hard towards us. This time the lever moved like palms on butter. The stone door slid to one side—to half its width, and then ground to a halt.

I stepped into the darkness. The air was stale but caused no distress. I guessed that the ancients had created air ducts to keep circulation. Eurydice stepped in behind me—we held our hands and moved cautiously. I removed a torch from my bag and prepared to light it. At that moment I felt the vibration of a mechanical contraption beneath my feet. I gasped—terrified that this was a trap and we would die a sudden, inglorious death, but that was not to be. In front of us, the dark passageway lit up with the gentle glow of lamps encased in translucent material. They came to life one after the other as if by divine magic. My mouth dropped in astonishment. We stood immobile, mesmerized at what unfolded in front of us. Elegant stone statues of ancient gods and kings, finely sculpted to human likeness and coated with fine dust, watched over cold cobbled floors.

Was this an abode built by men and gods together? I took the lights that showed us the path as an omen that the powers sought to encourage us forward. We walked about a hundred steps, and the passageway ended in darkness. I stood at the edge, wondering if we would plunge to death. Instead, once again, lamps lit up in a far distance. Soon, hundreds came to life, above us, and to our sides. And then a great fire lit up right ahead of us.

We had stepped into a magnificent dome surpassing anything I had ever seen—and I had been to Persepolis, Babylon, and Memphis. Those were mute monuments of stone and sand, but this felt alive—it felt our presence and reacted to it.

The dome was a large amphitheater with stepped stone benches all around. The fire at the center burned from a stone podium. On four corners stood statues of a man whose expressive eyes focused on the fire podium. He wore a large, intricately carved crown and a decorative cuirass with carvings of bulls and lions. One hand reached out to the heavens, and the other held a representation of fire.

Vibrant paintings in hues of blue, red, and yellow decorated the walls, depicting the lives of their empire.

A multi-level palace perched on a cliff overlooking the sea, with throngs of adoring people looking up to a King standing on an extended balcony.

A lilies, mandrake, and yellow rose garden alongside a long circular canal.

A giant central circular courtyard with the statue of a god—a bearded man, with majestic wings, holding fire in one hand and a stack of tablets in the other.

Rows of ships anchored near a curved harbor.

Women bedecked in jewelry and dancing to a man with a harp.

Warriors hunting a herd.

A dancer pirouetting in front of a bull.

A slender, royal woman standing before a crowd that bowed to her.

An old King and a beautiful young woman—his wife or daughter—beside him.

A giant man, naked and wearing a bull's mask, standing in what appeared to be a labyrinth.

A council of several men and women listening to the old King.

It was a glorious tapestry of an ancient era. In one section, men and women watched us in silent contempt as we walked by.

And then we noticed something on the floor—skeletons. Hundreds of them, with their degraded garments and jewelry still in place. Some headless and others simply splayed on the floor. I was horrified, and Eurydice closed her mouth with her palm. It was as if the freezing finger of death reached up from under us and touched my neck, gently caressing. My hair stood with terror—were the dead reaching to us? I uttered a prayer under my breath.

What had happened here?

Was this what the ancient writer meant when he said that the Lord had put people to the sword as they ate? We walked carefully avoiding stepping on the dead so disgracefully left behind. Three other passageways radiated from the dome—each next to a statue. On each entrance was a stone plaque with ancient writings; warnings or words of wisdom—we did not know.

We walked around—our breathing the only sounds apart from the hiss of the orange-blue flames that danced and burned.

"Where to next?" I whispered. She looked around unsure, and pointed to the passage straight ahead, opposite to the one we came from. As we walked into it, the lamps lit again. It opened to a chamber smaller than the central dome but still impressive in its size. On the floor were hundreds of stone beds and all around were shelves hewn into the rock.

On some were more skeletons—it was as if they were murdered in their sleep.

"Living quarters?" I said. The beds at the far end were on higher ground, larger, and ornate, signifying the stature of the sleeper. Several small baths and pits were carved into the stone. There were also more sealed doors.

Eurydice placed her hands below a small conduit in the rock wall.

"I thought water would flow to my palms," she said. We were beginning to expect wondrous magic at every turn. After a while, we realized there was nothing else here, and we returned to the dome to pick another passage. "This one is narrower and much longer," I said, as we passed two unfinished doors on the way.

"Are those guardrooms?" Eurydice pointed to the two rooms on the side.

"Could be. This does not look like a passage for the commoners."

The passage ended in steps that went down, and the floor of the chamber was several feet below us—we could see the entire level from where we stood. In the center was a large decorative stone vault. And radiating outwards, in concentric circles, were smaller stone vaults. We descended and walked up to one of the structures for closer examination.

These were not simple stone vaults.

These were containers with sarcophagi inside.

I heard Eurydice gasp behind me.

"Is that gold?" she said, placing her palm on the top of the lid of the vault in front of us.

I grinned. Every vault was inlaid with sheets of gold on the surface.

We walked around without touching anything. The one in the middle was the grandest with elaborate paintings on all sides. "They carved these vaults here and placed the sarcophagi inside them. Look at the designs; they are all the same. The only difference is the grandeur."

On each corner of the lid was a locking latch.

"Are we going to open one of them?" she whispered.

"Of course."

We opened the latches.

Then we stood at an angle on the bottom right corner of a smaller vault and pushed on the lid to the side.

It did not budge.

My puzzlement changed to realization. This time we stood behind and pushed it with all our strength. That force was unnecessary, for the lid glided forward. Underneath were tiny wheels on the grooved rim of the stone vault. The design was brilliant. We peered inside in the dim light; the glinting hinted at what was inside, but I wanted to make sure. I removed the torch from my bag and lit it and held it over the open space.

We gasped in unison and paused to absorb the breathtaking display.

The vault was filled with elegant gold-plated swords and crowns, lapis-lazuli and ebony decorative vases, silver and ivory goblets, gold and quartz musical figurines with intricately carved harps, silver ingots, red wood-carved boxes with thick gold padlocks, scepters, shining silk woven through series of gold rings. Buried underneath was a solid gold sarcophagus.

Speechless, we went to the next, and then the next, and another. Each one was similar, filled with precious artifacts—some with a sarcophagus and most without. It was by far the most spectacular collection of wealth I had ever seen. The treasure was unquestionably from various regions—Egyptian, Persian, Phoenician, Atlantean—no tactician would question why Eumenes sought this place— this would help him raise his armies and forge an empire.

"Let us go to the center," I said.

Could they be different?

We opened the vaults in the first concentric circle around the central vault. There were fifteen in all, of which thirteen were like the rest—filled to the brim. But two had nothing but a desiccated corpse with its mouth open. Eurydice screamed when a muscular rat jumped from within and scurried. For some reason, the builders had left these vaults empty in a hurry.

"The little demon is afraid of rats, who knew?" I teased, and she swatted my hand.

"What if the ancients placed a curse on this place?" she said, with a worried voice.

"The omens favor us," I said, with false confidence.

We finally went to the largest vault in the center. I gave the flame for Eurydice to hold, hauled myself on the vault and straddled the rim.

"Have you lost your mind?" she scolded me while making frantic gestures to the divine.

I made faces to annoy her further—and then I extended my hand. After a moment of hesitation, she grabbed it, and I pulled her up. We both peered under the orange glow. In the center was a massive, gold and lapis-lazuli sarcophagus of a pharaoh. Behind the pharaonic head was a large stone tablet with a script under the cartouche of the Pharaoh. All around lay grouped valuables, each one inlaid with gems. Near the foot was a flat gold plaque with ancient writings. On each side of the writing was a clear etch of the great pyramids I had seen long ago and heard much about. I wondered why a Pharaoh's sarcophagus was here. Who was he? Did the Atlanteans plunder Egypt?

I wondered what the writings said, and if they unlocked greater mysteries. We climbed down and looked at each other in disbelief.

"Do you question whether this discovery can alter the fate of empires?" I asked.

She seemed frightened at what lay ahead of us.

"Whoever finds it…" her voice trailed.

"Eumenes. No one else should find it."

"And you are confident there will be no bloodbath if he gets his hands on this?"

"I am confident of nothing…" I said. And that was true. I had no idea anymore how Eumenes might treat this.

My mind returned to the situation in the canyon below—what had happened? What would we find when we returned?

"What should we do next?" she asked.

"We explore the third passage."

"What if there are traps?"

"I do not think so. The ancients left this place with the intention to return—this was not meant to be a tomb."

She was not convinced, but her curiosity exceeded her reservation. I reached into one of the vaults and grabbed a handful of gold jewelry, a gem laid scepter, and several coins. She shook her head, but I pretended not to notice. When we were about to leave, she did a little of her thieving grinning mischievously.

I extinguished the flame on my torch, and we headed back to the dome. The final passage was much longer. We noticed three unfinished doors with guardrooms beside each one. When the passage ended, we stepped into another large chamber. Enormous lamps lit up all around us, flooding the chamber with eerie, reddish light and burning away the darkness.

Around us was a depiction of hell.

The chamber floor was bare except three stone vaults placed in a triangular formation. On each lid were grotesque carvings.

A man consuming a woman's entrails.

A group burning to death.

A city in flames.

An army with all decapitated soldiers.

A man contorted in pain with his heart exposed.

But that was not all. Three panels, one on each wall, depicted either what they had done or planned to do.

The first panel showed a city in flames. At a distance from the city was the shore and beyond that lay ships. Raining down from the sky were metal birds whose tails spewed fire. These were giant missiles launched not by men nor catapults. The shiny red, yellow, and orange hues bequeathed a demonic vibrancy to the panel which showed the impact of these fiery missiles on the ground—large fires and explosions engulfed the city, and the residents fled in terror.

We walked along the wall to the next one.

The second panel showed many Egyptians on the ground—their faces in agony and bodies covered in blisters. Some thrust swords to their bellies and others set themselves on fire. On the edge of the painting stood a man wearing an elaborate mask of a bull with two long horns. In his hand was a jar with the mouth of a snake, and droplets of an orange-red liquid fell from its mouth. What distinguished these paintings was the lifelike nature, unlike the beautiful, but flat artistry I had seen in Egypt or Babylonia.

"By the grace of all gods…" I said.

"Are these an artist's imagination?" Eurydice whispered as she stood next to me and gripped my forearm.

"Not if you believe the scrolls and the fables," I said, as my voice dissipated in the cavernous emptiness of the chamber. I studied the man with the jar. Evil oozed from him, and I felt his eyes from behind the mask.

I then turned towards the last panel and studied it from right to left.

The scene showed an extensive line of kneeling people, Egyptian and other, bound by chains at their necks. In front of them stood rows of people, but they contorted as if invisible demons tormented them. Blood gushed from gaping wounds on their bodies. To the far left, a row of Atlanteans soldiers held pipes that they pointed towards the dying. It was as if an invisible force came forth from their weapons and killed the enemy. A Pharaoh was depicted as running away, flinging his bow and arrows aside, despair and terror writ large on his face.

What terrified me was the alien methods on these panels. Who could fight an empire with such instruments of terror? After what I had seen so far, I had no reason to believe these were fictional. I went to one of the sarcophagi and noticed that the lid had a similar opening latch as the ones in the treasure room. We slid it and peered into the vault.

There was no gold coffin or jewelry.

Inside lay a mummified body of a man.

His shriveled face contorted in a scream.

The hands and feet were bound by a chain, and rats scurried about. A broken clay jar, like the ones shown on the wall painting, lay beside him.

I shuddered.

We both stepped back and knelt again, praying to the gods for our safety. Fear had replaced the thrill of the find. We then stepped into a chamber connected to another massive room—the weapons room with various devices whose purpose I imagined was what was on the panels. There were strange chariots—their rear a great metallic bulk, and the front with long tubes. Then there were many large iron spheres with protrusions on the surface. Resting against the walls were hundreds of metallic missiles with fins much like the wall panels. Each of those was the height of two to three men. On another side, large stone shelves that seemed to stretch to eternity held thousands of tubes that shot invisible power. From the ceiling hung thousands of jars, the jars of death depicted on the panels. And there were additional doors, all sealed, with pictures of angry contorting lions on each.

How much more was behind these doors? And what lay there?

"I have never seen anything like this," she said. "Could they be decoys meant to frighten the enemy?"

"This is too much effort to secure decoys."

"If these people were not destroyed—"

"They would have enslaved the world," I completed her sentence. "But the gods saw to it. They warned them not to test divine patience, but the Atlanteans paid no heed."

I placed my palm on the cool surface of the stone door and thought of my next move. But then a deep fear and sorrow rose in me—what should I do now?

Should I find Eumenes and hand him the secret? It would no doubt cause an eruption of violence until the matter was settled. But then if Eumenes' ambition flared—there was no question that the finds here would wreck a lot more destruction. And who knew what this would unleash?

And what if we somehow failed and someone else, perhaps Antigonus or even Ptolemy, secured this find? I had absolutely no doubt that they would unleash hell upon the world for those men had ambitions to surpass Alexander himself if they could.

Do I walk away? I could leave all this behind and go with some of my steal, and then hope to free my family. But that path would be paved by threat and risk at every step with little chance—and after all this effort, I might simply die or fail on the way, therefore dooming my family.

Was my wife's embrace worth risking a million innocents to death?

My head hurt. I cursed the gods for placing such decisions on a simple soldier! But we were not done yet.

"There will be an opportunity in the future to examine this, but for now we must return."

"Do you think there is more?" she asked.

"I definitely do. You saw there were more connected doors—what lies beyond one can only imagine."

"Do you think your men prevailed?"

"There is only one way to find out," I said, and we began to walk back to the dome. I had to decide the course of action based on the outcome of the battle that I hoped ended a while ago. We reached the central dome and spent a brief time admiring this wondrous place once again. Then we headed to the exit. That was when I noticed a figure far up ahead walking towards us.

No.

We ran back to the dome—I saw little point in trying to hide. Experienced soldiers knew how to search, and there was little time. We got behind the fire in the center and watched the man as he emerged from the passageway. He stopped in amazement.

Alkimachus.

Relief swept over me.

"Is the battle over?" I asked. I did not have to shout, for the voice carried in the vast spaces.

"Yes. This is quite a find, Deon, what is this place?" he said, looking around like a child in a town fair.

Not commander. Not captain. I was now Deon.

"I was not lying. How are the men? What happened to the enemy?"

He rubbed the bloodied armor on his chest.

"Most are dead, unfortunately."

"How many alive?"

"I don't know, five, ten?"

I did not understand the evasiveness. "What is going on, Alkimachus? We need to regroup and get the message out to Eumenes."

He said nothing as we watched each other from across the flames. And then he turned his face to the passage and yelled. "They are here."

As I watched in suspense, a large man emerged and stood next to Alkimachus.

Nekh-Aser.

We stared at each other as they stepped closer to the flames. Eurydice and I on one side of the stone podium and

Alkimachus and Nekh-Aser on the other. Then Nekh-Aser casually kicked a skeleton by his foot, and it shattered.

"There is nowhere to run, Deon."

"Didn't take you for a treasonous scum, Alkimachus, what are you doing with this backward dog?"

Nekh-Aser did not take the bait this time. He stood motionlessly—his dark eyes reflected the fire. Alkimachus continued, "Eumenes' time is up. You would know that if you listened to the reports."

"I was busy, as you can see."

"My loyalties switched to Antigonus before we met. The great man was intrigued by Eumenes' orders to find you. We decided to see this through."

"Brave of you to betray the man who you serve," I said.

"I am certain Antigonus would make you an offer. But it seems our friend here has other plans," he said, gesturing to Nekh-Aser.

"I am sure he does. But tell me Alkimachus, since when were you plotting with that brute?" I asked, but they continued to ignore my taunts.

"Only recently. You took me by surprise by moving from Sharuhen, but I knew Ptolemy's pursuit force was on the way. Like mature adults, we exchanged messages and came up with a strategy."

"You are a fool to think Antigonus and Ptolemy will align and share what they find here," I said.

"That is not for us to decide. We little men will find comfort with what we can and let the greater men fight for what is theirs," he said, smiling.

"A strategy that led to the needless death of so many men that looked up to you."

"You gave me no choice but to pretend until the end, and he would wait no longer," Alkimachus pointed at Nekh-Aser.

"You could preserve your dignity by holding up to your original oath to Eumenes."

Alkimachus laughed, and Nekh-Aser grinned from behind his hideous cage. "You are naïve. We are beholden to masters whose fates shine brighter on a given day. It is Antigonus' and Ptolemy's world now—it is time you bid goodbye to that secretary."

I shook my head in disdain. But if they were talking, they could be a way out. "That secretary killed two of Alexander's great generals and is still out there. And he excels all others in intelligence and compassion—the world is better with him in power."

Nekh-Aser began to swing his terrible instrument.

Alkimachus continued, "The road to glory has ended for Eumenes. Have you not heard? There is a death sentence on him. There is no way for you to establish contact with your master or for him to come here."

"What happened to our men, or did you hand them over to your Egyptian handler?"

"Most of them are dead, fighting for you, for a lost cause. The few remaining have run away."

Sadness enveloped my heart. These men had waited for months, followed our orders, and Alkimachus had led them to their death. "There is not much for me to say, then."

"But we both—" he pointed to Nekh-Aser and continued, "have come to an interesting agreement. We have no use for either of you, but you may want to hear this."

"And what is that?"

"The woman goes to Nekh-Aser, and we spare you."

I glanced at Eurydice—the terror on her face was palpable. Nekh-Aser grabbed his crotch and said in his raspy voice, "I will show her god."

Alkimachus shot a look of irritation but continued. "Consider it, Deon. There is much at stake here."

There comes a time in a man's life when the choices he makes dictate the direction of the river of life he floats on. I had escaped death for over ten years, away from family. I finally had a chance to end it all and walk away with riches to my family. Unfortunately, that meant a sacrifice—even if there was a connection between us. I wondered why I was fighting for a lost cause. I glanced at Eurydice. Her breathing was heavy, and her fingers trembled. Whether it was a tear that glistened from the corner of her eye or whether it was sweat I could not make out.

Our time was up. My voice conveyed my fatigue. "I am tired of the fighting Alkimachus. But for this to end what is my reward for handing her over?"

Alkimachus smiled. I watched Eurydice turn towards me in horror, but she stood immobilized.

"I am disappointed that she is worth so little, Deon," said Alkimachus, and they laughed.

"I got what I wanted from her," I said, coldly.

"You dirty bastard!" screamed Eurydice and turned towards me in a fury. I knew the deadly power of her attack, so gripped her hand swiftly. I leaned to her and hissed, "Stay quiet until I resolve the barter, or I will gut you here."

I stared into her wide eyes. Her lips began to tremble, and she swooned slightly. She was a fighter, but she would be no match for three experienced men. Besides, I knew all her tricks. I could break her like a twig if she tried fighting me.

"Go stand near that entrance," I commanded her, pointing to the door to the armory. I needed no distraction now. With unsteady steps, she moved back and stood as the rest of us watched. Flames crackled. For a distracted moment, I wondered how the fire was so pure. There was no smoke.

Then I turned to Alkimachus.

"Ah, my reward," I said.

Alkimachus leaned and placed his hands on his hips. "Let us be done with this."

I pointed at Nekh-Aser. "I want Nekh-Aser to pull out his cock and cut it off while singing an erotic song about his mother."

Nekh-Aser rushed towards us.

"Run inside!" I screamed at Eurydice and ran towards the armory passage. My feet crushed the brittle bones under my feet; another ignominy heaped on the unfortunates who had met their end here. We put some distance as we ran through the passage that led to the chamber with hellish paintings since we knew the path and they were cautious.

I whispered to her, "May the gods protect you, little demon."

She let out a little gasp of relief and then positioned herself behind a vault. Nekh-Aser and Alkimachus entered the chamber. They looked at the panels with their mouth agape and in wonder, before turning their attention to us.

"Give up. This is not our game to play," Alkimachus shouted.

I turned to Nekh-Aser, "Since she proved you a eunuch why don't you regain your dignity by fighting a man this time."

He moved towards me while Alkimachus eyed Eurydice. I watched as the two men separated.

It was time.

Eurydice readied herself for what was to come. Alkimachus had been deferential to her but never friendly. His actions today showed that no past relation mattered.

"I give you the choice of a merciful death," he said, raising his sword that glinted under the golden glow of the lamps. Eurydice focused on the surrounding. In the corner, she could see Nekh-Aser inch towards Deon. They were moving away from her.

Alkimachus advanced in measured steps.

She had her dagger in her right hand and a heavy gold seal in her left.

"A painless death would be boon compared to what he would do to a beautiful woman like you," Alkimachus hissed. He covered the distance and was at an arms-length from her. Eurydice braced for attack and hunched, like a lioness preparing to pounce on prey. Except that Alkimachus thought she was the prey.

The little demon.

That was what Deon had called her.

It gave her strength.

Eurydice's father had taught her something valuable about close combat. Warriors rarely fought for long stretches—death or flight happened within moments. The fantastic clash of swords and dancing around each other was good for theater.

For her, there would be no fleeing.

Alkimachus thrust his sword, and Eurydice stepped back to avoid the blade. He grinned and waved the weapon as it glinted under the dancing flames.

He rushed her again, toying with her.

Pretty little deer.

Ready for butchering.

Eurydice jumped behind the vault, causing Alkimachus to lurch with his hand extended. Then, at lightning speed, Eurydice smashed the gold seal on Alkimachus' wrist. He gasped in surprise and pain and drew his hand back. The smile vanished, and his face scrunched in rage.

Eurydice sprinted around the vault forcing Alkimachus to turn to face her.

She did not stop.

Instead, she lunged at him and in the final moment slid and slashed Alkimachus' tendons below the knee.

He screamed but swung his sword with impressive precision. The tip of the blade scraped Eurydice's shoulder and sliced her skin. She flinched but sprung back and ran again in the opposite direction. Furious, Alkimachus hurled abuses—he had never faced this tactic and worse, this was a woman!

"You will regret this, you fucking whore," he screamed. He chased her, slashing his sword in the air hoping to connect.

But Eurydice was quick on her feet. She changed direction and forced him to turn again. Alkimachus had forgotten all his training—anger fueled his actions now exactly how Eurydice wanted.

As he turned to face her, she aimed and launched the gold seal at his unguarded loins. As a teenager, she was an expert at throwing pebbles on a lake's surface, and her pebbles traveled across the water farther than any of her friends'. Alkimachus grunted, and he withdrew to a guarded position. Eurydice sprinted to his side for an attack from behind, but Alkimachus swung and caught her hair.

She felt his powerful grip and pain blinded her as he pulled her towards him. She turned, and before Alkimachus could swing his sword, swung her dagger low and stabbed him in the side.

Alkimachus' mouth opened in soundless agony. Eurydice did not stop—she withdrew the dagger and swung upward under his cheekbone. The serrated blade slid into his cheek like animal fat and punctured his eye.

Alkimachus' sword fell on the stone floor.

He collapsed screaming and covered his face as he rolled around.

She bent close to him, her chest heaving. Her dark hair dropped in front of eyes and glistened with blood that sparkled under the amber light. As Alkimachus flailed about, she smashed a knee on his chest and plunged her dagger into his chest. She heard his final tortured breaths and gurgling as blood welled up his mouth and nose. Alkimachus grunted and quivered until his body finally stopped moving. Eurydice stopped to regain her faculties and took a breath as the surge of strength in her body began to ebb. She then found the gold seal nearby and picked it up. It was time to find Deon.

She followed the sounds of struggle to find the two men on the ground. Nekh-Aser lay on the floor with Deon on him—his back on Nekh-Aser's stomach. Deon was struggling as Nekh-Aser choked him.

Eurydice approached Nekh-Aser and raised her dagger again. His fist exploded with stunning speed and smashed into her face. The force hurled Eurydice backward to the stone wall of another vault. The taste of blood in her mouth and sharp pain in her shoulder melded into a swirl of darkness.

CHAPTER 33.

KNIFE'S TIP

The world darkened as Nekh-Aser squeezed my throat with brute force. Blood rushed to my ears, and my eyes bulged. I sensed someone come near us, and Nekh-Aser relaxed his pressure as one hand released to hit someone.

I heard a loud thud and a gasp—a woman's gasp.

She was alive!

A heavy object dropped, rolled, and touched behind my knee. I crooked my leg to push it towards me and grasped it in my right hand as Nekh-Aser tried to regain his balance. I then smashed it to the metal cage that protected Nekh-Aser's jaw. The impact jolted my wrist, and Nekh-Aser screamed through the contraption.

Enjoy that the second time, you piss drinking pig fucker.

I rolled off him and gasped to regain my breath and clear my head. I had no time to search for my kopis. Nekh-Aser punched me hard on the ribs. It felt like a hammer slammed into me, and I doubled in pain. I mustered my strength and scrambled to my feet. The Egyptian was standing up—he looked like a beast rising from the underworld. I leaned back and kicked him hard on his chest, and he toppled over. I rushed and stomped my foot on his face again. The metal hinges snapped, and I heard the crunching sound of bones and teeth. The brute lost consciousness.

I crawled to the slumped figure of Eurydice. She was still breathing, but there was slick wetness down her lips and nose. She was injured but alive.

Where was Alkimachus?

I found Alkimachus lying dead in an expanding pool of blood, his face unrecognizable. Another in the extensive list of fools that underestimated Eurydice. I tended to her—she woke up after I wiped her face and dripped some water on her lips from the water bladder. She was groggy and tensed, but she relaxed once she felt my face with her palms. I tied the Nekh-Aser's hands and feet using necklaces and braces from the treasury.

Satisfied, I took a gulp of water and sat down to rest and regain my strength.

It was time to introspect.

Nekh-Aser finally regained consciousness. I sprinkled water on his face, and he came to clarity. Rage and fury burned in his eyes as he fought the restraints.

"If you nod your yes or no I could ease your way to the afterlife," I said, as I pressed the tip of my kopis on his chest. He did not respond.

"Are there people waiting for us outside?"

No response.

"Does anyone else know of this place?"

No response.

"Have they sentenced Eumenes to death?"

No response.

"Is Eumenes nearby?"

No response.

"Is Ptolemy nearby?"

No response.

"You gain nothing by silence. But your truthful answers can ease your suffering."

No response.

"I will even pray for your journey," I said, though my heart protested.

He grimaced. I persisted.

"If you have a last wish—a token to your wife—I could fulfill that for you."

Nekh-Aser strained to look at Eurydice who watched him. Then the Egyptian thrust his hips up and down while smiling through his blood-crusted, crushed mouth. His demonic eyes then turned on me in defiance.

I knew then that Nekh-Aser sought no redemption and no love existed in all the world to mend his dark heart. Eurydice struggled to stand, and I held her as she swooned. She whispered, "Let me…"

Nekh-Aser thrashed against the restraints when he saw Eurydice with her serrated blade. His muffled screams dissolved in the hollow of the immense dome. But as she was about to exact her vengeance, she hesitated, and I sensed a revulsion sweep over her.

She sat down first, and then she slumped on the floor.

Nekh-Aser's eyes smiled. I clubbed his head, and he lost consciousness.

I was not done yet.

Eurydice had lacerations on her arms, injured nose, and a dislocated shoulder. I wondered if the ancients had miraculous medicines. But we had seen no evidence, and I was not about to begin a new search in this condition. We limped to the central dome. No one else was here—it seemed Nekh-Aser and Alkimachus pursued us themselves. We ate some of the packed meat and drank more water. As energy returned, I let Eurydice rest and made a trip to the treasury with our bags. I threw out the heavier gold ornaments and filled our bags with exquisite gold coins. Those would still fetch a handsome sum if we survived long enough to barter.

After I came back, I had one more thing to take care of—Eurydice's shoulder. Physicians had taught me how to fix a dislocated shoulder. She screamed as I probed the joints and snapped her shoulder back. She recovered quickly, and it was time to move.

That was when it dawned upon me that we might be heading out to an ambush. Why would just Nekh-Aser and Alkimachus come here? Why were there no others backing them up? I knew Ptolemy was no fool—it was entirely possible that the Governor had someone else watching Nekh-Aser all the time. But we were exhausted—Eurydice was in no condition to fight, and I was hurt in many places. I could handle one man or two, but no more.

I had no choice but to try something I never wanted to.

I carried Eurydice back to the armory passage and let her lie in the darkness. Then I headed to the weapons chamber. The mute pictures on the walls watched me as I ran to the corner that had the magical cylinders and spheres that spawned fire. I picked one of the cylinders—it was about three feet long, heavy, and had a shiny metallic tint on it. Fine grooves were etched all along the circumference. On the side of the pipe was a lever, which, I imagined, was the mechanism to trigger it to bring forth its destructive power. I did not know what to do with the sphere, but I dropped two of them to a bag fashioned from cloth that adorned the statues. I ran back to the central dome and told Eurydice to stay where she was at the passage entrance.

Then I waited. It did not take long before I heard faint noises at the entry passage.

"Stay where you are," I whispered to Eurydice, and I moved a few feet from the entry. Nine men stepped out from the dim light — all of them Ptolemy's men. I did not recognize any of them, but the leader asked everyone to stay close and eyed us from across the steps.

"Where are they?"

"Dead, and you will be too," I responded. The leader's eyes went to the cylinder in my hand.

"Well, we have orders to arrest you and take control of this—whatever this place is," he retorted, looking around. His men had not fanned about, and that was an advantage.

"I know you will kill us at the first chance," I said, as my finger played with the lever. I had no idea what it would do, but I would find out.

One of the men laughed. "You are a smart one!"

"And you will be a dead one if you don't turn back."

The leader's expression changed from amusement to seriousness. "We can make this quick," he said, and they began to move forward.

This was it.

I rushed them—they were all bunched around their leader and still near the mouth of the exit of the entry passage. I pointed the cylinder just as I had seen in the wall panels—now I would find out if this weapon was endowed with magical powers or if I was only a fool—soon to be a dead fool.

The lever on the side did not move at first, but then it slid slightly. I felt the tension in it, and I pulled it hard again. There was a distinct metallic click—they froze in a surprise of what this "thing" was, and I stared at the end of pipe hoping for something to happen. Nothing happened.

"Are you going to club us all to death?" The leader laughed. Then they drew their swords and began to advance—panic rose in my belly. "We'll slaughter you like we did your men down there!"

I raised the pipe and pulled on the lever hard again. But this time the metallic click had a different tone to it, and the cylinder vibrated violently in my hand. The back end of it rammed into my shoulder, and vibrant yellow flame shot from the tip. The leader's head exploded in an instant, and two men next to him flew back as if slammed by an invisible hand.

I stood in paralyzed disbelief and stared at the remaining men—and they looked at me in horror. I pulled the lever hard again, and another fiery explosion followed, this time dropping two more men. Blood, pieces of flesh, and bone fragments flew into me. The remaining four turned and took flight, but in that instant, I knew what I had to do. I knew running after them would be futile, for my injuries prevented me from catching up. I tried to trigger the weapon again, but it would no longer shoot the fire.

I remembered the cloth-bag. I reached in and pulled out a cold, metallic sphere. The surface was smooth with no etchings or any triggering mechanism. With all my strength I launched it in the direction of the receding backs of my attackers, hoping that something terrible would happen when it struck them. The sphere arced in the narrow passage, the surface reflecting the golden light of the lamps, and contacted the wall just in front of the lead runner. And just as I imagined an angry Zeus launching fiery thunderbolts from the sky, white-hot fire exploded from the point of impact and engulfed every man around it. But no man ran screaming; it was as if they had all vanished from the earth—the fire had evaporated their flesh, and all that was on the floor was charred bones and bits and pieces of their garments. The acrid smell of burnt flesh filled the passage. The explosion had done something else too—pieces of wood and other material on the walls had caught fire, and the flames were beginning to spread to the roof of the passage. Like snakes of fire, flames licked the walls and climbed up, creating a spectacular sight like an orange blooming flower on the ceiling.

I leaned on the wall and composed myself—my mind finally coming to terms with what this unearthly power would give its masters. I returned to Eurydice. She held me and would not let go until I calmed her and that it was all over. She had heard the sounds and feared for the worst—and I told her what I had experienced.

"Why did the gods bestow them with such power and then destroy them?" She asked. I had only one answer—

"Perhaps the gods wanted to test the Atlanteans' ambition, and the Atlanteans failed," I said, unconvincingly.

It was time to return. When we returned to the passage, we realized our perilous state. The passage roof was enveloped in a sheet of fire, and the tongues were reaching into the corners of the dome, lighting up wood. We had to rush, or risk being burned to death.

I hurriedly placed two more metallic spheres in my bag. We gave one last look at the magnificent dome and hobbled back to the entrance, our hair singed from the flames just above our head and skin on the forehead burnt in places. We ignored the pain and goaded each other. Once we reached the entrance, we turned back to find the entire passage engulfed, and it was as if the gods had once again decided to punish the Atlanteans. We closed the stone door using the levers and slipped out of the narrow oblique opening. But before we exited, I flung another sphere through the passage. It exploded, and a great breath of fire emanated from the point of explosion and spread on the walls—the fire rushed at us like a monster with no form, but just before it reached us it arced upwards into an unseen crack. As we stood shocked, a great vibration began and caused the walls to collapse inward, burying most of the chamber with the levers to open the stone door to the inner passage.

I managed Eurydice with care and helped her onto the ledge and got her to safety. Sadness washed over me as I looked at the narrow opening on the side of the cliff. I had spent a life fighting, killing, maiming. And this discovery would only lead to more of it.

I then helped Eurydice farther back on the ledge and asked her to sit. I then reached into my bag and removed another sphere—I turned back to look at Eurydice who watched me quietly. Even in the cool air, sweat rolled off my neck and back. And then I aimed at the edge of the ledge and threw the sphere. It exploded on impact, and the fragile ledge collapsed. I rushed back as cracks appeared near my feet. Eurydice and I ignored our pain and rapidly moved to the narrow cliffside path. From where we stood, the narrow opening was now invisible, hidden in the fold of the mountain. There were other supporting structures on the ledge, and they collapsed as well. I also suspected that the shadows would no longer paint the complete picture as they did before.

We had found what we were set to do, and yet there was no joy in it. I looked wistfully in the direction of the second Atlantis—now hidden again, for how long only the gods knew. What we had seen was nothing short of remarkable—only a fertile mind could imagine what still lay undiscovered in the hidden city if it had not burned entirely. Surprisingly, there was little smoke from anywhere in the mountain, and it was as if the second Atlantis was hiding its secrets again. But for now, the wars of the Diadochi loomed to pit friends and fellow men against each other for years to come. The second Atlantis, if discovered, would only power the flames of destruction and turn it into a conflagration.

I returned to the location of the battle in the narrow cliff passage. There was death all around us—my men had fought bravely, but Alkimachus' treachery had ended their lives. We made way to our hidden campsite and ate. I applied medicine to our injuries, and we rested for the night. The next morning, we embarked on our journey home—and in the narrow paths of the cliff, we met some Nabatean traders. What had happened here? They wanted to know. "Some soldiers thought there was a treasury in the stones," I replied, and they shook their head. In hindsight, our plan of what to do after we found this was laughable. There was no way for me to get back to Eumenes and have him divert an army to this location. If the news I heard was true, Antigonus was on Eumenes' heels. Ptolemy had his men to our south. Seleucus was flexing his muscles in the East. How could Eumenes march an entire army, undetected, and hold and protect this location? The only thing that would happen was that the second Atlantis would fall into the hands of one of those men.

Plato was right.

Some secrets are best left unrevealed.

PART V

Now

"Revenge is not always better,
But neither is forgiveness"
—The Mahabharatha

CHAPTER 34.

MACEDON

Krokinos eyes me from across the courtyard. I count ten armed men who wait for his command. I had interrupted his dinner, but I was not bearing gifts for my lender. Today is the culmination of my long journey from the second Atlantis. I had tracked Krokinos to his villa and hired hardened mercenaries, once Alexander's soldiers themselves, to put an end to this story. I had put to good use what I had secured in the second Atlantis. Hiring a skilled force is extraordinarily expensive and I wished I had the backing of a general to help me free my family—but that was not to be. Whether this foolhardy mission would succeed or if my years of perseverance would end in all our demise was yet to be seen.

But I have no choice. I have to do this now before it is too late.

Six of my men stand behind me, and Eurydice is behind them, hidden. Her shoulder is much better, and she has regained full mobility.

"Not the visit I was expecting—" he says, as his eyes dart like a snake's.

"It is the type of visit you could have avoided, Krokinos, if you were a good human being," I said.

He laughs. A fake, dramatic laugh on a bony, ugly, beak-nosed face. He looks like a desiccated corpse in a nobleman's attire.

"Says the man who wanted to peddle in whores!" he cackles, and his men roar in approval. I doubt they know who I am, for I had arrived in surprise.

"That was a mistake long ago, Krokinos. And while you were pimping, I was out conquering empires."

"Not you. Alexander. You were just a horse boy. Where is my money?"

I would not let him bait me. "Where are my wife and daughter?"

Silence descends on the room like a cool curtain. Krokinos' henchmen realize that this dispute has bigger implications. One of them tries to speak, but Krokinos gestures him to be quiet. "First, the money. Then your wife and daughter."

"You mistreated them. That was not our agreement. I want to know that they are well."

Krokinos steps forward, but not close enough to be in my reach. He puts his palms forward. "The. Money. But I know you do not have it, Deon, otherwise you would not be here threatening me."

The scene is tense. No one makes a sound, and it is as if there are twenty lions in a room all hunched to spring. "What makes you think I have no money? I want to see my family to make sure they are unharmed," I say. I am wary as well. For all I knew, what I did may have been the most foolish act in the world, leading to all our deaths.

Now Krokinos' wife, Diona, steps from behind. She is barely taller than a dwarf but has a tongue sharper than an executioner's blade. "I told him," she says, pointing to her husband, "that worthless scum like you would never repay. You think you can hide behind your service; no one cares!"

"Be quiet!" he admonishes her.

But she does not back down. "We have been too patient with you. I should have sold your wife to one of our whore houses long ago, and she'd fetch a decent price!" She bobs her head up and down. I feel an urge to watch it roll on the floor. I choose to ignore her.

"Where do we go next, Krokinos? I need to see my wife and daughter first. Where are they?"

Diona is relentless. "They can take quite a beating! Even your arrogant little daughter, she has quite a mouth!" she screams.

My face feels like someone held a burning torch to it. I grip the handle of my kopis, and I hear someone else pull their sword out of the sheath. Suddenly every sword is out, and the threatening blades reflect light.

"How dare you invade my house and make demands!" she screams. Her face is red, and even I am surprised at the anger. But I have seen enough hateful, immoral people to know the poison in their minds.

"I am making no demand. I am only—"

"We sold them to Phrygian slave traders!" she screams.

"Diona—" Krokinos starts, but it is too late. My anger explodes, rising from deep within my belly and engulfing every fiber.

I lunge forward, and my men spring to action. Krokinos' men are surprised but scramble to a fighting position. Two men get in my way before I can reach Krokinos. I slam my shield to them. One of them falls and the other staggers. I thrust my kopis into the chest of the man on my right. He drops like a rock, without a sound.

Then I attack the second man on the ground and strike his neck. Blood spurts from the severed vessels. It is chaos all around me, and I know from the initial attack that Krokinos' men are just local thugs and we would slaughter them like pigs. I turn to see one of my men bleeding from a large gash on his shoulder, but his attacker is lying on the ground in his death throes. The swords clash all around me, and I look for Krokinos.

He is cowering behind one of his henchmen. I take an attack stance and his guard, after some hesitation, lifts his hands and deserts his employer. I grab Krokinos by his and push him against the wall.

"What did you—"

"They're here!" he croaks, "she was just—"

"If you're lying..."

"I swear I'm not, I swear on the gods!"

"Take me to them, and tell your men to stand down," I say.

We shout in unison for everyone to stop. After a few more metallic clangs the courtyard turns quiet. I survey the carnage—four of his men are dead, two more howl on the ground and the others have laid down their arms and kneel. One of my men is dead, and the rest stand with minor nicks.

I chose my men well.

As much as I want to go with Krokinos, I know I must ensure that this place is secure. I call one of my men, "No one goes out or comes in."

Then I look for Eurydice, where is she?

She is behind a large pillar. In front of her is a terrified Diona, whimpering. Eurydice holds her dagger to the woman's throat.

"Don't do anything," I tell her. Eurydice nods.

I head back to Krokinos and slap him on his head. "Take me to them." One of my men comes with me for safety.

Krokinos owns a large home, no doubt a result of his many ventures. Intricate paintings in red and green pigment dye adorn the walls. Dancers, gods, kings; all convey happiness, piety, and virtue. None that match Krokinos' values.

"Why are there no painting of snakes, hyenas, and vultures?" I ask.

He looks at me confused, "what—"

"Nothing. Take me to them."

We walk through two halls, another porch with a garden, a large room with a kitchen, and then finally a hallway that ends in stairs. I see a few servants and slaves, but the rest are either hiding or live elsewhere.

We come to the steps, and Krokinos hesitates. I shove him forward. It is not a basement—there is a door just a few steps below.

"Why don't you wait here? I will bring them to you," he says. I see his hands shake. He does not want me to go there with him, I realize.

It must be bad.

"I can slice your throat and go there myself, make your choice," I tell him, and push him down.

Someone has locked the door from outside. I feel anguish when I realize that this is like a dungeon. Krokinos has the keys to it. My heart beats faster as I wait to enter—the large wooden door creaks as Krokinos opens it. I push him forward, and my guard stays close behind me. The first thing that hits me is the smell—it like a foul wet blanket that falls on me. It is a hellish odor of piss, shit, pus, pain, tears, and misery.

My eyes adjust to the darkness. There are some lamps, and a small opening on the back allows a little sunlight. There are many hunched figures in the room.

I whisper to Krokinos, "Tell your servants to bring lamps, many lamps." I hold the tip of my blade to his lower back, and he squirms. He shouts the orders.

Soon, four housekeepers arrive, each holding two large lamps. I tell them to go inside and stand near each corner. The lamps fill the room and what I see takes my breath away. The place is no different from godless slave quarters I have seen in Persia and Egypt. The floor is dirty. There are bare straw mattresses all around, and the dwellers' meager belongings line up the wall—pots, clothes, small possession boxes. There are many people here—mostly women and children, and some old men.

They look emaciated, scared, and dirty. Very dirty.

I am terrified at what I will find. I do not recognize anyone. My wife and daughter could be in front of me, but I would not know them.

They surely would not recognize me.

"Apollonia?" I say, loudly. There is no response. "Apollonia?" I say again, and a woman comes forward slowly.

It is not my wife. This woman is too old. I shake my head at her.

"This is Deon. I am back!"

I hear a gasp to my side, and I spin. There is a woman right beside me. A girl stands behind her.

It is as if an angry demon ripped the heart out of my chest. It is my wife—but her lustrous hair is gone, her face is sunken, her eyes hide inside dark pits. She wears a torn, dirty gown that barely covers her upper body.

"Apo...?" I hesitatingly step forward, and she does not move. I no longer care. I step forward and hug her, holding her as tightly as I can. First, nothing happens and then she begins to sob uncontrollably. She shakes, and the vibrations travel through my arms and chest like the thundering hoofs of war horses. I cannot control myself, and all the years of sadness and guilt come over me, and I cry as well.

It is a strange sensation... crying. But my tears fail to cleanse the dirt on her. We stay that way without words. Krokinos stands deathly quiet. Apollonia extricates herself, and then she delivers a stinging slap. She slaps me again, and again, and my ears ring. I hear the girl scream and try to pull my wife back. My face feels like hot embers—what man allows a woman to hit him? Instinctively my hands shoot up, and I grip her neck like a vice. Then I pull her forward. She does not flinch.

My grip on her neck tightens. There is a conflagration in my mind.

"Why did you do this to us?" She asks, her voice a hoarse whisper and yet it has the power of a Scythian's arrow. It pierces me, and I feel the voice of a thousand angry gods cursing at me.

Asking me what man I had become.

I let go of my wife. She clutches her neck but says not a word. I hold her again. This time she does not pull back and instead pushes her head to my chest and sobs. There is only the sound of breath. She controls herself and pulls my daughter forward. She has been crying as well, seeing her mother. And maybe with fear.

My daughter is skinny and dirty, like her mother—but to me, she is the most beautiful girl in the world. The daughter I had thought of so many times and held as a chubby baby. But now she reaches her mother's shoulder. She looks like my wife, I think, and thank the gods.

"Your father," my wife says. Alexa does not move. I bend down and gently hold her to my chest.

She freezes.

It is understandable.

I am a stranger.

I am the man that took away her childhood.

I am the man that put her mother in such pain.

I am the man that grabbed the neck of her mother when I should be consoling her.

But I intend to mend the distance. I let my daughter go and turn to my wife. "Shall we go?" I ask her.

She nods.

"Have you been held here?" She does not answer—Krokinos scares her. I address the people. "You are all free to go, no harm will come to you. Do you object, Krokinos?"

He nods vigorously. But no one moves yet—I let them be. I will be back, but first, there are other issues to fix. I lead my family out, and my guard drags Krokinos along, and we come back to the courtyard. I walk to one of my men and borrow a thick wooden club. Krokinos' eyes widen in terror as I brandish it in front of him.

"You are going to tell me a few things, and you shall not lie," I say.

"What more do you want? You got your family!" Krokinos protests. His shifty eyes roam the courtyard.

"Why were they in a dungeon?"

"That was no dungeon, it was—"

I smash the club on his foot and feel the bones of his toes separate. He howls. I never knew his voice could achieve such a pitch. Two of my men stand him up. Krokinos balances on one leg. He gasps. "I swear no one told me you were coming back. I was planning to release them—"

I swing the club again, and his knee cracks like an eggshell. He bellows and screams until his voice is hoarse. I hear Diona pleading with us not to kill him.

My wife and daughter stand in one corner—my daughter's face hidden behind her mother. I nod at her to take my daughter away from this ugly business. My wife disappears in the corridors and returns with another girl—the same age as my daughter—and has them both retreat to a room.

Once Krokinos catches his breath, I ask him again. "Why were they in the dungeon?"

He gasps and wipes the drool off his mouth. His head sways. I order one of my men to bring Diona. They drag her next to her husband—her eyes see the far nothing. That is the look of someone who is visited by the same violence that they once unleashed upon others.

"Sale. I was preparing to sell them," he finally says. His voice is dry like corn left open in a desert.

"Why?"

"The price for slaves is picking up! That's why!" He nurses his knee with a trembling hand.

"But Governor Eumenes paid part of my debt!" I shout at him.

Krokinos says weakly, "I never believed you would return. Everyone is fighting everyone else around here," his voice trails.

My mind is a raging cauldron of emotions—Krokinos would have condemned my family to slavery, but then I had prevented it. I decide to threaten him and let go, but just then my wife speaks.

Her voice carries gently, but it is strong as steel. "He lay his hands on me, and not just to beat."

Anger roars through my blood vessels like the Hydaspes through a gorge. Krokinos is about to say something, but I yank his head back and slice his neck open with my kopis. Blood spurts all over, drenching his robe and his wife's face.

She does not react but instead begins to rock, murmuring.

Krokinos thrashes about clutching his neck, and I watch him. Air bubbles through the gash on his throat—his breathing slows and the light in his eyes fades, and his life seeps away. The floor is slick, and I step away from his contamination.

Then I turn to Diona. At first, my reaction is to kill her, but then I stop. I have seen too often the gentle nature of women transformed by the beasts that they lay with. Instead, I slap her hard, bringing her back to her senses.

She begins to wail, and I tell her to shut up. She finally listens.

"Free those you planned to sell. You will personally clean them, mend their wounds, and pay them a year's salary. If you try anything, you will die and so will your children. I will find them, and make you watch as I nail them to the posts."

She nods vigorously. And then she gets up and trudges towards the dungeon.

I decide to hold Krokinos' remaining goons. We disarm them and warn that any hostile action would lead to death. They say they have no conflict with us anymore now that Krokinos is dead, and only that Diona must pay them. I promise to take care of that. My heightened awareness and strength soon wear off, and after so many years my shoulders feel light. My chest no longer feels the constriction. I turn to Eurydice watching me—her green eyes quietly assessing the situation.

We all wash, cleanse, have the freed servants cook some food for us. It is a strange experience. Sitting around a table and eating good food, surrounded by happy-looking people, with my wife and daughter by my side. They are finally smiling, even though I know it will take years to expel the demons that now live within them.

Eurydice sits among my men, she does not talk, but I notice my wife and her trade glances several times.

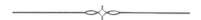

Once we eat, I summon Diona again. It is important to reiterate that she takes care of the household, and keeps her attack dogs at bay. She comes back, looking nervous. The men and women around the table look on as I issue my commands to her, and she listens without a word. I cannot see her eyes as they are downcast and hidden by her disheveled hair. Her pudgy face is further puffed by crying and stress.

"I want no disobedience, Diona. You will conduct—" I turn towards the table. That is when I feel an indescribable pain shoot through my lower abdomen; it is like a hot poker, and I scream. Through the shock and pain, I see several people shoot up from their chairs, and I see Eurydice move behind me.

There are noises.

There is screaming, and then there is a sensation of something sticky and wet on me.

My world descends into a blur of moving objects and strange sensations.

CHAPTER 35.

MACEDON

Eurydice eats quietly. There is levity in the room. Deon sits comfortably, with his wife and daughter by his side. They exchange glances, but not much is said. Deon's wife looks at her time to time. She is a beautiful, dignified woman, and she has been through much. The daughter is shy, but Eurydice can see the relief and happiness.

Deon summons Diona, the terrible wife of the dead lender. The woman radiates hate, and she listens quietly, head bowed, to what Deon is saying. Eurydice watches intently; she does not like Diona's false modesty. Every snake catcher knows that the viper never mellows. Deon stands up, and as he talks to her, he turns towards the table as if to address the rest of the group. It is then that Diona, a foot shorter than Deon, suddenly pulls out a short iron spike and drives it into Deon's side. He screams in surprise and turns, and Eurydice jumps up.

Deon stumbles around, frantically attempting to make sense of what had happened, and Eurydice dashes behind Deon. She unsheathes her serrated dagger and in one swift motion grabs Diona's hair, yanks her back, and stabs Diona in her chest. Blood springs like a fountain and drenches her, and Diona collapses in a heap. Deon staggers, and Eurydice steps back as several men rush forward to hold him.

Eurydice watches as Deon's wife scrambles to hold her husband and tends to him. There are orders to bring bandage and wine, and they lay him down to inspect the wounds. It seems that the spike did not drive deep into Deon but went through the corner of his side, sparing vital organs. Deon's wife cradles his head and gently caresses him, and the daughter holds his hand. They patch his wound as he groans and shakes.

She thinks of their journey.

The first time he had defended her.

His stupid jokes on the way to Alexandria.

The time he kissed her.

The frightening skirmish on the boat.

How she had saved him from death in the second Atlantis.

Their talk of a future together.

Eurydice smiles sadly, and she takes a deep breath.

He is home.

CHAPTER 36.

MACEDON

It hurt immensely, and they would not allow me to get up. I lay where I was for what seemed like a long time. The radiating pain begins to dull and throb. I stand with the help of two men and look around. There are many concerned faces—my men, who worry about their payments and bonuses, the Krokinos household who wonder what next, my daughter who looks at me with fear and perhaps a small hint of adoration, and my wife with a mix of relief, anger, and affection.

What I do not see are the green eyes.

Someone hands me a cane, and I hobble. I walk past the gaudily painted walls, the ugly green pillars, and I search. Eventually, I get to the courtyard which is now empty—the dead bodies taken outside the compound walls, and the ground still wet with blood.

There is no one there.

"Eurydice?" I whisper weakly, ignoring the presence of my men and wife behind me. I then walk outside the compound to where we had left our horses. It is silent there; the horses look at us and then get back to chewing the grass.

Eurydice's horse is gone.

I feel the soft longing spread through my body, under my skin, inside my chest. But I always knew, in spite of all my attempts, that Eurydice would never be the second woman.

When I turn, my wife looks at me. She is radiant, and her eyes know more than she lets. She leans forward and asks, "Who was she?"

I take a deep breath. I hold my wife's hands, and I tell her, "You are the angel for whom I have fought and lived, and she was the angel who brought me alive to you."

We say nothing more, and I walk back holding her hand.

I am home.

CHAPTER 37.

KNIFE'S TIP, SOME TIME BEFORE

Nekh-Aser wakes up in darkness. His face is in agony and his body hurts, but he feels relief that he is alive and can feel his hands and legs. But that cursed Deon has tied him up. The Egyptian knows he is strong and clever enough to break free. He wriggles his hands and pulls up his feet when he feels his knees hit a hard wall. He turns and tries again. His knees scrape stone on the other side too—he then raises his hands behind his head and feels another stone wall. He can also feel something softer with fabric cushioned between him and the stone wall on the right.

A slow fear begins to rise in Nekh-Aser's chest.

Where am I?

He maneuvers into a sitting position and feels better. And then he tries to stand, but this time his head hits a stone roof.

Intense terror grips Nekh-Aser once he realizes that he is in a closed space. His muscles spasm and sweat breaks out all over. His breathing becomes rapid as he rises again and tries to push the lid up—but nothing moves. No man on earth is strong enough to move a stone lid that weighs as much as a half-grown elephant.

He tries until he is exhausted. He feels for other openings, but there are none. His breath is hot and turns laborious as his heart thunders like a court drummer.

Nekh-Aser begins to shake and collapses—his cheeks hit the object next to him. His hands try to examine what it is.

It crumbles under pressure, and his fingers feel what appears to be a series of teeth.

The Egyptian begins to scream in his twisted mouth. The guttural sounds die in his throat. It dawns upon him that they have entombed him in a sarcophagus with the body of an ancient.

Darkness grips him like a vice.

His muscles contract and his chest feels like someone has placed a boulder on it. Tears stream from his face and soften the crusted blood on his destroyed jaw. He feels something run across his leg and bite into his thigh. He grabs whatever wretched creature it is and feels its bones crack under his grip; he throws it away in disgust, feeling its gooey after-matter and wet slickness in his palms.

He hugs himself and pulls his knees to his chest and breathes rapidly to calm himself—a technique some soldiers had taught him to assuage his terror of closed spaces. It takes a while, but he slowly regains his composure.

He thanks the gods—it is now time to work his way out methodically. He feels the grooves along the edge, and they end in what appears to be a latch. Nekh-Aser feels the ridges and senses a metallic track along the sides; it feels warm to touch. And that is when he hears the sounds—it's like the fluttering of wings in a room; like a gentle waterfall.

He wonders what it is.

The sounds grow in intensity and near him, and the softness gives way to cracks and a storm like rhythm.

He pushes his back to the stone wall, and it is very hot and singes him. He recoils from the pain, and soon feels that the air is beginning to warm. When he touches the stone above his head, it burns his palm, causing his skin to stick to its surface. Nekh-Aser screams through his bloodied lips and destroyed jaw, and by now his entire body is alive and pulsating with pain.

He begins to kick and flail and smashes his head on the stone walls.

The skin on his back begins to melt and peel and his exposed flesh sizzles against the heated stone.

His bowels lose control.

"No, father, no!" he cries.

But no gods listen to the wails of a man who had laughed at the despair of so many.

CHAPTER 38.

MEMPHIS, EGYPT

Ptolemy wipes sweat off his brow. It is hot and the sun beats down upon him and the umbrella offers little succor. But he is proud. Things are going rather well for the satrap of Egypt. After Perdiccas' foolhardy attempt no one has tried to invade Egypt, at least not until now.

Alexander's tomb is coming along beautifully. It is within the palace complex of Memphis and the central temple is surrounded by statues of angels. That Alexander rests in Egypt is of anger to the King's family, but Ptolemy knows that to have his body in his land lends great legitimacy to his rule. Ptolemy wants his dynasty to rule this land for a long time, and he has little interest in fighting with others or to expand his empire.

Egypt is glorious, rich, and he loves its customs and people.

Ptolemy has heard that Eumenes is somewhere in Asia, pursued by Antigonus. The tenacious little secretary has surprised Ptolemy. But his life or death is of no concern anymore.

There is trouble brewing in Greece and Macedon and Ptolemy knows he must watch the harbors of Alexandria and the entryway from Gaza for any invasions.

But today, the temple shines and he loves the beauty of god Alexander's tomb. Ptolemy smiles and holds his mistress Berenice's hand and dreams of a glorious rule ahead.

CHAPTER 39.

SOMEWHERE IN PERSIA

Eumenes lies on the floor, hungry, and thirsty. His parched tongue sticks to the roof of the mouth. He wonders how it all came to this.

The entire world was against him, and yet he had prevailed.

The enemy had done unto him what he had to Neoptolemus years ago. They had attacked the baggage train and held the Argyraspides' assets for ransom. In exchange, the traitorous officers had seized him and handed him over to Antigonus. What a shameful conduct! What gods would pardon men who handed their undefeated general to the hands of the enemy?

Antigonus had neither pardoned nor executed him—instead, he had confined Eumenes to a dungeon. But in the past three days, all supplies of water and food had stopped.

The door to the cell opens and a tall, well-built soldier enters. He holds a cup and pours some water on Eumenes' lips.

Eumenes asks him, "Why do you torture me so, Antigonus?"

The man mutters something. It sounds like he says he is not Antigonus. Eumenes is delirious. He continues, "My wife and children await me. It is time we end this rivalry."

The man watches without expression.

"In return, I shall reveal to you a great secret—one that can make our duo greater than Alexander."

The man inches towards Eumenes.

"My lieutenant, a man named Deon, should arrive any day now with news of the find. We can rule the world, Antigonus," says Eumenes. Though weak and exhausted his clever eyes still burn with hope.

"There is a city that Poseidon himself—"

The man moves behind and slips a noose around Eumenes' neck. Eumenes is too weak to struggle, and his knees collapse as the rope tightens.

His teeth cut into his swollen tongue. Before eternal darkness embraces him, Eumenes' mind plays the life gone by.

Alexander on a horse.

His wife pouring wine.

Craterus' head on his thigh.

Deon's face as he rode away to Egypt.

Callisthenes on the podium as the executioner strangled the historian.

CHAPTER 40.

ONE YEAR LATER, MACEDON

I walk back after the day's teaching—my legend, some true, and some made up, has made me a favorite tutor for the children of the rich in the region. I also offer protection and debt collection services but do it with great tact and kindness where I can.

The gods watch every man's deed, and they dispense justice as they see fit. I was the man that condemned his innocent family to years of fear and pain and forced them into a life they had not sought. After the short initial euphoria of return, the reality of our life, and my actions, hit us like divine bolts from the skies.

My daughter struggled to grow affection, and my wife never reconciled with what I had done, and what situation I had put them in. She was also unable to forget my affection to Eurydice, and that it had done nothing to dim the desire to return to her. Her family eventually found out the cause for their peril—that I had foolishly ventured into a partnership with Krokinos to open a "profitable brothel" to cater to the traders and the travelers. It is my eternal shame, knowing the brutal existence of those that toiled in these places, that I even attempted such a venture, my youth, and immaturity notwithstanding.

After much debate and recrimination, and then with calmer words and heavier hearts, we came to a decision, and Apollonia walked away with my daughter.

They returned to her parents, moderately wealthy producers of barley and olive. Four months ago, she married another man—a trader, and I have, from time to time, watched them all from afar. She seems happy, and I have no intention of trying to reclaim my space. My heart aches every day, but there is no one to soothe them.

I do dream of how a life of bliss would be with them.

Dreams where I mock fight with my wife about buying the finest drapery from the cheerful shopkeeper in Sidon, so I can stuff it in her mouth.

Dreams where we sit by the dwindling night fire and I regale them with stories of my battles.

Dreams where I feel their enveloping hugs and my wife caressing the scars of my past life, real and in the mind.

My daughter is growing to be the most beautiful young woman in Antigonus' empire, and I dream that she will marry Antigonus' son Demetrius. On that topic— Antigonus' men finally found me but left me alone believing the story that I had been defrauded and sent on a quest for a lost will. I still recount in vivid detail every terrible act of violence I have inflicted and endured. The wounds of my past are still painful—the body heals from blows, but the mind is not so resilient. My loneliness reminds me of what I have lost.

I think of my wife and daughter every day, and my love for them shines as brightly as ever.

I think of Eurydice too. She was a magnificent mystery when she rode with me and remained a magnificent mystery as she vanished like she never existed, leaving an eternal longing in my heart.

Neither the woman I came back to or the one I fell in love with during the way, are with me. It is the justice of the heavens.

Atlantis is a distant memory but etched in my mind like a script on granite. I have often talked about returning; I have often wondered how it came to be; I have wondered what rediscovery may mean to the world. But I know to leave it be.

Antigonus, Ptolemy, Seleucus, and a host of other characters—they fight for a vast empire, and yet none has so far been successful in achieving unquestioned supremacy. There is no news that anyone has found the second Atlantis. We get scant news of what is happening elsewhere—I only know that Antigonus and Eumenes are still fighting and chasing each other, and I have never had the chance or desire to reconnect with Eumenes again. I often think of how he is.

I come to my modest and empty house where I usually rest on a little clay platform until it gets dark. I notice dust raised in the distance, and my heart palpitates. The road to my house is the only one nearby and the only way one sees rising dust if there is a column of soldiers or riders. And soon I see riders.

I mutter under my breath and scramble inside to bring out my kopis.

There is no point in running. Within minutes the armed contingent surrounds the house in an arc. The riders have their faces covered in colorful cloth, and they wear grand flowing robes—green, blue, purple. They do not look like Macedonians or Greeks. They are heavily armed, and the man in the front is tall, powerful, and adorned in Asian jewelry. It is hard to see much with all the dust swirling around me.

"Who are you?" I shout, with my body hunched and my kopis pointing at them. It is a meaningless gesture if they wish to harm me, but I must do what I can. The leader dismounts but keeps his distance. He is wearing an elegant attire—a flowing blue robe common among Persian royalty. He removes the scarf across his face and reveals his impressive beard. My eyes widen in recognition.

"Pharnabazus?" I exclaim, and his face breaks into a smile as he steps forward to embrace me. The same man—a Persian Satrap—that led Eumenes' Asian cavalry against Craterus. My mind races.

"What brings you here?" I ask.

He looks behind, and another rider, shorter in stature, disembarks and comes forward. My eyes widen, and my heart skips a beat. Those piercing green eyes would belong to no one but—

"I wanted to thank you for bringing my daughter home," he says. His proud and affectionate eyes turn to Eurydice.

"Your daughter?" My tongue fails me.

Eurydice was Pharnabazus' daughter? I am shocked, angry, and relieved all at the same time. She hid the identity of her father all the time she was with me! Someday, I aim to know the true story of her life. But I am stunned at the revelation.

Pharnabazus grips my shoulders and his face conveys affection; he tells me sternly, "Someday you will know."

Eurydice removes her scarf, and she is breathtakingly beautiful. Her face brims with pride and her wet eyes sparkle. But I also sense a hint of anxiety.

"I have told my father of your courage, leadership, and protection. We thank you for bringing me home, sir," she says.

I smile weakly and nod. But I am relieved. She is alive. She is well. She steps forward and whispers under her breath as she bows to me, "He does not know."

Her mischievous eyes twinkle, and I see that she still holds great affection for me, and that is enough.

I nod imperceptibly.

I see her look behind me, into my house, perhaps anticipating my family to emerge. Her eyes question the silence, and I say, "They left me."

She says nothing and steps back.

"Why did you come all this way?" I ask Pharnabazus, for it is surely unusual to make such a journey only to thank me.

Pharnabazus' deep voice cuts the air, "Deon, there is much to share. You are an impressive man, for one great man had you in his mind and the other has you now."

I am puzzled. Who does he speak of?

"First, let me speak of a great man who has you on his mind now. Governor Ptolemy inquires about you; he believes you have the skills to help him with a mission."

Ptolemy? Did he not want to murder me?

"I shall speak of that later. But there is one more thing," he says, as he gestures an aide who brings me a beautifully handcrafted box.

On its lid is a symbol I have seen in the second Atlantis— three concentric circles with the symbol of a bull in the center. I say nothing, overwhelmed. The box is sealed with Eumenes' wax imprint and bound by sacred strings. Pharnabazus gestures me to open it.

"Governor Eumenes ordered that only you receive it."

I take the box from the aide and step away from everyone. Eurydice is curious; she leans forward, and Pharnabazus lays his palm on his daughter's head.

I cut the thread and break open the seal. Inside is a letter written in haste. It is for me but not addressed as such.

May this find you in health and happiness. The gods appear to have ordained that our quest remains unfulfilled. I have something else for you, and may you forgive me for not sharing this sooner. On my capture or death, I have instructed P. to find and give you a sheaf of engraved gold leaves. You will feel immense pleasure in reading them, of that I am certain, and find answers to many questions. In return, I command you to tell the fate of Eurydice to her father. My great affection for you remains, and I will embrace you in the afterlife. We will conquer the heavens.

I sit in shock. My legs are weak. I have often thought of Eumenes—a clever, brave, and subtly dangerous man who I admired more than anyone else in Alexander's circle. I wonder if my decision not to go back to him was wise. But it is too late now.

Pharnabazus watches from afar. The dust has settled. Cool wind brushes the nape of my neck, and I feel a sense of anticipation. With Eurydice looking over my shoulder, I pick up the first gold leaf and begin to read.

*In this with the blessing of the divine I speak the story of an empire that incurred the fiery **wrath of god**...*

THE END

THANK YOU FOR READING

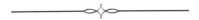

I would be immensely grateful if you took a few minutes to either rate the book or leave a review if you enjoyed it. This makes a huge difference to authors like me. You can also go to https://jaypenner.com/reviews for easy links.

You just finished the first book of the Whispers of Atlantis series. The next book, **The Wrath of God**, will take you to a fascinating world a thousand years prior, giving you some backstories on what Deon and Eurydice found.

Deon and Eurydice return in Book IV: Sinister Sands, but to truly enjoy the story, you will want to read Book II: Wrath of God and then Book III: Curse of Ammon.

If you are a history enthusiast, you will enjoy the flyby that will take you to all the major locations mentioned in this book.

https://jaypenner.com/the-whispers-of-atlantis/maps

Join my newsletter and get *"The History Behind the Book"* which sheds some light on some of the real history behind this novel.

Thank you once again for reading this book,

Until next time,

Jay (https://jaypenner.com)

JAY PENNER
HISTORY AND FANTASY

Choose your interest! A gritty and treacherous journey with Cleopatra in the Last Pharaoh trilogy, or thrilling stories full of intrigue and conflict in the Whispers of Atlantis anthology set in the ancient world.

THE LAST PHARAOH

WHISPERS OF ATLANTIS

https://jaypenner.com

ACKNOWLEDGEMENTS

My patient wife, who has had to deal with my "I'm writing a book" monologues, gave invaluable feedback as a reader. Her support was critical in getting through this book and its innumerable iterations. My young daughter, who surreptitiously read paragraphs standing behind my back, as I refused to let her read the chapters—because—well it is not for kids! But her questions, comments brought boundless joy as writing is no easy endeavor. She has many questions about Deon and Eurydice, and I tell her to grow up before I can answer.

References and Inspiration

- Anabasis of Alexander—Arrian

- The Ghost on the Throne—James Romm

- The Complete Works of—Diodorus Siculus

- Timaeus—Plato

- Quest for the Tomb of Alexander the Great—Michael Andrew Chugg

- Meet me in Atlantis—Mark Adams

- Dividing the Spoils—Robin Waterfield

- The Promise of Thera—Emily Vermeule

- Ancient.eu

Printed in Great Britain
by Amazon